THE
FORGOTTEN
ONES

ALSO BY STEENA HOLMES

THE FORGOTTEN ONES

STEENA HOLMES

Text copyright © 2018 by Steena Holmes
All rights reserved.

Published by Lake Union Publishing, Seattle

www.apub.com

Amazon, the Amazon logo, and Lake Union Publishing are trademarks of Amazon.com, Inc., or its affiliates.

ISBN-13: 9781503951754
ISBN-10: 1503951758

Cover design by Shasti O'Leary Soudant

Printed in the United States of America

This story is dedicated to my family. I love you.

Chapter One

DAVID

I always knew I was headed for hell; I just never expected it to happen like this.

It figures the devil decided not to wait until my cold and broken body was buried beneath mounds of dirt. No, he reached up and gave me what I always knew I deserved.

I never expected to live in hell before I was dead.

Who am I kidding? I deserve this life, this ending. If living in hell makes up for everything I've done throughout the years, then so be it.

Even if—and I hate to admit it—even if it means spending my final days in a cold and sterile hospital room.

Alone, until the end.

This is hell.

In all my eighty-odd years, I've done enough for God to turn His back on me, to ignore the pitiful prayers I've thrown His way. But this . . . this room, this body, this hell . . . it's too much.

My beautiful Gertie promised God loved me too much for this to be my life. My Gertie wasn't all there toward the end, her mind lost in its endless maze of the life she wished she'd had, so I knew not to place too much stock in her words.

I wanted to believe God wasn't vengeful. That He was loving, caring, and hell, even forgiving—for her. Not for me.

I am where I belong. I can gripe and complain all I want, but in the end, this is exactly what I deserve.

Scratch that. This is *better* than what I deserve, and I know it.

My hell is furnished with a thin hospital mattress with more lumps than the dirt road behind my house, a ridiculous number of tubes connected to every visible vein in my arms, and the constant beeping from the blasted machines reminding me I am still alive.

For now.

There is nothing else in my room worth noting. No get-well flowers from family members, no hand-drawn pictures from grandchildren. Nothing but a small television hanging from the ceiling. One with two volumes: whisper soft or thunderous loud.

When I'm lonely, I turn up the volume and count the seconds it will take for one of those nosy nurses to come running. Nine times out of ten she'll scold me for the noise and say something about letting others die in peace.

Die in *peace*. Is that even a thing? How does the nurse know, anyway? She isn't the one lying at death's door, waiting for it to finally open and drag her in whether she is ready or not.

Am I ready? Some days, when my body is on fire and I can barely breathe through the pain . . . hell yes, I am ready to meet death.

Truth be told, I've been ready to greet death for a while now.

But there's a difference between greeting death and accepting it.

Trust me, if I were twenty years younger and one hundred pounds heavier . . . well, I sure as hell wouldn't be here; that's for damn sure.

I turn my head so I'm not looking at the blank wall in front of me. Instead, I look out the same blasted window I've been staring at for days on end. Past the asphalt lot behind this small-town hospital and into the far-distant copse of trees that borders the edge of what once was my property.

The trees I planted when I first bought the land are so thick now that I can't see my house, but it is there. Taunting me. A reminder of what I've lost.

My past. My sins. My failures.

I hear the faint telltale squeak of shoes down the hallway. It takes a while, but eventually they stop right outside my door.

I count the seconds it takes the nurse to check her chart before she comes in.

I always know who is on duty by the amount of time it takes them to open my door.

The longer the wait, the older the nurse.

One. Two. Three. Four. Five . . .

The narrow shaft of light from the hallway that illuminates a path on the floor brightens as the door is pushed open.

Six seconds.

I scooch higher on my bed, ignoring the pain. A draft of air seeks me out, looking for an opening beneath the bedsheets before wrapping around my body, stealing the little bit of warmth still left. I pull on the blanket covering my all-too-thin sack of bones, knowing full well it will do little to stop the cold air.

"I saw that, Mr. Walker." The young one is on duty today.

I'd much rather have the baby tend to my needs than the old hag I am usually stuck with.

Nurse Brennley fiddles with the bedsheet, tucking it tight, as if knowing the chill is settling in. The moment she takes the five steps necessary to reach the locker-style closet in my room, I let out a small puff of air and smother the smile that always comes into the room with her.

She is a good girl. Her parents raised her right—unlike the hag who pretends to never notice the way my body shivers during the night.

Sometimes I pretend my granddaughter is like that—thoughtful and sincere, with the sweetest look in her eyes that reminds me of better days full of old pickup trucks and ice-cream floats.

They say life flashes before your eyes when you're about to die.

I tend to believe the memories of the life you miss surround you until that's all you see.

I see flashes of Gertie and Marie more and more, it seems.

"You should have buzzed earlier," she says. "No need for you to be freezing in here." Her gentle-and-completely-innocent smile is like warm honey. She unfolds a thin fleece sheet and settles it over my once-toned body.

I would grumble but I appreciate the warmth more than I want to admit.

"What happened to the heated blankets I got when I first arrived? If you're going to freeze me to death, I wish you'd get it over with already."

"Is that all you've got?" The look she gives me is a mixture of humor and concern. "I thought for sure you'd have a list of demands for me today. The other nurses warned me you were in a mood." She checks my vitals, reminds me to breathe in deep and let out the air slowly.

She then listens to my heart and checks my pulse, giving me a saucy wink as she does so.

"Still alive, which is nice to see. Wouldn't want to have our first zombie case while I'm on rotation." She keeps a straight face while she writes notes on my chart.

I can't tell if she really believes all that nonsense on the television or if she is just teasing me. Kids nowadays think the weirdest things.

Shortly after I'd arrived, I was shuffling through the channels when she walked into my room toward the end of her shift and found a show for me to watch.

God forbid, but I actually liked it.

She watched it for the story line.

I watched it for the violence.

At my age, watching people bash one another's brains in is about all the excitement I get most days. I much prefer the old

Westerns—cowboys, Indians, and saloons full of drunkards. But they only play those on the weekends or in the wee hours of the mornings.

"Is there anything I can get you?" She leans in close and lightly touches my shoulder.

I don't bother to hide the grimace that ripples across my face. Even the lightest of touches hurts.

"You see that little button right by your hand there? The one to numb the pain? It's there for a reason, Mr. Walker. You need to be using it."

I hate being scolded like a little child.

I know exactly what that little button is for and I don't want to use it. It is a game for me—how much pain can I tolerate before it is too much? Anything I feel here is nothing compared to what awaits me where I'm going.

Besides, if I can still feel the pain then it means I am alive and the cancer hasn't taken everything from me.

Yet.

"The day I have no pain is the day I'm dead." My chest pinches moments before I cough, the force sending spikes of torture through my veins. It takes a bit before I can even open my lips wide enough for the straw in the cup Brennley holds. I pull in a small mouthful of water and let it trickle down my throat before swallowing the rest.

"I'm sorry." Brennley wipes my bloodstained lips with a tissue.

"Don't be." I clear my throat, ignoring the rawness torn apart by what I swear are splintered pieces of kindling. "Don't be rushing me out of this room too soon, you hear?" I ignore the pointed look toward the blasted little button pinned within finger's reach, the one that will send waves of medication throughout my body, taking me to a place I crave.

A pain-free place. A place where I remain in a daze, oblivious to the reality I face.

I don't deserve that freedom.

"The only one rushing seems to be you." Brennley shakes her head as she writes more notes on my chart, probably mentioning the blood in my spit. "Your body needs some rest from the pain. That's why the doctor prescribed the medication. To help you, not kill you."

I grumble something I know she won't hear and stare out the window. The leaves on the trees are a bright green, but the sky is deathly gray for miles. Like my mood.

I hate summer. Nightmares begin in the summer. Marie left us one summer. Gertie died last summer . . . Bad things happen in the summer.

I have one request that I breathe in prayer day after day: I need to see those leaves change before I die. I don't need to see those same leaves fall to reveal barren branches. I don't expect to either. But I don't want to die during the summer.

Fall? Fine. Summer? Not so much.

"Any mail for me?" I hate to ask.

I ask this every day, hating myself every time too.

"Not yet." Brennley moves to touch my arm again but stops herself.

I nod.

"Ready for me to write that letter yet? Say the word, and I'll grab a pad of paper and pen."

"No." My lips set themselves in a straight line at the thought.

"You still have time. I even brought in some nice stationery from home, just in case."

These are the same questions we ask each other every day she comes in.

Is there any mail for me?

Do you want to send any more letters?

She never takes my no for an answer.

I am tempted to tell her no again, but I stop myself. What would it hurt to send just one more letter? I promised Gertie I would send as many as I could, but I think we both believed one day Marie would respond. She hasn't, and I doubt she will. I doubt one more letter will make any difference.

What more could I say? How often did she need to read the words? And yet *not* sending one feels like I am giving up. If there is one thing I'm not, it is a quitter.

"I heard you barely ate your lunch." Brennley turns the subject around, no doubt giving me time to change my answer.

"You call that lunch?" I wouldn't feed my poor dogs what they serve here. "Lukewarm piss water and green Jell-O? If you expect me to eat, it needs to be something edible."

"Did you even try the soup?"

I scoff. The soup was even worse. It smelled like my old septic tank in the dead heat of summer.

"I thought you weren't ready to die."

"Reverse psychology?"

"If that's what it takes." Brennley digs into her pant pockets. "Prove it."

Prove I'm not ready to die? I'm an old man with a body riddled with cancer. I can barely walk on my withered legs. I have to have my letters dictated because it hurts too much to hold a pen between my fingers. All my body wants to do is sleep.

Sleep until I never wake up.

Waiting for death sucks.

I finally understand the dejected look in Gertie's gaze as she waited to die, me by her side, forever trying to bring a smile to her face. I should have just let her go, back when she'd had the energy to ask it.

I couldn't do it, though.

Despite the mistakes I made, if I had to do it all over again, I still would have fought tooth and nail to keep her alive.

I stare out my streaked window. I always meant to die with no regrets. Told myself that I'd own everything I'd done in my life, refuse to blame others for my choices.

That's what a man should do after all, especially when there's a family to take care of. Shoulder the blame; carry the responsibility so others can live in peace.

It's what I did for my Gertie and what I tried so desperately to do for my daughter.

Marie never understood that, though.

~

A soft jiggle of the bed jolts me from sleep.

"Marie? You came." The words are torn out of my parched throat, the sight before me shimmering like the fairy godmother about to honor Jiminy Cricket's wish.

"It's just me, Mr. Walker. Time for your meds." The shimmer forms not into my fairy godmother but into the young nurse, who is now pulling the end of the blankets up from the base of my mattress before squeezing my big toe.

"Damn it!" I nearly shout as my leg jumps from the lightning shaft of pain racing from my toe to my groin. "Do you get your jollies from torturing me?" I breathe the words out while pressing down on the blanket in an attempt to work through the pain. I swear my heart rate is faster than it was when the neighbors' bull broke through the fence and charged.

"I'm sorry. I called your name several times, but you wouldn't wake up." The apology is genuine, but the explanation does little to help.

Why do they have to keep touching me? Why?

"You were mumbling in your sleep," Brennley says. "Were you dreaming of Marie?"

"She'd consider it a nightmare." The words come out full of regret.

"I'm sorry?" Brennley is looking at my chart.

I am acting like a monster. I should be thankful I'm not dying alone, that at least I am in a bed with constant care and not at home, where a concerned neighbor checking in on me would find my decaying body.

But I am beyond grumpy. Grumpy and disgruntled.

What secrets did I spill?

What lies did I reveal?

"I didn't hear a word. Promise." She holds up her hand in a way I can only assume is meant as a pledge.

Silly girl. Doesn't she realize I can read her like a book?

My stomach growls in rebellion, its sound louder than a cracked whip. I crave a good steak with a baked potato and fresh bread straight from the oven.

Crave it, but I know one bite into that steak and I'd be crying like a baby, the pain would be so fierce.

The doctors told me some nonsense about the nerve endings beneath my skin being sensitive due to the cancer.

It was all mumbo jumbo to me.

I know the truth.

I'm cursed, and it's my own fault too.

One day I brought home a simple woman who saw into the beyond, or so she claimed. I was desperate, needing reassurance that my Gertie would be okay despite cancer robbing her of speech.

That witch laughed the moment she entered our home. Cackled until the sound grated on my nerves and seared into my memory.

Even now, I can hear her.

She placed a curse on us both that day. I was sure of it.

She spouted some nonsense about knowing who we really were and that we needed to come clean before our maker—or else.

Or else my foot.

No one knew the truth. I'd stake my life on it.

So I kicked her out right then and there.

If she really knew who we were and what we'd done, she wouldn't have come in the first place.

That was the day Gertie got worse. And the day the pains started in my fingers.

That was the day I knew beyond a shadow of a doubt that God had forsaken me.

"Mr. Walker?"

I'd forgotten all about the nurse.

"I've got an hour left on my shift. I'll see about your dinner, and then we'll watch our zombie show together. After we work on your letter."

This is what my life boiled down to—being bribed like a five-year-old boy.

On a normal day, I'd tell the young kid where to go and who to go with. But my normal days ended when I was brought to this wretched room via ambulance. So instead I stare at the blank wall in front of me until she leaves the room.

I made Gertie a promise to right a wrong, and there was no way I was going to hell with a broken promise.

I think about what I want to say.

About what I hadn't said before that might make a difference.

Nothing.

Nothing I have to say could make a difference. After years of writing to my daughter, I came to that conclusion a long time ago.

But maybe . . . Maybe I shouldn't be writing to my daughter, but to my granddaughter.

Wouldn't hurt to try, right?

What would I say? How do you introduce yourself, explain your absence? I've said it before in letters I've sent throughout the years, but I never know if she's read them or not.

The one thing I did know was that I'd tell Marie how much I missed her. How much I loved her. How she would always be the child of my heart.

I do miss her. I was a fool. An old, stubborn fool unwilling to admit when I was wrong. Because of that, I lost more than I ever thought I would.

To say Marie was stubborn . . . well, that would be like schooling a zookeeper on the sleep patterns of a koala bear. All they did was sleep. Sleep, shit, and eat leaves.

She came by it honestly, though. I used to tease Gertie that if she were the walnut determined to remain uncracked, then Marie was the squirrel equally determined to eat that nut.

Gertie would laugh, but never once did she deny her daughter was just as stubborn as she was—if not more.

With that in mind, would Marie care that I'm dying? Probably not.

She has no reason to. I've always known that, to her, I'm already dead.

The sky bleeds brilliant shades of red, as if it's mourning along with me.

Some secrets are better kept hidden.

Chapter Two

ELLE

All I want to do is head home, put my feet up, and binge-watch the last few episodes of *Broadchurch* before falling into the deepest sleep my body can handle. I doubt I'll make it through the first twenty minutes, much less all the shows, but the battle between wanting to see how this season ends and sleep is real.

I have an hour to go before two blissful days off, and I can't wait. Pulling a double shift was my own decision. I wanted to be here, to stay with the family as they said goodbye to their newborn baby.

Life sucks sometimes.

Scratch that, life sucks *a lot*. In the pediatrics ward of the Kincardine General Hospital, I've seen too many babies born in distress, more tiny lungs unable to breathe than I care to admit.

The cafeteria is basically empty, other than a few fellow nurses sipping their coffee or downing a bottle of soda before heading back to their ward. It isn't a large area: fewer than a dozen tables; an *L*-shaped counter with coffee; a cooler area filled with sandwiches, yogurt, and other snacks; a basket of fruit; and then a hot station with fresh food made in the kitchen. The dinner rush is over, but the smell of fried chicken still lingers.

My own coffee mug is empty, but I am too tired to get up and refill it.

Maybe if I close my eyes, I can get a brief nap before heading back to fill out the rest of the file.

"Hey, Sleeping Beauty." Brennley nudges my chair, holding a carafe of coffee in one hand and a plastic-wrapped brownie in the other. "Figured you could use a refill."

"You're an angel in disguise." I barely wait for the last drop to splash into the cup before bringing it up to my lips and taking a sip. "Are you coming home with me?"

We share a two-bedroom apartment in the middle of town.

Brennley shakes her head. "I'm going to sit with one of my patients for a bit and watch *The Walking Dead*. If you're asleep, I'll keep quiet."

"David?" He seems to be the only patient Brenn is focused on lately. From the way she describes him, he is a cranky old ogre with the heart of a teddy bear—and all alone.

I'm glad she has someone to watch her zombie shows with, though. She talked me into watching an episode once, but my dreams after were too morbid.

"I'm not sure how much time he has left. I'm trying to get him to send his daughter one more letter." She sits down, looking as tired as I feel. "I heard about the baby." She reaches out and squeezes my hand. "You okay?"

I nod. It's hard to not become invested in my patients, even if they are only a few hours old.

Especially when they are only a few hours old.

"I can't believe his daughter hasn't come to see him." Brennley fills the silence between us. "I don't think he's had a single visit, come to think of it. Can you imagine how sad that must be? To die alone?"

I think about it all the time, if I'm being honest. Other than Mom and Grace, I have no other family. I'd like to get married one day. To find someone to fall in love with, to share a life together, maybe even bring a child into the world and be the mother I always wished I had, but I can't.

I won't.

It wouldn't be fair to that person, to that child.

Mental illness runs in the family, and I'm living on borrowed time until it's my turn. I experienced firsthand what it's like to grow up with an unstable mother, and I swore I'd never do that to my own family.

It's why I'm a pediatric nurse. I love children, so I use the job to fill the void in my heart.

It has to.

My phone buzzes on the table and Mom's photo fills the screen.

"Hey, Mom." I cover a yawn with one hand while holding the phone with the other. I am surprised she is calling midshift but then remember I'm not technically supposed to be here.

"Everything okay, Elizabeth? We expected you hours ago." Her voice is smothered with concern.

The guilt of making Mom worry slams into me like a rear-end fender bender.

"I'm okay. Sorry, I totally forgot about dinner. I'm still at work." I rub my face and shake my head at Brennley, who smacks her forehead with the palm of her hand. She obviously forgot too.

"Are you all right?"

I can picture her, hand to either her throat or chest as she thinks of the plethora of reasons why I'm still at work.

"One of my families lost their baby today. I wanted to stay with them until they were ready to leave." It hurts just to talk about it, the weight of their sadness heavy on my heart.

"Oh, Elle. I'm so sorry. Come home, please? I'll pour you a nice glass of wine, and you can tell us all about this little one." She was breathless, her voice soft and hurried.

I'm not sure if it is from worry or excitement about something or if she is in the middle of one of her moods.

Since my first year as a nursing student, every annual performance review has said the same thing: Elle Myers becomes too attached to her patients. It's my greatest strength and my biggest weakness, but no matter how hard I try to remain detached, I'm unable to do so.

Mom once told me she worried the weight of all those deaths would become too heavy for me to carry, that I'd crumble and find I wasn't strong enough to get up.

I wish she had more faith in me, but sometimes I secretly wonder if she's right.

I want to tell her I'm too tired to drive the forty-five minutes to her house in the country, but I know if I don't go, she'll stay up all night worried about me. Once she becomes fixated on something, she won't let it go. Right now, she's fixated on making sure I'm okay. She needs to see me every time I'm off work.

Brennley and I have talked about requesting a transfer to the hospital closer to Mom, but I'm hoping this is just a phase she's in.

"I just need to finish some paperwork; then I'll be on my way. I'll text when I leave. How does that sound?" It sounds exhausting to me, but I won't let on just how tired I am.

"Don't be too long, okay? Grab some coffee to keep you awake. I don't like you driving at night."

I stifle a yawn and nod, then remember to tell her I'll buy a large coffee and will see her soon.

When I hang up, Brennley gives me the most pitying look she can muster.

"Guess *Broadchurch* will have to wait." I shrug. "I can't believe I forgot—and that you didn't remind me." I mock frown and say, "You always remind me." She loves coming with me to Mom's house whenever she can, which isn't as often as she'd like.

"Guess I'll see you in a few days." She finishes the last bite of her brownie before pushing herself to her feet. "I promised David I'd see

what I could finagle from the kitchen that might tempt his taste buds."
She leans down to give me a hug. "Let me know when you arrive, okay?"

I take another sip of my coffee, willing it to work quickly. I need
that jolt of energy.

"How did your mom sound, by the way?"

I chuckle. "Frenzied. She's in the middle of getting ready for her
showing later this summer, and you know how she gets when she's
painting." Mom has a habit of becoming frazzled, withdrawn, and lost
within her own world while she paints. She loses track of everything—
time, people, and I can't count how many times she's forgotten to eat,
even when the food is right beside her. When she does come up for air,
she's either filled with nervous energy or she's completely silent, lost
within her own psyche. Then, she barely registers the people around her.

She's a creative person with mental health issues. Nowadays, that's the
norm, what you expect. Mental health is such a part of our lives now—
whether because of the media or groups and outpatient programs—that
it's become more acceptable.

But when I was a child, it wasn't the norm. It was hushed up and
never discussed. This powerful secret destroyed so many lives.

Mine included.

Chapter Three

I used to believe wishes were like fairy tales: all you had to do was make one, and your happily ever after would come true. I grew up in a world where teapots talked, fishes sang, and a click of my heels could take me anywhere I wanted.

I don't believe that anymore.

I was six when the Cheshire Cat became scary, a bringer of nightmares; eight when I feared the Beast's transformation; twelve when I understood my mother had more in common with Maleficent than I had with Aurora.

It wasn't that she was evil. On her good days, she'd call me "Lizzie" and she was Glinda the Good Witch. Full of sunshine and rainbows. We could do anything and everything together. Most days, she was like that—happy, cheerful, and bright.

But every so often, there were periods of darkness. She'd beg for my forgiveness. When she couldn't get out of bed, when the slightest touch sent shards of pain through her body, and the faintest of whispers rang like bells within her head.

There were no stories on those days. No tea parties among the wildflowers, no backyard games or lazy hours spent on the tire swing.

I never knew when those days would come, but even as a child I watched for the signs.

Still, as an adult, I watch for the signs.

Like right now.

I'm about to open the door to my childhood home, and there's a deep, paralyzing fear inside me. Am I about to step into a nightmare? I never know what to expect. Even on the best of days, when I know Mom is okay, that fear is still there. Always there.

Like a nurse about to start a midnight shift in the middle of an emergency, I breathe in deeply and turn the doorknob.

If there's music playing, Mom's flitting about from room to room.

If it's silent and dark, curtains all drawn, Mom isn't well and I need to be quiet.

If it's just silent . . . Mom's out in her studio and I can breathe easy.

I'm prepared for any of the three.

The curtains are open, but there's a stillness to the house—a good sign.

Despite the fact I come home most of my days off, it's always weird to walk through the door . . . that feeling of it being home—*my* home—is gone. I'm not sure when the change happened, but it's there. Subtle. But there.

My apartment with Brennley is light and airy, white with splashes of brilliant colors throughout the rooms. It has a cottage feel, which is perfect since we're blocks away from Lake Huron and love to spend our days by the water. Mom's house is quaint and homey, done in muted tones that offer feelings of warmth and quiet.

The first thing I notice in the kitchen is Patches, a stray cat I brought home when I was nine years old. She's sprawled out on the kitchen counter, waiting for the wedge of sun that will shine in from the window above the sink in the morning.

"Did you miss me?" I steal her away and cuddle her close, rubbing my chin against the top of her head. She accepts my hug for a moment before arching her back and escaping my hold, returning to her chosen spot on the counter with a hearty meow.

I open the French doors leading out to the backyard.

There is only one place Mom would be at this time of night.

Of all the places on the property, this is probably my favorite. Our apartment isn't big enough for a garden, so we make do with planters on our small back deck.

A winding pathway runs through her gardens, leading from the back deck to her studio. I set it myself last summer, after several of the hand-made stepping-stones Mom and I made when I was little cracked and broke over the years. It's a fifty-foot walkway now, lined with decorative stone chips and staggered rocks. Birdbaths, benches, and garden gnomes are set within the bushes and flowers. This was my haven, from the spring through the late-fall months. My thinking place when I needed to work through issues. My safe zone when everything else around me twisted into whirlwinds of chaos. Here in these gardens, I found peace.

I grew up loving the feel of dirt between my hands. I knew the names of flowers and how to plant them before I knew how to count. Mom and I used to spend hours out here, playing in the grass, her teaching me the difference between weeds and flowers. I try to think about those good times, when there was a smile on her face as she taught me the different meanings behind the names of rose bushes we planted, why the irises liked the sun better than the hydrangeas did. But there are also moments when the memory of Mom ripping through the garden, pulling out the flowers I'd so lovingly tended as punishment for not completely following her mysterious rules, crashes into me. It's those moments I push away, try to forget.

I take my time along the path now, bending here and there to pull out a weed, to check the soil for moisture, to pluck a dead branch. I only have a few rose bushes now, and they are all thornless. My favorites are the miniature Cinderella roses, with their soft pink petals, and the smooth mauve Prince Hybrid Tea rose. Once, when I was around twelve years of age, Mom forced me to sit in among the rose bushes as a punishment for not eating all my dinner. Then, the bushes were overgrowing and there wasn't much space between them. The sundress I wore provided little protection from the thorns—I still have a few scars along my legs, arms, and on my left thumb, where scratches became infected afterward.

By the time I make it to the door of Mom's studio, my hands are streaked with dirt and my shirt is wet from getting caught by the sprinkler after turning on the hose, but the lethargy and exhaustion I felt during the drive have dimmed.

"Is it safe to come in?" I ask as Mom sways back and forth to the music blaring from her headphones, oblivious to my presence.

I've always enjoyed watching her work. It's fascinating how she's able to create an image from something she's seen and make it come to life. When I was younger, she would paint garden landscapes. My favorite hangs in her bedroom—two little girls having a tea party in the middle of wildflowers, with an old shed in the background.

She used to tell me stories about those two little girls. For years, I believed they were real. For a while, they even became my imaginary friends.

I know better than to make myself known by touching her, something that inevitably startles her. Last year, I tapped her on the shoulder after waiting for almost thirty minutes for her to turn around. Mom's reaction? She flung her paintbrush and paint in the air and curled up into a ball, rocking herself in shock. That one little unexpected touch took her three days to recover from.

It only takes about fifteen minutes for Mom to pull the headphones away and notice me this time.

"Elizabeth! You're finally here!" She sets her paint jar on the bench, wipes her hands on her apron, and smooths her hair before she comes over to give me a hug.

Mom is the only person who calls me Elizabeth. I generally prefer Elle, but Mom is stubborn in her refusal to never, ever call me that. It's Elizabeth or Lil'bit.

Apparently, when I was younger, I used to beg Mom for a little bit more time to play, to sleep, or to read stories. I said it enough that she started to call me Lil'bit, which is funny because it's also how I pronounced my own name as a child.

My first-grade teacher made the mistake of calling me Ella. Her own daughter was named Elizabeth, and Ella was her nickname. When Mom found out, she threatened to pull me out of school. Her reaction was a tad . . . severe . . . but I was already learning to expect that Mom's reactions would never make sense.

I've never understood what's so wrong with being called Ella. Mom once tried to explain, saying it was too similar to her own name—except it isn't. Anna Marie is my mom's full name.

Just one more entry on the list of unanswered questions I grew up with.

"It's so good to see you." Mom's eyes shine with light and laughter.

"I'm sorry for not calling to tell you I'd be late."

"You probably forgot about coming out, didn't you?" Mom wags her finger, but I can tell from the lift in her voice she isn't upset.

"So what do you think?" Mom sweeps her arm over a collection of paintings hanging from wires, sitting on stands, or leaning against boxes and other knickknacks in the studio.

It is a bit more crowded than the last time I was out—and that was only a few days ago.

"These are all from our last trip, aren't they?" I ask.

Canvas after canvas of quaint Tuscan homes from the trip the three of us took last year. Three of us being my mom, Grace—her companion—and myself. Three months in Italy . . . it was amazing. While Mom painted, I explored. I've always wanted to travel extensively, and once I even dreamed about being a historian and working in a museum.

"What do you think of the colors?" Mom asks, biting her lip.

The colors are warm—browns, purples, reds.

Warmth is good. Warmth is healthy. Warmth means . . .

"I think I'm almost ready for the Toronto showing." Mom stands to the side, arms stuffed into the pockets of the apron she wears, with a thousand-watt smile that lights up the room.

I don't even bother to smother my own smile. I can count on one hand the number of showings she's held in the past five years.

One.

Two planned showings had been canceled months in advance because the stress had been too much for Mom to handle.

"You got the time off, right? You'll be able to come? We can do that girls' weekend we've talked about doing too."

Despite her tall stance, I catch the slight stoop of her shoulders that indicates a lack of confidence in herself.

"I wouldn't miss it." I can't help myself. I wrap my arms around her and squeeze tight, ignoring the stiffness of her hold. It only takes about two seconds before she relaxes and pats me on the back.

"Okay, okay. I know it's a big deal, that I've canceled all the others. But"—wisps of hair escape her bun as she shakes her head—"don't make it out to be more than it is, okay?"

My brows rise toward my hairline. *Make it more than it is?* Everything inside of me is jumping for joy, twirling around like a little girl in a tutu.

I know better than to let that show.

"What's left on the to-do list?" I ask instead.

"Grace mentioned needing to still organize the food and drinks. We have a caterer but haven't selected the menu yet." She pulls out a notebook from her apron and flips through the pages. "We also need to organize shipping the crates, and I need to figure out which pieces to send."

"The gallery should help with the shipping, right?" At least, they had in the past. It was always part of the agreement.

Mom nods. "Just need to schedule it." She pats me on the cheek. "I'm so glad you're coming. Have I said that yet? Grace and I have made some plans. She says I need some fun in my life once the show is over."

Well, color me a rainbow. Fun? Who is this woman speaking?

"Sounds like a plan to me. Where is she?" I'd almost expected Grace to be here in the studio, since she hadn't been in the house when I arrived.

It's not very often she leaves Mom alone. All my life, from the time I was a newborn, Grace was always there. She was Mom's nurse, companion, best friend—and my second mother. All rolled into one. She is also older than Mom, something I all too often forget.

"She went over to the Moweses' for a cup of tea. She left a plate from dinner in the oven for you. She made your favorite. It's too bad you couldn't make it in time."

My stomach rumbles at the idea of dinner. There was nothing I loved better than Grace's homemade macaroni and cheese, along with strawberry shortcake for dessert.

"How about I make dinner tomorrow night to make up for it?"

"What if we were to cook together, like we used to when you lived at home? Remember?" My mom's gaze has that far-off look; she must be thinking about a time when life was simpler and happier.

Cooking with Mom was fun, especially when I was younger. We wouldn't follow recipes; we'd just combine whatever we thought would taste good and make a story out of it. We'd pretend we were living in Prince Charming's castle and had to make the prince and princess a meal they'd never forget, or we'd be the bakers in Belle's small provincial French town, or adventurers trying to lure Tinker Bell and her friends out to play with fairy cakes.

Mom leads the way out of the studio, holding the door for me.

"How come Brennley didn't come with you?"

"She's spending a little extra time with one of her patients. He's not doing too well. She doesn't think he's going to last much longer, I guess." His death is going to hit Brenn hard.

"Oh, that's too bad. Doesn't he have any family to sit with him?"

"There's no one, which is why Brenn's there. He has a daughter, but they've been estranged for years, from what I gather. She's helping him write a letter to her, and then they're going to watch *The Walking Dead* together."

Mom and I wrinkle our noses at the same time.

"I never could get into that show. I don't understand why such a sweet girl is so into watching zombies eat other people." She pats my hand. "That show gave me nightmares for weeks after she coaxed me into watching an episode."

I laugh, considering the same thing happened to me.

"Seems she found a kindred spirit in David Walker."

Mom stops ahead of me, right beside my Cinderella rosebush. She pivots on the ball of her foot.

"What did you say?" she demands.

"That she found a kindred—" I begin with caution.

She shakes her head. "No, the name. What name did you just say?"

Mom vibrates as she waits for me to repeat it.

"David. David Walker? Why, do you know him?"

"That name will never be mentioned in my presence again! Do you understand me, Elizabeth Myers?" Her eyes are now a cold gray, rather than the warm blue they had been earlier. Her shoulders are rigid, and her hands curl into fists. "I'm serious." Spittle flies from her mouth.

I stand there, deeply rooted, like the rosebush I planted years ago as a surprise birthday gift for Mom. I watch her walk away from me along the stone pathway and into the house, her steps measured and heavy. Then she closes the door behind her, leaving me out there all alone.

What just happened?

What did I do?

But most importantly, who the hell is David Walker?

Chapter Four

I rush inside, but Mom is already hiding.

Go figure.

David Walker. Other than hearing the name from Brennley for the past few weeks, it isn't familiar to me at all. Mom's reaction was unexpected, to say the least. Full of anger, hatred, and outright contempt, which is odd since I've never seen her react like that toward anyone, ever. I want more information.

I need to understand my mom's reaction to that name. The only one who can start me on the path of getting those answers is Brenn.

Hey. Made it here. Funny story. Mom asked where you were and when I explained the situation with David, she kind of went . . . nuts. I think she knows him, or of him but she won't tell me how. Any clue?

I wait to see if she'll respond right away, considering she is probably just getting home.

OMG. Girl, have I got a story for you! I'm still here with David, but let me call you later okay? I think I'm going to be a while.

But trust me, you'll want to stay up for this. I think . . . I think David knows you. Or knows of you. TTYL.

What? What does she mean, he knows me? I have no clue who he is, other than what she's told me. What is going on?

I hate when you do this! Call as soon as you can.

I pour myself a glass of wine and walk through the house.

The photos of myself as a child haven't been moved, a few more first editions of books have been added to Mom's collection, and a hand-braided rug I can only assume Grace made is now a focal point in the living room.

One thing that isn't anywhere in this house are photos of my mom as a child—or of her parents. I really don't know anything about my grandparents. They weren't people my mom liked to talk about.

From as far back as I can remember, the only family I knew was Mom, Grace, and myself. No one else. My father has never been in the picture. He left my mom before I was born—and preferred to parent from a distance once he found out about me. We chat a few times a year—birthdays, Christmas, and such. The last time I saw him was at my graduation from nursing school a few years ago. As for my grandparents, I think they both passed well before I was born. I have no exact details because anytime I asked questions, Mom would change the topic.

All the stories I know about my mom's childhood are from before she turned six years old. Those were the only memories she wanted to share, she'd tell me—the only memories worth remembering.

I've often wondered if something happened to her as a child, something that would explain her manic moods. Grace has confirmed time and time again that this is just the way Mom is. Has always been.

26

Is it genetic? I pray to God it's not. Grace has reassured me over and over that I have nothing to worry about.

I hope she's telling the truth, but I have a feeling she isn't.

I'm just waiting for that proverbial other shoe to drop, for the signs I'm always on the lookout for to materialize.

Standing at the window, I jump at the long honk from Grace's car as she pulls up beside mine. I've been so lost in my thoughts, I didn't even see the glare of her lights from the driveway as she turned in.

I rush outside and reach for the bags Grace has loaded on her arms after giving her a quick and awkward hug. "Here, let me take those."

"Thank you, love, but I've got these. Grab the rest, will you? Mrs. Mowes loaded me up with more vegetables than I expected." Grace gives me a soft kiss on the side of my cheek before she heads into the house.

To say I love Grace would be a bit of an understatement.

"Did you get the plate I left?"

"I did, thank you."

"Your mother mentioned why you stayed late. How is the family?" She looks me steady in the eye before giving a small nod. "How are you?"

This time she gives me a real hug, her arms wrapped tight around me. She lightly rubs my back before pulling away. I catch a sheen of tears in her gaze, and it warms my heart to know she understands me so well.

"I don't think it'll ever get easier. I feel for that family."

"Of course you do. It's what makes you such an amazing nurse. I'm sure one day, when they're able to look back, they'll appreciate you being there for them. Is your mother still out in the studio?" Grace pours herself a glass of wine, then empties the remainder of the bottle into mine before we sit at the kitchen table.

"She's upstairs."

27

She gives me the look—the one that asks why and what happened. I know I have to explain.

Maybe Grace has some answers for me.

"I'm afraid I might have set her off. I mentioned that Brennley has been spending time with a patient named David Walker. He's dying in the hospital right now."

Grace looks off into the distance. There is a sadness in her eyes when she looks back to me that catches me off guard.

Her posture at this moment reminds me of a painting I'd once seen called *The Woman in the Red Dress*. Her bowed shoulders and defeated gaze are the same. It worries me.

"She reacted rather . . . strongly when I mentioned his name. In fact, she told me to never mention him again, but didn't explain why. Do you know?" I ask.

By Grace's long sigh, there's clearly more to this than I could have imagined.

"It's not so much *who* he is, but more what he means to your mother." Grace shakes her head. "Sadly, that's not something I can answer." She twists around and glances up the stairs. I can see a whirl-wind of thoughts run across her face. "I doubt she'll be down anytime soon." Grace breathes in deep.

The smile she forces her lips to fold into bothers me.

"What do you think about having a bonfire?" Her attempt to change the subject is obvious. "We can make s'mores, drink wine, and you can tell me how life is treating you in Kincardine?"

Grace starts to rise, but I grab her hand to stop her.

She slowly sits back in her chair.

"That's not an answer, and you know it."

No response.

"There's obviously some sort of connection between Mom and Brenn's patient." I don't even bother to make that sound like a question.

Grace's unwillingness to talk about it tells me all I need to know. Her shoulders sink, and the woman I consider my second mother suddenly looks older than she ever has.

Gray highlights are sprinkled throughout her hair, her wrinkles more pronounced than I remember, and despite her neat and presentable appearance, I realize Grace looks tired.

I don't *ever* remember her looking tired.

When Grace sighs, her whole body deflates. It is like watching a person's spirit escape in the moments after death, leaving only the shell of who they were behind.

"This really is something your mom needs to explain, love. I'm sorry."

Once Grace decides she isn't going to say anything, she rarely changes her mind. Especially when it comes to Mom.

Despite there only being the three of us in the family, there are enough secrets to make the house feel crowded.

"There are things that happen to us that . . . change us. Your mother is a very emotional woman, and what might change one person can destroy another. That's the fight your mom deals with on a daily basis, Elle—trying not to let the weight of all the hurt and pain she carries destroy her." She winces, like the words are barbed.

"There are things in your mother's past I don't even know about. A lot of things. But I do know"—she leans forward and grabs my hand, her grip tight and earnest—"that she has always loved you. That love forged who you both are today."

That love also destroyed me time and time again. If it wasn't for Grace and Brennley, I'm not sure I would have made it to adulthood alive—much less be the person I am today.

"Should I be worried? Brennley is going to call me tonight to tell me something about David. She says she thinks he knows me."

Grace looks pained. She rubs her face, exhaustion comparable to what I feel etching her face too. "What she tells you may seem dramatic and life altering. You may be forced to make a decision. Choose what is right for you—not for your mom. Okay?" She releases my hand, wipes her eyes, and stands.

I wait till she's gone upstairs, then go to sit outside. It is peaceful. Off in the corner, just past the deck and close to a small breakfast nook, is a water fountain Mom had installed years ago. I pick the chair closest to the fountain and run my fingers beneath the flowing water for a minute, then wipe my wet hand on the cushion.

I check my phone and notice a message from Brenn telling me to call when I can.

She answers on the first ring.

"You are not going to believe what happened tonight!" The words blast from her mouth before I can even say hello.

"Remember that letter I was helping David write? Elle, I think it's for *you*. I'm serious. I know I haven't said anything until now, but the things he tells me, the things I hear him say in his sleep . . . I know you said you have no grandparents, that they died before you were born, but girl . . . I think David Walker is your mom's father."

She lets the bomb drop with supersonic speed, not thinking about the potential damage. The Hiroshima-type mushroom cloud envelops me as I try to take in what she's said.

"Did you hear me? I know it's a lot to take in. I wish you were here. Or I was there, so I could explain it better. But he dictated his letter and then had me address it to your mother. Your mother, Elle! What are the odds? Do you think she knows? You have to tell her. You have to."

I pull the phone away from my ear to mute her constant chatter. The noise is too much, too overwhelming. My whole life is imploding.

It can't be true. My grandparents are dead. They died years ago. From what Brenn has told me, this man is estranged from his daughter because of something horrific he did in the past. We've both spent too many hours on the couch trying to figure out what he could have done to elicit dying alone.

There is no way he's my grandfather.

No way.

"Are you sitting down? I'm going to read the letter to you. I really think you should meet him, Elle. I think you'd like him, and he seems to have a lot he needs to get off his chest."

Dear Elizabeth,

You'll have to forgive this old man for not writing sooner. Your grandmother had me send you a letter years ago, but I'm not sure you ever received it. Just like I'm not sure you'll ever read this one.

I hope you do.

I'm not sure if you know about me. Or care to know of me. Or even want to.

But I'm dying, and I regret not getting to know you.

You would think saying those two words—I'm dying—would get easier with time. But I'm an ornery old bugger, and if there's one thing I don't like to admit, it's this: I've lost.

There's no beating death.

You can't get through life without regrets, and God knows I have a multitude of them. But as I lay here, alone, there's only two that seem to matter.

If you came to see me, I'd tell you about those regrets. That's my way of asking if you'll come to see me, by the way. I'm not so good at asking for things, not when it comes to myself. But I'm asking.

I'd love to meet my granddaughter before I die.

David.

P.S. Marie, I miss you. I miss my daughter.

It's been too long. There's something I'd like to tell you . . . will you come see me before it's too late?

I wish I could say my life changed after hearing his words.

I wish I could say that all the questions I've ever asked have been answered.

I wish I could say that I finally understand the things my mom kept from me, things I don't even know that I should know . . . if that makes any sense.

I wish I could say all that and more. Except the reality is, hearing that left me with more questions than answers.

Well, that's not true. I have one answer. I now know who David Walker is.

My grandfather.

I want to race up to Mom's room, pound on her door, and demand she explain why I've never heard about him before. Why she's never given me the letter he said he sent years ago.

I have a grandfather.

He wants to see me.

Should I go?

The answer seems obvious.

But whatever I decide will affect Mom, sending her into another of her tailspins, where no one makes it out without wounds.

Am I willing to do that?

I tap my phone against my knee and stare out over the yard, contemplating.

Grace told me to choose what was right for me.

David Walker is dying. Whatever decision I end up making, I need to make it soon.

I glance up to my mom's window and notice her standing there, holding a portion of her curtain back. Watching me.

We stare at each other. Then, with a snap of her wrist, the curtain closes, masking her from my view. Almost as if she hopes to become invisible.

Chapter Five

The urgent whispers between Mom and Grace, the soft voices raised in argument, make me pause before knocking on her bedroom door. I can count on one hand the number of arguments I've ever heard these two women have.

All my life, I've lived shrouded by secrets.

"It's time, Marie. Time to tell her."

"There's nothing to tell. Nothing she needs to know."

I can hear the tears in Mom's voice as it breaks.

"You wanted to protect her, and you have. She's an adult now, with a life of her own. She deserves to know the truth."

I rub an area on my forehead where a headache is beginning to form.

I deserve to know the truth? What could be so bad that I need protection from it? David Walker himself?

"What truth, Grace? Whose truth? Mine? His? Hers? No. I can't do that, I can't . . . I can't go there. You know that. Please . . ."

Now Mom is crying even harder. The guilt from being the reason for those tears chips away at the frustration I was feeling about being left in the dark.

"The decision may be out of your hands, and you need to be prepared for that." Grace's tone of voice is almost too hard to hear.

"Did you know?" There is an urgency now. The tears and the anguish are gone.

I can't hear Grace's response. For the longest time, no more words are said.

Minutes later, Grace opens the door. She doesn't seem too shocked to find me standing there as she shuts the door behind her.

I wish I had the courage to knock, to walk into Mom's room and demand to know what is going on. But something holds me back.

Fear, maybe?

Fear that I'm not ready to learn the truth? Or that maybe I won't be told the whole truth? Fear that Mom is standing on the cliff of sanity and, after months with no psychotic episodes, I will be the catalyst for a new one?

"Come downstairs with me, Elle. Your mother needs a little time alone." Grace gently leads me away from Mom's room and down the stairs. She doesn't say anything else. She just goes into the kitchen, opens another bottle of wine, and pours us each a glass before leading the way outside.

"Nothing good ever comes from eavesdropping." Grace looks at me over the rim of her glass while she takes a sip. "I know you want to talk about David Walker, but I'm not the one you should be talking to."

No, the woman I need to be talking to is upstairs, trying to calm down.

"Is she okay?"

More than anyone, I trust Grace to tell me the truth when it comes to Mom.

She shrugs. Not really the answer of confidence I was hoping for.

"I keep wondering, you know . . . when it's my turn." The last thing I expected to say is the only thing I can admit. This isn't the first time I've mentioned my fear, and it won't be the last.

Brennley had made me a solemn vow years ago that she would always be honest with me when it comes to the signs of mental illness. We have talks every few months about how I am doing, and she is supposed to bring up things she might have noticed or was worried about. So far, nothing . . . no signs, no signals, no symptoms. But that doesn't mean that one day I won't end up like my mother.

"Bipolar is hereditary. We both know that. I haven't shown any signs yet, but—"

"You won't either," Grace says with a slight shake of her head. This isn't the first time I've had this talk with her.

"Elle, your whole life is stress. You handle it on a daily basis at work, as well as here at home. Look at you, today—you stayed to help a family deal with the death of their newborn and you didn't collapse. I think it's time you stop giving in to your fear and let yourself live for once." Grace lifts her feet and rests them on the patio coffee table.

She looks relaxed and comfortable, which is surprising, considering everything that has gone on tonight.

I catch her glancing up to my mom's room. Then she gives a small sigh and sips her wine.

"Will she come down?" Grace knows my mom's moods better than I do.

"Your mother isn't the fragile flower you make her out to be, Elle. You need to give her more credit. She's stronger than she lets on." Grace looks at me, and that tiredness I saw earlier deepens right in front of me. "Will she come down? No. She's stubborn that way. Which means you'll need to go up there to discuss this with her."

"Brenn called. She told me the truth." I wait for a reaction. "David is my grandfather. She read me a letter he wrote to me."

Grace leans forward and rests her elbows on her knees. I catch a flash of something . . . regret, maybe? The emotion crosses her face too quickly to be sure. She sits back in her chair and looks off into the distance.

"Go. Go talk to your mother," she says. "Nothing good will come out of any of this, but it's too late to turn back time."

She leans her head back on the cushion and closes her eyes, dismissing me.

I knock on Mom's door before opening it. She sits curled in her corner chair, legs tucked beneath her, a book on her lap.

I've always loved her room. It's an oasis of calm. I used to come in here as a child, snuggle up in bed with her, and listen to the stories she'd tell me. She'd braid my hair, let me brush hers, and we'd cuddle until we both fell asleep. Her room seemed so magical to me. One wall is lined with photos taken during her trips, another with framed pictures I drew as a child. A small corner bookcase is full of novels, journals, and little knickknacks. A vase of flowers is always on top of her dresser.

Back then, it seemed like the largest room in the house to me. Now it seems small and confined. I feel smothered, like I can't breathe. It's a new feeling. One I don't like.

"Can I come in?" I wait just outside the door for her permission.

I can't read the look on her face or in her eyes, but from the sudden stiffness in her shoulders, I know this isn't going to be the easiest of talks.

"Of course you can. I'm sorry I didn't come down earlier." She sets the book to the side.

I perch on the edge of her bed, hands behind me, flat on the covers.

Now that I am here, the words won't come. One moment they were on the edge of my tongue; the next, gone. I can't help but feel frustrated.

It must show on my face, because Mom leans forward and rests her hand on my knee.

"I'm sorry."

I nod even though I am not sure what she is apologizing for.

For her outburst earlier?

For not telling me about David?

For keeping her past a secret?

"Brennley called. Her patient dictated a letter to her, one that was meant for his granddaughter. But he added a few lines to his daughter, who happens to be named Marie."

She looks at me with . . . surprise? Shock? Regret? I can't tell, but she pulls her hand back from me.

"Guess who the granddaughter turns out to be?" As hard as I try, I can't keep the accusation from my voice. "Who is David Walker, Mom?"

She purses her lips into a thin line and narrows her eyes. She casts a furtive glance my way before staring down at her entwined hands.

I could just leave it. I can see the signs that say she doesn't want to talk about him. But I am tired of secrets, tired of giving in, tired of always placing Mom first and never making myself important enough.

"You told me my grandparents were dead. I didn't think I had family, but it turns out I live in the same town as my grandfather. Who happens to be dying."

She just looks at me, her lips tight together, as if refusing to allow the words to come out.

"Why haven't you told me about him before?" I lean forward and rest my elbows on my knees, my voice even more insistent than before. "Why keep him a secret? He's dying. What is it going to hurt?"

"He died a long time ago, as far as I'm concerned." The flat tone of her voice surprises me. "I never kept him a secret. I told you what you needed to know."

"You told me he was dead."

She shrugs.

This feigned indifference, like she couldn't care less that he is still alive, blows the smoldering embers stoked inside of me into red-hot flames.

"I want to meet him. I'm *going* to meet him." The words come out without thought and stay there, between us, like an unwanted present.

A heavy silence falls in the room.

My natural instinct is to bridge the gap, to step into the role of peacekeeper when it comes to Mom's moods . . . but Grace's words about her being strong stop me.

I never really thought of Mom as being strong.

I've never really seen her as strong.

She's always been weak, delicate, vulnerable.

What if I've been wrong?

"I'd rather you didn't." Mom lifts her chin but keeps her face a mask. "But do what you want."

Surprised, I don't know what to say. I thought for sure she'd fight me on this, demand I not go, guilt me with words about love and respect. Anything to dissuade me from going to see him.

"Do you want to know what his letter said?"

She snorts. "I don't want to know anything about him. Don't tell me about your visits, don't tell me the lies he shares, and don't mention me to him. Ever." Mom pushes herself to her feet and stares down at me with her hands planted hard on her hips. Her chin wobbles, as if it is all she can do to hold herself together. "Do you understand me?"

"I do." This all seems anticlimactic. I was expecting theatrics, hysterics. Not a woman who smolders with anger while maintaining a calm appearance.

"He said that he wrote me before—is that true?"

"He had no business writing you." The words are wrenched from her clenched mouth.

I take that as a yes.

"How many letters did he send?"

With a sigh, Mom rolls her eyes and shakes her head. "For Pete's sake. You were a child. Too young for him to play his games with your head. That's what he does. Plays games." She turns her back to me and stares out her window. "All I wanted to do was protect you, Elizabeth. You were my angel, and I wanted you to remain as innocent as you could."

For a few years, we went through a phase where Mom felt *less than* as a mother. That she'd let me down, that she'd failed at raising me. She'd overheard me once say that Grace was more of a mother to me than she was, and she took that to heart.

Literally.

She pulled away for months, withdrew into her own little world, and painted landscapes full of cemeteries. She would drive to hamlets and little towns to sit in their graveyards, sketching for hours on end. When she came home, she'd lock herself in the studio and paint canvas after canvas.

Painting was how Mom exorcised her demons.

Those graveyard paintings were what caught the eye of a collector who recognized her talent. One thing led to another, and she had her first showing in Toronto when I was ten years old.

In the years that followed, Grace raised me while Mom hid herself in the studio.

"Protect me? From what? From who? Why did you have to lie to do that?"

"What you consider a lie, I consider a means of survival. I didn't want to share you with them. They didn't deserve you—still don't, as far as I'm concerned."

She turns, and the far-off look in her eyes frightens me.

She is going there. Back into that place in her mind where she hides herself. I can see it happening right in front of me, and I know nothing matters anymore. Not what I say, not what I do. She will go there anyway.

Why? What was so bad about her childhood that it would affect her like this?

"Some secrets are best left hidden. Some closets should never be opened. The skeletons are too, too many," she says, wringing her hands.

"Too many?"

What does she mean?

Mom grabs my hands, her grip strong. Her thumbs press hard into the soft spots between my thumbs and forefingers.

"Don't go. Please, Elizabeth. For me. Don't go." Tears run down her face. Her hold starts to hurt. I don't think she realizes what she is doing, so I jerk my hands from her grasp and rub the area, sure to be bruised come morning, before pulling her close for a hug.

"It's okay, Mom. I promise. I'll be okay." I whisper those words over and over while she sobs in my arms.

I don't know what happened. I don't know what went wrong.

The only way to find out is to meet David Walker myself.

Chapter Six

DAVID

There's one ceiling tile off in the far corner with a cross on it.

I can never decide if someone stood on their tiptoes to draw it or if it is a water stain.

I asked one of the nurses once—Ms. Crankypants, as I think of her—if she could see the odd-looking mark. The look on her face after glancing over at it was a mixture of exasperation and irritation, with a little bit of concern thrown in.

Apparently she didn't see it.

I see it again today, though.

Is my mind playing tricks on me? Is the guilt so strong that it's showing the one thing from my past I can't bear to deal with?

Or am I just going crazy?

I stare at that cross and ignore the light knock on my door.

I know who it is. I know why she's here. Why the hell would I welcome her?

It's Ms. Crankypants herself. She warned me she'd be back to check on me after breakfast. She wanted to take some blood earlier, and if I had the strength, I would have tossed her out of the room.

Wishful thinking, I know.

"I noticed you were a little chilly earlier, so I heated up a blanket for you." Ms. Crankypants, or rather, Nurse Amy, walks in with said blanket in one arm and a cup full of something—disgusting, no doubt—in the other.

"I never said I was chilly."

"No, you never do." She places the blanket at the edge of my bed, her fingers brushing against my feet. Her touch is featherlight. "Why do you think I'm always touching your toes and fingers?" She pulls the blanket up gently. The weight is a slight burden, but the warmth immediately spreads across my cold and achy skin.

"Harrumph." I don't say thank you. I won't. It's her fault I'm cold. Why can't they turn up the heat in this room?

"You're welcome. Now, try the smoothie I brought."

I eye the cup she sets on my tray with suspicion.

"It tastes good. I promise. Better than what they make in the cafeteria too."

"The pigs I raised as a boy wouldn't eat the slop they serve here." My nose wrinkles at the first hint of strawberry as she opens the lid for me to see inside.

"It's pink," I grumble. I'm sure it tastes good, and the saliva on my tongue is already pooling, but she doesn't need to know that.

"Do you have to complain about everything?" She *tsks* before replacing the lid. "Of course it's pink—it's made with strawberries picked fresh this morning from my garden. I even added a little banana to it. Try it."

I'm not hungry. My stomach can barely handle anything I do try to eat, but I miss food.

More than I thought I would.

I can't hold the cup myself, which means I need Amy to hold it for me.

I hate being spoon-fed like an infant.

"Not bad, right? Gertie used to love my smoothies . . ."

I grunt in response to the memory of my wife while continuing to sip.

In the end, smoothies were the only things Gertie could drink. And she did love Amy's smoothies.

"It's passable," I finally admit after a few swallows.

"I'll leave it here in case you want more." She brings the tray hovering over my bed closer and situates the cup so all I have to do is lean forward slightly to reach the straw.

"How is the pain level, David?"

"The same as it is every day. I'm alive and breathing. Stop fussing and leave me in peace. Don't you have other patients to bother?" I settle back against my pillow and look out the window.

"What are you trying to prove? Don't forget, I've known you for far too long. You're not as grumpy as you pretend to be. Take the pain meds—it's why your doctor prescribed them." She reaches for the button pinned to the bedsheet and pushes. "No need to try to impress me, if that's what you're going for," Amy continues. I look at her out of the corner of my eye. "My husband is as cantankerous as you, and I put up with him just fine."

I listen to the sound of her shoes squeak away on the tile floor until there's nothing but silence. She's either gone into another patient's room or back to her desk.

Either way, once again I'm alone.

I should be used to it by now. I've always known I'd end up alone on my deathbed, but I assumed I'd be one of those who died from a sudden massive heart attack or went quietly in their sleep. Not like this.

This is torture.

This is hell.

I flick through stations on the little TV on the wall until I find a baseball game. What I wouldn't give to sit outside, feel the wind on my face, with a beer and dog in hand while watching my favorite sport in person.

Hours tick away until I can't stand to listen to that second hand *tick-tick-tick* a moment longer. I'm ready to yell for a nurse to come throw the damn thing away when there's a knock on my room door. Amy pops her head in.

"David, are you in the mood for a visitor?"

I'm caught off guard by the hint of excitement in her voice.

A visitor? For me? Who the hell would come to see me now? I've been stuck in this room for a solid four weeks, and other than a parade of nurses and my pansy of a doctor, I haven't seen another soul.

For a moment I think maybe it's Marie, but I squash that quick enough.

Not even the promise of me dying would be enough to make her visit.

"If it's that pastor, tell him not to waste his words," I say moments before hacking up a lung. I lunge forward from the effort, and my body bends in half as I fight to catch my breath.

Within seconds, Amy's at my side. Her daggerlike touch on my back has me shouting through my coughing fit, which only increases the pain I'm in.

"Try to breathe, David."

I shoot her a nasty look but do as she says and focus on opening my airway until I'm not coughing anymore.

The pain is too much. Too fast. Too sudden.

"Between one and ten, David. What's the pain right now?"

"Eight." The truth comes out before I have a chance to stop it.

Amy hits the button at my side, and I count the seconds it takes for the drugs to hit my system.

One. Two. Three. Four. Five. Six. Seven . . . ahhh.

"Better?"

I nod.

"Do you need a few moments, or think I can send your visitor in?"

She tidies the blanket on my bed.

"Who is it?" I keep my voice low as I look from the nurse, to the door, and back at the nurse.

"It's not the pastor."

"Who?" I repeat.

"And ruin the surprise? Not on your life." Her eyes twinkle. "You can come in!" Amy calls out as she straightens. "I'll give you some time to talk." She winks before leaving the room.

I'm never one to put much stock in phrases like "time stood still" or "lost in the moment," yet as I watch a young woman walk into my room, that's exactly what happens.

She's a stranger. Someone I've never met before. She's a young woman. Pretty for her age. I can imagine the boys are all after her, with her long brown hair, clear blue eyes, and summer freckles sprinkled along her cheeks.

Gertie had freckles like that too, when we first met. Said they were sun kisses or something equally as ridiculous.

"David Walker?" The young girl stops just short of my bed, her hands gripping the handle of her purse.

"Depends on who's asking." I attempt a smile, but it obviously comes across as more of a grimace from the way she takes a step back. "I'm kidding, girl. Relax. I'm David." I clear my throat, suddenly feeling very nervous.

She looks familiar.

"I'm . . ." The girl loosens her tight grip on her purse and fiddles with her hands. "I'm Elle." She shakes her head. "Elizabeth. Your . . . granddaughter."

Granddaughter. That bomb drops, and it's as if I've been blown to bits.

My granddaughter.

I'm frozen. I can't think. Can't form a word. Can't—

"Brennley is my best friend and roommate. She . . . she told me about the letter." She swallows hard before lifting her chin.

Well, that little sneak. She never said a word when she was in here the other night.

"I never thought you'd get it, truth be told. I only did it to appease her." My voice comes out gruffer than intended.

"I'm glad you did."

I can't stop staring at her. Despite her height, she's a tiny thing. Delicate, even.

"So am I." The words tumble out like ice cubes from one of those automated machines.

I can't believe she's here.

Maybe miracles do happen. Maybe God hasn't forgotten. Maybe . . .

Elle doesn't blink, flinch, or smile. She doesn't back away as she holds me accountable for not being in her life by staring me straight in the eye.

So much like Gertie. If there were ever any doubt . . .

"Thank you." My eyes smart, and I have to look away.

She doesn't need to see an old fool crying.

"I don't understand."

The dryness in my throat feels like a burned piece of toast without butter to soften the edges.

She doesn't understand? I don't either.

I don't understand why all of a sudden my heart caves in on itself with pain, why my eyes flood with tears I've refused to shed, and why knowing my granddaughter came here alone kills any tiny flicker of hope that Marie would forgive me.

I look away from Elle's beautiful face and stare up at the white tiles above me, forcing myself to get a grip on my emotions.

"Thank you for coming." My mouth is full of dust, like in the old days when I'd forget I'd left my windows down a notch in the truck and drive on a newly sanded dirt road. I attempt to swallow, forcing the imagined grit down my throat. I try again. "You didn't have to, I know that. But thank you."

Elle's gaze flickers around the room like a hummingbird. "I wasn't sure if I would, to be honest." She winces. "It's not like I know you or owe you anything . . ." She continues to take in my sparse room, as if memorizing every little detail, and then sinks into a chair. "I wish I had known who you were earlier. Brennley often talks about you. Does anyone know you're here?"

Of all the questions she can ask, should ask, this is one I'm not expecting.

"Why would they?"

Her gaze focuses on the bare wall across from my bed.

I try to view my room through her eyes.

Cold. Barren. White. Single bed. One nightstand with a phone I have no need to use and a book Brennley brought me to read. Two chairs: the one she's sitting in and another by the window that's draped with an old blanket Gertie knitted years ago. I keep it there so I have something to look at, something from home. A small television hangs from the corner, and my food tray is now off to the side, beside my bed. There's a small wardrobe where my bag, shoes, and spare clothes hang. Not much else.

This room looks lonely.

"Why wouldn't they? There must be someone. Friends or relatives or . . . ?" Elle rubs the back of her neck as her cheeks go red.

"You're here. That's what matters." The words come out before I can stop them. Hopefully she won't read into them too much.

Or maybe that's exactly what I want her to do.

"Guess I'll bring flowers if I come back."

I might be dying, but I'm not deaf.

I heard that *if.* Heard it loud and clear, and I know that if there's to be any chance of her coming back, I need to do something—and quick.

"How is your mom?"

The sigh that follows my question is full of regret. I shouldn't have asked.

She looks away from me, fiddles with the purse, and that's when I know she won't answer.

Or doesn't have an answer, maybe.

"Forget it." I want to take the question back. "I'm sure that daughter of mine wants nothing to do with me, which is answer enough." It takes an effort to keep my hands still. Nervous people flit about, their bodies in constant motion. "Why don't you tell me about yourself?" I still can't believe she's here. In the flesh. I want to learn as much about her as I can before she leaves.

Because she will leave. They always do.

So when she smiles, my heart hurts a little less.

"You said you're Brennley's roommate. How long have you known each other? What do you do? Do you live here? Married?" I don't see a ring, but that doesn't mean anything nowadays.

"Brennley's been my best friend since high school. I'm a nurse here at this very hospital, in pediatrics. I've worked here for a few years now. Not married, and I doubt I ever will be."

"Why wouldn't you get married? You need someone to look after you. Women shouldn't be alone. It ain't right."

She laughs, and the sound takes me back years. To piggyback rides, pillow fights, and tickle monsters.

To a time when things were simple and my family was whole.

"I'm not alone. And why would I want to get married? I'm quite happy with my life. If men can be alone, why can't a woman?" Her eyes sparkle with a challenge.

"So you're one of those women's lib folks, I take it. Sound like your roommate. Guess that's why you get along and all."

"We're modern-day women." She leans forward in her seat. "Nothing wrong with that, is there?"

"I'm a truck driver, sweetheart . . . and I'm old to boot. Back in my day, a woman's place was in the kitchen rearing children. Not out in the streets burning bras and all that other nonsense."

The way her brows rise almost to her hairline tell me what she thinks of that comment.

I'm not going to apologize, though. I told the truth, and there's no apology for that.

"So . . . you drove a truck?"

The fact she had no idea tells me a lot. "Your mom never really talked about me, did she?"

Elle shifts in her seat, clearly uncomfortable.

"Never in my whole life."

I'm not going to let my disappointment ruin this. She came here for a reason: curiosity. I can live with that.

"I dropped out of school to help my dad, who was a farmer, then took up driving long hauls across the country. Met my Gertie, settled down, and the rest is history."

Life was different back then, much simpler.

My chest pinches, and as hard as I try, I can't still the cough that tears through my already-raw throat. I grab a tissue and cover my mouth.

I don't need to look at it to know it's covered with specks of red—blood from my lungs.

One more way my body is betraying me.

The look on my granddaughter's face says she understands what's happening to me. At least she doesn't jump up like a crazy woman, concerned about a little blood. Might be good to have a nurse in the family.

She hands me some water, brushing against my arm as she does so. I inhale sharply.

My hands shake as I struggle to take the offered water. I manage to jab myself in the lip with the straw.

"Damn it all," I grumble.

"I'm sorry."

Elle sounds stressed, unsure, and more apologetic than she should.

"I forgot . . . Brennley did tell me you were sensitive."

Sensitive? Yeah, that girl likes to use that word too often. Sensitive skin. Sensitive heart. Sensitive emotions, when she thinks I don't notice the tears in her eyes.

By the time I manage to get a little bit of water, I'm exhausted.

"So you're dying." Elle sits up on the edge of her chair.

I appreciate how she says it. Not as a question, just a basic fact. Like talking about the weather or how gas prices keep going up.

"According to the doctor. Every day I wake up, it's supposed to be a blessing. Some days it's more like a curse." *Most* days, more like it.

Although, truth be told, meeting my granddaughter today is worth it all.

I've waited for this day. To make right a wrong. To meet Elizabeth. To apologize to Marie.

One out of three ain't bad. I could die tonight and all would be right.

"Cancer?"

One word, but it's all that's needed. When I nod, she nods as if understanding. Except no one can ever understand cancer. I learned that with Gertie. Cancer is a nasty disease.

An awkward, prolonged silence ensues.

"So that girl told you about my letter and you—what? Took a day to decide to come see me?"

Am I a little hurt she didn't come right away? Maybe.

Elle shrugs.

"Thought you might wait to see if I died or not first."

The bitterness tastes vile, and my regret is instant.

"I was out at my mom's. I start my shift in an hour, but I thought it would be nice to pop in to see you first. I could come by during my dinner, or after shift, if you'd like."

I *harrumph.* "Why?"

"'Why' what? Why spend time with you? That should be obvious."

"No. Why come see me at all?" It shouldn't matter. But it does. Maybe it's a pride thing. Maybe it's honest curiosity . . . but the need to know is strong.

"I always thought you were dead, and it turns out you're not."

There it is. Everything I suspected but didn't want to know.

Marie promised us we were dead to her that one summer, when Gertie came home after being in the hospital for more years than I like to remember and wanted to see her daughter. Marie met us at the door, arms crossed over her chest, and made it known we weren't welcome.

Guess she kept that promise.

It was completely one-way, however. We kept tabs on Marie, as much as we could. Gertie filled a photo book with newspaper clippings of Marie's shows and her art.

I'd never been so proud. My little girl. The daughter of a trucker and a housewife, a famous painter.

We saved up some money and bought one of her pieces from a studio years ago. It's still hanging in the living room back home and will go back to her once I die.

I don't own much of value—in fact that's probably the only thing worth stealing. But what I do have will go to my girl. What she does with it is up to her.

I fully expect her to burn it all.

"I guess . . ." Elle stops, crosses her legs, and recrosses them. "I guess I wanted to get to know you. I've always wanted to be part of a family, to know my history . . ."

"So it's a history lesson, then." Makes sense. I doubt Marie would have been forthcoming about her past . . . that was something we drilled into her from a young age.

What happens in the home stays in the home.

What happens with the family stays with the family.

That day, on Marie's doorstep, she flung that back in our face.

If family was all *she* needed, then she didn't need us. She created her own family.

"I grew up hearing about fairy tales," Elle said. "I thought I lived one when I was little."

Her smile nips at my heart. I've missed so much of her life.

"I always thought the big bad wolf came and ate my grandparents. To find out that didn't happen . . ." She trails off, as if lost within her memories. "Call me curious. But I'd like to know about my mom's childhood. I'd like to know her history. My history. Your history."

She looks at me with those big blue eyes of hers, and I know all she has to do is ask and it's hers for the taking.

"Your mother always did love stories. When she was younger, I would tell her one every night I was home. Your grandmother would look for secondhand fairy-tale books, like the Grimm brothers, you know? I have a bookshelf full of those. Every fairy tale you could imagine. Your mother knew them all, by heart too. Eventually I would start making up stories, combining fairy tales to catch her off guard." I chuckle at the memory. Oh, how she hated when I did that.

"Like having Little Bo Peep join Alice for a tea party?" The smile that stretches across Elle's face shows remnants of Marie's smile when she was younger and Gertie would promise she could make cupcakes for a tea party. Like mother, like daughter. And like grandmother, because Gertie would smile like that as well.

"Exactly like that."

Marie might hate everything about me. About us. About her life growing up. But it gave me a sliver of satisfaction to know my stories had lived on.

"Guess your mom figured out my secret."

Elle's forehead wrinkles. "Your secret?"

Like a little kid being offered a jar full of his favorite candy, it's everything I can do to keep the excitement from showing on my face.

I love stories. Love telling them. Love reading them. Love hearing them.

I have a feeling my granddaughter is the same.

"Every story holds a kernel of truth. Some more, some less. It's all in the telling." I chuckle before looking Elle directly in the eye.

"Why don't I tell you a story?" I could drag it out, make her return . . . if she's curious enough.

Her eyes light up, then narrow. "What's the catch?"

"It's just a story," I say. "You came because you want to know more about your history, about our family . . . so that's what I'll tell you."

I watch her carefully. I might not be a smart man—I never finished school, don't have a fancy degree—but I know people.

Just like I know my granddaughter is caught in my snare.

She's curious.

She'll stay to listen to my story, come back to hear more, and maybe—just maybe—I can finally right a wrong.

"You promise not to lie?"

Marie must have warned her something fierce for her to not trust me.

"I don't lie." I am many things, but if there's one thing I pride myself on not being, it's a liar. "Regardless of what your mother has told you, I never lied to her. A parent's job is to protect their children. If that's a sin, then so be it. I'm already a condemned man. One more stone thrower won't matter."

Elle's nose wrinkles with distaste. "I'm not calling you a liar, it's just . . ." She leans forward. "But that's what I just did. Sorry." She reaches out and squeezes my forearm.

I jerk. It's hard not to. The amount of pressure she uses has the same effect as slamming a hammer onto my thumb. I suck in a deep breath as she pulls back, a look of horror on her face.

"Oh no. I'm sorry, so sorry!" She stands and looks around uncertainly. "I can't believe I did that again."

"Stop your blathering." Shockwaves of pain reverberate up my arm and then through my body, every nerve electrified.

I breathe in and out until the pain is somewhat manageable.

"I'm sorry."

"Don't." I swallow hard. "The nurses here hurt me worse, trust me. Not Brennley, though. Not on purpose, at least." Hopefully my I'm-not-in-pain-so-don't-blame-your-pretty-little-head smile will be believed.

Elle sits back down, pulls her chair closer, and gently lays her hand beside me on the bed. I notice she's careful not to touch me but is close enough that I know she wants to.

It matters. More than she could know.

"Why does it hurt?" she asks.

I'm surprised she asks, considering she's a nurse. But then, maybe they don't deal with this stuff on the floor where she works.

"Did you know the big man upstairs"—I point toward the ceiling— "likes to play games? He's a practical jokester, all right. I used to tell my Gertie that my worst nightmare would be not being able to hug those I love. Guess the big guy's in a mood to make nightmares come true. Not only does it hurt to hug, but any touch is painful."

I have no idea what my granddaughter believes—if she goes to church, believes in God or Buddha, or is an atheist. She might be horrified by what I've just said or find it funny, who knows? I don't really care. I'm not going to heaven, I already know that, and nothing I can say or do will change it.

God might forgive, but He sure as hell doesn't forget. Despite what the preacher said, there is a limit to His forgiveness—and I surpassed that years ago.

"Life isn't always fair." Elle tilts her head to the side. "You must have done something awfully fierce to get played such a bad card."

She's teasing. I can see it in the quirk of her lips and relaxed body position, but it hits closer to the truth than she knows.

I struggle with what to say. Something witty? Gruff? I don't want to scare her off, but I'm not going to lie.

I'm saved from having to do either by a knock on the door.

The nurse pokes her head in.

"I hate to break up this party, but the doctor is here, David. You probably need to get ready for your shift, Elle."

Elle stands and gathers her purse.

A moment of panic hits me. She's going to leave. I've wasted all this time with her.

I reach out to stop her, just shy of touching her.

"You will come back, right?" I ask. Beg. Plead. "Please?"

The smile I see on her face makes me feel like a child granted the wish of a lifetime. It eases the pinch of panic in my heart.

"Of course I'll be back. You have a story to tell—or did you forget?"

Chapter Seven

Elle

Stories.

He wants to tell me stories.

I'm not sure what I was expecting from a visit with a man I've never met. A man Mom refuses to acknowledge. A man who is my grandfather. Being told a story wasn't at the top of the list.

I shouldn't be surprised though, really. After all, Mom is a story-teller. I was raised on stories. So why wouldn't my grandfather tell me one as well?

I just hope it's not going to end up like a fairy tale. I've had enough of those to last me a lifetime.

David Walker. He surprised me.

I'd prepared myself to meet a monster. A sociopath who gets off on playing mind games. A man with a dark past I know nothing about.

I thought I would be able to walk away with closure.

Grace said to meet him with an open mind and to walk away complete.

That's what I fully intended to do. Except I'm now walking away with the intention of returning.

He's either a master manipulator or a genuine old man waiting to die in a cold hospital room.

I check on him a few times during my shift, but he's always asleep. I don't have the heart to wake him up. Brenn is on shift now and promises to text when he's awake.

So rather than head home, I go to the next-best place.

The beach.

I love Kincardine. Love the small-town feel, the Scottish bagpipe band that parades down the main street every Saturday evening during the summer, the markets held in Victoria Park on the weekends, the way the town comes together when tragedy hits. The day both Brennley and I were offered positions at the hospital, I couldn't have been happier.

Plus, Kincardine is close to Mom yet far enough away that I can live my own life. A win-win situation, in my opinion.

Grace brought me here first, for a day at the beach when I was around thirteen. We walked through the town and ate french fries from a double-decker bus down at the beach. Mom had stayed home to paint. That was probably the one and only time I ever visited this beach. Otherwise, it was only a town we'd drive through. But the memory of that day always stayed with me.

Station Beach is popular today. Waves lap the sand, sunbathers recline on their towels to soak up the summer sun, and children chase after the ridiculous number of seagulls in search of scraps of food.

I bury my toes deep into the sand and sit, head down, arms wrapped around my knees. I need to process today. I won't be good company for any of those passing by wanting to say hello.

My first instinct is to call my mom with a range of questions that won't leave me alone.

I send Grace a text instead.

She calls me within three minutes.

"How did it go?" she asks, real interest in her voice.

"Okay, I think. He's sleeping right now, so I'll head back when he's awake." I stare out at the water and think about dipping my toes in. There's a nice breeze coming off the lake.

"Sounds like you're at the beach. I'm jealous."

"You should bring Mom. We can spend the day here," I suggest, despite knowing she'll decline on Mom's behalf. "They say it's going to be a hot summer."

"Your mom has mentioned heading to Southampton for some smoked salmon, plus I hear there's a bakery there not to be missed."

That's her subtle way of saying a beach day is a good idea—just not in Kincardine.

I don't say anything for a moment.

"Are you okay?" Grace asks. "Do you want to talk about the visit?"

I lean forward and play with the sand. "He's . . . not quite what I expected," I admit.

"No, he's not."

"Wait. You've *met* him?"

"I've known David Walker for a very long time."

What? Why didn't I know this?

"You never told me that." The story I have been led to believe was slightly different. That Mom and Grace were introduced by Mom's doctor. So, what? I grew up believing *another* lie?

"It's a long story, Elle. And one that's not all that important. Not right now."

"I think it is. I'm a little tired of all the secrets and lies, Grace." It was one thing for Mom not to be completely honest with me—but Grace? This hurts.

"Elle . . . omission doesn't always mean there's a lie involved. It means you weren't ready to know the truth. That's all."

I stare up at the sky, watch the birds as they fly overhead.

I get it. I do. I was a child to be protected. But I'm not anymore. Still, I'm at a loss about what to think or how to feel at the moment. Yesterday my world was small, narrow. The only worry I had was wondering when Mom's next psychotic break would occur. Today my world is so much larger. I can't seem to take it all in.

I've got a grandfather who is dying.

I've got a mother with secrets she won't reveal.

"He has a story he wants to tell me."

There's a quick inhale of breath.

"A story? About what?" Grace asks.

"About Mom. About him and his wife. About what life was like for them when Mom was little, I'm guessing." I'm intrigued, I'll say that much.

"Be careful, Elle. Please."

Again with the warning.

"What's so evil about him?" I ask. I wish someone would be open and forthright with me.

"Not evil," Grace clarifies. "Just . . . be careful."

"Why?" I want to know. I need to know.

There's silence on the other end of the phone. I'm not sure if Grace has hung up or not. I check my screen and see a full set of bars, so I know the connection is fine.

"Just remember," Grace finally says, her voice soft and low. "A story is just that: a story. Don't try to find a hidden meaning or look too closely at the tale he's weaving. It's one man's version of a life he probably dreams about. The history between your mother and her parents is . . . complicated. A story is always biased, never one hundred percent factual, and it's based on perception. In this case, a dying man's memory. Things aren't what they seem, and words can always be twisted. You know that."

"So basically"—I stand, dusting the sand from the back of my maxi skirt—"it's only a story and I shouldn't take it as fact. I asked him not to lie to me, Grace. I don't think he would make up something just to satisfy my curiosity." At least, I hope he wouldn't. But considering he is a complete stranger to me, who knows?

"A story is just a story, love. There's always an element of truth. But remember, it's just an element."

I listen to the care in Grace's voice, to the concern and to the warning. I hear it, but I'm not sure it's necessary.

David Walker is an old man on his deathbed. He says he's full of regrets. Him telling me a story has more to do with unburdening his own heart than anything else.

"I'll listen to him, Grace. He's lonely and he's my grandfather, for whatever that's worth. Whether he deserves it or not, this will give me closure."

I hope she hears the conviction in my voice.

"I trust you, Elle. Your mom was wondering when you'd be back. I think it would help her if you were able to come home a little more often right now."

If I don't go home soon, Mom will think I'm choosing David over her, which isn't the case at all. But that's how she will see it.

"I can come early in the morning, if that works." As long as I left by dinner, I'd be back in time. It would make for a long day, but I'm a nurse. I'm used to long days.

I hang up and heave a very long sigh. No matter what I do, I'm bound to hurt someone: David Walker, if I leave. My mother, if I see him again. Grace, if I'm not careful and I get myself hurt.

I spend close to an hour on the beach before heading back to the hospital.

Part of me is excited.

Part of me is nervous.

Another part of me wonders what the hell I'm doing.

And yet, I don't turn around, don't head home . . . instead, I find myself standing at the nurses' desk, waiting for Brennley to get off the phone.

"Hey. I didn't text you, did I?" she says.

"I just thought I'd stop by before heading home. Mom wants me to go back out in the morning, so I'm going to leave bright and early."

"Gotcha." She checks her watch. "Will you be up when I get home? We have a lot to talk about. I need to know what's going on with David and your mom."

When I roll my eyes, she chuckles. It isn't that I mean to be sarcastic; it is more out of frustration.

"Don't be too angry with her," she says, as if reading my mind. "I can't fathom what would make someone pretend their parents were dead. Give her a chance to explain, if you can."

Explain? I don't think that's something Mom wants to do. I'm not even sure she's ready to. Grace said she was stronger than I gave her credit for, but I'm not so sure.

When I open David's door, he looks like he's sleeping.

Or at least, I think he is. His head is turned toward the window, the blanket covering him moves with his breaths, and there is a stillness to the room that makes me pause.

I'm not sure how long I stand there, but it's long enough to create an impression of him in my mind.

My grandfather is an old man. He's thin, frail-looking, and with only a little bit of hair on his head. His face creases with wrinkles when he smiles, and the skin on his hands—on his arms, even—is translucent.

I move to take a step backward, to leave the room. He turns his head.

His gray-blue eyes stare at me with a steadiness, measuring me, judging me while I stand there.

Do I pass?

What does he think when he looks at me? Does he see a thin and mangy girl trying to find her way in the world, or a confident woman willing to take the world by storm—what I hope I portray?

"You came back."

The roughness of his voice surprises me. I find myself wanting to reach out, to comfort him. Knowing you're about to die must be a hard thing to live with.

"Of course." I sit next to him and place my hand briefly beside his, careful not to touch him this time. "Turns out I'm a sucker for stories."

I've always found it amazing how easily a simple gesture can transform someone's physical features. David Walker has become someone I want to get to know, someone who intrigues me. I can't imagine him being a monster, like my mom made him out to be.

I realize looks can be deceiving, and it's entirely possible this is all a ploy, an act . . . but for some reason, I don't think so.

My mom lives in a fantasy world, one of her own making. I know this. It's completely possible she's made her parents out to be the monsters she believes them to be . . . but in fact, aren't.

I am willing to give him the chance to prove Mom wrong.

No one deserves to die alone.

David's hand shakes as he reaches for his cup of water. I struggle with whether I should help him or not—until there's a knock on the door.

"David, I see you've met my roommate. Imagine my surprise when I realized your granddaughter is my best friend." Brennley places her arm around me in a tight hug. "I couldn't believe it," she confesses as she reaches for the chart hanging on the end of the bed.

"You could have given me a heads-up, kid. I almost had a heart attack when my granddaughter walked into the room. Then my death would have been on you."

There's a half grin on David's face. A devil's smirk, my mom would say.

"You keep saying you're going to die and yet you're always here when I walk in," Brennley teases. "He's not as scary as he thinks he is." She winks.

"It's hard to die when you're always here bugging me." David shakes his head.

"Then I guess I'll keep it up!" She gives a slight wave before leaving the room.

Both of us sit there awkwardly.

"No lies, right? That's what you asked of me earlier."

"Right." I don't like the sound of this. I twist the ring Mom gave me a few years ago—a sterling silver band inset with garnets, a simple design with my birthstone.

"I sent a lot of letters over the years. I figured that was my last. I never believed you'd get it, let alone visit me before . . ." He doesn't finish. He doesn't need to.

If it weren't for Brennley, I wouldn't be here. My heart hitches at the thought.

Regardless of my earlier purpose in coming, I want to be here, right now, in this moment with him—David Walker.

"I'm here for a reason, I guess." The smile I give him is genuine.

When he reciprocates, that part inside of me that I didn't realize was lacking . . . fills up.

"Guess we better get started then," he says. He glances out the window, and I wonder what is out there. It isn't the first time I've caught him looking in that direction, nor is it the first time I've noticed his gaze seems to be . . . elsewhere? As he stares out the glass window into . . . what?

A field. With trees in the distance.

He breathes in deeply before turning his gaze back toward me.

"Ever since you left, all I've been able to think about is what I'll tell you. What story could I possibly share that would tell you everything you need to know." He swallows hard and twists his hands together in his lap.

"Anything you tell me will be more than I know now," I say warmly.

The acceptance in my voice must have been clear because he dips his chin toward his chest.

"I guess in the end," he begins, "you start thinking about the beginning."

Chapter Eight

DAVID

June 1956

The stormy clouds overhead had opened up, and rain pelted David as he ran from the diner to his truck. He splashed through puddles; the bottoms of his jeans were completely soaked by the time he got the door open and climbed inside.

What was supposed to be a bathroom break turned into coffee with other truckers, resulting in his staying longer than he'd intended.

He turned the wipers up full against the torrent of rain, barely able to see past the flare of his headlights.

Rain was the last thing he needed. He had an hour and a bit before he would pull into his driveway, and he was exhausted.

With miles ahead of him, David unwound the cap of his thermos and carefully poured the fresh black coffee he'd gotten at the restaurant into his mug. The suspension on his truck bucked more than a rodeo bull when it came to bumpy roads, and they only got worse the closer to home he got. He'd spilled many cups of coffee on his lap throughout the years, thanks to these roads.

The rain covered the road ahead, and his beams barely cut through the darkness, so David almost missed the two figures walking on the side of the road.

He leaned forward to get a better look, slowing down as he did so.

Of all nights to be hitchhiking, tonight was one of the worst.

He pulled over and flashed his lights to snag their attention.

He didn't like what he saw the moment they turned.

A young mom holding tight to the hand of a small child, her other hand raised to shield her eyes from the rain.

The child she held on to didn't look up.

David cleared the passenger seat beside him, throwing his bag of clothes, lunch sack, and jacket on the floor.

"Thank you," the girl said as she lifted the child up into the cab and followed quickly behind. She carried a backpack, which she placed at her feet as she pulled her child onto her lap.

They were both soaked right through.

"Where are you headed?" David asked.

He'd picked up his fair share of hitchhikers in the past, but never one with a small child.

"Anywhere, really. The closest city, if possible." She rested her cheek on the child's head, but the look in her eyes said not to mess with her.

"Girl or boy?" David asked. He couldn't tell from the way the kid attempted to burrow beneath her arm.

"Girl." She helped the child in her lap sit up. "Her name is Isabel Marie, and she's not a fan of the rain. Are you, Bella?"

David caught the soft kiss she placed on Bella's forehead and recognized right away the love of a parent.

"I've got a little girl at home, probably about the same age. Anna Marie. She's not a fan of the rain either," David offered up, waiting to see if Bella would deign to look at him.

She did. She peeked out from beneath her mother's arm and gave him a soft smile, one that reminded him of a similar smile waiting for him at home. The darkness had to be playing with his mind because he could have sworn he was staring at the face of his own little girl.

"I'm David." He handed the mother the cup of coffee he'd just poured. "You look like you could use this." He pulled his flannel jacket off the floor and laid it over her and her daughter.

"Thank you." She took a sip of the coffee and held it tight in her hands.

David turned the knob for the heat as far as it would go. The girl's jeans were soaked right to the skin, and she shivered as she sat there.

"Hey, Stickshift. That you? Everything okay?" His CB radio blared with a greeting from a driver who passed him on the road. "Need me to stop?"

David reached for the receiver. "All good. Just picked up a traveler and bundle. Thanks for checkin' in, Singer."

"You got it. Give your woman a kiss for me tonight. Tell her I miss her," Singer replied.

"Will do. Safe travels," David signed off.

He could tell from the questioning look on the mother's face he had some explaining to do.

"Singer is an old friend from school. He got his name after not realizing his switch was on and we were forced to listen to him sing for over an hour. The guy has a horrible voice, but he helped to keep a few drivers from fallin' asleep that night. I'm known as Stickshift, thanks to this old girl. She's got a small motor and it's a pain to change gears goin' uphill, especially when you're up north with a full trailer. Those hills aren't fun."

"I'm familiar with handles," she said, dismissing his story. She kept her hold on her daughter tight. "What was that about your wife?"

The smile on David's face grew. "Ahhh. Singer was best man at my wedding. Him and Gertie bicker like brother and sister whenever they're together—and trust me, they're together often. He lives just down the road and always seems to know when she's got an apple pie in the oven. She now makes him his own just so I can get a piece or two."

She relaxed her grip, her elbows dropping a few inches.

"You're not from around here, are you?" David asked once she'd drunk half the cup and leaned back in the seat with a small sigh.

The girl shook her head. "How'd you guess?"

"Well"—David pointed behind him—"for starters, the closest town is that way."

The girl grimaced before she looked out the window and stared at the passing fields.

"Up ahead," David continued, "is all farmland, countryside, and the lake."

"Are you sure?" the woman asked. "I thought the map at the truck stop said otherwise."

David caught the way her hold tightened on her daughter again.

"I've been driving this route for years. Pretty sure."

Poor kid.

"I'm headed home, and I can almost guarantee my wife will have a pot of soup on the stove and some fresh bread to go with it." He knew it was a long shot, but from the look on her face, it might be her only shot. "We've got an extra bedroom and hot water. Get a good night's sleep, have a hot shower, and eat some good homemade food."

He let his invite sit between them for a little. No doubt she needed to mull it over.

"Are you headed back into the city tomorrow, then?" she asked.

He shook his head. "First thing Monday morning. I don't work weekends. I can drop you off then."

The choice seemed pretty clear to him, but he gave her time to think about it. *Sure, she could leave first thing and catch a ride back to the city, but would she be fool enough to give up a soft bed and food?* He hoped not.

"What do you think, Bella? How does a hot bath and soup sound?" she said quietly to her daughter.

"And a friend?" the sweet little voice asked.

She looked over at David. He nodded.

"That would be nice, thank you. It's been a bit since we've slept in a real bed." She yawned, as if to prove just how weary she was.

Her leg bounced, and she played with a lock of her daughter's hair as David drove down the long, empty road. They passed farmhouses along the way, a few windows shining bright off in the distance.

It wasn't the first time he'd picked up a stranger along the side of the road, but it would be the first time he brought one home with him.

As long as it's a good day for Gertie, all should be fine.

Otherwise, he would be back on the road tomorrow with his guests, headed toward the city.

"I'm Judy." Her voice broke the stillness in the truck.

"Nice to meet you, Judy. Are you hungry? I think I've got some crackers in the bag, half a tuna sandwich, and maybe even some home-made cookies if Bella would like them."

He handed her his lunch sack, pretending to ignore the way her hands shook as she opened the bag and how quickly she reached for the food inside. The cookie Judy handed to Bella was wolfed down in no time.

When was the last time that girl had a good meal? He thought about his daughter. *No child should go hungry—that isn't right.*

He'd make sure Gertie filled up their bellies and sent them on their way with extra food too.

"Why is your truck smelly?" Bella piped up after she'd eaten another cookie. Her nose wrinkled with disgust.

"Is it?" He waited for them both to nod. His daughter often said the same thing. He was a truck driver; what did people expect? "I don't notice it anymore, but it must be why my Gertie insists I have a shower the minute I walk in the door. I haul cattle, and them cows, they rarely smell nice."

Bella sat up straight in her mom's arms. "Cows? Can I see?"

"Not now, sweets. It's nighttime, remember? The cows must be sleeping," Judy said.

"My trailer is actually empty," David said. "But we've got some cows I can show you in the morning. How does that sound?"

Bella nodded enthusiastically before she started to cough. She wiped her runny nose with the sleeve of David's jacket, and he caught the look of embarrassment on Judy's face before he turned his attention to the road, pretending he didn't notice.

About halfway home, David glanced over and noticed Bella had fallen asleep. Judy remained wide-awake, half turned in the seat and staring out the front window.

"So you're headed to the city, huh?" he asked, hoping to strike up some conversation and get to know Judy a little bit more. "Do you have family waiting for you?"

She snorted. "What family? They disowned me when I was eight months pregnant and refused to give Bella up for adoption, despite their orders."

David didn't like the sound of that. *If there's no family, then where is she going? Is she on the run? All she's carrying, besides her daughter, is a backpack. Surely she has more than that?*

"Cities have shelters, and that's what we need."

"So you're all alone, then."

Her hold tightened around her daughter. "I've got Bella."

"What about the father?" A part of him hoped she'd say he was either dead or stationed overseas.

"I don't want to talk about it." There was a weariness in her voice that didn't go unnoticed.

"Sorry. It's none of my business, I know. I just . . ." David really didn't have the words, didn't know how to express himself. He saw Bella, saw the resemblance to his own daughter.

What man could pass up having that in his life?

"Matt, my boyfriend . . . he's not really father material. More interested in getting high and drinking beer than being the father Bella needs, you know?" Judy pulled the sleeves of her long plaid shirt down over her hands, as if hiding them.

"How long have you been on the run?" David decided to call it like he saw it, despite the flash of fear that flared up in her gaze.

"Does it matter?"

He shook his head. "No. Just wonderin' is all."

He slowed down to turn from Highway 9 onto Country Road 3. Judy sat up and looked around.

"Still got a bit till we get to my place. If you can, try to get a little shut-eye. I promise to wake you up when we get close."

Judy hid a yawn behind her hand. "I'm good. Are you sure your wife won't mind us staying for the weekend? I don't want to impose . . ."

"Gertie mind? Nah. She might grumble about it being so late and the bed isn't made up, but just you wait. She's a true mother hen if I ever met one. Always has been. She likes to take care of others. Trust me, it'll be fine. Besides, she'll love having another little one in the house."

He did his best to keep the worry from his voice.

Bella coughed again, her whole body shaking from the force.

"How long has she had a cold?" Anna Marie had had a cough like that during the winter, and it seemed like it lasted forever.

"It's just a summer cough. Getting wet tonight probably doesn't help. I have some Vicks I'll rub on her chest when I put her to bed." Judy rubbed her daughter's back and gently rocked her in her arms.

"A nice warm bath would help, I'm sure. Don't worry, almost home."

He wished the girls could see his house as they drove up. He could imagine Bella's reaction to the huge yard, the swing set, and slide play area he'd created for his daughter.

He slowed down as he drove through the hamlet of Bervie, the town he called home. He'd grown up in the area, bought a section of land from his father, a farmer, and made a home with his wife. His parents had both passed on, and portions of their land were now rented out to various other farms.

David was a truck driver, not a farmer.

Thankfully, Gertie didn't mind. She was a town girl and knew nothing about crops or farm life. He'd had to teach her to garden, even. But when it came to vehicles, his girl could get lost in an engine with the best of them. He used to call her "a princess with a wrench instead of a crown." When they needed to change a tire on his truck while driving to Niagara Falls for their honeymoon, she insisted on doing it herself.

She was the best thing to ever come along in his life, and he knew it.

He pulled into the long driveway just off the highway and parked the truck. Gertie stood in front of a window, the light from the back room highlighting her. He waved once he opened the truck door and the light turned on.

"Hang on. I'll help you out." David climbed down and rushed over to the passenger side, opening the door and holding out his arms for Bella. Judy helped Bella step down so David could reach her.

By the time they were both out of the truck and David had retrieved his lunch sack and jacket, Gertie had the door open for them.

"I missed you," he said.

She gave his cheek a slight pat.

"You're late, you smell, and you brought guests."

He searched her face to gauge her reaction. At her slight smile, he knew everything would be okay.

"Is my angel still awake?" he asked.

Gertie's brow rose toward her hairline.

"David Basil, it's after ten at night. You can apologize for not tucking her in when she wakes in the morning." The look she gave him said he would be apologizing for a lot more than just being late.

"I see another little girl who needs to be in bed too. After drying off." Gertie waited for Judy and Bella to approach. She reached for the bag Judy held, and after hesitating for a moment, the girl relinquished it into his wife's hand. "Her mamma too, if I'm not mistaken."

"Thank you, ma'am." Judy's quiet voice barely carried over the *pat-pat-pat* of rain on the roof.

"Child," she said, running her hand over Judy's arm, "you're soaked. Let's get you into a hot shower, shall we? Your daughter too." She led the girls into the house.

David did what he did best.

He followed after his wife.

"You know what to do. I'll give you five minutes," Gertie said to him before ushering the two through the house and up the stairs toward the spare bedroom and bathroom.

David remained in the back room, where he'd set up a small shower stall next to the laundry. If there was one thing his wife hated, it was the smell of cows he brought home with him every night. She'd love it if he could start hauling something else, but this was the life he knew and he was comfortable with it. He worked for a trucking company out of Paisley that hauled livestock across Canada. They'd taken him on after he dropped out of high school. They treated him fairly. He was a loyal man, and until they proved otherwise, he'd remain with the company.

He tossed his jacket and shucked off his pants and shirt, placing them in the waiting washer. He stepped beneath the lukewarm water and quickly soaped up. Gertie had given him five minutes—considering the states of those two girls, he'd be lucky if she waited that long to turn on the water upstairs. Once that happened, his lukewarm water would turn bitter cold. If he wasn't clean by then, it was either suck it up or else.

He washed, dressed, and went to the kitchen. Gertie was already there, heating up the soup on the stove and placing bread in the toaster for him.

He loved this moment of the day.

Life could get crazy, work could get busy, but coming home and being in this room . . . it makes everything disappear.

Home meant a spotless kitchen with fresh-baked bread on the counter, his wife waiting for him with a smile, and his little girl at peace. Home meant love and security and family.

"Girls taken care of?" he asked as he snaked his arm around her waist and breathed her in deep. She smelled of home, everything he held dear. The only thing missing was having his sweet angel wrap her arms around his neck as he held her close.

God, but I love my family.

"Judy's giving her daughter a bath, and then she'll have her shower. Wherever did you pick them up from?" She turned in his arms and laid her head on his chest.

She was listening to his heartbeat, counting the rhythm, hearing his soul. He thought it weird when she told him it was her most favorite sound, but after several years he understood why. The steady sound of his heartbeat calmed her after worrying about him on the road all day. He was home and he was safe. She would say that was all she needed in this life—him at home with her.

She didn't say that often lately. There were other needs she had that they didn't talk about, needs that broke her heart whenever they weren't met. She had always wanted a large family, and all they had was one daughter.

For him, that was enough.

But not for his Gertie.

"Between Teviotdale and Harriston. Poor kids were soaked right on through. She drank all my coffee, so I'm not sure how she'll sleep tonight."

"She'll sleep. That girl has been running on instinct and adrenaline for far too long. Once she lies down in that bed with her daughter all safe, she'll sleep, and she'll sleep well. Anna Marie will be happy to have someone to play with in the morning." Gertie turned back toward the counter when the toast popped. "Hand me the peanut butter, will you?"

"Figured they might as well stay the weekend," David said as he rooted in the cupboard for the jar. "She's headed into the city to stay at some hostel and look for a job, I imagine."

"She *what?*" Gertie's hand paused in midair. "She's not on her way to family or such?"

David grunted. "She's got no place to go, no job, and from what I could see, very little to call her own. That's not the type of life you live with a child."

He couldn't help but think of his wife and daughter in that situation. It bothered him a heck of a lot more than he wanted to admit. They had no family to run to if anything ever happened to him on the road.

What would Gertie do in her shoes?

"That little one is sick. You know that, right?"

"With a cold." David filled his bowl with soup from the stove and sat at the table. First bite, his stomach rumbled.

"She's also got a fever, David." Gertie brought over the plate of toast and bit into a piece.

"What do you suggest, then?"

Gertie's long, hard sigh held the weight of two innocent lives. "I'm not suggesting anything tonight. Let them stay for the weekend, and we'll go from there."

David nodded in agreement.

Having Judy and Bella here might be a good thing, no matter how long. Give Gertie something to focus on and someone for Anna Marie to play with.

God knew, they both needed it right about now.

David glanced at his wife's tiny frame as she stood and headed to the counter to make more toast.

It'd been a rough week for them all, and David hated that he'd been away for the past two nights.

"You okay?" he asked her.

She sounded fine, and she looked like she was holding things together despite the dark circles beneath her eyes. But his wife . . . she knew how to hide things from him.

"I'm fine, David. I'm . . . fine. Life happens, you know?" She gripped the edge of the counter.

He knew she was anything but fine.

"I love you," he said softly.

This time, she did look at him.

"I know, love. I know."

He just hoped his love was enough. Most days it was. But lately . . . lately he wasn't so sure.

Chapter Nine

David was itching to get out into his garden. He'd looked at it early that morning, after feeding the chickens and fetching the eggs, and saw it needed a little bit of tending.

He'd learned from experience that if you didn't keep on the weeds, they'd destroy any hopes of fresh veggies in the fall. Usually Gertie would be out here during the week, watering the seeds and keeping an eye on things, but the last two weeks had been somewhat of a disaster. The garden was probably the last thing on her mind.

Not that he blamed her.

After his smoke and daily morning walk around his property, he trudged into the kitchen, basket of eggs in hand. He was surprised to find his wife already up and making fresh bread.

Maybe having Judy and Bella here is exactly what Gertie needs.

"Morning, love." David placed a gentle kiss on his wife's cheek while she kneaded dough on the counter. There was a flour streak on her cheek that he was tempted to leave. It looked cute, but he knew he'd get a scolding if she found out.

"Oh good, you got the eggs. Were there many this morning?" She peered into the basket he'd set on the counter and softly counted them.

He could tell her exactly how many eggs were in the basket, but it wouldn't matter. She'd still count them. She loved to count things, that

Gertie of his. Even though he didn't understand her fascination with numbers, it kept her happy, which is all that mattered.

"Eight. Well, isn't that nice? Perhaps I'll have the girls help make a cake for dinner since we have plenty."

"You're too good to me, love. Fresh bread *and* a cake . . . I'm a spoiled man." He nudged her slightly and was happy to see a rosy bloom on her cheeks.

While she finished kneading the bread, David poured himself a cup of coffee and sat at the table. Yesterday's paper waited for him.

He hadn't even gotten halfway through when he noticed Gertie at his side, hands on hips and giving him the fiercest scowl he could imagine.

"David Basil Walker! You haven't heard a single thing I've said, have you?"

David took a sip of his coffee and pushed the paper he'd been reading to the side.

"I was reading about the new grocery store coming into Kincardine. Did you read that?" He pointed toward the article in hopes of distracting her, but it didn't work.

"Yes, yes, I know all about the new store. It's all anyone is talking about these days. But that's *not* what I was telling you." She threw her hands up in the air and murmured a few choice words beneath her breath.

He didn't even want to imagine what those words had been.

"I asked you if you'd heard that little girl cough all night long? I don't like the sound of it." She pulled out a chair and sank down. "I wanted to go in and offer some medicine, but"—she leaned forward—"the door was locked," Gertie whispered while worrying her hands together.

David leaned forward and whispered back. "You'd lock the door too, if you were in a stranger's home." He caught the way Gertie eyed the stairs off to the side, and for a moment he thought for sure Judy had overheard. But when he looked, no one was there.

"I know." Gertie nibbled on the edge of her lip. "I just . . . all I kept thinking about last night is what if it was myself and Anna Marie?" She bit her lip again; then a look of resolution came over her face.

"I'm not letting them leave until Bella is healthy. That's all there is to it." Gertie pushed her chair back and stood.

David leaned forward again, resting his elbows on the table. "You can't make her stay. You know that, right?"

"I won't need to, David. I'll have a little chat with her after breakfast. I'm sure she'll agree."

Arguing was pointless once Gertie got an idea in her head.

Before long his little angel skipped down the steps, her fists stuck to her eyes as she rubbed the sleep away. She padded over to him and stood quietly by his side until he swung her up into his lap and gave her the tightest hug he could.

"There's my sleeping beauty." He rained kisses all over her cheeks until she giggled. She wound her arms around his neck and squeezed as tight as she could—barely tight at all, but David pretended otherwise.

"Someone's getting stronger, Mama. What are you feeding this child?" he teased. Deep inside, he wished it were true.

Since she was born, their daughter had been sickly. First, she couldn't keep anything down and had to be rushed into surgery to fill a hole in her stomach. Then the fevers started. They wouldn't go down, no matter how often Gertie prayed and gave her lukewarm baths. She was still all skin and bones, still came down with way too many colds for his liking, and they probably coddled her too much because of it.

Gertie looked over and winked. "It must be all the eggs she's been eating."

"I'm growing, Daddy. I'm growing." Anna Marie squeezed once more before she let go and cuddled into his lap.

David rested his head against hers. "You sure are, sweetheart. Growing more and more each day."

"You didn't tell me my story last night, Daddy." His daughter rested her head on his chest and curled her legs up.

"Sorry, love. I was a little late getting home, but I promise I'll tell you a story tonight, okay?" He kissed the top of her head again before finishing his cup of coffee.

"Promise?" She placed the palms of her hands on his cheeks.

"Promise." He didn't smile but he did wink, which brought out the dimples on his daughter's sweet cheeks.

"Daddy?" She leaned in close, so close their noses touched. "How come there's a little girl sleeping in the other bedroom?" She whispered, as if unsure if the little girl she'd seen was real.

"A little girl?" David wrinkled his nose before giving her a kiss on her forehead. He glanced up at Gertie. "I thought the door was locked?"

Gertie shrugged. "It was when I checked in on them before I came down here."

"Well, now . . ." David considered how to tell her about their guests.

"Anna Marie," Gertie interrupted, "how would you like to help me with breakfast? I thought we could make pancakes." Gertie reached for a bowl from the cupboard and brought it down.

Anna Marie jumped off David's lap and rushed over to Gertie's side.

"Pancakes? Is it a special day?" She placed her hands together as if praying and looked up with hope in her eyes.

Gertie squatted down until she was at eye level with their daughter. "It sure is. Daddy brought home some guests last night, and I have a feeling you might have something in common with one of them."

Anna Marie inhaled, pressed her praying hands to her nose, and squealed.

"I do?" Her voice was bright, airy, and full of excitement.

"You do. Any guesses what it might be?" Gertie's eyes twinkled as she looked to David before focusing on their daughter again.

David's heart filled with contentment as he watched the two people he loved more than anything else. They were the reason he woke up each morning and why he worked so hard each day.

"We like pancakes?" Anna Marie asked.

"Well, I know *you* do"—Gertie touched Anna Marie's nose—"but that's not it."

Anna Marie's tiny facial features furrowed as she tried to think of another possible answer. Before she could, there were footsteps overhead, the sound of a toilet flushing, then the sound of water flowing through the pipes.

David, Gertie, and Anna Marie all fell quiet.

Anna Marie turned to stare at the stairs, excitement building up inside of her until she couldn't stay still and ended up jumping up and down in place.

There was a wariness on Judy's face as she walked down the stairs, Bella held tight in her arms.

"Good morning, Judy," David said. "Gertie and Anna Marie were just about to make some pancakes. I hope you're hungry."

He watched Bella, but she barely even moved at the mention of pancakes. Her head was snuggled tight into her mother's neck. For a moment, he thought maybe she was asleep.

"Pancakes sound delicious." Judy hurried over to Gertie's side. "I was wondering if you would happen to have anything for fevers, for Bella?" Judy asked.

Gertie wiped her hands on her apron. "I sure do." She went over and placed her hand on Bella's forehead.

David didn't like the concerned look in Gertie's gaze.

"She's burning up. Let's get her into a lukewarm bath to help bring her temperature down. The medicine is upstairs. David, will you bring her up, please?" She didn't wait for him to respond, just ran right up the stairs toward the bathroom. Within seconds, the water was rushing through the house's pipes.

"Judy, would you like me to carry her?" He didn't want to presume, but from the exhaustion he saw in Judy's eyes, he knew she wouldn't say no.

"Thank you," she said as she gingerly transferred her daughter into David's arms.

Bella whimpered slightly. He was shocked at how much heat radiated from her skin.

"Anna Marie"—David looked at his daughter—"could you get Bella a glass of water? She's probably thirsty."

"Is she sick, Daddy?" Anna Marie didn't move.

"Well, she's not feeling too great, sweetheart. Can you help me, like I asked?" He waited for his daughter to give him a solemn nod.

"David? Bring her up here, please," Gertie called down the stairs.

"Coming, love," he replied, careful to keep his voice down so as not to startle Bella.

He made his way up the stairs, Judy and Anna Marie trailing after him. He set her down on the bathroom floor and held her until she could stand. Her body shook from the effort, but Gertie was there to hold on to her.

David slowly edged out of the small bathroom, letting the two mothers take care of the situation.

Anna Marie stood in the hallway, a plastic cup in hand, worrying her lip.

"Is she going to be okay?" she asked softly.

David took the cup and handed it to Judy before she shut the door. David scooped his daughter up into his arms.

"With her mommy and your mommy looking after her, you bet she's going to be okay. Tell you what . . . how about you and I go downstairs and attempt to make these pancakes? Think you know the recipe?"

"Mommy keeps it in her recipe box," Anna Marie whispered into his ear.

David kept an ear toward upstairs, listening to the soft murmurs of Gertie and Judy. He hoped the little one was okay.

By the time Gertie made her way back downstairs, he had a plate of pancakes sitting on the table along with some fresh maple syrup. The kitchen was a bit of a mess, but Gertie didn't seem to notice, for which he was thankful.

She was a stickler for a spotless kitchen.

"Judy will be down shortly. She's reading Bella a story, trying to get the little one to sleep."

"But it's just morning, Mommy," Anna Marie piped up from her chair at the table.

Gertie picked up a cloth and began to clean, as if on autopilot. "Her body needs to sleep to fight off the fever and cold, Anna Marie. Hopefully the fever will break, but in the meantime"—she turned to David—"do you have any plans for the day?"

"Thought I'd work in the garden for a bit, maybe run into town. What do you need?"

"I'll make a list, if you don't mind. Maybe you can take Anna Marie with you?" Gertie asked, not looking at him as she turned on the tap to fill the kitchen sink.

Take Anna Marie into town with me? Without Gertie being there as well? Bella must be sicker than I thought.

Gertie didn't like their daughter leaving her side.

"Of course I can." He kept his tone sterile, the concern he felt hidden beneath a calm veneer.

~

Four hours later, David pulled into the driveway, parking his pickup close to the old shed. He nudged Anna Marie, who had fallen asleep on the short ten-minute ride home.

He hitched her up in his arms and carried the bags of groceries Gertie had asked him to pick up, along with some extra medicine for Bella.

He wasn't sure what to expect when he walked into the kitchen, but happy expressions on both women's faces were the last thing he thought he'd see.

"How's everyone doing this afternoon?"

"We thought you got lost or something," Gertie answered.

"Where's my new friend, Mommy?" Anna Marie climbed up onto a chair, rested her elbows on the table, and cupped her face with both palms of her hands.

"Bella is sleeping upstairs, love," Gertie said. "I made her Grandmama's soup, and it worked its magic. Her fever broke, and she's finally resting comfortably without coughing."

"It's really a miracle," Judy said, casting a hero-worship gaze toward Gertie. "I can't thank you enough."

"We know what it's like to have a sick child, trust me." Gertie buried her head in the bags he'd brought home.

"Bella and I"—Judy pulled a leg up tight against her chest in the chair—"we've been through a lot, but I've never seen her this sick. I was scared. Really scared. I was telling Gertie earlier that I don't know what I would have done if you hadn't picked us up, David. Thank you."

David grunted, not wanting to make this out to be more than it was. "It's what any decent person would do."

"The appropriate response is *you're welcome*." Gertie gave him a sidelong look.

"You're welcome." He rolled his eyes at his wife before nodding his head in reply to Judy. "Now, if you ladies don't mind, I'm going to go do some man work, like change the oil in the pickup. Call me when it's time for supper."

David escaped outside and busied himself with work that was mindless. Changed the oil. Cut the grass. Cleaned the inside of his truck.

~

For the next two weeks, Judy and Bella stayed in their home. It was like a fresh wind blew in and all their problems—the grief, the unease—disappeared with their appearance. David would come home in time for dinner and play with the girls, tell them stories before bed each night. Stories about little girls who became best friends, fairy tales about princesses who became sisters, and anything else he could think of. They ate it up—especially Bella. After the two weeks, she was over her cold.

It was amazing how alike the two girls were. Despite Anna Marie being the older of the two, they practically shared a wardrobe. Once they discovered they both shared the same middle name, they begged to be called Marie One and Marie Two, but that was nixed right away.

One night, David came home from a run with news for Judy. He wasn't sure how the news would go over, especially with his wife and daughter.

"I found you a job, if you're still looking for one." David sat at the kitchen table and went through the flyers that had arrived in the mail, trying to make his announcement without much fanfare.

Judy and Gertie were standing at the sink. Gertie was washing the dishes, Judy drying them.

His gaze remained on the paper in his hand, even though he didn't really focus on it. Rather, he waited to see how the girls would respond.

"Really?" Judy didn't stop drying a plate, but he heard the hesitation in her voice.

Interesting.

"Molly at the truck stop in Teviotdale put up a Help Wanted sign in the window today. I told her I'd mention it to you."

"Where would she stay?" Gertie half turned to look at him as she asked.

When he looked up at her, she was holding a dishcloth in one hand. Her other hand rested on her hip, leaving a growing wet stain on her apron.

"Molly knows of a place where she can rent a room." David didn't know all the details, but he figured it would work out fine.

Gertie frowned, her brows knitted together tighter than the hat she'd made for him last winter.

"And who is going to take care of Bella while she works? Did you think about that, David Basil Walker?"

He held up his hands in mock surrender. "Hey, hey, don't shoot the messenger. I'm just giving Judy some options. She's welcome to stay here for as long as she needs to, but she probably wants to be on her own. Don't you remember how that felt, Gertie? I'm sure she'd like to get on with her life."

Gertie's lips thinned until they were barely visible, and her hands shook enough to grab David's attention and make him a little worried.

"You don't need to leave." Gertie turned to Judy and reached out her hands. "Stay here for as long as you need. God knows I could use the help around the house, and our girls get along so well . . . it would be a shame to break that up."

The smile on Judy's face faltered. "Gertie, I . . ." She looked to David like a wide-eyed cat caught between two rabid dogs. "I don't know what to say," she finally mustered.

"Stay for the summer, at least." Gertie wouldn't let go of Judy.

"Gertie, your hands are dripping wet," David interjected.

As if shaken from a daze, Gertie released Judy and wiped her hands on her apron.

"I'm sorry," she said. She swallowed hard, glancing over at David, looking for help. She let out a long sigh.

"You've both been so kind." Judy's smile seemed genuine. "Would you mind if I slept on it and let you know tomorrow? I'll admit the offer is tempting, but I don't want to intrude and take advantage of your kindness."

Take advantage? If she only knew.

David was torn. He realized Gertie was grabbing on to Judy and Bella like a lifeline. He wouldn't take that from her—not now, not after recent events.

But . . . we barely know the woman and her daughter.

For the past two weeks, he'd noticed a change at home. When he arrived at night, no longer did he walk into a quiet house or find his wife silently sobbing when she thought he wouldn't notice. There was a pep in her steps, laughter in her voice. Rather than dwelling on the past and their losses, she talked about the future, planned summer fun for the girls, and even sat outside with him late at night by the bonfire—something she hadn't done for a few years.

Gertie needed Judy.

Anna Marie needed Bella.

And what did David need? He needed for his family to be happy, to be at peace.

"Take all the time you need to decide," David said. "We'd love to have you here. If you'd like, consider it room and board along with a small stipend. You can help with the garden, watching Anna Marie, and giving my wife here some much-needed rest." He studiously refused to look at his wife, knowing she was probably throwing death looks his way.

"I don't need rest," she grumbled. "But the company would be nice."

David stood up from the table and went over to give his wife a nuzzle on her neck.

"David!" She pushed him away with a laugh.

"If we were to vote on it, I have a feeling you'd be outnumbered, Judy." David wound his arms around Gertie's waist. "Gertie wants you to stay, Anna Marie wants Bella to stay, and I want the women in my life happy. So . . ." He winked at Judy, who shook her head in mock exasperation.

"So I guess I'll stay," Judy agreed.

Gertie's breath hitched with surprise. David was even a little shocked she agreed so easily.

"Well, then, I guess it's official," David said.

"What's official, Daddy?"

Anna Marie pressed her face tight into the opening between two wooden rails on the staircase. Bella sat on a step above Anna Marie and did the same.

"Aren't you two supposed to be getting ready for bed?" David pretended to growl as he stalked over to the stairs.

Anna Marie giggled. "Daddy, you're supposed to tell us a story! Remember?"

David lifted his hands high in the air before dropping them dramatically. "Remember? Remember? How could I forget? You've only reminded me a dozen times since supper, you little monkey."

He stood at the foot of the stairs and prepared himself to run up, indicating he wanted to play a game of chase. Anna Marie stood and crossed her arms.

"What's official, Daddy?" she repeated.

David looked toward Judy. "You want to tell them, or should I?"

Judy went to stand directly beneath where her daughter sat.

"Bella, how would you like to stay here for a little while longer? We can work in the garden and play at the beach and—"

"We can *stay*?" Bella asked, her voice laced with more excitement than if she'd just been handed a chocolate cake and told it was all hers.

"Yesssss!" Anna Marie turned and wrapped her arms around Bella. "It worked! It worked!"

"What worked?" David smothered a smile at his daughter's reaction.

"We made a wish and it came true." Anna Marie reached for Bella's hand, and together they ran up the stairs, giggling the whole way.

David's heart swelled as he listened to his daughter's laughter. This was all he wanted—for her to be happy. He would do anything and everything to hear that sound each and every day.

Anything and everything.

Chapter Ten

I have a new friend who is just like me.

Mama says we look like two peas in a pod, and if it wasn't for our giggles, she wouldn't know which one was me.

We even share the same name.

Mama says we're like sisters. I've always wanted a sister, one that I can play with and will play with me.

We both like the idea so much that we've decided to be sisters. Now and forever.

We even spit on it, which was gross because Mama says it's not ladylike to spit.

Mama is sleeping. She's been sleeping a lot. My sister's mama says that sometimes a body needs to sleep the day away before it can be well. I didn't know my mama was sick but she must be because she's sleeping a lot of days away.

My sister and I are baking cookies today and are going to have a tea party in our special place.

There's this place behind the shed where there are lots of flowers. We like to come here and talk with our other sisters, the ones no one sees. But we do and we hear them.

They say we're all sisters. One day we'll be able to play together.

Chapter Eleven

ELLE

I guess in the end, you start thinking about the beginning.

Those words stay with me all night.

By the time Brennley makes it back to our apartment, I am halfway through a tub of Ben & Jerry's ice cream. One look at me and she grabs her own spoon, joins me on the back deck, and thankfully doesn't say a word until the whole container is gone.

"That bad, huh?"

I snort. "I don't know. It was . . . weird." I am still trying to process everything, looking for some hidden meaning in the story he told me. I try to picture Gertie and my young mother, the love that was obviously between them. But every time I try to fix it in my mind, the image hazes over until I'm not sure what I am seeing, like the morning fog over the lake.

"What happened? What did David say? What do you think of him?"

I can tell she is nervous about my first impression. For some reason, she's really fallen for David. When he dies, it is going to hit her hard. I don't feel that same level of devotion—at least, not yet.

"He told me a story. But it wasn't quite what I expected, and I'm not sure how to handle that. He insinuated some things about my grandmother I never knew, painting a picture that completely goes against the little that Mom has said to me."

I feel pulled in two different directions, and it isn't a comfortable feeling.

I share the story with Brennley, who sits staring out across our small deck while I speak. By the time I am finished, she has tears in her eyes. For the life of me, I don't understand why.

"He loved Gertie so much." She wipes the tears that stream down her face. "I can't imagine having that kind of love, can you? She was his world. For all his gruffness, he misses his wife so much, his heart breaks over and over."

That's the difference between Brenn and me. She romanticizes life and looks for the good in everyone, while I look behind the words to search for what's not being said. She's the yin to my yang.

"Give him a chance, Elle. You should have seen the smile on his face as he fell asleep tonight. I've never seen him so . . . peaceful."

"But are Judy and Bella real? I've never heard of them before."

She shrugs. "I'm not sure if you can take everything he says as truth. His mind isn't seeing things as clearly as before. He could be lost in the past, or a past that he prefers to remember. I've heard of that happening a lot."

So he could be lying, then? Or maybe not lying, but rather not remembering the complete truth?

~

On the drive up to Mom's, with a sky draped in hues of raspberry and orange, I try to focus on the man and not the story. I focus on how I feel about meeting the man I should have grown up calling *Grandfather*. I can't shake the betrayal, the sense of loss. It's like a part of me I always knew was missing has been found, but it's too broken to replace.

I find Mom and Grace outside. I left my apartment at five in the morning, unable to sleep, but never would I have expected to find them out here so early.

Out in the country, mornings are magical. Watching the sunrise over the fields, catching the glittering diamonds of dew on the flower petals, listening to the wake-up calls of nature—you don't get this living in town.

We used to sit by the fire in the morning like this when I was younger. There were times Mom had insomnia and never slept. Grace would bring her out here and build a fire. After a few minutes, the crackle would have Mom closing her eyes and getting a few moments of rest.

Has she not slept again?

I grab a cup of coffee and join them, sinking into an Adirondack chair, draping a waiting blanket around my shoulders to ward off the early-morning chill. I ignore the fact both Grace and Mom are staring at me, as if waiting for revelations about my visit.

Grace seems anxious.

Mom seems almost resigned.

The crackle of the fire is the only sound between the three of us. I draw my legs up close to my body, clasp my fingers together, and watch the flickering flames. I love how they move, like modern jazz dancers swaying to music.

When I was little, we would sit out here during the summer nights, roasting marshmallows. Mom would weave stories about the flames.

There was a period of time when I was fascinated by dragons. And so Mom would tell stories about dragons who lived beneath those flames, their bodies covered by the burning coal, scales in brilliant hues of red, orange, and even blue. Those dragons would come alive when the fire was lit, the smoke proof they lived and watched us.

The ones I loved best were of the dancers, though. She could weave the most magical stories about them within those flames—I would have sworn I could see them.

"He reminds me of you." I swallow hard and watch the shift in my mom's eyes as she stops staring at me and looks back into the flames.

"I'm nothing like him."

The words are full of daggers and sharp edges, with a hint of warning.

Grace gives a small shake of her head, a gesture I decide to ignore. "All he wanted to do was tell me a story."

Mom bolts from her seat and glares at me. Though she leaves her words unspoken, her gaze is doing plenty of yelling.

I stare back, not backing down. She's kept this man from me for my whole life, made me believe a lie—and I'm not sure why.

Brennley was right. The love my grandfather has for my mother shines like the sun in all its glory, welcoming a new day full of light and hope.

I didn't admit it last night, but listening to him, I was transfixed. Not by his voice, but by the way his eyes glistened with tears, the way they would widen with delight as he described how it felt holding his little girl in his arms, hearing her laughter, being lost in her smile.

For Mom to have declared him dead to her all these years, I know something terrible must have happened. For the life of me, I can't figure out what. It is like the answer dangles there, on the tip of her tongue, but she refuses to let go of the words, the pain, the memories.

She heads back to the house, her footsteps heavy on the paved walkway.

"He told me a story about you and Bella," I call out.

Mom doesn't stop, doesn't hesitate, doesn't even look back toward me. She keeps right on going, as if I haven't said a word. The only way I know she's heard me is by the very distinct slam of the French door behind her.

I wince.

"Don't take it personally." Grace, as usual, tries to bridge the gap between us.

Don't take it personally?

I don't.

I learned a long time ago never to take her outbursts personally. It was just how she reacted when I wasn't the perfect daughter, when I decided to have my own opinion, be my own person rather than the little princess doll she wanted me to be.

There were a few years, as a teenager, when I tried to conform. I tried to be the girl Mom wanted of me, but it was hard. The expectations of being the perfect daughter, of anticipating her moods and knowing how to navigate the world of Marie's mind, was exhausting. The more I focused on her, the more I lost myself—until Grace stepped in and reminded me my role was to learn, to grow, and to experience life. Her role was to take care of Mom.

That moment of freedom . . . it was exhilarating. I left for school and had goals of working at a city hospital until Mom had a breakdown, collapsing in her studio and calling for me. The guilt of not being there, of not taking care of her . . . it was too much, too heavy. I didn't need to say a word to Brennley. She started looking at the job boards and found openings close to home.

And here we are.

I feel the pressure again to conform, to toe the line, to place Mom's emotional well-being before my own peace. But I won't.

I decided to place my own needs first, even knowing she would be upset.

I went to see him anyway.

She warned me she didn't want to hear anything about him.

I shouldn't have been surprised by her reaction.

"How did he look?" Grace asks.

"Old." That isn't adequate enough. "Like a man ready to die."

"Was he happy to see you?"

"More like surprised."

Doleful, Grace plays with her empty coffee mug. "Guess fate has a way of working out in the end. You finally met your grandfather, and all you have to say is he's old and ready to die?"

"I expected a monster, and instead I found a very sick old man. All he wanted was to tell me a story."

"And all you wanted was to hear that story, right?"

"Right." I sigh. "Except it wasn't the story I thought I'd hear, you know? I expected it to be about Mom, about my grandmother, about him. But instead, it was about two other people who came into their lives. I have no idea why it's so important."

"Two others?"

"Why would he tell me a story I'm not interested in? What kind of game is he playing with me?" I speak over her, giving voice to my thoughts.

"Why would you think it's a game?" Grace asks.

I lean forward in my chair, elbows on knees. I stare into the dying flames.

"Mom warned me he'd play games with me. Maybe that's all it was. A game to see if I care."

"Care?"

"Care enough to go back, to find out more. There has to be a reason Bella and Judy were so important."

"Did you say *Bella*?" Grace stares at me with an anxiety-ridden gaze. I nod.

Grace worries her lip before standing. "I'm going to go check on your mom. There's sand in the pail for the fire when you're ready to come in."

"Do you know her?" My question stops her.

Grace rubs her temple before releasing a sigh that deflates her whole body.

"Bella." She looks toward the house. "She . . . isn't real. Whatever story he told you, the likelihood of there being any truth to it is slim."

Grace squeezes my shoulder before she leaves me to sit by the fire alone.

I hug my knees tighter and listen for the sound of the door to close while I watch the dying flames before me.

I think back to when I left the hospital last night. David fell asleep while telling the story. I sat there for a bit, watching him, taking in everything I saw. I realized that the man in that bed . . . he wasn't what I'd expected.

He isn't a monster.

He isn't a grandfather either.

He is just a man, dying.

I feel sorry for him.

He promised me a story. He also promised me no lies. But can I trust him?

I hadn't been sure then and I definitely wasn't sure now.

Moments before I left the room, he woke up and reached out, as if to stop me.

I reached for his hand before I remembered the pain that touching him caused.

"Will you come back?" he asked.

I wasn't sure how to answer.

Part of me wanted to, but meeting David Walker, my grandfather, hadn't been what I thought it would be.

"Of all the stories you could have told me, why that one?" I slung my purse over my shoulder and waited for his answer.

"You wanted to know more about your mother." I caught the way he gripped the edge of his blanket in his hands as he said it.

"That wasn't about my mother." I stated the obvious. "That was about Judy and Bella, two people I've never met and have never heard of before."

"Are you sure?"

"Of course I'm . . ." The look he gave me made me pause. I was pretty confident I'd never met those people before.

"You should ask her." David's eyes closed. "I know you don't have to, but I'd . . . I'd like it if you came back."

"I'm really glad I met you." I couldn't give him the answer he craved, even if he was dying. I ran my finger over my chapped lips, pulling at some loose skin. "I would like to come back, but . . ."

"But my daughter asked you not to, and disappointing her once was hard enough. I understand."

And yet the hurt in his voice, the dejected look on his face, increased my guilt tenfold.

Whether I returned or didn't, I was going to let someone down.

"Even though I've known you for only one day, I'm glad we met." I wished I could have shaken his hand or touched his shoulder or even placed a kiss on his cheek.

I guess life is about having to deal with unfulfilled wishes and hopes.

His eyes opened, and I caught the single tear that trickled down his weathered face.

"Meeting you is all I ever wanted." His sandpapery voice hit my tender heart hard.

I didn't say anything. I didn't go to him or even lift my hand to wave goodbye. I just gave him one solid look, eye to eye, before I turned and left the room.

I didn't cry on the drive home, but the tears flow freely now as my head drops to my knees.

I want to go back. More than anything. I want to spend whatever time I can with the grandfather I just met.

But there are so many questions that I need answered, and going back can only mean more questions.

He wouldn't tell me what I need to know.

Grace for sure isn't going to.

So that left Mom.

Except I run the risk of setting her back mentally and emotionally, and she is in such a good place right now.

It isn't fair to her.

It isn't fair to Grace.

It isn't fair to me.

When Mom's moods come on, when she withdraws and internalizes everything . . . she changes. She becomes a different person. A person I don't like. A person who scares me.

It isn't that she becomes sad and depressed.

It is more.

There were so many times in my life when I wasn't sure if I was the crazy one or if it was her. Things would happen—things that didn't make sense.

I would get sick.

A lot.

In fact, the only time I ever get sick is when Mom has one of her episodes. It's like my own body, my own mental state, is linked with hers.

I wipe the tears from my face and get up to dump sand on the smoldering fire. I wait till it dies down, until the dragon is asleep, before I head into the house.

All is quiet on the main floor.

Patches winds her way between my ankles, doing her figure-eight dance. I pick her up. Listening to her purr, having her body vibrate close to my chest, calms me.

"What are we going to do, huh?" I nuzzle my nose into her fur before whispering a small prayer for clarity.

Whenever I was little and unsure or unsettled, I would climb into bed with Mom and beg her to tell me a story. It was always my favorite time with her.

She'd gather me close and tuck me beneath her arm. She'd weave a story while playing with my hair. Before long, I'd fall asleep, curled close and feeling safe.

My steps lead me to Mom's room.

I know she is expecting me because her door is open.

She sits on her bed, legs tucked beneath her, hands folded over an open book.

"Come join me." She pats the cover beside her.

She looks . . . comfortable and at peace, which was the last thing I expected coming up here.

A soft gust of morning breeze blows in through the open windows, the curtains billowing.

"I like it when you're home. Have I said that yet?" The look on her face is tender and warm. "This house feels so empty when you're not here."

I climb onto the bed, lean against the plush pillows.

I always did like her bed.

"I miss you too."

I'm not sure what's happening. Why the sudden change? I know enough to go along rather than question it, though.

"Will you come out and spend the summer with me? We live so close and yet it seems so far. Could you take some time off, maybe? We could go away, go on a trip out west, or rent a cottage in the Maritimes, on the ocean?" She reaches for my hair, twirls a lock with her fingers, her voice soft and gentle.

"Maybe after your showing?" I suggest.

"Yes, after the showing. Of course. But you'll think about it?" She sighs and drops my hair from her grasp. "I know I could get lost in my painting all summer, but I want to spend time with you instead."

I search her eyes for a hint of what's going on in her brain. Does she care about her father at all? Even have a sliver of concern that he's dying? Is this her way of ignoring the truth? Or is she trying to find ways to keep me from visiting him again?

"We could head to the market for fresh berries and baking," she continues. "Maybe take some day trips and explore, like we used to do when you were little."

"Mom? Who is Bella?"

It isn't what I meant to say, but the subject needed to come up eventually.

She picks imaginary pieces of lint from the bedcovers, not answering me.

I let the question sit between us.

"You've always loved stories, Lil'bit. If you're going to spend your summer listening to his, then I guess I need to tell you mine."

Her tone changes with her words. The ease, the lightness—gone. The accusation and disappointment—cutting.

"Will you tell me about Bella?" All I want is for someone to tell me the truth.

"Do you remember the stories I used to share when you were little? Stories of two sisters who weren't?"

I nod. "That was you and Bella?"

But Grace said Bella wasn't real.

Unless she assumes Bella is a mere figment of David's imagination.

Mom leans back against her pillows and removes the book from her lap. She closes her eyes, head tilted toward the ceiling, a sad smile on her face.

"I used to think I had the best daddy in the whole world. He was my everything, which is as it should be between a little girl and her father. I followed him around like a puppy dog, wanting to spend every moment I could with him. For a time, I would cry whenever he'd leave us in his big dirty truck that smelled like the farms around us.

"We lived a simple life back then. Momma took care of the house, tended the garden, and could make the most delicious meals. She was strict but loving, firm yet soft. She had a dream once, to have a home filled with children. I think having that dream unfulfilled . . . it eventually destroyed her."

"Was there a Bella?"

"Yes. She was my friend, my playmate, my sister. I loved her and hated her all at the same time.

"She was my magical friend. I found her one morning, fast asleep in our guest bedroom, and I thought maybe God had answered one of Momma's prayers and given her a little girl to love.

"Bella was . . . well, she was sweet and good. You remind me of her all the time. She loved to dance and sing and draw. I used to be so envious of her drawings. Momma would tack them up on the walls all over the house, so proud of the pictures, so happy to have another daughter to love.

"Bella didn't have a bad bone in her body. Everyone loved her. Daddy would take us out for picnics on the weekends he was home. We'd walk through the fields around us until we found the perfect spot for our sandwiches and cookies, and then he'd tell us a story.

"The stories were always about two sisters who weren't. They were princesses and bakers, dancers and farmers. They were anything and everything, and they made us wish we could be like them.

"In many ways we were.

"That whole summer, we did everything together. Once Daddy realized how much Bella loved to draw, he brought home pads of paper for her to use. She'd carry those around with her everywhere, wanting to capture everything she saw. She went through so many pencils. She left those pencils everywhere, until finally Momma had enough and created Bella her own area for art supplies.

"That's when I realized we all saw things through different lenses.

"Bella viewed life by her drawings.

"Momma viewed life by her emotions.

"Daddy taught me to view life by stories.

"That summer, everything changed for me. I gained a sister, but I lost my family. Or rather, I had to start sharing my family with someone else. There were days I found it too hard.

"Bella was always by my side. When she first arrived, she slept in the guest bedroom because she was sick. Once Momma nursed her back to health, she shared my room, my bed, my toys, and even my clothes.

"Momma told us we were now sisters, and so that's what we became. Until we weren't. She appeared one morning after I'd wished for a friend, and she disappeared with a wish as well."

Tears cascade down Mom's face once she finishes her story. I reach for her hand and squeeze gently, reminding her I am here, that she isn't alone.

She leans her head down till it rests against mine, and her breath brushes against my cheek.

"What did you wish?"

The whisper of her breath on my skin stops.

The weight of her head against mine eases up.

The warmth of her hand in mine disappears as a shudder runs through her body.

"I wished her dead. And then she was."

Chapter Twelve

I wished her dead. And then she was.

Mom's words haunt me. I imagine a little girl vanishing into fields of grass, one moment there and the next, gone. Or her body floating lifeless in a lake. Or walking aimlessly along dark country roads, never to be seen again.

My imagination gets the better of me, and I find myself eyeing Mom with suspicion.

I wished her dead. And then she was.

Does that mean Bella had been real? Or was she just an imaginary friend?

Who is telling the truth, and who is living in a fantasy of their own making?

My instinct is to trust Grace. She's never lied to me before, whereas all my life Mom has filled my head with stories and lies.

And David? Well, it's hard to trust the words of a man you've only just met.

For years, Mom told me stories of two little girls.

For years, I assumed those girls were us. She'd always let me choose the names—sometimes they'd be ours, sometimes they'd be names I made up. But the girls were always imaginary, stories created within Mom's imagination.

Except I now know her story holds notes of realism and memories of things she hasn't wanted to admit.

Maybe if I merge the two stories together, I'll get a semblance of something that I can understand.

I find Grace sitting outside on the patio, Patches in her lap, nursing a cup of coffee while waiting for me to join her.

"Everything okay?"

I rub my face with my hand.

Everything okay? Not by a long shot.

"She stopped talking."

I left Mom curled up on her side, a blanket thrown over her body to ward off the morning chill from her opened window. She'd retreated inside herself, into her memories, her fears. I knew there was nothing I could do while she was like that.

"If you're determined to visit him again in the hospital, there are things you need to know beforehand."

The resignation in Grace's voice should warn me, but it doesn't. It gives me hope—hope that I'll learn more truth.

"What kind of things?"

"Things that require a lot more coffee than this. It's too early to get into it, and my thoughts are still too muddy. Why don't you make breakfast? I'll check on your mom, and we'll talk later." With her shoulders stooped, Grace heads inside, leaving me to sit alone once again.

Why does it feel like everyone is withholding things when it comes to David Walker?

I eat breakfast alone.

Grace takes a tray up to Mom in an attempt to coax her to eat.

I wait for that talk with Grace, but she never reappears. She opts to stay with Mom for the morning.

I don't need to be told.

That spiral I've been so worried about? Mom is on it for sure, and I am the only one to blame.

We've been through this before, many times. For various reasons. Sometimes it happens for no reason. Once, we were on a road trip and stopped in a town for a bite to eat. She recognized someone, or thought she did, and almost collapsed. It took three days for her to get back to normal. Another time, she was reading a newspaper and wouldn't leave bed for almost two weeks, that paper clutched tight in her hands the whole time. I never know what the catalyst will be, but I am always ready.

I grew up knowing I had to be always ready.

It took years for me to realize that I wasn't responsible for her emotional instability. In my head, I know this. And yet the guilt is always there.

I take my coffee and my phone and head out to the back deck.

There is one person I know who might be more willing to give me answers than either Grace or Mom.

"Mitch Myers."

My lips widen in a smile as I hear my father answer the phone. He lives in northern Alberta, working on the oil rigs. It's been too long since we last spoke. We don't have the best relationship, considering he'd basically been an absentee father until I turned eighteen, but we are working on it.

"Hey, Mitch. It's me."

"Elle, this is a surprise. How are you? Everything okay?"

"All is well. Listen, I have a question for you. Do you recognize the name David Walker?"

Part of me expects him to say no immediately, and I think I was hoping for that. Maybe because then it would mean this secret hadn't just been kept from me, but from the man my mom once used to love.

But all I get is silence.

"You still there?"

"How is the old b . . . ugger?" Mitch has a thing about swearing in front of me, which I never understood.

"So you do know him?" Like a wheel punctured by a nail, I deflate in my seat.

"I take it you don't? Sorry, Elle. I had no idea she . . . well, I should have guessed she'd keep him from you. She has a thing about secrets and keeping people apart, doesn't she?"

I catch the dig but don't deny it or try to stick up for Mom. She kept Mitch out of my life until I was eighteen. She always promised she'd tell me when I was an adult about the man who chose to walk away from her and us, who didn't want to be part of our family. On my birthday, she handed me a box full of cards and letters from him.

He'd written me every year, on my birthday and Christmas. I spent days poring over those cards and letters, the anger inside building as the realization of what I'd lost grew. Mom had kept a man who obviously wanted to be a part of my life away from me.

"He's dying." Two words, but the inhale from Mitch says I've caught him off guard.

"I'm sorry, Elle. I only met him the one time, but it was enough to know he wasn't someone to mess with."

"When did you meet him?"

Mitch laughs. "He tracked me down, believe it or not, after I broke up with Marie. It took about a year for him to find me. He was the one who told me about you. Demanded I do right by you, to be honest. Marie wouldn't have it. I abandoned *her*, and that's all she focused on."

Of course. Leave it to Mom to jealously guard me from anyone who could possibly love me more than her.

"How's Marie handling this? Are you okay?"

Mitch and Mom dated about a year, until he couldn't handle her mood swings and arguments any longer. He left before finding out she was pregnant with me. He had no idea about her dissociative identity disorder—not that it would have changed anything. He still would have left.

"Thrown for a loop. But then, it's not the first time I've had to learn about something so life changing." I instantly regret my words.

"Life has a habit of doing that. Thanks for letting me know about David. Was there something else you wanted to ask?"

"Did Mom ever mention a Judy and Bella to you?"

Mitch groans.

"Oh, come on, kiddo. You can't expect me to remember every person in your mother's life, can you? That was a lifetime ago."

"So you never met any of her friends? A best friend or . . ."

"Of course I met her friends. We didn't live in seclusion, but she didn't have many either. I don't remember anyone named Judy or Bella, though. Sorry."

We spend a few more minutes catching up with each other before he mentions he is running late for work.

It's nice to talk to him, but I hang up feeling a little disappointed he couldn't shed any more light on the situation.

My fingers drum on the kitchen table as I picture Mom curled in a ball on her bed, her pillow stained with tears, Grace quietly beside her.

I have two choices: stay or leave. Head home, or head upstairs and be the daughter Mom needs me to be right now.

I opt to stay.

With a smile plastered on my face and honey infused in my voice, I knock on Mom's bedroom door and step in.

The scene I pictured downstairs is the complete opposite of what I see.

Grace is the one relaxing on the bed, and my mom is standing on a chair in her closet.

"Elle! Oh good. Come and help, will you? You're taller than I am."

She climbs down from the chair and points to the top shelf.

Grace pinches the bridge of her nose.

"What's going on?" Mom's closet is immaculate, her clothes color coordinated on hangers, her shoes and bags neatly displayed on shelves.

"There's a box up there I need you to grab, if you'd be so kind."

She moves out of the way so I can take her place. The box is at the very back of the top shelf, tucked into the corner, and apparently normally hidden behind a blanket or two she's swiped to the side.

The box is wood, with hinges on the back. It almost looks like a music box, but it is too large for that, and it looks handmade. I pull it off the shelf, surprised at the weight of it in my hands. Before handing it down, I blow at the dust covering the lid.

Mom blows lightly across the lid too, particles of dust billowing up and off the box. She reaches for a tissue on her nightstand and wipes it clean with extreme care.

I've never seen this box before. Never knew she kept it in her closet. I want to stand on my tiptoes to see what other things she has hidden up there, but I restrain myself.

"What's in there?" I take the corner chair and sit on the edge.

Grace releases a long sigh as my mom gently lifts the lid. Her fingers shake noticeably as she sets it down and peers inside.

"Grace is expecting me to have a relapse. She thinks I'm emotionally frail and is concerned that this nonsense with you visiting . . . him . . . is going to prove too taxing for me." She folds her hands neatly in her lap and looks more composed than I could have expected.

"I didn't call it nonsense," Grace mutters.

"You're right. *I* did." Mom pats Grace's knee like a mother placating a child who doesn't know any better.

"How are you feeling, Mom?" I'm not sure what's happening right now.

"I'm fine, Elizabeth. I wish you and Grace would stop treating me like a fragile flower or one of your newborn patients. Trust that I can handle this."

Something isn't right. I can feel it. The look on her face is too serene, the vibe in the room too calm.

My whole body is tense, poised to act on that flight-or-fight instinct. I'm ready for the bogeyman to jump out of the closet or for the big bad wolf to climb from beneath the bed and present his fangs.

"You're an adult, and"—she pauses and bites her lip, leaving an indent of her teeth—"I need to accept that. If I could wish this whole damn situation away, I would. But I can't change fate, as Grace reminded me. You always were a curious child, always wanting to know more about the stories, about the stories behind the stories. This is no different."

She pushes the box toward me.

Grace sits there, silent and watching Mom like she always has.

I place the box in my lap.

"Is Bella real?" I ask.

The soft *tsk* from Grace tells me she wishes I'd leave the subject alone, but Mom, surprisingly, nods.

"It's in the box, Lizzie. Everything I told you earlier—it's there."

The box is full of drawings.

"Did Bella draw these?"

I quickly look through the papers. Some are pencil drawings, others crude crayon images, but all were drawn by the hand of a small child.

"She did. It's all I have left of her—of the girl that was brought home to be my sister. They took her away from me because of something I did and then made me pretend that she never existed . . . but they forgot about these."

Mom made Bella out to have talent, to have drawn these amazing pictures that covered the walls of her house. But these . . . these were just childish drawings.

"This is the one she made of our home. Look at the detail, the way she drew herself in that window, waving down at me while I was picking flowers for the dinner table." Mom caresses the crude crayon outline of a home and a stick-figure child in the window.

I steal a look at Grace, careful to not show my thoughts on my face. It wouldn't matter anyway, though. Mom is so lost in the drawings she takes from my hand that I could stand and scream at her and she wouldn't pay me any attention.

She might think she is okay, but she isn't.

She is on the verge of a breakdown, walking along the yellow brick road of delusion.

Bella wasn't real.

She was an imaginary friend.

She was the creation of a lonely child.

She was the reason Mom survived whatever hellish childhood she lived through—and there was nothing wrong with that.

I watch her lose herself in her past, in the cherished friendship of a little girl only she knew.

I feel hopeless.

Hopeless and angry.

Grace tried to warn me. She told me to be careful, to guard my heart when it came to David Basil Walker. I didn't listen.

Not completely.

I thought I could handle meeting him. I thought my heart wouldn't grow attached, that I was only there out of curiosity. The need and drive to learn more about my mother, about my family, the only reason for going.

I asked him for one thing: not to lie to me.

He promised me he wouldn't.

Except, that's all he's done. Lie.

Bella and Judy—they weren't real.

His reasoning for telling me a story that is false is beyond anything I can imagine. What kind of man does that to someone he just met, someone who is family? Why lie when you're about to die? What is inside of him to make him spend his last days caught up in something that isn't even real?

Real is this . . . my mom on the verge of losing herself once again.

That is real, and that is all that matters.

Chapter Thirteen

Mom is . . . off. Different. She lives somewhere in between reality and one of her stories.

She talks about Bella a lot the rest of my visit. She retells stories from my childhood, but she changes the tales from being about her and me and makes them to be about her and Bella.

Maybe Bella is me. Maybe Bella is the imaginary friend that sustained her through being an only child. Maybe . . .

There could be a lot of maybes in this scenario, and my fear is that I will never really find out the truth.

Am I okay with that?

Grace told me to get closure but to be careful I don't become obsessed with David. Maybe I read into it too much, but the way she stressed *obsessed* makes me think she noticed a sign of mental instability in me.

God, I hope not, because I'm not sure I can let this go.

I have questions. Questions I want—no—I *need* David to answer. Questions about my grandmother and about my mother as a child. Questions about their mental health.

Had my grandmother been as emotionally unstable as my mother? Were the signs there? What kind of help had there been for them?

I shudder involuntarily at the idea of the treatments available back then. They were horrific.

Maybe that's what happened here. I don't know. But I want to find out.

~

The hospital is relatively quiet when I arrive before my shift.

My sandals squeak on the linoleum-tiled floors as I head toward David's room. The only sound in the hallway is the muffled shouting of a man from one of the rooms.

Amy, one of the older nurses who has been here since forever, stops me.

"I didn't believe it when Brennley told me, but it's true, isn't it?"

I nod.

"Blow me over with a bazooka. Who would have thought? I knew your mom. Well, I knew of her. I think we played together a few times before . . . well, before school, I guess. We all like to make claims we know the famous painter Marie Walker, but the truth is, we all know David and Gertie. There was a time rumors were spread that Marie had died. Did you know that?"

Are you kidding me? She died? What the—

"Of course, imagine our surprise when there was a big write-up in the paper about her being discovered by some collector. Kincardine is known for its sunsets, the pipe band, and now for a farm girl with the skill of Monet."

I can't help but laugh. *Monet?*

"She's not *that* famous." I say the line I grew up repeating over and over. "And I promise you she's not dead either."

"Then where is she?" Amy is known for her bluntness.

"She's preparing for a showing in Toronto." The explanation is weak, I realize that, but Amy is also known for being a gossip.

She joins me on the other side of the station and looks down the hall. "He's her father. She should be here."

It will be a cold day in hell before Mom steps foot in this hospital.

"He missed you yesterday. He suffered through a sponge bath in hopes you would have come to spend time with him."

"Is he doing okay?"

"He's not having the best of days." She sighs heavily and rubs the back of her neck. "I gave him a sedative, which should knock him out shortly. Unfortunately, that means he won't be up for company." She glances at her watch and frowns. "Are you on shift tonight?"

"I can always check in on him during my break. How bad is it?"

"The weight of his gown hurts his skin today."

I swallow hard. I can't even imagine the pain he must be in.

"The doctor increased his medication. It won't be long now. I'm surprised he's lasted this long, to be honest. Having you come in the other day . . . that gave him a reason to live."

"Would you happen to know his address? I'd love to stop by the house and see it for myself." My curiosity is working overtime. It'd be nice to walk through the house Mom grew up in. I tried asking both Grace and her, but neither would tell me.

Amy's eyebrows squish together. "Offhand, no. I'm sure it's in his files, but"—she pauses, thinking—"if you were to stop by the coffee shop on the corner of Broadway and Queen, you might find old Charlie there. He and David were friends, but the old man refuses to let me tell Charlie he's in here. You could though. He might even give you directions and even tell you a story or two about the old grump." She winks before returning to her station, burying her head in some paperwork, effectively dismissing me.

Considering I have a little over an hour till my shift starts, I run down to the coffee shop on the corner. Even if Charlie isn't there, I can still get a good cup of coffee before I start—a requirement before a hospital shift.

It's empty save for three older gentlemen who sit off in the corner, mugs of coffee in front of them. No one says a word as I walk in, but I have a feeling it isn't as if I've interrupted anything. They've probably been sitting there for a while in silence.

I order an iced coffee at the counter and ask the server if one of the men in the corner is Charlie.

"Boys? This girl here is looking for Charlie. Play nice, will you?" She hands me my cold coffee. "He's the one in the gray T-shirt," she says in a loud whisper.

All three men turn to look at me as if I were a bright pink unicorn that magically appeared.

"You sure you're looking for Charlie? He owe you money or something?" A man with a cocky grin leans back in his chair and motions me over.

"One of the nurses at the hospital suggested you might be here." I hold my iced coffee in my hands and stand there, feeling more awkward than when Mom caught me kissing Chris Veysey when I was sixteen.

"What can I do you for?" Charlie lifts his chin as I step closer.

"She mentioned you might know David Walker?"

Charlie nods.

"He's in the hospital, is he? How's the old bastard doing?" There is no emotion on Charlie's face, no hint of whether he considers David a friend or not.

"You should go find out for yourself."

No one says anything until Charlie cracks up with a snort.

"Guess I should." He studies my face for what seems like an eternity. I'm not sure what he is looking for, but he must have found it because he dips his head in a nod.

"What can I help you with?" he asks.

"I was hoping you could give me directions to his house. I know it's out of town, but I've only lived here a year or so and still get turned around on those country roads."

"You family?"

I shrug.

"Must be Anna Marie's kid. Haven't seen her since she was a child. David said she was a famous artist or something?"

This catches me off guard.

"You knew my mother?" My voice is mixed with both excitement and incredulousness.

"Child, we were practically family." The wrinkles on his face deepen as he looks at me, puzzled. "Been a long time since any of us talked with David, though. He's a bit of a . . ." Charlie shares a look with his friends. "Well, things happened, and we all lost touch."

"Like what?" The words come out quickly. Too quickly.

He frowns.

"Well, your grandmother wasn't well. When your mother left . . . things changed." By his look, he assumes I should know all about this. As much as I want to press further and ask more questions, I hold my tongue.

I wait as Charlie pulls a pen from his pants pocket and draws a map on a napkin.

"You'll find his place about fifteen minutes away. He know you're heading there?" He holds the napkin out but doesn't let go.

"This looks simple enough. Thank you." I give him my brightest smile while ignoring the question and hope that's enough to make him let go of the napkin.

"He'd probably appreciate a visit or two, if you have time," I suggest.

"You don't know David very well, do you?" Charlie chuckles. "Seeing any of us is the last thing that man would appreciate."

"Last time I saw David, he told me to rot in hell," one of the men mutters.

"Your grandfather made it clear a long time ago he didn't want friends. If he's dying, he's going as he always has lived: alone. Sorry to say," Charlie says without a hint of emotion in his voice.

It's as if he really doesn't care that my grandfather is dying.

That says a lot. About both him and David Walker.

"So *is* your mother a famous painter?" Charlie asks.

"She's good," I say.

She'd grumble if she knew just how famous she seems to be in this town. She is well known within the art world and has sold enough paintings that she can retire happy and never lift another brush.

"She always was a funny child." Charlie looks out the plate-glass window.

There's something in his voice that piques my interest even more. "You said you were practically family?"

Charlie shrugs. "For a while, yeah. Best man at their wedding. There when your mama was born too."

"You were Singer?" At the beginning of David's story, I remember him mentioning another truck driver.

Charlie laughs. "Haven't heard that name in a long time." He continues to chuckle but soon has to pound his chest with his fist as he struggles to breathe.

He pulls out an inhaler and uses it.

"Yeah," he eventually says. "I'm Singer. David and I used to drive for the same company. Gertie . . . well, we grew up together. Our parents figured we'd settle down one day and marry. Might have happened if she hadn't met David. Once she did . . ."

He begins to draw circles on the table with his finger, not looking at anyone as he does.

No one interrupts him. I turn to leave, but then he stops and looks at me.

"You look like her. Gertie. You've got her eyes."

I smile. I can't help it.

"Hope that's all you got too," he mutters.

If I were looking for confirmation that there'd been mental health issues in my family, his statement just nailed it for me.

"Can I ask what happened between you and David? He told me you were best friends."

"For a while, sure. And then one summer, he told me Gertie wasn't up to visitors for a while. In the end, that turned out to be for a long time. I didn't see much of my old friend after that. He started taking longer hauls, barely home, I guess. Saw him here and there at the truck stop, but that was about it. Eventually stopped seeing Gertie in town too. Few years ago, noticed David was back in town, but . . . too much time gone by, I guess." Charlie's shoulders slouch, his head tilts down till his chin hits his chest, and he's lost in memories.

I notice one of the men nod at the door. I take the hint.

"Thank you," I say softly.

As I walk back to the car, I think about everything Charlie said—and didn't say.

What caused David to pull away from his friendships? How bad had Gertie gotten?

Chapter Fourteen

It doesn't take much convincing to get Brennley to come with me to David's farm.

I follow the directions on the napkin, driving out of town and taking one of the side roads off the highway. It's a gravel road, and dust billows up behind me. We pass a few farms with towering windmills in the distance. Brennley notices the black mailbox with the name "Walker" in faded yellow paint.

I pull into the driveway and stop the car, taking it all in.

"Wow." Brennley throws open the car door and jumps out onto the driveway, turning round and round with the widest of eyes.

From the way David described his home, I pictured something small and quaint.

It's anything but that.

It's a large corner lot. The driveway starts and ends on two separate roads, the house in front of the driveway and a dilapidated garage on the other side.

I imagine David driving up in his truck, parking off to the side in that patch of gravel to the right of the house.

I envision where the garden he planted was, think about my mother running around with Bella—real or imagined—playing tag and hide-and-seek in the tall grass, or catching butterflies along the old wood fence, overgrown now with wildflowers.

I take a photo of the house and then, keeping my phone in hand, snap other images as we walk down the driveway.

"You said farmhouse, but this . . ." Brennley shakes her head. "I was thinking *Anne of Green Gables* style, you know? Not *Little House on the Prairie.*"

It isn't *that* bad.

The house is old; that's true. The roof looks like it would tear apart in a windstorm, and the siding is just faded yellow wood. At one time it was probably a really nice-looking home. I imagine Mom playing with her dolls on the ramshackle porch—now just a heap of broken rails, beat-up stairs, and overgrown garden beds.

We walk behind the house to find the back door locked and the windows covered in dirt. With a tissue from my purse, I clear enough of the dirt away for us to see inside. In the far corner there is an old washer and dryer, a large freezer, and a closet full of coats and work boots.

I walk around the backyard, through the dense lawn full of mushrooms, imagining where the clothesline would have been, the gardens, the chicken coop. I think about David's story and mourn for a childhood I never had.

Maybe I would have grown up here too, knowing my family, playing in the fields, gathering my own eggs from the chicken coop, having tea parties with my grandmother, and learning how to bake in her kitchen.

"It just needs cleaning up a bit. I could see it being a really nice family home back in its day." Brennley stands beside me, solemn, probably imagining the same thing as I am:

What would this have looked like when my mother was young?

I sit on a large tree stump in the middle of the yard. My phone rings.

"Hey, Mom." The smile in my voice is genuine, even if a little sad.

"What's wrong? Are you okay? Where are you?"

She sounds okay, normal. None of the singsong pitch from the other day.

"I'm okay." I ignore her other questions, unsure how she would respond to knowing where I am.

"I couldn't remember when you said you had a day off again. I was hoping it was tomorrow. I thought maybe we could go for a drive to Southampton, eat some smoked salmon, and watch the sunset on the beach?"

Southampton is a small beach town about forty minutes away from my mom's house. Heading to the beach to watch the sunset and eat smoked salmon from a newspaper wrapping was something we often did when I was younger.

While I like the idea of going, Mom's neediness is disturbing. This isn't normal, not for her.

"It'll be a couple of days. I have the night shift for the week."

"I wish you could come sooner. What are you doing right now? Are you home?"

I hesitate.

"Elizabeth, where are you?"

The struggle about whether to lie or tell the truth is real. I look toward Brenn, knowing she heard Mom's question. She's no help.

I'm not going to lie. If I accuse her of keeping secrets, of lying to me since I was a young child when I asked about who my father was . . . I would be just as guilty now if I lie about my whereabouts.

"I'm sitting on a large stump in the middle of the yard where you grew up."

Silence. For the longest time.

I walk around the yard, finding the post for what I assume was the clothesline. It's covered in weeds. The other end is a good thirty feet or more away from me, and a rusted wheel is attached to that end. If I close my eyes, I can imagine a woman standing here, hamper resting on one hip and a little baby on the other. Would she have set Mom down on the grass to play while she hung the wet laundry? The woman I picture is weary, sad. From my experience with women who suffer multiple miscarriages, I feel sorry for her.

I turn my attention to the large, run-down garage to my left. It's an L-shaped building that looks like it might have been painted yellow once upon a time, to match the house. Now there are broken boards, missing boards, and it looks more stained with yellow streaks than anything else. Not quite like a building found in a horror movie, but it could be close if seen at night.

A gravel path wide enough for a vehicle leads to garage doors that have seen better days. I don't think it's been opened for years, if the weeds along the edge are an indication. There's a window streaked with dirt, which Brennley is currently trying to rub clean with a piece of tissue from her bag.

"There's a really old truck in here, Elle. You should see it. And a whole crapload of tools and . . . stuff. Wow. I think I'm actually seeing my first evidence of a pack rat." She tosses the blackened tissue to the ground and dusts off her hands on her jeans. "Not sure I want to go in there, to be honest. Doesn't look safe."

Taking a peek into an old garage holds no interest for me, so I continue my walk around to the front of it.

Nothing but a large window and an old wooden door that's blocked off by two pieces of wood nailed across it.

"I haven't been there in years," Mom finally whispers. "I couldn't imagine why you would go there."

"Because it's where you grew up." I turn to look at the house. "From the stories you told me, I think I'm looking at your bedroom window. I remember how you used to tell me about looking down on your daddy as he worked in the garden or on his truck. How you would say good night to the moonbeam on the cornfields behind the house . . ." I look over my shoulder to where the chicken coop would have been, and I smile.

"How I would count the chickens every morning from my window as they left the coop to stretch their legs." Mom reads my mind. "How does it look?"

What a strange question to ask.

"The garage?"

She sighs, as if the answer should be obvious. "The house."

"Old." I don't know how else to sugarcoat it. "Like an old farmhouse except minus the farm." I know this isn't what she wants to hear. "Could do with some new siding, new porch." I try again. "The gardens are a disaster, but"—I gaze up at the cloudless sky—"I can see you here, as a little girl. It's cute and—"

"Do me a favor?" Mom interrupts me.

"Sure?"

"Go home. Please. Leave the past where it belongs, where it can't hurt anyone."

This time it's my turn to sigh.

"The past only hurts us if we let it. I'm just trying to understand."

"There's nothing to understand." Mom's voice says there's a lot to understand, but she isn't the one about to explain.

Which is why I'm here. I don't see the harm.

"There wouldn't be if you'd only tell me the truth."

She hangs up on me. I can't say I'm too surprised.

What is she trying to hide? What did she walk away from when she left home? What happened that changed David so much that his friendships were destroyed?

"Um, Elle . . ." Brennley waves me to her side as she peers into the dirty glass window of the garage. "You've got to see this."

I track my way through the long grass and prickly weeds, then nudge her to the side so I can look through the area she's streaked clean with the palm of her hand.

I do a double take, not really sure what I'm looking at.

"We need to get inside." Brenn grabs hold of the wood blocking the door and tugs hard. "Come help," she says with a grunt. She pulls so hard she almost falls backward.

We spend the next half hour trying to pull those boards off, getting our hands full of splinters. We finally find a crowbar at the side of the house and manage to remove the barricade.

The door isn't locked but it takes a few good pushes, hip nudges, and leg kicks to get it open.

The inside is a disaster. Like a tornado had blown through—or an angry man crazed with rage. Broken furniture looks like it was flung every which way. Books litter the floor in piles, children's costumes cover mounds of toys, and there are shards of glass that sparkle in the late-morning sun.

The smell turns my stomach. No doubt there are dead animals lying in the wreckage somewhere.

But it's the object in the corner that catches my attention.

A dollhouse, intact. A little faded by the sun and covered in cobwebs and dust, but the rooms are full of doll furniture.

Everything else in the room is destroyed but this dollhouse.

A dollhouse that looks exactly like the one I used to play with as a child.

On the wall above it, there's a drawing covered in a light dust. The edges of the paper are curled, but the image is unmistakable.

Two little girls—same color dresses, same color hair, same bright smiles—side by side, looking like they're hugging each other.

But the names above the girls really catch my attention.

Anna Marie and Bella Marie.

Chapter Fifteen

Before I head back to Mom's place, I spend more hours than I can count at the library, straining my eyes by looking through microfiche.

Brennley had the great idea of seeing what we could find to corroborate David's story about a hitchhiker and child in the area. There is nothing. I can't remember if David said where Judy was from, so we search all the local newspapers—plus the main city ones—from the mid-1950s for any missing people or children. Trying to comb through those is exhausting.

Brennley seems to thrive on the challenge and told me to leave the hunt to her while I calm Mom down.

She has called me at least three times a day for the past three days— since we visited the farmhouse. Grace finally had to send me a text asking me to come out. She said Mom was on the verge of a panic attack, the suspense of not knowing what I found too much for her.

Mom is now staring at the photos I took on my phone, scrolling back and forth, not saying a word.

I can almost pick out which image she's looking at by the way her nose scrunches or when her finger hovers over an image before scrolling to the next one.

Mom finally sets the phone down, pushes it across the table toward me.

"You didn't go into the house, right?" she asks.

"The door was locked."

Her lips press together until they're white.

"Did you . . . did you bring anything back?"

I shake my head. I wanted to. I thought about tearing that picture off the wall, of bringing the dollhouse and its contents home, of taking some of the children's clothing, washing it up, and asking her about it. But I didn't. I left it all there, as it was.

"Could you?"

The whispered words hold the haunting tone of the final chord of a funeral march. The hairs on my arms rise, and shivers dance along my skin.

Seeing those photos must have really touched her.

"I could. Or . . ." I know this is a long shot. "You could come with me?"

Mom rubs her hands over her face, the tips of her fingers scratching so hard against her cheeks that they leave lines as she presses down.

I take that as a no.

Her fingers drop from her face. She grips the edge of her chair and stares down at the blank screen of my phone.

"Can you tell me about the dollhouse?"

It is eerie how identical it is to the one Grace gave me as a birthday gift when I was a little girl. I loved it. It was handmade, a farmhouse complete with a wraparound balcony and porch off the upstairs bedroom. Mom and I spent weeks decorating it, painting the walls, finding material to use as curtains in the windows, putting up wallpaper. We would look everywhere for furniture and dolls that would fit it.

I played with that house for years.

It sits in Mom's studio now, in a corner along with tea sets, my dolls, and other toys I want to keep for my own children. She's used it a few times in her paintings—sometimes in the background haunting the images, sometimes the focal point.

"He . . . your grandfather"—Mom looks like she's swallowed a snake—"made that for you."

Well, color me a unicorn. I had no idea. I knew it was handmade, not something you'd find in a toy store, but I thought Grace custom ordered it or picked it up at a market somewhere.

"Did you know that?" I ask.

She shakes her head.

"Not right away. When I did find out, it was too late. You loved that dollhouse so much, and—"

"*We* loved it, you mean. You spent just as much time decorating it and playing with it as I did."

I never needed an imaginary friend growing up. I had Mom.

A ghost of a smile graces her face, the memory of my childhood welcome between us.

"How did Grace get it from him?"

Grace told me she knew him but never expanded on that. Apparently she knows him better than she let on.

"I never asked."

"Because you didn't want to know, or because it didn't matter?"

"Elizabeth." Mom shakes her head. "Why can't you leave things alone?"

"What happened that was so bad you wrote your parents off as dead?"

She flinches but doesn't bother to respond. She turns and pours herself a cup of the fresh-made iced tea that is sitting on the counter.

"Why is this so important to you?" She takes a sip of her drink and sets the cup down hard on the counter. "I've asked you to leave it alone, yet you keep pushing it—pushing me. You know I'd rather not talk about that time in my life."

I'll admit, for a moment I feel a measure of guilt because she's right. I won't leave it alone, and I do keep pushing her for answers. Even when she's made it clear she isn't going to give me any.

"I'm having a hard time wrapping my head around the fact you lied to me."

"You don't know him like I do, Elle. You can't understand. I wanted to protect you from him, from them. They're . . ." She presses her lips together, refusing to say anything more on the subject.

I swallow back a groan full of frustration.

"What are you arguing about this time?" Grace says, opening the French doors, clippers in one hand and fresh-cut flowers in the other.

I wait to see if Mom will say anything. She only lifts her hands before dropping them to her side, as if to say, *Who knows and who cares?*

Grace looks to me. I pick up my phone and show her one of the photos I took.

As if in slow motion, Grace sets the flowers down on the table, the clippers next to them, and sits. Her hands plant themselves in her lap. She stares, rapt, at the image of David Walker's house, the one I took when I first arrived.

I slowly scroll through the photos of the house, the yard, and the grounds. I take my time when it comes to the images of inside the garage.

"Oh my . . ." Grace covers her mouth with her hand, eyes wide as what is on the screen registers.

The shock and horror on her face mirror what I'm sure had been mine when I first opened that door to the garage and stepped inside.

"You found it like that?" Her eyes are unfocused. She lifts her gaze from the screen to me.

"I didn't touch a thing."

She presses hard on her chest, her fingers digging into her skin as she rubs the area above her heart.

"Why . . . I don't . . . how could he . . ." Grace fumbles with her words.

"Marie, have you seen these?" She twists in her seat and looks over her shoulder.

"Why couldn't you just listen?" Mom says. Her words are soft, mournful.

"I don't understand." Grace scrolls through the photos again and stops at the most disturbing one. The one that shows the room completely destroyed.

"Why would David have this? What . . ." She struggles to find the words I can't even put thought to.

"That was *our* room." Mom let her words settle among us all. "He destroyed it. I used to play in there for hours. It was a sanctuary." She looks at Grace. "Do you remember that? We would sit in there, have tea parties, and I'd play with my dolls while you read? It was the only place I felt safe.

"He destroyed my sanctuary." She pounds the counter with her fists. "What kind of father does that? Was he trying to hide something? Forget what he did? What she did? You can't erase sins like that." She turns to me, her eyes ablaze with anger. "Don't let him fool you, Elizabeth. Don't you dare feel sorry for what he's going through. He deserves to burn in hell for what he did." Her face contorts as her muscles contract and her lips pull back in a feral grimace. With utter contempt, she spits on the floor and then storms up the stairs to her room.

Silence reigns between us as we listen to Mom's heavy footsteps. Moments later, her bedroom door slams shut.

Grace sighs.

"So it looks like you found his house."

Nothing like stating the obvious—something that isn't normal for Grace.

She fiddles with her hands, entwines her fingers together, her knuckles cracking as she does.

"How was he today?"

I shake my head. My tongue is stuck to the roof of my mouth, my throat parched as sand on a scorching day. I take a sip of my iced tea, wet my lips before clearing my throat.

"He has his good and bad days." I scratch the back of my neck.

"So how did you find out where he lived?"

"Charlie."

The corners of Grace's lips lift at the mention of his name—for a brief moment. I almost miss the movement.

"Do you know him?"

Grace chews on a fingernail and doesn't answer.

"Seriously, Grace?" I roll my eyes. "Fine. Don't tell me. What is with all the secrets?" I am starting to get heated, my voice rising in octaves, my hands flying like crazy.

"The past is like that Russian matryoshka doll I bought you when you were only six years old, the one that nests together. You separate one doll to find another inside, and you continue this until there are no more dolls to separate. The first time you played with those dolls, you became so frustrated because you just wanted to reach the baby. I think there were over twelve dolls you had to open before you got to that baby, and then she was so tiny—too tiny for you to really play with." Grace draws circles on the table with a finger.

I remember Mom telling me stories using those nesting dolls, how each was a mother at a different stage in her life, always protecting her younger self. Looking back, I can see that she was talking about herself, I think.

"Your mother has a lot of layers to her, Elle. You can't hope to get to the bottom of her past without carefully unwrapping each one of them. Those nesting dolls are like her secrets. You can't expect to uncover it all at once."

Chapter Sixteen

DAVID

It's easy to remember all the mistakes made in life when you are at the end of it.

Sitting beside me is one of them—one I'd rather not remember.

I don't say the words, don't actually voice how I feel, but damn it's good to see Charlie again.

"Out of all of us, I thought I'd be the one to go first, you know?" Charlie hunches his shoulders as he rests his elbows on his knees. He's not looking me in the eye.

I envy him the movement. The last time I sat in a chair and attempted to touch my bony elbows to my knees, I almost died from the pain.

"Life has a funny way of twisting expectations." My throat vibrates with my garbled words, causing my voice to deepen until it sounds like I grumble the words on purpose.

"Gertie always said if my drinking didn't destroy my liver, my smoking would. Said she'd never forgive me for forcing her to attend my funeral."

I eye Charlie with the look of man who knows too much.

"That's why you stopped, ain't it?" Not sure why I ask. I know that's why the old bugger stopped.

Also why he never married.

He was in love with my wife. Always. I knew it, Gertie knew it . . . hell, everyone around us knew it. He was still my best friend, though. I knew he'd never betray my trust.

Until he did.

"I'm sorry, David." Charlie wipes at the moisture on his face.

I look away. A man needs a bit of privacy to control himself.

"Nothing to be sorry for. We all made mistakes. I should be apologizing to you. Except . . ." I look at him then and force a wiry smile onto my face.

"Except you swore you never would. Not surprised." Charlie leans back in his chair, crosses his arms over his chest, and grins like we're teenagers again, getting away with the latest stupid stunt we've pulled.

Despite the years, Charlie knows me. Well, he knows the me that I was before I pushed him away.

I couldn't handle him knowing those secrets.

Couldn't handle him knowing how broken our Gertie truly was.

Couldn't handle sending him to a place of no return. It would have destroyed him.

So I destroyed him instead by giving him the easy way out.

"No sense changing now just because I'm about to die." I lift myself slightly to get a sip of water, then ease myself back down. Nurse Crankypants increased my pain meds before my granddaughter came for a visit, but not enough to numb the pain completely.

"Might make those gates above swing open for you."

There's a slight twinkle in Charlie's eyes. Or maybe tears. Either way, I ignore it.

"Don't know unless you try." Charlie stares at the medical equipment to the side of him and grimaces.

Probably realizing one day this will be his life, his fate.

"Those gates are bolted shut against me," I remind him. "I've made my peace. You just treat our girl right when you see her. You hear me?"

Charlie jerks his gaze toward me, his eyes wide, his jaw slack.

Guess he wasn't expecting to hear that.

"Don't know why you pushed me away. Figured you had your reasons." His lips tighten until his chin resembles a prune. "But I sure as hell didn't like being kept in the dark." He leans forward in his chair and rubs the swollen knuckles on his hands.

The groan that comes out of my chest at his words, at the question in his voice, at the memories they bring back to the surface—it hurts like hell.

"No sense in rehashing the past, Charlie." I stare at the wall in front of me, fixate on a crack about an inch long.

"Why the hell not? It's just us in here. We used to be brothers, man. David, the day you told me to leave and never come back . . ." He slams his fist down on my mattress, the power of it vibrating along all the nerves of my body.

I suck in air between my clenched teeth, the sound a high-pitched whistle; keep my gaze unflinchingly on that crack.

"I lost my family, man." Charlie whispers, oblivious to my pain.

I swallow hard, count to five silently before attempting to speak.

I have to add another five before my teeth unclench.

"Leave it be. Nothing can change what happened. I wish to God that were untrue."

Charlie was a crappy poker player when we used to play. Apparently he still is. I read everything he wants to say but doesn't on his face. The way his eyes narrow while the scenarios of what could have happened play in his head, the flare of his nose as the questions cross his mind, the tightening of his lips when he realizes I will never give him the answers he needs.

He loved my wife. We all knew it.

But Gertie chose *me*.

Charlie respected Gertie's choice and stepped back, choosing to maintain a friendship rather than lose her altogether.

I loved him like a brother. Demanding he leave us, never come around our home again . . . it killed me. But I had to protect Gertie. She came first.

She always came first.

Everything I've ever done was for her.

Nothing short of death is gonna stop that.

"I met your granddaughter," Charlie says instead.

I can't help but smile at the thought of Elle.

"She's got Gertie's fire." Charlie smiles as well.

"Pity the poor man she marries," I chuckle. I wasn't surprised Charlie noticed that as well.

"How is Marie?" he asks, as if he has no idea about the estrangement between us.

My smile falters. I play with the sheet covering me, wishing more than ever I had something more than a skimpy gown on.

"It's like that, is it?" There isn't even a question. He sees and understands.

Regrets? Yeah, I've got a lot. Not reconnecting with Charlie is one of them. Even after Gertie's death, I could have. But I let my pride get in the way instead.

I deserve to die alone.

That's not happening now, with both Elizabeth and Charlie back in my life. I refuse to feel any guilt about it.

"She's more her mother's daughter than she wants to admit." I clear my throat.

Charlie starts to laugh, slapping his knee in the process.

"What's so funny?"

"Sounds more like she takes after you. Once you make up your mind about something, there's no changing your course. Take us, for example."

I want to argue but stop before the words leave my lips. I shrug instead. He's right, and we both know it.

The longer Charlie's face wrinkles with mirth, the more annoyed I become.

"If you're only here to laugh at me, you can leave. I don't need to die with the sound of your voice stuck in my head, thanks very much," I grumble.

Charlie stands, but the smile doesn't disappear.

"You grumpy old fool. You're not getting rid of me that quick. You able to drink coffee, or they just giving you water?" He eyes the tray that hovers over my bed with only a glass of water on it.

The mention of coffee has my taste buds going like crazy.

"If you can sneak it in and it's lukewarm, I could force it down."

Charlie looks down at the watch on his wrist. "I'll be by for visiting hours tonight, then. Decaf?"

I shudder but nod.

"Getting old sucks. Don't tell anyone, but I had to switch to decaf almost ten years ago. The damn coffee had me thinking I was having a heart attack once." He steps close and lays his hand on my shoulder.

I freeze but refuse to say anything. My shoulder is being crushed—or at least it feels like it—but there's no way in hell I'm letting Charlie see the pain he's inflicting on me.

"It's good to see you, brother." He squeezes it before releasing my now-bruised skin.

I nod. All I can think is that he needs to leave, right away, so I can hit the damn buzzer and get some relief.

Elle is on her way.

~

An hour later, pain numbed to manageable levels, I watch the clock *tick-tick-tick* its way around while waiting for my granddaughter to arrive.

Not sure I can handle another day without seeing her. Having her work here is nice.

When I close my eyes, I see her face. I see my Gertie's smile, my Marie's eyes. I see a past that never happened, and it makes me wish I'd been a better man. A different man.

Maybe in the hours I have left with my granddaughter, I can be.

I hear her walk down the hall. I've asked Nurse Crankypants to keep the door open. The squeak of her flip-flops along the floor catches my attention.

I'm ready for her.

The moment her bright striped skirt comes into my room, all the shadows that haunt me disappear and the sun blazes through the window, warming even my ever-cold body.

"Oh good, you're awake." Elle sets a bulging bag down on one of the chairs and flashes me her familiar smile.

Her mother used to smile the same way when she was a teenager. It filled her whole face, ending at her eyes. When Marie smiled, everyone around knew she was happy. They couldn't help but smile back.

"I would have been here earlier, but"—she reaches for the bag she set down—"Grace wouldn't let me come empty-handed."

Grace.

The way Elle watches me, I know she's trying to gauge my reaction to hearing her name.

"What's all in there?"

She pulls out multiple containers of various sizes.

"Nurse Amy is going to store these for you in the staff fridge. Grace kind of went . . . overboard."

I count seven containers.

"There's three different types of puréed soup, three different fro-yo flavors, and a watered-down smoothie made from fresh fruit."

"Fro-yo?" *What has Grace sent me now?*

She lifts a lid on a container and shows me what looks like ice cream.

"Fro-yo. Frozen yogurt. Fresh fruit and cream, no sugar. It's good, trust me." She replaces the lid.

"You said something about soup?" My stomach grumbles. I sipped piss water earlier and forced it down, knowing my body needed it.

"She didn't want them to be too thick but figured you'd had enough of broth, so there's tomato, cauliflower, and even a cream of potato."

She catches the hunger in my gaze and begins to giggle like a schoolgirl. She sets the three containers on the tray beside me.

"Please tell Grace thank you," I say after I've finished all I can handle of the soup. They all taste delicious, as I knew they would.

Grace always loved to cook.

"Why don't you tell her yourself?" Elle nods toward the phone at my side.

I snort. Good try, girl. If Grace wants to tell her about our connection, then she can do it. It isn't my story to tell.

"How do you know her?"

Elle tries to appear relaxed, but I can see her body vibrating in the chair with the need for answers.

"There's a lot of things in my past, child, that you don't need to know about. Grace is one of them. Unless she wants to tell you." There are so many secrets in my life. Just because I'm at the end, they don't all need to be uncovered. "Put that shovel away. Stop digging. You have questions. I get that. Ask me, and I'll tell you what I can."

Disbelief radiates from her in waves.

"I said I'd tell you what I can. Doesn't mean it'll be everything you want to hear."

"I met Charlie."

I nod. He said as much earlier.

"Went to your house."

I cover my shaking hand with the edge of my blanket. Charlie didn't share that bit when he dropped by.

"Why?"

Elle crosses her leg, readjusts her skirt, wastes time when she could be answering me.

"There's nothing there for you. Nothing for you to see." The soup in my stomach curdles.

I thought about burning everything to the ground, myself along with it, but couldn't.

Had she found the containers of gasoline in the back room?

She wouldn't have gone into the garage, right?

"Is it so hard to believe I want to know more? Why wouldn't I go to my mom's childhood home?" she asks, blinking rapidly while looking off to the side.

"Wasn't what you imagined, huh?" I don't have to think hard about the stories Marie would have told her. The kid probably thought it was a castle full of princesses.

"Not quite," she admits. "I always imagined a farmhouse with a white picket fence, surrounded by beautiful gardens."

"We used to have gardens." And they were beautiful. I'd pick Gertie a rose or a bunch of wildflowers every day I could. During the winter, I'd buy a bouquet and place it on the middle of the kitchen table for her to see when she eventually came down the stairs.

"I always assumed Mom got her love for gardening from her mother, but I guess it came from you, didn't it?"

To know Marie loves to garden, well, it chokes me up a little inside. I clear my throat and edge the corner of my lip up into a half grin. She can run away from us all she wants, but we are there, always on the outskirts. No matter how hard she tries, she can't completely erase us from her life, from her heart. That, well, that means a lot.

"A man's gotta have a hobby. The flowers made my Gertie happy, but she had more of a black thumb than anything else."

"Will you tell me more about her? About Gertie?" Elle worries her hands together in her lap, her whole countenance suddenly unsure.

"Darlin', I'd take any chance I can to talk about my Gertie. Your grandmother was the love of my life. There was nothing I wouldn't do for her, and she knew it. All she had to do was bat those beautiful brown eyes of hers, and I was a goner."

When I close my eyes, they're there, those eyes so full of emotion. Some days she'd build me up to be a better man with just a look; other days she'd tear my insides apart until I didn't know where she began and I ended.

"How did she die?"

I sigh, the air emptying out of every hollow space in my lungs.

"Cancer. Throat."

Two words that destroyed my life.

I don't look at my granddaughter. I can't. I'd talk about Gertie all day, but not about her death.

I won't tell her what it was like, watching Gertie in so much pain.

I won't tell her how devastated she was at losing her voice.

Or how nasty chemo can be.

I won't tell her about the years following Gertie's treatment when we waited for the other shoe to drop. Or how wrecked we were when it did.

No. I won't tell her any of that. That isn't a story my granddaughter needs to hear.

"Did she smoke?"

I snort. "Not a day. Doctors said it was secondhand smoke. God has a sense of humor, did you know? I loved that woman with all my heart and in the end, I was the one who killed her."

Elle inhales. "I'm sure you didn't—"

I lift my hand from the bed, stopping her.

"I've come to terms with it. There's no going back, not in this life. But cancer runs in our family, so you be careful, you hear me?"

Her forehead creases as she frowns. "What kind?"

"Does it matter? Once it starts growing, it doesn't stop. Do me a favor—just stay healthy, okay?"

She leans away. My gruffness must be too much.

"Sorry." I breathe in and out, in and out.

She doesn't say anything for a minute, and neither do I. The sound of my labored breathing echoes in my ears, and I try to calm myself. Get too worked up and Elle will leave. God knows if I'll see her again.

"I'll be careful."

It's amazing, the effect her voice has over me. Those three words, spoken in her soft voice, relax my lungs. The air flows easier.

"Thank you."

My head bobs like one of those dancing baby Jesus dolls Gertie gave me for my truck. In the beginning, before we lost so much, she had a sense of humor, that girl.

"Wish you'd told me you were going to the house," I say. "I'd have warned you not to. The place isn't safe. Don't go back, okay?" I need her to promise me. I need to know she won't go digging around in graves meant to be left alone.

She watches me. I can see the questions dancing around her head. She's trying to find the answers within my own gaze.

"Will you tell me another story?"

"Will you promise not to go back to the house?"

She pauses.

"No."

That's when I know what she's seen. It was inevitable, I guess.

"What is it you want to know?"

What will I tell her? How will I explain? I wanted the chance, the opportunity, to right a wrong.

My time is close. Death hovers, impatient to take its due. I need more time, time to fix the mistakes I've made.

If I believe in guardian angels, then I know Gertie has to be working her magic up there, arranging for this moment to happen.

"Thank you for visiting me," I say to my granddaughter. "You don't have to. I'm sure . . . I'm sure you left here with more questions than answers. I wouldn't have blamed you if you thought I played you."

The polite response would have been to say that wasn't the case, that she wanted to come. But I'm not going to push her. Not going to demand answers I don't deserve.

"You did play me. Let's call it what it is. But I visit because that's what families do, don't they? Give second chances? Whatever happened between you and Mom, that's for you to work out." She sighs. "Or not work out. I knew I'd regret not coming, not giving you another chance to tell me more about her."

I can accept that.

"What do you want to know?" I ask again.

I should be warned by the way she takes a moment to gather her thoughts. By the way she sits up straighter, squares her shoulders, stiffens her neck.

"Tell me about the playroom," Elle demands.

Chapter Seventeen

Two mommies in the house isn't always fun.

My mama is feeling better. She's not sleeping so much anymore and my sister's mama is teaching us lots of new things.

I bring the eggs into the house every morning from the chickens.

Mama gets to make breakfast for us all now too.

She's so busy that she doesn't play with me much anymore, but I have my sister to play with. We do lots of things now together, and sometimes I forget what it was like when it was just me and Mama.

Sometimes I miss it.

I told my sister that once and she got mad at me. She locked me in the closet when everyone was outside and I couldn't get out. My mama didn't even miss me until it was time to eat.

I got in trouble for hiding except I wasn't hiding.

Chapter Eighteen

DAVID

July 1956

A cloud of dust rose up off the side road, and David recognized the rusty red Ford truck turning down his driveway.

"Your other favorite pain in the ass is here," he said to Gertie as he handed her a paper bag filled with flour, sugar, and other items she'd put on her grocery list.

"Oh good. There's an apple pie with his name on it in the cooler. Let me go grab it. Keep him out here, will you?" She rushed into the house, the screen door slamming behind her.

What is Charlie doing here?

David had just seen him in town—and wasted a good half hour with him while they drank coffee at their favorite diner.

David stood in the middle of his driveway, arms crossed, frown fierce, as Charlie parked his rugged truck in the middle of his driveway and stepped out.

"What's going on?" David asked.

"Nothing." Charlie placed his hands in his pockets and looked around. "Thought I saw Gertie out here with you as I drove up."

David nodded. "She just went into the house to get you an apple pie."

A smile the size of Lake Huron spread across Charlie's face. "Well, I'll just pop in and see how she's doing, then." He rounded the front of his truck, making his way toward the door, when David blocked him.

"She'll be right out."

"Ohhhkayy?" Charlie stepped back, his gaze fixed on the door, waiting for Gertie to appear.

"What's up?" David asked, grabbing his attention. "I thought you told me you were going fishing today? Don't see any ponds out here, or a pole in hand."

Despite the teasing, he wasn't happy to have the unexpected visit.

For the past month, David had worked hard to keep Charlie from dropping by.

Not an easy task, considering the man was his best friend. The guy was normally there for dinner every weekend and sometimes would even stop in for coffee and a sandwich over lunch if he was driving by with a load.

With Judy and Bella staying on, Gertie wasn't comfortable with Charlie coming around anymore.

So far, David had met the man in town, mentioned Gertie wasn't feeling up for company, and that seemed to have done the trick. Charlie was familiar with how Gertie worked. When she wasn't up for company, he knew better than to drop by unannounced.

"Pole's in the back. Thought I'd see if you and Anna Marie wanted to join me. It's been a while since I've seen the tyke."

Just then, Gertie nudged the door open with her hip, carrying a pie in her hands. She beamed the brightest smile David had seen in forever.

"I bake an extra pie, and you come calling. How does that seem to work, Charlie Daniels?"

His eyes lit up brighter than a sparkler on a hot summer night as he stared at the pie. He wrapped his arms around Gertie and gave her a solid kiss on the cheek before taking the offered pie and bringing it close to his face, inhaling like he was a starving man.

"I love you, Gertie Walker. I should have asked you to marry me while I had the chance," Charlie teased, winking over at David.

Gertie swatted him on the arm.

"That's what you get for taking your time, isn't it? Besides"—she stepped away from Charlie and stood at David's side, linking her arm through his—"once you introduced me to this handsome man, my heart was lost. Instantly and forever."

David's chest swelled with pride as his wife squeezed his arm. He leaned down, whispering in her ear that he'd show her how much he loved her before claiming her lips with a long and endearing kiss.

She was his. Every so often, Charlie needed to be reminded of that.

"You doing okay, Gertie?" Charlie asked.

Gertie looked up at David, her forehead creasing briefly as she frowned. The next second, she pasted a smile on her face.

"All good, Charlie. Thank you for asking. I haven't been feeling the best for a bit, but today's a good day." She patted David's hand while she talked.

David caught the concern on his friend's face and gave a slight shake of his head—not a big enough one for Gertie to notice, but one Charlie could see.

"Just miss you and these pies, that's all. Thought I'd come to steal your husband and daughter away for a few hours to fish. We could fry them on the grill after."

"I'm sorry, Charlie. Anna Marie is starting to get a summer cold. And, well . . ."

David gave Gertie a sharp look.

"You don't need to explain. I know how you are about her health," Charlie said. "What about you, David? Or are you playing nursemaid?"

David's brows rose at the mock challenge.

"Go. It's good," Gertie said softly.

David looked toward the house, but the pull to fish—something he hadn't done yet this summer without the girls tagging along and scaring away their dinner—was strong.

"Regular spot?" David asked.

Charlie nodded.

"I'll meet you there. I'll grab some sandwiches and beer. Just don't catch all the good ones."

He waved at Charlie as he drove away. Then he gave his wife a stern look.

"Summer cold?"

Where had she come up with something like that? Anna Marie is fine.

"I don't mess with our daughter's health. He knows that." The shrug of her shoulder told him she didn't think anything of lying to their best friend.

She might not, but he did.

"You can't hide our guests forever, Gertie. Eventually it's gonna come out that they're here." Gertie was adamant that they stay at the house, not go into town where questions could be asked.

To say she was paranoid at the moment was like saying his chickens laid eggs. It was obvious.

Normally, David wouldn't give in to her paranoia, but after everything the past few months . . . all he wanted was a stable home where his wife felt safe.

Gertie was happy, and she hadn't been happy for a long time.

He'd do anything to keep that smile on her face.

"Can't we just enjoy our family in private for now?" Gertie busied herself with the laundry on the line, not looking at him.

"Gertie, love." David went over and gently laid his hand on her back. "Judy and Bella are our guests, not family."

Gertie whipped around, her eyes crazed. "How can you say that? Of course they're our family. God brought them to us to love. Those girls . . . they have no one else, just us. Of course they're ours." Her body shook, and little tremors along her skin vibrated beneath the palm of the hand he rested on her arm. "God knew I needed them." Gertie's eyes filled as she stared up at him, imploring him to understand. "He took our babies away, but gave us others to love."

David pulled his wife in close and tucked her head beneath his chin. He didn't want her to see the concern, the doubt, the worry on his face.

Maybe I shouldn't go with Charlie.

He'd hoped having Judy there would be good for Gertie, for her state of mind.

Have I made a mistake? Have I only made things worse?

Gertie had made him promise he'd never let her become like her mother and yet . . . the signs were all there.

"You go fish. We're fine here. Judy is resting, and I've got the girls making her get-well cards. This afternoon they can help me pick vegetables for dinner." Gertie pulled away and turned back to the laundry.

"What's wrong with Judy?"

Her hands went still for a moment before she busied herself again with the wet clothes. She wasn't answering him right away. He didn't like her silence.

"Gertie?"

"She's a little under the weather, is all," Gertie muttered.

"Again?"

He didn't like the sound of this. She'd been "under the weather" too often the past few weeks.

Since he left so early in the mornings, he didn't usually see Judy or the girls until dinner. Normally, Judy would be helping Gertie set the table when he arrived, but too many times lately he'd come home to find her up in bed, "resting."

Always resting.

"Is she sick? Pregnant? A cold? What is wrong with her?" David couldn't figure it out.

"The poor girl is under the weather. That's all, David. Think about the strain she was under before you found her. Now that she's here, safe, her body is telling her she needs to rest."

The look she gave him, her cheeks flushed, her gaze flighty . . . he didn't like it.

"As long as that's all it is," he mumbled.

He kept his thoughts to himself as he made some sandwiches and grabbed a few beers from the fridge in the garage.

He made sure to check in on the girls before he left. He was tempted to head upstairs to see about Judy, but by then Gertie was in the kitchen, making a fuss over the mess he'd made with the bread.

He made a promise to himself to talk to Judy later, to see for himself how she was feeling.

"You better get going, or Charlie's going to think you stood him up." Gertie rushed him out the door, pushing on his back until he was out of the house.

"If I didn't know any better, I'd think you were getting rid of me on purpose. First it was to run into town for supplies I know I bought just last weekend, and now this. Is there something I should know about?"

Unease pricked at his conscience. The flash of guilt that lit Gertie's face briefly only increased that feeling.

Today wasn't a normal day. The last time he hadn't listened to his gut, he'd come home to find his wife lying on the bathroom floor, blood pooling beneath her as she miscarried one of their babies.

"Maybe I should stay home. I can help with the girls and even take care of dinner."

"You'll do no such thing, David Basil Walker. Now go. Scoot, and don't come back until you've got enough fish for dinner."

Her lips thinned into straight white lines. Panic set in her eyes as he walked toward her. He could tell she was about to lose it on him.

"On one promise," he said before she could say anything else. "I want you to get those girls to lie down, and you along with them. I know you're tired, so don't bother denying it. You tossed more last night than a puppy trying to get comfy on his new blanket." He kissed her forehead and stared directly into her wary eyes.

"Promise me, Gertie Walker, or I won't go. I'll haul you up to our bed myself if need be." He wriggled his brows as he said it, knowing how she'd react to his threat.

Her cheeks flushed, and the wisp of a smile played on her lips.

"Not during the day when the girls are up!" she whispered.

"Then promise me."

"I won't sleep a wink tonight, and you know it." There was a challenge in her voice that he happily met.

"Guess I'll be helping you get to sleep, then." He kissed her quickly on the lips. "Promise me."

He wouldn't let it go. The last thing he needed was for her to be exhausted. He wasn't happy about leaving today but knew she'd only get prickly if he stayed.

Tomorrow he'd stay home and watch over her and Judy. He'd take a few days off work if need be. Wouldn't be the first time.

"I promise. Now leave."

She stood there on their back porch, hands on hips, until he drove away.

The niggling sense that something was wrong remained, even as he watched her figure disappear in his rearview mirror.

Chapter Nineteen

When David walked through the door three hours later, cooler in hand, he was greeted by two little girls singing at the top of their lungs while Gertie stood at the kitchen sink, head bowed, shoulders slumped, fingers clenched tight along the edge of the counter.

"Whoa! A little quieter girls, please!" David had to raise his voice to be heard over them.

The girls stopped singing abruptly. Gertie slowly turned her body to face him. There was a rigidness to her movement that let David instantly picture the scenario of the past few moments.

"What's with all the noise?" He set the cooler full of fish down on the floor and looked at his daughter. "Anna Marie?"

Her gaze dropped instantly to the floor, hands at her sides. She peeked at Bella constantly.

"Don't you look to Bella." David squatted down and lifted her chin with his finger. "Look at me. What's the rule for inside the house?"

"Inside voices."

He could barely hear his daughter's words.

"Was that an inside voice?"

She shook her head, lower lip jutting out so far he could have set a penny on it.

"Sounded to me like that was an outside voice meant to wake up the neighbors' chickens, right?"

Anna Marie nodded.

"We just wanted to play house, Daddy."

"But do you have to be so loud about it?" Gertie muttered.

David, back on his feet, handed his wife the cooler full of fish. "Brought home dinner, as requested. All cleaned and deboned. Give me a minute to clean up, and I'll get them on the grill."

He eyed the two little girls, who stood still as statues.

"I see only one outcome out of this. We can't have outside voices happening all the time in our home, but you're two little girls who have very loud voices that need to be heard. Isn't that right?" Both Bella and Anna Marie looked up at him then.

His daughter nodded her head enthusiastically, her eyes twinkling as she read the tone of his voice and realized they weren't in trouble.

"I think they need a room of their own to play in. What do you think, Mommy?" He turned to Gertie, who stared at him in absolute confusion.

"I can clean out that front room in the garage a bit, and the girls could play out there," he mused.

Currently, that room was full of boxes and tools and cast-off truck stuff, but he had enough room in the main garage for the tools and equipment. Some of the boxes could go to the dump. He could clean it up nice, add some shelving to the walls, maybe give it a fresh coat of paint. The girls could play house there all they wanted.

Gertie nodded. "You'd make sure it was safe? No loose nails, no tools lying about?"

"I'll even put a lock on the door going to my garage so they can't get into things."

She studied the girls, whose eyes shone with excitement.

"It could work, then. But only after they apologize to Judy. You probably woke her up with all that caterwauling."

Bella gasped. "I forgot Mommy was sleeping!" She cast a dirty look Anna Marie's way.

David frowned.

"You can help set the table and get some fresh flowers from the garden for your mother, then, Bella. After you've written her a note to say you are sorry."

Gertie must have caught the look too, considering the briskness of her voice.

She opened the cooler lid and sniffed at the fishy smell. "I'll rinse these off while you clean up."

The house remained quiet until dinner was ready.

Judy sat at the table, as white as David's bleached Sunday shirt, but she maintained a gentle smile directed toward her daughter.

"If it isn't Sleeping Beauty," David teased, pleased to see her out of her room. He didn't like how pale her skin was or the dark circles beneath her eyes.

"Who could sleep with all the singing down here? I'm just sorry I missed it." Judy held Bella's hand while nudging Anna Marie gently with her shoulder.

"I'm sorry, Mommy." Bella leaned her head against Judy's arm.

"You said that already, love." Judy laid a kiss on the top of her daughter's head.

Throughout dinner, David talked with the ladies about his idea for the playroom in the garage. He carefully watched the uneasy dynamic at the table, how Bella remained glued to her mother's side, needing to be in constant contact. How fevered Gertie's gaze remained as she watched everyone at the table. The brightness of her smile and the softening of her features as she listened to Judy talk with both Anna Marie and Bella.

Yet she refused to look at her husband.

Anna Marie remained a mystery too. She would speak when spoken to, ate everything on her plate without complaint, and even offered to grab any last-minute items they needed before Gertie had a chance to rise from her chair. Her smile was quick, her posture stiff, and the cheerfulness in her voice forced.

What is going on with my girl?

While the girls worked on chores, David brewed a cup of tea for Judy and sat with her at the table.

"You're not looking so good," he said, making sure his voice was low enough not to be overheard.

"I'm not feeling so good," Judy admitted, her hands wrapped tight around the mug, eyes fixed on the table.

"Gertie says it's just a summer flu?" David hoped his wife was right, but the more he watched Judy, the less he believed that was the case. Something was seriously wrong with her. She needed a doctor.

"Maybe."

That wasn't the voice of one who believed it either.

"Anything you need, just say it."

Judy looked at him then with a mixture of hope and disbelief.

What is going on?

"I need to get away from here. To see a doctor and . . . just get away." Judy paled even more as she tilted her head toward Gertie and the girls, who were washing dishes.

"Get away?"

Judy sighed.

"I appreciate your opening your home to us and welcoming us with open arms, but"—she looked down and frowned—"your wife needs help, David."

David leaned back in his chair, thrown by the harshness of her words despite their soft delivery.

Of course she needs help.

That's why he had asked Judy to stay. She'd just lost another baby two weeks before they showed up, and having Judy there to help with household chores or even to keep Anna Marie occupied had been a godsend.

"That's why you're here. I thought you were okay with that?" He leaned forward, elbows on the table, voice still low.

"I'm okay with helping around the house, and I was okay with Bella playing with Anna Marie. But . . ." She paused, as if weighing her words.

"Oh, just spit it out," he said. The faster she said what was on her mind, the sooner he could get her back up the stairs and into bed. Every minute she sat there, she drooped. He didn't like it.

"There's something not right with Gertie." She covered her mouth as she yawned and tried to blink away the fatigue written all over her.

David pushed his chair back and held out his hand to Judy. "Come on, let's get you back up the stairs before you fall asleep on me." He kept his voice chipper, friendly, as if he were only concerned for her health. Deep inside, her words worried him.

He wanted to ask her more, but not with Gertie and the girls around.

"Everything okay over there?" Gertie stood at the other end of the table, drying her hands on her apron.

Judy's grip on David's arm tightened. She lifted her gaze to him, and he could read the silent plea in her eyes not to say anything.

"Just going to help Judy up the stairs before I take the girls out for a night stroll to see the cows. She was basically falling asleep at the table."

He put his arm around Judy's back and led her to the stairs. He could feel Gertie's stare right in the center of his spine.

"I can bring up some more medicine—"

"No!" Judy almost shouted the word, interrupting Gertie. "I mean, it's okay. I think if I can just get a good night's sleep, that will help."

Gertie rubbed her hands together, the frown on her face deepening.

"I'll bring up some chamomile tea, then. That always helps me sleep."

For a moment, it looked like Judy was going to decline, which would only make Gertie more suspicious and more insistent.

"Thanks, love," David said as he started up the stairs. Judy followed at his side. "That's probably exactly what's needed."

He could feel Judy's body shake. He wasn't sure if it was from the exertion of climbing the stairs or if it had something to do with her earlier comment.

He opened her door and stood there while Judy stepped into her room and sank down on the edge of the bed.

"I don't want that tea."

"Why?" He kept watch on the stairs, not wanting anyone to sneak up and overhear their conversation.

When Gertie called Judy and Bella part of their family, he understood the feeling—even though he'd felt the need to remind her they weren't.

He thought of Bella as his niece and Judy as his sister. Her being so sick right now ate at him.

"Something's not right, David. I . . . I don't want to accuse Gertie of doing something to me, but . . ." Her shoulders slumped forward as she rested her head in the palms of her hands. "This isn't a cold or the flu. It's something else."

David had been taught that it was a man's responsibility to see to the health and well-being of those in his care. Whether that was family, friends, or even employees. His father always took care of those around him, making sure the men who worked on his farm had enough food on their plate, that their own families were taken care of, and that those who lived under his roof were healthy, fed, and clothed.

A feeling of failure haunted him. He not only had let his wife and daughter down but also was letting Judy down now.

"What did you mean downstairs?" he asked.

"You know exactly what I meant. That's the real reason I'm here, isn't it? Not to help with dishes or laundry or weeding or washing floors. You asked me to stay because you're worried about Gertie. Why haven't you taken her to the doctor?"

The words settled into a bubble in his throat. That bubble grew until it blocked his airway and suffocated his soul.

Why haven't I?

He was too afraid to. He hadn't been sure if it was all in his head.

There were little things—things he'd started noticing that seemed out of character.

He attributed it to losing their babies.

She was grieving, and some days she was lost in that grief.

If I take her to the doctor, they might . . .

No. I'm not going to entrust my wife to a doctor, a doctor who would put her in an institution.

An institution like where Gertie's mother lived because she had also gotten lost in her own grief.

"What do you need? Tell me, and I'll take care of it." He cleared his throat. "We need you, Judy. More than you know."

He let his words, his request, hang there between them.

She searched his face, his eyes. He knew the next moment she was going to say she couldn't stay, except . . . she didn't.

"Take me to a doctor, David. Please?" The anguish in her voice gripped him.

For a moment, he couldn't think of any words to say.

"David?"

He stood tall, shoulders back, and nodded. He could fix this.

"There's no office open tomorrow, Judy. It's Sunday."

If only the doctor made house calls. But then . . . it would mean the doctor seeing Gertie, and well, she isn't ready.

"Could take you to the hospital, though," he suggested instead. "You'll sit there all day, and they're known to be short-staffed on weekends, but . . ." He stuck his hands in his pockets and shrugged. "Otherwise, I can see if the doctor can fit you in first thing Monday. I'll go into work late."

She shook her head before climbing onto the bed and lying down.

"I don't want you to miss work."

With her eyes closed and hands tucked beneath her cheek, he thought she looked angelic. A pale angel, but an angel nonetheless.

"Let's see how I'm feeling tomorrow, okay? I'll just . . . sleep . . . for . . ."

David remained in the room, watching the girl he considered his younger sister fall sleep midsentence. He didn't like what he saw.

Her skin was only a shade darker than the white pillowcase on her bed, ripples of pain spasmed across her skin, and her knees moved up to her stomach—a classic pain-and-protection move.

She's right. This is more than a summer cold. But what?

In any case, he needed to have a serious talk with his wife.

By the time he got back downstairs, the girls were sitting at the table with mixing bowls in front of them. Gertie was nowhere to be found.

"Where's your momma, buttercup?" David ruffled Anna Marie's hair.

His daughter shrugged, focused on the spoon in hand and the ingredients inside her bowl.

"Bella?"

Bella looked up, completely wide-eyed. "She's outside, Daddy David."

Sucker punched right in the throat, David froze at her words.

"Just Mr. D., honey."

Where had that come from?

"Momma Gertie said I could call you that now." Her forehead crinkled as she looked up at him, obviously confused.

David sighed. "You've got a momma upstairs, love."

It was wrong to confuse the poor girl.

"You girls keep doing what you're doing. I'll go see what's keeping . . ." His tongue tripped over how to refer to Gertie. Momma? Mrs. G.? My wife? "That woman of mine."

The words were awkward, just like this whole situation.

Momma Gertie? Why would she be telling that young girl to call her that?

He was still shaking his head as he walked outside.

She wasn't in the garden or checking on the chickens. The lights in the garage remained dark, so there was really only one other place she could be.

With a heavy heart, he headed toward the back of the garage, where they'd planted a large section of wildflowers.

Gertie loved to go there. When Anna Marie was only a baby, she would bring out a blanket and they would lie there together, among the wildflowers. As Anna Marie grew, Gertie would bring her out there for tea parties and tell her stories about why the area was so special.

David didn't like it. There were too many memories. Broken dreams. Heartache associated with this patch of wildflowers.

Wildflowers, and four white crosses.

He found her kneeling between the crosses, hands in her lap and a serene smile on her face. She spoke quietly to the children she'd— *they'd*—lost too early.

"Be nice to her when she comes? Okay? She'll be there to look after you, to make sure you're all doing well. She's gonna be your other momma until I can come. She won't love you like I do, but her love will be enough."

What is she talking about?

David stood to the back, sure she knew he was behind her.

"Your new sister, she's fitting in well. She's a smart one too, that girl. She knows how to read and write, and you should see the pictures she draws. Anna Marie really likes her. I told her today she can start calling me Momma Gertie. You don't mind, do you? She can't replace you in my heart, but having her here . . . it helps me not be so sad. I know I haven't been out here as often as I should, but Judy needs my help right now. She's not well, and for the first time in a long time I feel needed. You'll get to know her soon. Remember what I said and be nice to her, okay?"

David really didn't like what he was hearing.

"Hey, love. Everything okay?" David knelt behind her and wrapped an arm around her waist.

"Just talking to our babies. I wasn't able to get out this morning like I normally do."

Before the girls awoke, Gertie would be out here, wrapped in a blanket, to say good morning. She said it helped calm her, soothe her soul.

"Who were you talking about just now?"

She didn't answer him. In fact, she acted as if she hadn't even heard him. She kissed her finger and brushed it against the wood cross, like a caress. She then repeated the gesture three more times before standing and wiping the dirt and grass from her knees.

"I forgot to bring a blanket out with me," she mumbled.

"Gertie?" He wasn't going to let this go.

"I miss her, you know? I know she's dying and soon she'll be the one to care for our babies. I just wanted to prepare them." She ran her hands along the edge of a cross, cleaning away the dust or pollen that had gathered.

A sense of unease filled David's veins.

"Who?"

When she didn't answer right away, he asked again, more insistent this time.

"My mother, of course."

David felt like he was living in a whirlwind. He had a hard time following Gertie's line of thinking.

Her mother? Her mother isn't dying. She's fine.

They'd just visited her a few months ago at Easter. If anything were wrong, there would have been a phone call.

"Why do you think your mother is dying, love? What did I miss?"

She rolled her eyes at him as she wound her arm through his and started to walk toward the house.

"I know you're trying to protect me and all, David, but I'm not some fragile flower. I wish you would stop treating me as such."

His mouth opened, but no words spilled out.

Protect her? Damn straight, I am. Fragile flower? Right now, that's exactly what she is.

He tugged her to a stop.

"Gertie Walker, I don't understand a word you're saying. Why do you think your mother is dying?"

"Because she told me so."

She told her so? How is that possible? Her mother never calls. She can't call. She doesn't have phone privileges.

Gertie's mother was in psychiatric care and certifiably crazy.

Chapter Twenty

Sunday mornings were meant for peace and quiet.

Not for arguing and hissy fits, but that was all David was getting while sitting at the table, trying to drink his coffee.

Is a little bit of peace too much to ask for?

He cocked his head toward the stairs, trying to figure out what was being said behind Judy's closed door, but it was all a bunch of garbled mumbo jumbo.

Bella and Anna Marie sat at the top of the landing, both holding their heads between their hands. Neither one said anything.

He tried to coax them down, but they wouldn't budge.

Anna Marie sat like a stone because her mother had told her to wait there. David didn't know why Bella wouldn't move. He figured she was either scared of what Gertie would do if she did or she wanted to stay as close to her mom as she could.

There were too many cooks in the kitchen—or in this case, too many mothers under one roof.

It was making him crazy.

Judy's door opened and Gertie came stomping out, sweeping past the girls with barely a look as she marched down the stairs, muttering beneath her breath.

David didn't bother to stop her as she passed him. He knew better.

He knew better than to speak as she banged cupboard doors open and closed in a frenzy, didn't offer to help as she tore through cabinets looking for who knows what, and certainly didn't ask what was wrong as she stood there, hands on hips, with the fiercest frown he'd ever seen.

"Anna Marie!" Gertie stopped looking around the kitchen and focused in on their daughter. "Where is that bottle of medicine I had you put away yesterday?"

David's grip tightened around his mug at the deadly stillness in her voice.

Anna Marie didn't respond.

Gertie's mouth tightened until her lips turned white.

"Now, Gertie—" David tried to get his wife to calm down, but he was stopped from saying anything further when she turned the force of the wildfire gaze in her eyes on him.

"I will deal with this, David." Each word was measured carefully. She turned from him, back to their daughter.

"Anna Marie, I expect an answer. Now." She stared up at their daughter with straighter accuracy than an owl diving for his food.

"It's . . . it's in my room, Momma."

Anna Marie's voice trembled as she clutched her knees together within the grasp of her locked hands.

"Why is the bottle of medicine in your room and not in the cabinet like I asked?"

The words were said in a flat tone, neither rising nor falling—but that didn't mean there was no emotion.

Oh, there's emotion there, all right.

It was very rare to see Gertie address their daughter this way. She was strict but wasn't one to yell or scream or dole out unearned punishment.

David would have preferred the yelling, truth be told.

When Anna Marie didn't reply, Gertie went to stand at the foot of the staircase. She looked up.

"You don't want me to go and get the bottle, do you?"

Anna Marie shook her head.

"Then I suggest you go and bring it to me." When their daughter didn't move, Gertie placed one foot on the bottom step. "Now!" she screeched.

David let all the air out of his lungs.

"Why would she hide the medication from me?" She turned, directing the question to him, her arms flailing. "Does *everyone* around here think I'm poisoning the poor girl?" Her body shook as a tremor tore through her, forcing David out of his seat with worry. "Why would I do that?" She waved him off and crossed her arms over her chest, her brows knit together in confusion.

"I never said that, love," David said. He held onto the edge of his chair, uncertain if he should remain where he was or go to her.

"But you've thought it, haven't you? That would be the only reason why Judy has been so sick."

The accusation flung his way shocked him.

"We should take her to the doctor."

He slowly sat back down in his chair and rubbed the back of his neck. He didn't like where this was going.

"Like they would do anything." The scorn was real as she dismissed his idea, like he knew she would.

Gertie hated doctors and hospitals. To be honest, he didn't blame her.

"Who said you were poisoning her?" The words came slowly to his tongue.

Could Gertie be the reason Judy is sick?

"Our daughter." Gertie spat the words out like they were orange seeds.

"Anna Marie?"

That doesn't make sense at all. If Anna Marie felt that way, she would have said something to me.

She always talked to him about things she was scared of or worried about. Always.

"Is that why she hid the bottle, then?" That, he could imagine her doing.

He glanced over to find their daughter's face hidden between her knees.

He frowned.

"Anna Marie, go get that bottle. Please." He kept his voice calm and quiet but full of authority.

His daughter looked up and nodded. She stood, her back straight as she headed to her bedroom.

"Judy."

"What?" David shot Gertie a look, feeling utterly confused.

Gertie stood only a few inches away. "Judy blamed me this morning, refusing to take any more after I suggested it." Her chest swelled as she breathed in deep and held it before letting it rush out of her with a gust. "Like I would do that to our daughter. Doesn't she understand that? I just want her well." She covered her face with her hands. "I need her well." The cry in her voice would have felled him if he'd been standing.

David gripped the edge of his seat to steady himself.

"She's not our daughter."

He hated having to say it. Hated what saying it meant.

The slap across his cheek shook them both to the core.

Bella gasped.

Anna Marie let out a cry from the top of the landing, where she stood with her hands holding a bottle tight to her chest.

Gertie's mouth hung open. She looked from his cheek to his eyes and back to his cheek.

David stepped back and sucked in a deep breath.

"Oh, David, I'm so sorry. I'm so sorry." She reached out to touch his skin, but he pulled his head back in time, not ready for the contact.

"She *is* our daughter. Why don't you understand that?" Gertie looked lost, confused, out of control. "God brought her to us for a reason, David. She could be the first baby we lost . . . ," she pleaded.

David didn't have the words that needed to be said.

She'd never slapped him before. They fought, for sure. They raised their voices. But physically hit each other? Never.

David's father had slapped his mother around, and he'd sworn to never be like that with his own family.

He didn't like the wildness in her eyes.

"Gertie, I need you to sit down."

She didn't move. Her eyes were saucers that remained fixated on his cheek.

He went to her, grabbed her arm, and led her to his chair. He helped her to sit.

He kept his hand on her shoulder, letting her know without words that he wanted her to remain seated.

"Daddy?"

David turned his focus from his distraught wife to their daughter.

She walked down the steps with slow precision, her hands tight against her chest as she cradled the bottle between them.

"Were you hiding this from your mother?" he asked her.

Anna Marie stared up at him with eyes opened as wide as her mother's, but she neither shook nor nodded her head.

"Bella?" Judy appeared in the doorway of her room, leaning heavily against the frame.

The sound of her weak but desperate voice froze everyone in place.

"Bella?" Judy coughed, her voice even weaker. "Come help me, please."

Bella jumped up from where she sat rooted on the step and ran toward her mom, hugging her tight.

David's hand tightened on his wife's shoulder.

Judy whispered some things to her daughter before they slowly made their way to the stairs. She leaned heavily on the railing as she took one slow step at a time.

"I'd like to leave, David. Please."

Her flushed cheeks blazed bright against the white backdrop of her skin. Despite her weak appearance, the strength behind her words was clear.

Gertie's body began to tremble beneath David's hand as she twisted in the seat.

"I think we all need to calm down." David tried to broker peace, but Judy wouldn't have it.

"You promised me we could leave at any time—I just had to say the word." She paused as she took another step. "I'm saying it."

"No!" Gertie cried, her hand unsteady as she reached out to Judy. "You can't leave." She turned to him, her body trembling with emotion. "David, she can't leave."

Gertie's grief-stricken face started a war in David's heart.

Her attachment to the girls wasn't normal. He knew taking Judy and Bella away would probably destroy her. But Judy was sick—that much was obvious. She needed medical attention.

He was damned no matter what he did.

"Please, David!" Judy pleaded, her voice cracking from the strain.

She wobbled on the stairs, and David rushed to steady her. He made it just in time. The moment his arm went around her waist, her knees buckled and half her body fell forward. The only thing that prevented her from crumbling right there on the stairs was him.

"Judy!" Gertie pushed herself to her feet but didn't move toward them.

"Momma!" Bella cried as she stood there, frozen, large tears now streaming down her face.

"It's okay, love." David tried to console the young child who had become dearer to his heart than he'd thought possible.

He swung Judy into his arms, balking at her slack form.

Every spare ounce of color disappeared from Judy's face as her head rolled backward against his arm. Only the whites of her eyes were showing.

There'd been only a few times in his life David had ever been scared.

Every time Gertie told him she was pregnant.

Every time Gertie lost another baby.

One night on the road when he jackknifed across highway lanes during a snowstorm.

And right now.

"She's fainted." David's voice shook like he was driving his truck on bumpy back roads.

That broke whatever spell Gertie had been under. Her bowed body straightened, reminding him of the picture of his father in his military uniform that his mother had hung proudly in their hallway.

Stern. Commanding. In control.

"Bring her to the couch."

Her hand went out for Bella to grab hold of, fingers wiggling impatiently as she waited for the little one to slowly climb down the stairs alongside David.

"Hurry up, child. You're in the way." She grabbed Bella and pulled her down the remaining two steps before rushing into the living room and tossing the dolls Anna Marie had been playing with earlier to the floor.

"Put her down here, David." Her voice was as steady as a drill sergeant's.

Five steps away from the stairs, David stopped and turned slowly and carefully so as not to jostle Judy.

He took in the couch, his wife's crazed eyes, and then Bella's scared ones.

None of this is right.

Not the way his wife was acting, spiraling out of control while pretending she was anything but.

Not the scared children who stood between them.

Not the sick girl in his arms.

"She needs to go to the hospital," he decided.

"Not like this. She needs to be awake. She can't leave like this." Gertie ran to him and pulled on his arm, pushed at his back until he set Judy down on the couch.

Those were the longest seconds of his life. He waited for the tiny fluttering of her lashes to let him know she was conscious.

"David, please!" she begged him once she opened her eyes and realized where she was. "I can't stay here."

"Here is exactly where you need to stay." Gertie pushed David to the side and fussed over the girl. "You fainted. You're not strong enough to go anywhere right now. Just rest."

Judy struggled to sit up, leaning on her elbow for support. "Gertie, please . . ."

"I don't understand why there's an issue. I just want to help you," Gertie stressed. She knelt down in front of the couch, hands folded in her lap, head bowed as if praying.

Judy pushed herself up and attempted to stand. She struggled to her feet. Gertie stood in her way and reached her hand out to David, silently begging him for help.

In two seconds flat, he was there. He bent as if to pick her up, but Judy planted the palm of her other hand flat against the wall. "Let me walk, please."

They were halfway through the kitchen when Gertie rushed to her feet. "No!" she called out as she ran toward them, arms out wide as if to stop them.

He ignored her.

"You can't take her away, David. God told me she'll be fine. We just have to have faith." Gertie dodged him, then positioned herself in his way.

"She's not fine, Gertie. Look at her." Judy's hand clutched tight to his arm. He knew she was ready to collapse at any moment. The only thing keeping her upright was her willpower.

"Don't take her. Please."

"She's *sick*." He was getting tired of the conversation. It was leading nowhere, and he needed to get Judy to the hospital.

"You can't take her from me, David!" Gertie's fevered voice was pitched high. "I can't lose another one." She stepped backward, toward the door, and stumbled. "Please, don't do this to me."

Anna Marie ran past him and stood in the doorway leading to the back room. With her arms stretched out, legs wide until her body resembled an *X*, she barricaded him from leaving.

"Anna Marie, move." His voice was stern.

"Don't take her from Momma, Daddy!" his daughter cried out.

The panic on his daughter's face was too much for him.

"What the hell is going on here? Move out of the way, both of you. This girl is sick and needs a doctor. Now!" He didn't stop himself from shouting out that final word. He was glad he hadn't because it shocked both his wife and daughter enough to make them move.

Gertie stepped to the side, and Anna Marie's arms dropped.

Nothing was said for a sum of five seconds. Then large tears dropped from his daughter's lashes and she rushed over to Bella, grabbing hold of her hands.

"I'm so sorry, Bella," Anna Marie said.

David paused as he took it all in.

It's all too much in such a short time. Not even ten minutes have passed from the time Judy appeared at the stairs, and yet it feels like a lifetime.

"I can't lose another child, David. I just can't." Gertie sank down to the floor, her words hardly distinguishable as she crumbled before him. "Please don't do this."

David swallowed hard. The guilt was a heavy weight on his heart, but he knew what Gertie was asking of him wasn't right.

Nothing about any of this is right.

"David. Please? We need to leave." Judy's insistent whisper confirmed it moments before her knees buckled beneath her. He caught her in time and swung her up in his arms again, her head rolling slightly against his arm as she fell unconscious.

Bringing Judy and Bella here was a mistake.

He should have turned the truck around or asked Singer to pull over and return the two to the truck stop once he realized they were headed the wrong way.

I never should have brought them to our house, introduced them to my family, or taken them in as if they belonged.

I should have recognized how fragile my wife's state of mind was a long time ago and gotten her the help she needed.

So many things fall on my shoulders.

But I'm not going to have Judy's sickness or even her death on my shoulders too.

"You can't leave, Bella. We're sisters. Sisters don't leave each other!" Anna Marie called out.

"David, don't do this." Gertie reached out, grabbing his arm and pulling it hard toward her, catching him off-balance.

He stumbled and his legs twisted together as he fought to stop himself from falling over.

That's when it happened.

Judy's head hit the wall.

"Shit."

His grip on Judy loosened as he struggled to regain his footing while watching her head.

She fell from his arms.

He tried to grab her, but he was too late. Her head thumped against the edge of the step from the kitchen to the back room.

The sound of that thump held the power to stop time.

For a moment, everything and everyone stood still.

David couldn't breathe.

Judy just lay there, her head twisted at an awkward angle, her body unmoving.

One second everything was still, a bubble of stillness. Every sound, every breath was muted.

Until it wasn't.

All noise came rushing back as Bella screamed for her mother.

In the midst of all that chaos, David bent down to his knees and checked Judy's pulse, hoping, praying that there was one.

Except there wasn't.

David wrapped his hand beneath Judy's head to move her. He lifted his gaze with horror, his hand slowly revealing blood-coated fingers to Gertie.

"Oh no." Gertie shook her head, not wanting to accept what he showed her. She picked herself up from the floor and ran to the girls, turning them so they faced the opposite direction.

"Run upstairs—now. Go on. Don't turn around. Don't even look. Anna Marie, you take Bella to her room and close the door. Promise me, now. Go on." She pushed the girls gently toward the stairs.

Bella fought to stay behind. "Wake up, Momma. Please, please wake up."

"*Shhh*, honey. It's going to be okay," Gertie said soothingly as she waited for them to do as she'd asked. "Straight to your room," she reminded them as they hesitated.

"What's wrong? Momma? Please wake up! Make her wake up. Please!" Bella begged as Anna Marie led her up the stairs.

David couldn't respond. He tried. He opened his mouth for the words to be said, but they wouldn't form on his tongue.

Even after the bedroom door closed and Gertie turned to stare at him with questions in her eyes, he heard that little girl's voice.

He would forever hear her asking him to wake her momma up.

The moment the girls' bedroom door closed, Gertie was at David's side, untying her apron from around her waist and setting it beneath Judy's head as a cushion.

"That's not going to matter. She's dead." David uttered the words with deadly calm.

"She can't be dead. We just need to move her."

Gertie shook her head as she bunched up her apron even more, adjusting the angle of Judy's head and then tugging her body so her head would lay on the floor rather than propped against the step. "Head wounds bleed more than they should. Remember that time when Anna Marie fell off the swing and hit her head on that rock? She was fine, even with all the blood. She was fine. Judy will be fine too. She will be. She's fine," she continued without taking a breath, a frenzy to her voice.

It was as if she needed to get the words out in order for them to be true.

"She's not *fine*, Gertie. She's dead." He couldn't believe what he was saying.

The sight of Judy's white face, the pooling blood beneath her head . . . it's too much.

David staggered to his feet, grabbing the wall for support.

Gertie ignored him. She checked Judy for signs of life, her pulse, the feel of nonexistent air coming from her lungs.

Everything came crashing down on David.

What have I done?

What did I do?

What just happened?

He prayed for the young girl to move. To open her eyes. For her lungs to rise and exhale the air trapped inside.

He prayed for her mouth to move. For the blood to stop. For her fingers to reach out.

He *needed* her to be alive.

"What did you do?" Gertie accused him, her voice hoarse, hard, and full of hatred and disbelief. "Why didn't you listen to me?" she wailed. "God told me she'd be fine. Why couldn't you just have *listened* to me?"

David waved his hands in front of him, waving away Gertie's accusations.

"I should have listened to her. I should have taken her last night, when she begged me."

The horror of what just happened curdled his stomach.

"Listen to her? Listen to *her*? She accused me of poisoning her! Why would you listen to her and not believe me! It was . . . it had to be Anna Marie. That wasn't the first time she's tried to hide the bottle from me . . . she must have poisoned her." Gertie turned to him, her eyes feral. She stood and stepped forward, her feet steady, her face hard. "What have you done?"

"Anna Marie? God, Gertie . . . how could you accuse our daughter? What is wrong with you?"

The words lashed out with the strength of a whip, his intention to strip his wife down to the bare bones and force her to see what she was doing.

Accuse our daughter? Is she that far gone?

He searched for any flinch in her face, for the telltale sign of guilt.

But it wasn't there. No blink of the eye, no downturn of her lips, no glancing away.

Instead, she kept her gaze on him, her chin lifted high.

"You were the one who killed her, David. *You*. If you'd just listened to me, I could have handled this. She would have been okay. But no. You had to freak out and tear our family apart. This is your fault."

She stood directly in front of him, body straight as a two-by-four piece of wood. He was as flimsy as a kite string drifting against a strong wind.

She poked him in the chest, right over his heart, her fingernail digging into his skin.

"You're always taking my children away from me. You're never there when they're ready to be born. Always on the road, leaving me alone to deal with the pain of having to say goodbye. You think you can talk me out of it every time I want to try for another baby, thinking you know best. But you don't. You don't know best. So God brought us these two to take care of and you've ruined it. You've *ruined* it."

The hatred that emitted from her while she ranted scared him.

David didn't know what to say or what to do.

He watched his wife transform from a woman undone to a woman with a mission.

"Gather Judy up. We'll take her to join our babies. She can watch over the little ones."

"What?" Her words now had the same effect as her earlier slap. "No, Gertie. No. We have to call the police. Let them know what happened. Her parents need to be told."

We have to right this wrong. We have to.

"*We* are her family. We are the ones who loved her. We are the ones who will take care of her."

"She's dead, Gertie. Dead."

How many times do I have to say it before she'll believe what's just happened?

"Stop saying that."

"What about Bella?"

"She's ours."

"Gertie . . ." David shook his head. "We have to find Judy's parents. We have to—"

"No!"

"Gertie."

"David, no one is to know of this. No one. We'll lay her with our little ones, and no one will know. It'll be our secret. Just us."

"It's not just our secret, Gertie. What about Bella?"

"No one knows they're here."

He couldn't believe what he was hearing.

"We can't keep her a secret."

"She is ours. Our heaven-sent daughter. Our gift from God. We'll make up a reason why she's here. Maybe she's your sister's daughter and we're taking care of her? It doesn't matter. I'll homeschool the girls. It'll be fine."

"It won't be fine."

The need to laugh hysterically hit him despite the gravity of the situation.

Judy is dead. I killed her.

"You need to do this for me, David Basil Walker. You go out and dig a new home for our girl, and I'll take care of all this here."

"I'm not putting her in the ground. The authorities need to be called. Her family—"

"*We* are her family."

They stood there, chests heaving, hearts pounding, bodies shaking as they stared at each other, willing the other to back down.

This was the moment that could change all their lives.

I will lose my family forever if I call the police.

I could lose my family forever if I bury Judy in the backyard and pretend like nothing happened.

One scenario was definite. The other a possibility.

But he'd sworn to love and protect his wife. Even knowing things weren't right in her mind, that she wasn't okay. He would do whatever it took to help her get through this.

Even if it means burying this girl next to all our stillborn children.

Chapter Twenty-One
ELLE

My ears are ringing by the time David finishes his story. At least, I hope he's finished. I'm not sure I can handle sitting here for another minute while he feeds me more lies.

That's what they have to be: lies.

Does he really think I'm going to believe he killed someone and covered it up? That my grandmother was sick enough that she would not only poison someone but then bury her in their own backyard? That's insane.

He paints a bleak picture of insanity, but I'm not buying it.

David lies there, staring out the window, his face soaked with the tears that began flowing the moment he started talking about what Sundays were supposed to be like.

He almost had me there. Almost.

But Grace's words ring in my mind over and over. After today, I finally hear them.

Everyone has their own version of the truth. His is mired with age. It has to be.

David is using his blanket to wipe his face, an obvious avoidance tactic so he won't have to look my way.

Not that I mind. I'm not sure I've schooled my features yet.

"You must think I'm a blathering idiot," he mumbles into the blanket.

Think? That would be a yes.

I give a slight shrug of my shoulder instead of saying the words. He catches the gesture and nods, as if understanding. He shrugs himself.

"Not only are you a blithering idiot, but you're also a tired and cranky old man who needs his rest," says Brennley.

I jump when I realize she's standing right next to me. How long has she been there?

"I'm telling my granddaughter a story." David frowns. "That doesn't make me tired or cranky."

The look my best friend gives him says otherwise.

"Fine. Whatever. I'm allowed a little crankiness at this stage of the game. You're too young to know any better." David rolls his eyes.

Brennley squeezes my shoulder, then leaves.

The heavy weight of uncertainty settles in the two feet that separate us.

"Never seems to be enough time, does there?" David says.

I lean forward and rest my hand on the sheets beside his arm, careful not to touch him.

"I don't think there will ever be enough time."

"When . . . when you were at the house. Did you see the crosses?"

I shake my head.

I hadn't seen any crosses. But then, I hadn't walked behind the garage either. According to his story, they should be there.

Now I'm not sure if I want to look for them. I'm not sure I believe his story.

They wouldn't have buried Gertie's stillborns behind their home, would they? She would have been rushed to the hospital each time she miscarried. Right? I realize this would have been in the fifties, but they weren't *that* backward—despite being in a small town.

I can't believe that David would willingly bury the body of a hitchhiker either. Or then have the audacity to raise that girl's child as his own.

Besides, I would have met Bella—wouldn't I? She'd have been more than just my mother's imaginary friend.

Unless *David* is the one not right in the head.

Considering the stories he's telling, that's a very real possibility.

"They're there. They're proof of what I did." His voice is rough.

I decide to play his game.

"If it's true, why are you telling me?"

"Because I was wrong." He won't look at me.

"Wrong? About what?"

"All I wanted to do was protect my family." His eyes clench tight and his fists gather the blankets beneath him into a ball. "My Gertie . . . she wasn't well."

I roll my eyes. *Wasn't well* doesn't really seem adequate. The woman, if the story is even half-true, had serious mental issues.

I don't mean that to sound harsh.

More of a reality.

A woman who suffered so many miscarriages or stillborns . . . it was understandable that she'd suffer from some sort of depression. She should have been medicated—hospitalized, even. Like her mother.

The fact I can't seem to call her my grandmother doesn't escape my notice. I'm not sure I'm ready to accept her—or the version of her I'm being fed—as family. Not yet.

"Was there no help for her?"

I think about my own mother and her own mental health. Thank God for Grace and for medication.

But what does that say about me?

"The only help would have been to institutionalize her. Her own mother was already in one. I couldn't do that to her. Or to Anna Marie.

She deserved to be loved by her mother, to get her hugs and kisses, to be taught how to garden and bake. I couldn't bear the thought of taking her for weekend visits that would eventually turn into no visits at all. That's no life for a child."

I think about the relationship Mom had with her parents, how she considered them dead for all these years. I wonder which would have been better.

"You think I'm lying, don't you?"

Do I tell him the truth? Or do I let him live the fantasy he has going right now?

Honesty is the best policy—isn't that what they say? Honesty is the first book in the series of your life, Mom used to tell me. How you start is just as important as how you finish, so why not start with honesty and see where it leads?

What a crock, now that I think about it. But considering the lies he's been feeding me, the least I can do is give him a dose of the truth.

"I still don't understand why you're telling me the story of two people I don't know. Judy and Bella mean nothing to me. The little details you're giving me about my mother . . . you're barely scratching the surface. And . . ." I stand. "I don't know, to be honest."

"But you believe there's a Bella."

I know he wants me to believe, to trust what he's telling me. But I can't.

"I believe Bella is the imaginary friend my mom created as a young and lonely child."

David's brow creases. The wrinkles fall into one another until his forehead resembles one of those wrinkly dogs—a shar-pei?

"Is that what she told you? Is that the lie she believes even now?" He heaves a heavy sigh. "She had an imaginary friend when she was younger, yes—but only after Bella died."

There's something on his face. He has more to say, but I'm not sure I want to hear it.

"I think you need to rest." I rise and gather my bag. I hold the handles with a firm grip.

"I'm not lying, child. If you don't want to believe me, I get it. I'm just a dying old man talking nonsense. That's what you're probably thinking, aren't you?" He stares straight at the wall, his mouth puckered in a fierce frown.

That frown reminds me of one I grew up with. My mother would often give me that same look when we argued.

I hated it on her, and I hate it on him.

"Your story is a bit hard to swallow." I step closer, my hand reaching out automatically before I catch the slight tensing of his arm muscles. "I need time."

Time for what, I'm not sure. To verify his story? To talk to my mom? To see what she will say?

"Go to the farm. Look for the crosses." His lips relax into something more like acknowledgment than frustration. "Then you'll believe. Hopefully it won't be too late."

I mumble something about hoping he sleeps well. I tell him I'll be back when I can. Then I leave and walk mindlessly down the hallway.

Brennley is waiting for me.

"It looked like I interrupted something pretty intense in there," she says.

"You could say that." I love Brenn like a sister, but how do I tell her David just admitted to murder? Even if it's true?

"Was it another story? Did he tell you more about Bella and Judy, or did he focus on your mom this time? Did you get any answers?"

When I don't answer right away, she gives me a hug.

"It's okay," she says. "If the story seemed odd, it's normal. They tend to do that, as the end nears." She gives me a gentle smile, as if to be encouraging.

I'm not sure why the idea relieves the weight on my shoulders. I should have remembered that from the nights we'd sit out on the deck and she'd share things about her patients with me.

There would be times she'd be in tears, knowing that sometimes it's their way of saying goodbye.

~

I wrestle for more than a day with the decision of whether to return to the farmhouse and search for the crosses.

If I do, it means I want him to be telling me the truth.

If not, it means I've decided he isn't.

I hate not giving people the benefit of the doubt, of judging them based on others' reactions.

Is he just a dying old man with a handful of memories that aren't real?

Or is he a man with a burdened heart, needing to tell the truth while he still can?

That's what I wrestle with the most.

What's the benefit to the truth being told now? Am I ready to hear that my whole childhood has been a lie? That my grandmother was a killer?

A *killer*?

I don't believe it.

Why is there such a need, deep down inside me, to know the truth? What is bothering me the most? The lies, or the fear of just how unstable Gertie was and what that means for my mother—and possibly for me?

What will I do if I find the crosses? If they are really there?

The idea of those little babies being buried behind the garage has my stomach in knots.

~

A long shadow covers the farmhouse and all the grounds as I turn into the driveway. Everywhere else the sun is shining brightly, the grass flowing with a gentle summer breeze, like the waves along the shore of Lake Huron.

I shiver, and it isn't from the breeze that brushes my skin.

The real shadow over David's property is coming from the clouds that hover above, but the tiptoe of fingers along my spine taunts me as I step out of my vehicle and stand in the middle of the driveway.

I had a dream about this home last night. Or rather, about my mom playing in the yard as a little girl. There were chickens running around like crazy and my mother twirling in circles, birdseed flying everywhere from her hands. Towels blew on the line with a breeze similar to the one today, the weight of their dampness causing it to creak as it swayed. While I stood there, almost in the same spot I am in now, my mother continued to turn in circles, her laughter as bright as the sunshine. Then it became something more, sinister almost in nature. I remember hugging myself and calling out for her to stop, saying that she was going to get sick, but she continued to spin round and round and round, her maniacal laughter now haunting. Finally she collapsed to the ground.

Everything was still then, in my dream. I watched as the birdseed dropped to the ground, covering her. I screamed in horror as those chickens rushed toward her, pecking at that seed until they tore into my mother's skin.

And yet all she did was laugh.

I woke up with a start, all the hairs on my arms on end. My scalp hurt, as if I'd slept with my hair in a ponytail.

There's something about this house—something that doesn't sit right.

It's more than just the hovering clouds over the yard. More than the shivers of unease along my backbone. More than the knot of twisted pain in my stomach as I make my way across the driveway, past the garage, and to the back.

The long grass brushes against my calves as I walk behind the deteriorating garage. I see its warped boards, rusted nails, and chipped paint again as if for the first time. The bottom half of it is covered in a jungle of vines and weeds.

I'm not sure what I expect.

I think a part of me believes if there truly is a graveyard, it would have been kept intact, similar to the playroom at the front of the garage.

If being the operative word.

There's nothing, though. No carefully kept section of the yard, no small white crosses to signify a burial ground—nothing to indicate David's story could even remotely be true.

The whole area is overgrown. No one has been back here in years. There's a rusted body of an old tractor off to the side but nothing to indicate this was an area often visited, as portrayed in David's tale.

I retrieve the crowbar we used to pry the boards off the front of the garage the last time we were here and run it through the tall grass, back and forth, back and forth.

I hit something.

A dirty piece of wood, straight but with a pointed end . . . so it would stick into the ground. My heart sinks.

I edge the wood more into the open and notice it's what I hoped *not* to find.

A cross.

Old, worn, discolored, and weathered, but undeniably a cross.

I sink to my knees.

I really wanted this not to be true. Such a large part of me didn't want to believe any part of his story, but I can't ignore this. This is hard evidence. This tells me that even if a single part of his tale is shrouded in truth, it's possible the rest is as well.

This cross represents everything I wish I could ignore.

Not just the possibility that there is a murderer in my family—which in and of itself is difficult to comprehend—but that I could be sitting on the graves of babies Gertie miscarried, children she spent time with in the mornings talking to, possible brothers and sisters to my mother.

This place, this grave site—could it also have been the catalyst for Gertie's mental breakdown?

I climb to my feet and stumble backward. Away from the cross I've unearthed. I round the corner, not paying attention to where I'm going, only knowing I need to get away from there.

And yet, I can't leave.

That playroom Brennley and I discovered, the one David mentioned in his tale, pulls at me. I can't get it out of my head. Everything in that room but the dollhouse was absolutely destroyed. Why?

I asked David about it, but he refused to answer.

That level of damage was meant to obliterate everything in sight, erase any and all memories.

But why?

There's only one reason I can think of. The weight of it shrouds everything else.

Guilt.

Guilt for Judy's death. Guilt for Gertie's instability. Guilt for losing Marie and possibly for letting her down, for not being there to protect her from Gertie's mental issues.

There'd been a deep need in David to destroy everything in the room that contained a memory he couldn't bear to dwell on. Yet he didn't touch the dollhouse or the drawing on the wall.

Why?

Chapter Twenty-Two

When I walk through the front door, the first thing I see is Mom sitting on the couch in the living room.

She doesn't notice I'm home. I breathe a sigh of relief as I walk by unnoticed.

"Elle, is that you?" Grace stands at the kitchen island, hand poised in the air, holding a knife. "I didn't realize you were coming tonight." She gives me a soft smile. "Come help me, will you?"

I take the knife from her hand and work on cutting the vegetables she had set out on the counter.

"Your mom is in the mood for stir-fry, and I had some chicken in the freezer. Hope that's okay?"

"Anything will be delicious." I focus on cutting the carrots the way I know Grace likes. Pinkie length, thin slices. She's very particular about how the veggies are cut.

"How are things?" Grace casually asks.

I look over my shoulder to find her standing at the stove, her back rigid, her hand in midair, waiting for my answer.

"If you're asking after David, he doesn't have much time left."

She sighs while her shoulders slump.

"He told me a far-fetched story that at first I found a little hard to swallow. Brennley says this can happen sometimes toward the end, so maybe none of it was real."

"I'm sure it wasn't too bad," Grace finally says as I finish with the vegetables.

"If you consider a murder confession to be not 'too bad' . . ."

The spoon she is holding clatters to the floor.

"Excuse me?"

I fill a glass with water and sit at the kitchen table and mask my face with a calmness I don't feel. I have just accused my grandfather of murder.

"Mental instability, poisoning, murder. It was all there. Wrapped up in a nice red bow. Of course, I didn't believe him. Not at first, but then I went back to the farmhouse and found a cross behind the garage . . ."

Is it too much to hope that someone will level with me for once? I feel angry for being played . . . even though I know it isn't fair to Grace.

There's a look of horror on her face. I suddenly feel ashamed for using her as my proverbial punching bag.

"I'm sorry, Grace. That wasn't . . ." I don't know how to describe the tidal wave of feelings rolling inside of me. "This is all messed up, you know?"

"What did he tell you?" Every movement she makes is of forced calmness.

I rub my face and the back of my neck while taking a few deep breaths.

I give her the short version of David's story, ending with my thought patterns once I saw that cross and the destruction of the playroom.

"Each detail on its own isn't enough to complete a story, but put two and two together and—"

"You don't always end up with four, you know that. It all depends on the measurement scale you use."

I roll my eyes out of habit. I don't need a mathematical lesson just now; I need someone to explain what is going on.

"Look behind the stories, Elle. What do you see?"

I think about this. Take away the story, take away the hurt and anger I feel at the secrets that circle this family. What am I left with?

"I see a man who loved his family. I see a broken child and now a broken woman."

"You know what I see? I see a family that is trying to heal. Is that so bad?" Grace leans forward, rests her elbows on the island.

I shake my head. She's right. Until I found out about David, I always knew the cracks within the mold of what made us a family were there, but I never understood why. There were too many secrets, too many lies. At least now I know. Or know *something*, anyway.

"She's never said anything to you, right? About her friends being poisoned or buried behind the family barn?"

I have to ask.

Grace just looks at me, a bored expression on her face.

"Right." I roll my eyes, as if the answer is obvious. "Of course she didn't, because Bella and Judy weren't real."

When there is no response from Grace, I look toward where Mom is sitting and lean forward, imitating Grace's posture.

"I mean, who does that? Even back then, in the fifties, who would bury their stillborns or miscarriages in the backyard? That's not possible, right? It has to be against the law, at least."

Grace has a way of letting a person know just what she thinks by the brief lift of an eyebrow and quirk of the corner of her lips.

"You seriously believed him?" she asks.

I rub the back of my neck.

"He insisted he was telling me the truth."

She nods. The same way a doctor nods when you tell him you're at death's door and all you actually have is a bad cold.

She's placating me. She knows it. I know it, and yet I don't let that stop me.

"Maybe that's his truth . . . ," she eventually says.

"What do you mean, 'his truth'?"

Grace pats my hand before pushing the chair back and returning to her place at the stove.

"Exactly what Brennley said to you. His mind could be playing tricks on him. Nightmares become reality. The real world, the pain he's in—that's become his nightmare."

With her words, the reality of David's situation sinks in. That man—my grandfather—is dying. It's something I really don't want to focus on, something I don't want to face day in and day out. Any minute, Brennley might call and tell me he's passed away. I know this. I expect this. Every time I think of it, I want to rush to his side so he won't die alone.

"Why haven't you gone to see David?" I'm not 100 percent sure where that question came from—nor am I sure who was more shocked that I asked.

Me, or Grace.

"Why would I?"

Good question.

"I thought you knew him. He hired you, didn't he? To look after Mom?"

I watch as Grace opens the cupboard to her right, carefully takes out three plates, sets them down on the counter, and then closes the cupboard door—all with a controlled fury.

I almost wish she'd slam the doors and throw the plates like I know she really wants to.

The angrier Grace becomes, the more controlled her body movements. It is a sure sign I've just crossed a line I had no idea was even there.

"Sorry." I'm not sure what exactly I'm apologizing for, but the quick smile on Grace's face tells me I made the right decision.

"Elle, honey. Do me a favor, okay?" She pauses as she pulls out silverware from the drawer. "If you're going to continue to visit him, listen to his stories—and then forget about them. I think it's wonderful that you're spending time with him, that you've given him something to smile about before he dies. That, more than anything, probably means more to him than you realize."

"What about the playroom, then?" Yes, I know. I'm like a cat with a piece of string, unable to leave it alone, wondering where the ball of yarn is and how much I can unravel before my world falls apart.

"What about it?"

I shrug. "He said he made it for Mom and Bella, to keep them occupied and give them a place to play that wasn't beneath Gertie's feet."

Grace smiles. "I can see Gertie appreciating that," she says softly, lost in thought. "She wasn't one for chaos, and two little girls with their toys and energy . . . she probably had her moments when it was all a little too much."

"If Bella was real," I remind her.

Grace rubs her face. "Right. Obviously, if the child was real."

"I brought some things home for Mom from the playroom. Well, from the dollhouse." I look back at my mother, still engrossed in her book.

Grace sets a pan on the counter, gives it a quick stir before she wipes her hands on a tea towel she's thrown over her shoulder.

"What kind of things?"

I reach for my bag, which I'd set on the floor beside me. I pull out the items I've brought.

A small doll, a bed, and a rocking chair—all things that would fit within my old dollhouse in the studio.

Right then, Mom appears at my side. She squeezes my shoulder hello before she notices the items on the table.

Gasping, she drops the book in her hand. It lands on the floor by my foot with a loud thud.

No one says anything. Grace and I watch Mom as she picks up each piece and looks it over with apparent tenderness. She strokes the hair of the tiny doll I found, straightens the nursing gown she wears, and then gently places her on the bed.

When Mom finally looks up, her eyes are full of tears.

"Thank you." She wraps her arms around me and squeezes tight. "These were Marie's. Daddy brought this for her as a special gift. I loved this doll, but she would never allow me to play with her—said she was special." Mom clasps her hands over her heart as she gazes at the doll once more.

I look at Grace.

"Mom, *you're* Marie."

Mom nods. "I know." Her voice is dreamlike, soft, but higher pitched than normal.

"So this is *your* doll, then, right?"

Mom tears her gaze from the doll and looks at me. I watch as a cloud sweeps over her pupils. There's a blank look, as if she isn't there. Grace comes over and places her hand on Mom's arm, which is all it takes for Mom to shake herself out of her memory.

Her laughter is off-putting—and more disturbing than the laughter from my dream last night.

"Of course it's mine," she finally says. "From when I was a little girl. I can't believe you found them."

I don't know what to say. Or how to act. So I stand there like an idiot while Mom blathers on.

"Marie, why don't you sit down?" Grace pulls out a chair. "Elle is going to help me set the table, and then we'll be ready to eat."

"You're upset, Lil'bit." Mom reaches for my hand. "Why?" She twists to look at Grace. "What did I do?"

"Nothing, Marie." She shoots me a look, shaking her head slightly. "Just sit, and we'll get the table set. Won't we, Elle?"

I ignore Grace and her obvious attempt at distraction.

"Who were you talking about, Mom?"

The confusion is still there but not like before.

"What do you mean?"

"You spoke about yourself in third person. You said the doll was Marie's and that your daddy had bought it for her as a special gift." The words come out silky smooth, covering my intense concern.

Mom picks up the doll and holds it close to her heart. "I remember when he brought it home for me. It was so special. I played with Isabel forever. Even brought her to bed at night. I couldn't sleep until we were both told a bedtime story."

"That's what you called the doll? Isabel?"

Mom nods.

I look at Grace and see the same questions on her face.

Bella could be a short form of Isabel. Is David telling me stories about my mom's *doll*? Had *he* made the imaginary friend real for her?

"Thank you," Mom says, oblivious to the silent interaction between Grace and me. "Thank you for bringing Isabel home. We should go put her in your old dollhouse." Her eyes light up like nighttime sparklers. She gathers the doll and furniture in her hand and leaves the house, heading out to the studio.

My grip on the top of the dining chair tightens as I try to make sense of everything.

David told me stories about Mom and Bella.

A doll, not a child.

"Your mother is just confused." Grace stands at the door, staring out after Mom. "She's been living in the past all day, poring over photo albums."

"Grace, was Gertie mentally unstable? Like my mom?" The question hovers between us, and for a while it doesn't seem like Grace is going to answer.

"Your mother has always suffered from dissociative identity disorder." Grace measures her words. "You know this."

That's not what I asked, and she knows it.

Grace clears her throat while she draws random lines on the table with her finger.

"Your mother never knew her own grandmother. It wasn't because she was dead, but . . . because she was institutionalized. David didn't learn about it until after they were married. I don't think it was something Gertie told many people about."

I lean forward, place my hand over hers to stop the movement.

"So my great-grandmother really was mentally unstable. I wasn't sure if that was true."

Grace nods.

"Mental health has come a long way since that time. The medications available now help tremendously, as you know."

What I know is that Mom needs to be heavily medicated at times.

"What about before that?"

Grace shrugs.

"Is there a way to find out?" I can hear the desperation in my voice. Grace hears it too. She covers my hand with hers and squeezes.

"Do you really want to?" she asks.

Part of me is saying yes, I really do. The other part screams that it won't matter.

My shoulders drop, and I can feel the beginning of a headache forming.

"My great-grandmother was crazy. My mother's unstable. So what does that make me?"

"Fine," Grace says with more conviction than I feel. "You are fine."

"For now. But how do I know that won't change? The fear is always there—you know that."

It's the one thing that haunts me, that keeps me separated, segregated from everyone who tries to get close. I'm not just protecting myself; I'm protecting them too.

I know firsthand the effect of mental illness.

"It's good to know your family background, to be aware. But don't let it derail you. You've got your whole life ahead of you. Embrace life. Stop getting buried in the past."

Buried.

The moment she says the word, images of white wooden crosses fill my mind.

Every story has a nugget of truth. That's what Mom taught me.

I've never felt more confused in my life. I'm getting mixed messages from Grace. A strong and very clear message from my mother. Who the hell knows what type of message I'm getting from David?

I rub my head, and Grace immediately reacts. She heads for the cupboard beside the stove and pulls out a bottle of pain relievers. She hands me two small, clear liquid pills.

"When David dies, you'll stay here, right? With Mom?"

The pill bottle drops from her hand, hitting the tile floor with a loud thud.

"Why would you say something like that?"

"Because he's the one who hired you."

I know the answer—that she will of course stay. This is her home, we're her family, and the death of the man who hired her won't change that. I just need to hear it.

There's something in her face, in the way she stands, shoulders tilted forward. The way her eyes slowly close as she inhales.

I'd hurt her with my words.

"I'm sorry," I say.

"No, you're not." She stands by the patio door and looks out in the direction of Mom's studio. "If you were, you never would have asked that."

I want to argue but don't bother. The words just came out of me, without thought. So she was right.

It's something I've been thinking about, something I've been mulling over, wondering . . .

"You are my family, Elizabeth Myers. You and your mother. This is my home, and it's the only place I have ever—or will ever—belong. I don't appreciate you questioning my love for you both."

"I'm sorry, Grace." I stand to give her a hug. Her body is stiff, unbending. Despite my apology, she isn't ready to forgive me. "I'm just trying to find out the truth."

"The truth isn't always what you assume it will be. You're expecting a dying man to provide you answers when all he's doing is grasping on to what little life he has left. Reality isn't his friend. Memories are. But those memories aren't pure. They're caught up in what could have been and what should have been—and he can't tell the difference anymore."

I search Grace's eyes. They are filled with hurt. With pain. With grief.

"I didn't mean to hurt you with my question," I reiterate.

She brushes me off.

"Go see your mom. Spend time with her, please. Dinner can wait."

Grace turns away from me then.

I follow my mother's footsteps along the path I created toward the studio, where music is blaring loud enough I can hear it halfway there.

I open the door, but I can't see her—not at first.

What I see is a new painting. Far from finished, but of an image I saw many times in my childhood. A familiar backdrop of wooden slats, a field of green grass dotted with wildflowers.

It's a scene from her childhood that she keeps locked in her psyche and uses as inspiration when she's in between feelings, she used to tell me. When she can't understand the emotions inside of her, she paints this. Brown-flecked wood boards. Swaying grass. Growing blooms. Once it was on canvas, then her emotions would open up. Sometimes the sky would darken until it was a thunderstorm and the grass was trampled by hail. Sometimes it was a beautiful summer day and she'd paint a children's tea party. Other times there would be a lonely feel to the canvas. A forgotten doll, a broken cup, one lone dress shoe . . .

Seeing this canvas now tells me a lot about Mom's emotional state.

She's confused.

I'm to blame.

Chapter Twenty-Three

I'm not sure when the roles changed between us.

I think it was gradual, for me at least. There was a time I knew Mom would always be there, protecting me, taking care of me. And then I began to protect her, take care of her.

There was a period in between when we were almost equals.

That's never a good place for a child to be with a parent.

I watch her now, in front of the dollhouse, where she's rearranging furniture and humming along to the music that's blaring so loud, my ears throb to the beat.

I remember when we would do this together—decorate the dollhouse, move the furniture around, and play. That was when we were equals, playmates.

We would spend hours decorating the house until it was perfect.

Back then, we both had our own favorite dolls. We picked them out once, during a trip to the city. There was a store full of dollhouse kits, furniture, and anything else you could imagine. We would go and walk through that store, make lists of what we wanted to get the next time we were there. We would always leave with one item.

We made a special trip when I was seven so we could pick out our dolls.

I called mine Ida, after a story Mom told me about a little girl and her little flowers. It was one of Hans Christian Andersen's first fairy tales. A little girl discovers why her flowers look so tired in the mornings. They would attend balls every night, where they would dance until the wee hours. It was one of my favorite stories. For years, I would place little daisies and rose cuttings on top of my dolls' beds so they could sleep during the day and then dance at night.

Much like Ida, I would creep out of my bed at night with the hope of catching my flowers in the act.

Looking back, I don't think I ever did.

Mom's doll was named Zelena, after the Wicked Witch of the West. Mom would bring home all sorts of books from the library that we would read together. Our favorite was a series about the land of Oz. The name *Zelena* used to conjure up someone who was evil and looked hideous. She would have a large wart on her nose and a brilliant green face—much like the character in the movie.

Ironically, it really means grateful and kind one.

Mom liked that Zelena was someone completely misunderstood. She was a person with two characters living inside of her—the evil witch everyone assumed her to be as well as a person with a kind soul.

"Hey!" I call out after turning down the volume on her stereo.

She turns, a sweet smile on her face. She's holding the doll I brought home in her lap.

"Every so often, I'll place a cutting on your bed in here. Did you know that?" she says.

I lean in, and sure enough, there's a drying rose on my doll's bed. Ida sits in the chair beside the bed.

"That's still one of my favorite fairy tales." I pick up the rose and lightly touch one of the petals.

Mom's smile is a little too bright.

"You used to ask me to read it to you all the time. We'd go out in the field for a tea party and tell stories about the balls all the flowers attended the night before."

I sit down on the ground beside Mom, dying rose in my hand.

"I remember," I say after a while. "A few times, you woke me up when the full moon was out and a gentle breeze was playing with the grass. You would tell me there was a ball going on. You'd turn on some soft music, and we'd sit there, huddled in our blankets, and hope to catch a glimpse between the grass blades."

She nods. "You'd always fall asleep, cuddled close to me, while we watched."

She reaches over and takes the rose from my hand, places it back on the doll bed.

"I wanted you to grow up knowing what magic felt like," she says.

I did.

I must have said that out loud because she frowns, her chest heaving as she lets out a long breath.

"Until I ruined it all." Mom releases Isabel and reaches for her doll, Zelena. "There's a lot of evil people in the world, Lil'bit. But not all of them are bad. You just need to look deep enough, long enough, and you'll see it. You don't listen to what they say, but you look at what they do. Remember Mr. Mowes? For the longest time, you were so scared of him. We'd go for walks through the fields and see him with his cows in the distance. You'd beg me to turn around. Do you remember?"

I remember.

I remember how that man scared me. How I'd wake up screaming because he'd be in my dreams, that stern frown on his face and him waving his arm at me. He'd lost his hand in the war. While he normally pinned his shirt over his stump, the first time I saw him it was out there in the open for all to see.

I was only a little girl. That stump, with its puckered red skin, scared me. He told me that that was what happened when little boys and girls didn't listen to their elders.

"I'll never forget the day you realized he wasn't so scary," Mom says. "We were walking the fields and saw one of the small calves lying down. You were so frightened for it—you thought it was going to die."

She looks off into the distance, and I know she's looking out over the fields, to where we'd stood that day.

"So you told me"—I finish the story for her—"to run and get Mr. Mowes. He was on his tractor. I ran as fast as I could and started jumping up and down to get his attention."

I recall being scared.

"You were such a brave little soul," Mom says.

I don't remember being brave. I was a scared little girl, but fear for the calf overshadowed my fear of Mr. Mowes.

"He propped me up on the seat in front of him and drove his tractor over to where you stood. I could barely hear him over the noise, but I do remember him telling me the calf still needed a name. He asked if I had any suggestions."

Asking a little girl to name a baby animal was like offering her a lifetime supply of ice cream.

"What did you call it?" Mom asks.

"Gimp!" We both say together.

The calf had only twisted its leg in a gopher hole.

We used to feed Gimp carrots and celery we picked from our garden. Mr. Mowes kept that cow around even though he could have sold it or used it for food. But we'd named it, and named farm animals stay—according to Mrs. Mowes.

I cried so hard at Mr. Mowes's funeral. He died doing what he did best: taking care of his cows. He had a heart attack, and his older son found him late one night out in the barn. He'd become family, and it hurt to lose him.

"You were so scared of him in the beginning. Until you discovered there was another person beneath that crusty exterior of his."

"What are you trying to tell me, Mom?"

Her shoulders droop and she gives me a look I can't quite read.

"Not everything is a lesson, Lil'bit."

Okay. I don't believe her, but I will leave it be. I look at the doll-house with new eyes.

David made this for me.

My grandfather.

Does it hold new meaning for me now that I know? Does it make it more special knowing it isn't something Grace picked up from a market or a store, but something that was made with love? For me?

It does.

"Did your mom play dolls with you when you were little?" I ask.

I want to know more about Gertie. David's story hovers there, something I could touch. I want to mold it, to look deep at all the layers. To see the meaning behind the words.

I don't believe anymore that there was a Bella or a Judy. Not real people, anyway.

But created for my mother's benefit? I think the tangible proof is there, within that dollhouse.

Isabel, or Bella, is very real. In doll form.

"No." It is like the weight of the world settled onto her shoulders. "My mother wasn't the type to get down on the ground and play dolls with me. She spent her time cleaning the house, ensuring not one speck of dust settled on her precious furniture. Or she was out in the garden, tending to her vegetables. She didn't have time for play."

I can't imagine. I feel sorry for Mom and want to return that smile to her face.

"I think"—I reach out and place a hand on Mom's leg—"one of my favorite things about my childhood is the relationship you and I had.

You made it so special, magical . . . I truly believed we lived in a fairy tale." I let the truth of how I felt as a child shine through my words.

"When did you stop believing?" she asks.

When? That's easier to answer than it should be.

When Mom stopped being able to take care of me due to her depression. When I had to be the one taking care of her. Helping her to the bathroom. Making sure she showered—somehow knowing she shouldn't take a bath. When I had to be the one feeding us with toast, bowls of cereal, and heated-up cans of soup on the stove.

When I realized that asking her about my grandparents was enough to send her into a spiral.

That's when the fairy tale became a nightmare, one I was too young to be equipped for.

But I don't say that. I can't. She isn't looking for me to be honest with her, she's looking for me to ease her own guilt.

"We lived in our own little world, didn't we? Those were the best years of our lives. At least, of my life." There are tears in her eyes and they break my heart. "I wanted you to have what I never did," she says.

"What was that?"

She pats my hand, a sweet smile full of memories on her face. "A childhood full of love and happiness. I wanted you to know how loved you were, how important you were to me. *Are*, to me," she clarifies.

"I love you too, Mom." I lean my head onto her shoulder.

"It wasn't enough, though, was it?" she asks. "It's not enough, even now? You always had to ask. You were always full of questions, needing to know the story behind the story, and you wouldn't accept no for an answer. It's why you're so good at what you do, why working with patients is so perfect for you. You care about who they are and listen to their stories." She plays with my hair as she speaks.

It feels nice. A reminder of when I was little and she'd run her hand over my hair, soothing me whenever I was sad or unhappy.

"Life doesn't always work out the way they do in fairy tales, love. Sometimes there are no happy endings."

I sit up, stretching my back until I hear a slight *pop*. "All I've ever wanted was to know the truth, Mom. To know my past. I thought my grandparents were dead, but David isn't. I don't understand. I can't even pretend to know what happened to you that would create the need to distance yourself like you did from your family—"

"No, you can't. No one can." She cuts me off.

"But I'd like to, Mom. I'd like to."

She shakes her head, begins to breathe hard, and her hands start to shake.

"You can't understand, Lil'bit. You can't. My mother . . . I hated that woman, don't you understand? I never wanted you to grow up hating me."

"I could never hate you," I say softly, my hand on her arm.

"You would have, though," she insists. "If you'd grown up like I did. Secluded. Not allowed to have friends. Locked away where no one could see me or know about me. One day I was driving into town with my daddy to get groceries, and the next day I wasn't allowed to step a foot outside of the house—not even to play outside in the field." She shakes her head while tears roll down her cheeks.

"My mother was crazy, Elizabeth. She should have been locked up in a hospital, not raising a small child." She stands and walks in a circle.

"David . . . he told you he was a truck driver, right?"

I nod. I don't want to say much, don't dare break whatever spell has come over Mom to make her open up like this.

"He was never home. I think it was easier for him to not be. For a long time, he would always get home in time to tuck me into bed and tell me a story. But, little by little, he began to take longer trips. Instead of coming home every night, it turned into every other night, and then eventually he was only home on weekends."

She stops to stand in front of a canvas of a growing storm, full of browns and grays.

"He left me alone with her and didn't care what it did to me."

The agony in her voice is enough to push me off my seat. I move to stand beside her.

"I'm so sorry, Mom."

She looks at me then, and the clarity in her eyes . . . it's unexpected.

"He wasn't my father, Elizabeth. Not the way a father should be. He was supposed to protect me, take care of me, love me, treat me like the princess he made me think I was. He betrayed me, and I swore"—she turns away and hugs her body—"I swore he would never get the chance to betray you too."

"So that's why you told me he was dead?" If that's the truth, then I understand. Not completely, but enough.

"He was dead to me the day I left that house. He's always been dead to me. I didn't lie to you."

"He's alive, Mom."

"It doesn't matter." Her arms drop to her sides and she returns to the dollhouse.

"You are my family." Mom's voice is soft, empty of emotion. "You and Grace. That's all I need."

Her hands shake as she turns from me and focuses on the dolls, moving them around, smoothing their hair, picking up the furniture and looking at it closely—all but ignoring the fact I am standing behind her.

In fact, I'm not even sure she remembers I'm there.

Chapter Twenty-Four
DAVID

A summer storm rumbles through the air, and I count the seconds between each flash of lightning and roar of thunder while the rain spatters against the window.

Plop-plop-plop-plop.

Living by the lake means fantastic summer storms.

I used to love watching them with Marie when she was little. If the lightning was far off, we would sit outside underneath the protection of the back porch.

Sometimes it would rain.

Other times it would be a dry storm. Those made my arm hair stand on end when lightning struck.

Right now, the rain is pounding against my window. If I were a betting man, I'd say it was about to hail and hail hard.

Hail is never good.

It destroys farm crops, vegetable gardens, rose bushes, and everything else in its path.

Gertie hated the storms, but me, I loved them. I slept like a growing teenager when it stormed at night. I never had any problems sleeping through thunder loud enough to shake the house, and I would always wake up wide-eyed and ready to go, whereas Gertie would be up all night, huddled beneath the blanket, and a zombie in the morning.

Gertie never did well when she didn't get a solid eight hours of sleep.

There's a knock on my door, and before I can gather the strength to croak, "Go away," in walks Charlie, carrying a tray of what I hope is coffee.

Nurse Amy always refuses to give me even a sip of the stuff. She's the devil incarnate.

I said that to her once, and she just laughed.

Said she'd rather think of herself as the devil's wife, thank-you-very-much.

I snorted.

"I brought you a fancy cold coffee with lots of ice. Your nurse said it was okay." He holds the door open and peeks down the hallway. "*Geesh*, she's kind of militant, isn't she? You'd think since you're about to die she'd let you eat or drink whatever the hell you want." Charlie sets the tray he's carrying down on the food table, sticks a straw in my cup, and brings it close enough to my mouth so I can sip the damn thing.

Dying destroys any normality a man wants to have. I shit in a diaper—that is, I would if I had anything left in me to shit—pee in a tube, and I can't even get it up during a sponge bath. What's having an old friend basically hold your straw against all that?

"Stop scowling," Charlie grumbles. "You think I want to be holding your drink like you're a mewling baby?"

I'd tell him off but he might just take the drink away, and it feels soothing going down my throat.

My mouth, throat, and stomach are all on fire today, and so far nothing can dampen the flames.

"How are you doing?" he asks. I notice the uneasy look he gives the machines to my right.

No doubt he's thinking about the day he'll end up here, in this bed.

I hope he has nightmares about it.

"Remember when we found that rabid dog up near the Routers' farm when we were kids?" I say instead. Wouldn't be right to tell him what I'm really thinking, considering he did bring me coffee.

"Yeah. I also remember my dad handing me the gun and telling me to 'do the right thing.' First time I killed an animal."

"Wish you had that gun now," I mumble.

Charlie frowns, then looks at the monitor again. My heart rate just spiked.

"Don't say that, man," he says. "You've got your granddaughter back in your life. Surely you want as much time with her as you can get."

True. I do. Seeing her, watching the expressions flitter across her face, the way she holds herself—it's like having Gertie back.

"She's the spitting image of her, ain't she?" Charlie asks.

Funny how he knows what I'm thinking.

"Do you get to talk much when she's here?" He finally sits in the chair beside the bed.

"I tell her stories about her mom when she was young."

Charlie fiddles with his cup and sits up straighter. Doubt he caught me noticing. But I notice. What else is there to do?

"How young?" He stares at his cup.

"Young." What does it matter? "Before school," I clarify.

I could say, *When you were still in our lives,* but I don't. No need to rub more salt in the open wound.

"Ah." Charlie nods. "Marie was a fireball back then. She changed afterward, though. Lost some of that . . . spark."

Changed? Lost that spark? Who is he to say that? What right does he have to judge my little girl?

"How would you know? You never came around."

Charlie's lips tighten until they're a solid white line. Then he barks, "Whose fault was that?"

If I could, I'd punch the sucker right where it hurt.

"You might as well leave if all you're going to do is bring up the past like that. It is what it is. Leave it alone."

Charlie grumbles something beneath his breath as he sits back in the chair and sips his own iced coffee.

"What's that?" I ask. I shouldn't have. I really don't want to know what he said.

"The boys say hi."

That's not what he said, but I don't push it.

I know the past will always be there, between us. We both have regrets. But what does he expect to happen now? Nothing can change the past. There's no magic eraser strong enough for that. Besides, it's not like it was all on me. Sure, I told him to not come around, to leave us be, but he was the one who didn't argue, who didn't force himself back into our lives.

He walked away like it didn't matter.

I'm not going to lie and say that never bothered me.

"I'll admit, I'm surprised you came back." Back into my life, back into this room. I didn't expect it.

"You want to die alone, is that it?" Charlie leans forward, the muscles on his arms still visible even at his age—mind you, the varicose veins are there in droves too.

"What does it matter how I die?"

"It matters." He leans back, arms crossed. He glares at me.

I glare back.

"What kind of stories are you telling your granddaughter?" he finally says after a very long minute has passed.

"The girl wants to know more about her mother. You can't know who a person is until you know their past. So that's what I'm telling her." It annoys the hell out of her, but sooner or later she has to learn life isn't to be lived with ribbons and bows. Life is hard, and it sucks even at the best of times.

"All of it?" He frowns, as if questioning my method. "Or just parts?"

"Just one part. But there's enough there. If she looks hard enough, she'll see it for what it is."

"What's that?" Charlie asks.

I don't know how to answer without telling him. It's there, on the cusp of my lip, wanting to be said.

But I can't do that to him. Or to Gertie. That wouldn't be fair.

"That mistakes were made," I say instead.

Charlie's eyebrows become one straight line.

"Mistakes? What mistakes could you have possibly made?"

Oh, come on. He knows me better than that. This is the man who sobered me up enough to get me home before my father skinned my ass for telling him off when I was a teenager.

"It's amazing what you'll do for the women you love."

"You're placing this on *Gertie*?" He half rises from his chair.

"No, I wouldn't do that. It's all on me."

My wife, my daughter . . . they weren't to blame. I am.

Charlie settles back down. "What did you do that was so wrong?"

I turn my head and watch the hail I was expecting earlier bounce off the window with a *ping-ping-ping* sound. They're just small morsels of ice that will melt in no time.

What I wouldn't give to be outside now, even with the weather as it is. At least it would be better than the recycled air I'm breathing.

"You did it for Gertie." Charlie coughs, turning my attention back to him. "That's what you said to me once. What was bad enough to make you push me away?"

I did it for my family. I don't say that out loud, though. Charlie doesn't need to know. He wouldn't understand.

That fire is back, burning everything inside me. My back arches as the flames lick at my soul.

"You okay? What's wrong? Do I need to call the nurse?" Charlie pushes himself to his feet and reaches for my call button.

"I'm fine," I grind out from a clenched jaw.

I deserve this fire, this pain. I breathe through it, knowing this pain will soon be my life, once I die.

"I need a drink, please." I struggle to get the words out.

He holds the straw against my lips. I sip as much as I can with greedy intentions and feel a modicum of relief.

"Do you want me to leave? Get the nurse? What can I do?" There's a mixture of panic and concern in his voice.

It feels good to know I'm not alone.

What can he do? There's nothing to be done. No words to be said, no gestures to be made, no reparations that can change what happened.

I hit the button for medicinal relief and wait for it to set in.

"I'm okay," I eventually get out.

Charlie sits back down and watches me closely.

What's he expecting to see?

"Ever feel like you crossed a line you never saw?" Charlie asks out of the blue.

"What the hell are you talking about?"

Charlie jolts, like he didn't mean to say what he just said. He climbs to his feet.

"How can a man think with all these machines blaring?" Charlie smooths the creases in his pants.

What is that about?

"What line did you cross?"

He shakes his head, and I know he isn't going to tell me anything.

"Fine. Whatever." I lift my hand enough to wave him away. I've enough demons to deal with on my own. I don't need his.

"I wasn't asking you to," he says.

Guess I spoke out loud.

"Surprised you heard me," I said, rolling my eyes, "considering all the machines working to keep me alive."

They aren't loud, though, and after a while, you learn to mute them so you hear nothing but silence.

"Look, maybe this was a bad idea." Charlie grips the edge of the seat with his hands. "I thought we could put everything behind us. We're grown men after all."

"Sounds to me like you've got something you need to get off your chest. Better hurry up." I swallow. "I don't have much time left. Don't be asking me for forgiveness or to give you peace or any other type of crap that happens with these deathbed confessions, you hear?"

"Why do you have to be so crotchety?"

"Because I can."

"What happened to the man who loved life and saw the good in everyone? When did you become so damn negative?"

I snort. So damn negative? Live my life, go through the hell I've walked through, and then ask that again.

"Life doesn't always work out the way you want. You should know that, Charlie." I close my eyes, tired. Tired of dealing with the emotional crap Charlie is dragging up. Tired from lying here, waiting for the end to come. Tired of living a life I never wanted to live.

"You're right," Charlie says. "I've got something I need to get off my chest. I should have said this to you years ago, but you wouldn't have listened. You would have told me to mind my own business and to walk the hell away."

"Mind your own damn business and walk away," I say.

We look each other straight in the eye until his gaze slips. I grin.

"Seems to me I'm the only one walking anywhere right now. So shut up, old man."

I clamp my lips tight. If the man's got something to say, then I'll let him say it.

Charlie walks the length of my room a few times before he stops at the foot of my bed.

"What took you so long getting help for Gertie?"

My jaw drops. That's not what I expected him to say.

"Get help for Gertie? What do you mean?"

"You know exactly what I mean." He punches the palm of his hand, and the slap of flesh rings like a bell in my rather small room. "Don't play dumb, David. It doesn't suit you."

The beep from the heart monitor increases until all I can hear is an agitating *beep-beep-beep-beep*. I glance at the machine and try to slow my breathing, my chest rising like an accordion until I take in one solid breath and hold it, counting to three—which is about as long as I can go without it hurting—and let it out through my nose.

"Say what you mean," I finally say to Charlie.

"I already did." His jaw is etched in stone as he glares at me.

"What type of help was I supposed to get for Gertie, Charlie? It's not like we were swimming in cash back then."

"That's not what I'm talking about, and you know it."

No, I don't.

The day I told Charlie to leave and never come back, Gertie's state of mind wasn't obvious. She was sad, on edge, and exhausted, but that was life then. Raising our daughter, taking care of the house, the chickens, and herself—it became too much.

Judy was supposed to help. She was supposed to relieve some of that pressure on Gertie so she could relax and get rested up.

The day Judy died, our lives changed drastically.

But Charlie had no idea, nor should he have.

"Something was wrong with her," Charlie says, the words tearing from his soul.

I wince. Not from the accusation, but from the pain in Charlie's voice.

He believes I betrayed him. Betrayed my wife. He couldn't be more wrong.

"You knew it." The accusation stands between us. "You knew it and did nothing. Why?"

"Did nothing?" He should know me better than this. Or he did, at one time. "You don't know what you're talking about. I did everything I could for Gertie, for my daughter."

"Right," he spits the word out. "That's why you started taking longer loads? Because you were doing it for Gertie? She needed you home, not on the road."

"I was home."

Charlie's grip tightens until his arthritic knuckles are whiter than my bedsheet.

Even as I say the words, I know them to be a lie.

I took longer trips. That much was true. I did what I could to not be home.

But not for the reason Charlie thinks.

"What makes you think you knew what my wife needed better than I did?"

I'm not sure I want to hear the answer.

"Because I was the one there for her, you jackass. While you were logging more and more hours, taking as many long-haul shifts as you could, I was there, taking care of your wife."

I lurch upward at his words.

"How dare you, you son of a . . ."

Everything goes crazy. All the monitors are shouting, and Charlie starts yelling for the nurse. All I can do is fall back as electric shards of pain pierce my body and everything goes black.

Chapter Twenty-Five

I don't want a sister anymore.

She's mean.

She broke all my pencils into pieces and now I only have one left.

Her mama said I get no more pencils for a week. She thinks I broke them all in a tantrum.

But I didn't have a tantrum. Sister did.

She got mad because Mama put my picture up on the fridge. I thought it was a nice picture, of our new family.

Sister is meaner than the bumblebee that stung my arm.

Meaner than when the sky screams at night with thunder and lightning.

Meaner than the scariest monsters you could ever imagine.

I tried to be mean back, but I only got in trouble and had to sit on the stairs for a whole hour.

I don't want a sister no more.

No more.

Chapter Twenty-Six

DAVID

September 1956

"The girls need to be in school, Gertie," David argued with his wife as they worked in the garden, pulling up vegetables.

"I'm homeschooling them, David. The girls are too smart for kindergarten. Look at them—they both read and write almost better than we do. I found an ad in the paper for a homeschool group located in Hanover. I'm just waiting on the materials to arrive. I can teach them from home, send in their tests and exams, and we'll be fine." Gertie was hunched over a section of peas while his fingers were deep in the dirt, pulling up potatoes.

"They need to socialize. Being out here, alone—it's not healthy."

"David Basil Walker"—Gertie stood and glared at him—"don't you be telling me how to raise these girls when you're off trucking for days on end and don't bother coming home as often as you should."

He hated arguing with her, but he also hated watching Bella deteriorate.

"Besides, how are we going to explain her? Have you thought of that?"

"My sister . . ." David didn't bother to finish his sentence. It wasn't the first time they'd argued about this, and he already knew how she would reply to his suggestion.

"No. We'll do things my way. It's worked out fine, and it'll continue that way." Gertie arched her back with a groan. "I'm taking these peas in to clean them. Bring the potatoes when you're ready. Let's end this talk now, all right?"

David watched his wife cross the yard with the basket of vegetables on her hip and knew he'd let her down.

He'd let them all down.

He focused on the speck of white he could see in the distance, behind his garage. The white of the crosses hidden in the long grass. The cracks in his heart widened.

What they'd done was wrong. Burying that girl back there, not notifying the police, covering up everything that had happened a few months past . . . it was all wrong.

One look at Bella confirmed it too. That girl needed to be with family—her real family, not the people who'd killed her mother.

"Daddy?" David looked up and caught Anna Marie running toward him. Bella slowly walked behind her. "Can we go play in our playroom? Momma said we had to talk to you first, to see if you wanted any help or not."

His daughter buzzed with energy while Bella looked ready to crumple in a ball. Gertie said she'd been having nightmares of late. It looked like she could use a good nap.

"Sure, go play. Or read, or whatever it is you girls like to do in there. Bella, love, I could always use a new drawing for my truck."

Bella perked up at the sound of her name. The sweetest of smiles grew like he knew it would after she realized she could draw a picture for him.

That was the only time the girl smiled anymore. She loved to draw, would spend hours and hours sitting at the table, drawing pictures for her mom. Gertie put a stop to it, said it wasn't healthy to get lost in her thoughts like that so much. Now she could only draw when they gave her permission.

David gave her permission every time he could. He didn't think it was right of Gertie to take away the one thing that sweet girl loved more than anything else, but every time he gave his opinion, he was told he was favoring the girl.

Of course he was. She just lost her mother.

"Bella, you need to play with me, not color!" Anna Marie stomped her foot on the grass.

"Princess . . ." David added a little growl to his voice, which made his daughter immediately contrite. Her head dropped, her fists unclenched, and he heard the word *sorry* come from her lips, even if it was half-hearted.

"Bella, you run along while I chat with Anna Marie for a moment."

David brushed his dirt-covered hands on his jeans and joined his daughter on the grass. Her legs were crossed, and she was picking blades of grass with her head bent low.

"What's going on, love?" David picked his own blade, brought it to his lips, and whistled.

Anna Marie's head popped up.

"Do that again, Daddy." She leaned toward him and watched as he showed her how he pinched the blades between his finger and thumb.

She copied him, and together they blew grass whistles until he caught a smile playing with the corners of her lips.

"Are you ready to talk now?" David asked. He had a feeling he knew what was wrong, but he wanted to hear her admit it.

"Bella's supposed to be my sister, but she doesn't like playing with me." Gone was that soft smile, and in its place was a pout fit for a toddler.

"I think Bella's still sad, moppet. You would be too, wouldn't you, if you lost your mommy?"

She nodded with heavy dips of her head before she shrugged. "But she's got a new mommy. She should be happy now."

If only it were that easy.

"She needs time, love." He'd remind her as much as she needed.

"Momma says I am responsible for her smiles."

David frowned.

Why would Gertie say such a thing?

"You just worry about your own smiles"—he tilted her chin with a finger—"and you let us take care of Bella, okay?"

Anna Marie nodded, but he knew she didn't take his words to heart.

How could she, when Gertie is saying something different?

"Are you doing okay?"

The moment she looked up in confusion, he knew she didn't understand why he was asking. It was the same thing he asked over and over when he was alone with her. Was she okay?

"Are you doing okay, Daddy?" She turned the question on him. Her hand rested on his arm, and she seemed concerned as she stared up at him.

"Why do you ask?" He tried to mask his surprise at the question.

"You killed her mommy, Daddy. Does that make you sad?"

His throat collapsed and he couldn't breathe. Her words gripped his heart like a fist and squeezed. He thought for sure he was having a heart attack.

He beat his chest with the palm of his hand until something opened up and air filled his lungs.

He expected accusation, distrust, fear to be in his daughter's gaze.

He was a monster. A killer. Shame covered him like moss. He was so entrenched in what he'd done, it covered up everything good about him.

"Go play, love." He could barely look at his daughter, he was so disgusted with himself.

To hear those words come from his baby's mouth—it was too much.

All of it is too much.

He sat there for a long time, lost in thought, until Gertie laid her hand on his shoulder.

"David, what's wrong?"

He looked up at her with tear-stained cheeks, embarrassed to be found like that. Wasted. Wrecked. Weak.

"Our daughter thinks I'm a murderer. A monster." There was no one else to talk to, to admit this to. Even though his wife wasn't strong enough to be his support, he needed her to be.

Gertie held out her hand, and with a sigh, David unfolded his body from the ground and stood.

"She couldn't love a monster, but she loves you. What happened was due to a series of unfortunate events. One day, she'll realize that." Gertie reached out to caress his cheek, but instead of seeming like a loving gesture, it was condescending, patronizing.

"It was more than a series of unfortunate events," David repeated while closing his eyes, trying to block out the sound of his daughter's words.

They were going to haunt him for the rest of his life.

He was a murderer. Intentional or not—that no longer mattered. The moment he'd let Gertie talk him into burying Judy behind the garage, he sold his soul for his wife and daughter. There was no turning back.

He needed to find a way to be okay with that.

"Go play with your daughters, David. Don't get lost in what happened, just focus on what we have now. Two beautiful girls to raise as our own."

His wife vibrated with an assurance he didn't feel.

They walked to the garage together and stood outside the door while they watched the girls.

Their playroom was everything a little girl could hope for, everything his girls deserved.

Gertie was right. They're both my daughters. That's the life I live now.

When Bella glanced up from the corner table, pencil in hand, the ghost of a smile appeared on her face.

Maybe she'll be okay. Maybe we'll figure a way through this. Maybe Gertie is right.

"Daddy, come play with me." Anna Marie jumped up from where she lay on the carpet, dolls spread out. She looked from Bella to him and frowned. "Come play with *me*," she repeated more forcefully.

Gertie nudged him hard in the side.

"You need to focus on Anna Marie too," she whispered to him. "She's hurting just as much as Bella. Don't forget that."

Is this what my life is going to be like from now on?

He felt like the rope in a game of tug-of-war, his daughter on one end . . . but he wasn't sure who held the rope at the other. His wife? Bella? His soul?

If it was his soul, he'd already lost. He wanted Gertie to get through this unscathed. Since Judy's death, he'd watched his wife's mood improve a little every day. She wasn't as sad, lost in the past like before. She was present, had a purpose, and was more of a mother to those two girls than she'd ever been.

If there was ever a silver lining, this was it. He'd ignore the shadow over their lives for as long as he could.

"Why don't you come play as well?"

Gertie chuckled. "Unlike you, I need to clean these vegetables and get dinner started if you're wanting to eat while the sun still shines. Go play with the girls, remind them their daddy is always there for them."

Her eyes blazed with fire, but the heat wasn't a welcome one—not for him.

While he agreed that Bella was becoming a daughter to him, hearing Gertie say it sent shivers down his spine.

Bella was already her daughter. That bond had been instantaneous. There was no doubt in his wife's mind that God brought Bella into their lives, and it didn't seem to faze her that someone had to die for that to happen.

Knee-deep in Judy's grave, shovel in hand, David had made a vow to do anything and everything to protect his family, even if it meant burying this secret, if only his wife could be healed. He didn't want their daughter to grow up not knowing her mother's love, and he couldn't imagine a life without Gertie in it. After burying the girl next to their other children, Gertie had stood at his side with a bouquet of wildflowers she'd picked. She'd laid them on Judy's grave, then bent down and whispered words David couldn't make out.

"She'll take care of them now," Gertie said to him as she entwined her fingers with his. "I can rest now, knowing they're not alone." She laid her head on his shoulder, her eyes full of tears. She hummed the lullaby she used to sing to Anna Marie every night.

After that day, there were no more daily picnics or visits to the graves with the girls.

After that day, Gertie would go out there alone on Sunday mornings before breakfast. She'd share about her week, tell stories, and say a prayer. But instead of coming back into the house with red-rimmed eyes, she'd greet him with the brightest of smiles.

His Gertie was a different woman, one he wasn't sure he recognized, but he wasn't one to kiss a donkey on the ass.

Gertie leaned up to kiss his cheek, another thing that had changed in the last few weeks. She was quick to show affection, more so than before.

Yep. My Gertie has changed. Better or worse, doesn't matter.

She'd say that Bella was a gift from God, but David knew better.

God had nothing to do with it. The devil had tricked him, made him a deal he couldn't pass up.

One day, he'd have to pay his dues.

Chapter Twenty-Seven

The girls had made a story corner in their bedroom. They'd sneaked quilts from the closet and any extra pillows they could find. The two of them were as snug as two lazy dogs in front of a fire.

Bella's eyes were drifting closed, while Anna Marie was buzzing with excitement.

"I've missed your stories, Daddy." She cuddled up to him and nuzzled her head in the crook of his neck and shoulder.

David placed his arm around her and pulled her in tight for a hug.

The past week, he'd been away every other night due to longer hauls. The extra money meant a little more security for him and Gertie. He was going to pass it up when they'd offered him the route, but Gertie told him not to, that they'd survive with him not being home every other night.

"What story should we tell tonight?" David asked. Despite the stack of books on the floor beside them, David preferred to make up his own stories for his girls.

Anna Marie glanced over at Bella with a fierce frown on her face.

"Bella, you need to wake up. You can't sleep through Daddy's stories."

"But I'm tired," Bella mumbled. If they remained quiet, the girl would be out in a few minutes.

David didn't mind, but apparently Anna Marie did.

"Tell her she has to stay awake!" she demanded.

He lifted an eyebrow and waited for her to apologize. He didn't take kindly to his daughter telling him what to do like that, and she knew it.

"Please, Daddy?" Her voice softened with her second request.

"Bella, do you want to help tell the story, or would you like to climb into bed?" If the girl was really tired, he wasn't going to keep her up.

"Bella, you can pick first, if you'd like," Anna Marie offered, her voice singsongy.

David tried to mask his surprise. His daughter rarely let Bella choose the directions of the stories.

"Can you tell a story about my mommy?" Bella inched an eye open, her voice peppered with liveliness.

David bent his head down a little to get a good look at her.

She doesn't look tired at all, so why is she faking it?

"His stories aren't real, silly."

"They could be. They could be real, if we believe in them enough." Bella rustled around until she sat up, her back against the wall, blanket pulled up tight to her neck.

"Every story is rooted in truth," David reminded the girls. It was something his own father had once said to him—moments before the belt came off because he'd been caught lying.

"How about I tell you a story about two little girls who were best friends?" he suggested.

Bella's nose wrinkled.

Anna Marie shook her head.

"I want a story about two sisters, Daddy. Like us." She leaned over and smiled at Bella.

The hesitant smile she received in return seemed to satisfy her.

David took his time thinking about what story he'd create. While the girls waited, they settled into more comfortable positions.

"One day, two little girls were playing in the field. They weren't paying attention to how far they roamed from home. The sky started to get dark, and thunder shook the sky. The girls were scared and afraid they wouldn't make it home in time. It started to rain, so the girls ran for shelter in a nearby barn a farmer used to store hay for his cows."

"Was it a smelly barn?" Anna Marie asked.

"What do you think it would smell like?" His daughter always loved to ask questions. She didn't just want to hear the story, she wanted to experience it.

"If it's raining, the hay would smell. If it's an old barn, I bet there are a lot of spiders and mice."

Bella shuddered at the words.

They'd already established that Bella wasn't a fan of either. She screamed whenever she came across a mouse in the field and wet her bed once when she found a spider on the ceiling over her. Both Gertie and David had run into their room because she had screamed like a banshee.

"I bet there were lots of spiders and mice. One of the girls didn't want to go in, right Daddy?" Anna Marie gave Bella the side-eye.

David sighed.

"It's hard to face a fear sometimes, love." He set his hand on Bella's foot and gave a slight squeeze, wanting her to know he was there for her.

"The thunder kept rolling in the clouds, and the loud bangs scared the girls. The one little girl—"

"Hannah," Anna Marie interrupted him. "Her name is Hannah."

"Okay . . . Hannah wrestled with the barn door to get it open and then ran straight for a pile of hay, hiding herself inside it. The grass wasn't wet, but it smelled really bad."

"What about the other girl?" Bella asked. "What did Julie do?"

Julie, huh?

"Julie was scared. She didn't want to go in the barn, but she didn't like storms either, and she was getting wet. Hannah yelled at her to come join her, but Julie stayed outside, too afraid to go in."

Bella shuddered again. "What if there were spiders in the hay? Or mice?"

"Maybe there's baby mice and they were scared of the storm too?" Anna Marie piped up. "I bet Hannah found some babies who were crying because their mommy was gone and so she put them in her lap and petted them until they all fell asleep."

"What happened to their mommy?" Bella leaned forward, staring at Anna Marie's lap as if she could picture the mice there.

Anna Marie grabbed a teddy bear and started stroking it, petting it as if it were real.

"I bet their mommy was caught by a cat who ate her so quick." Anna Marie smirked while Bella's eyes filled with tears. "Why are you crying, Bella? You don't even like mice."

"But . . . but . . . they're just babies." Her lips quivered, and David knew he needed to get control of this story—and fast.

"The mommy mouse was fine, Bella. She was out in the field looking for food for her babies. Hannah"—he looked down at his daughter— "saw the baby mice and knew they needed their mommy, so she gave them space and tried hard not to frighten them."

"But the thunder was scary, right?" Bella asked, moving past the mice to another of her fears.

"It was scary, but Julie knew Hannah was there and she wasn't alone. The girls sat in a corner, and while the storm raged overhead, do you know what they did? They made braided bracelets from the hay, ignoring the storm until finally the sun poked through the boards of the barn."

"They made it through?" Bella's eyes were wide and bright.

"They made it through the storm. Do you know why?" He wrapped his arms around both girls and pulled them close. "Because they had each other. They were never alone. They knew no matter what came their way, whether it was a scary storm or facing fears of spiders and mice, they were stronger together."

"You're my sister, Bella," Anna Marie said, breaking up the silence following his story. "You'll always be my sister. Okay?" She held out her hand, which Bella took.

David watched as they shook on the declaration.

"And you'll always be my girls." He placed a kiss on the tops of their heads before getting to his knees. "Hop up into bed and let me know when you're ready to be tucked in."

David waited out in the hallway, half listening to the girls as they scrambled into bed and got comfortable.

"What if I don't want to be your sister?" Bella said.

David stepped closer to the barely open door.

"You have to be. Your mommy is gone, and you're all alone now," Anna Marie said, pure conviction in her tone.

"My mommy is gone because of you."

David winced at the heartache so clear in Bella's voice.

"Not true. Daddy was the one who killed her."

A stone fist grabbed his heart and twisted.

"I can leave whenever I want."

The false bravado brought tears to David's eyes.

What have we done?

What have I done?

This is all my fault. All of it. I'm the one who brought them home. I begged Judy to stay, even offering to pay her and give her a roof over her head to keep her daughter safe. I placed my needs, my family's needs, over hers.

And now she's dead because of it.

"You'll never leave." A bed creaked. When David peeked through the door, he saw his daughter resting on her knees, finger pointed toward Bella.

"You will make Mommy sad if you leave, and I won't have her be sad." She brought her hand down and climbed beneath her covers. "Just be a good girl, Bella, like Mommy said, and everything will be fine. You're my sister now, and we'll always be together. Besides, your mommy is protecting my brothers and sisters, and she'd be sad if you didn't stay so she could one day protect you too."

David was chilled to the bone at his daughter's words.

Who is this little girl? What happened to my sweet, kind, always-full-of-laughter little girl?

His princess had turned into the ugly stepsister, and he knew if he didn't do something about it, she'd become the black fairy he used to tell her about when she was misbehaving.

David opened the door, letting them know he was there. He didn't say anything at first, mainly because he didn't know what to say.

"Daddy, Bella said she'd be my sister. For real. Isn't that"—she spread her arms wide and beamed a smile at him—"wonderful?" She giggled, a high-pitched sound that made the hair on his arms stand straight up.

"What's going on in here?" Gertie stood beside him. "You girls are supposed to be asleep already." She rested her hands on her hips and looked around the room. "What in the world?" She spied the bed of quilts and pillows in the corner.

"It was story time, Mommy." Anna Marie snuggled beneath the covers, wiggling until she was comfortable.

Bella lay like a plank of wood, straight and stiff, the covers pulled up tight to her chin.

"I expect this cleaned up first thing, is that understood?" She gave the girls a stern look. Bella nodded her head while Anna Marie giggled.

"Will you say prayers with us?" she asked.

That's when David silently stepped out of the room.

His role was to tell stories. Gertie's role was to teach them about God.

God won't listen to a single prayer I utter. Why would He, when I've broken one of the Ten Commandments?

Thou shalt not kill.

Even my daughter called me a murderer.

"Now, you know what to say, girls. I'll start and you go after me, okay? Our Father, who art in heaven, hallowed be Your name. Thank You for Your protection, Your mercy, and Your justice. Continue to guide me as I raise these daughters You gave us, my birth daughter and my heaven daughter."

David left then, not wanting to intrude. He waited downstairs, set the kettle puttering on the stove, and buttered a piece of homemade cinnamon-raisin bread.

When Gertie joined him, she said, "The girls want you to tuck them in before you go to bed. You didn't tell them you were leaving in the morning, did you?" She took the knife from his hand and buttered her own piece. "They're going to be sore disappointed not to find you at the table for breakfast."

"What about you?" David asked. "Will you be sore disappointed too?"

She set the knife down in the sink, then turned to wrap her arms around his waist.

"I'm always sad when you're not here. But these girls, they keep me on my toes, that's for sure."

He looked for the haunted whisper of exhaustion in her gaze, for the circles beneath her eyes. He saw none of that.

Instead, he saw a tired but content woman—and he saw a future exactly the opposite of what they'd almost lived.

"Do you want me to ask for a shorter route?"

She shook her head. "Goodness, no. I like being able to buy good cuts of meat at the market rather than the ones on sale. Besides, we're doing fine. I promise."

He believed her, he really did. It's why he didn't press her about taking shorter routes.

The kettle sang, and Gertie poured water into the two waiting cups, dunking a tea bag in each a few times.

"How has Anna Marie been?" David asked. "With everything that's happened?"

Gertie's brow knitted together as she handed him his tea.

"What's happened?"

"Judy."

She waved as if the mention of the girl buried in their backyard was of little consequence. "She's fine, David. Trust me. She loves having Bella here. The girls are like two peas in a pod. Some days I can't even tell who is who, you know what I mean? I swear they could be twins. If Bella smiled more, why, even Charlie wouldn't be able to tell them apart."

"She doesn't smile because she's sad."

"Oh, I know that. I'm just saying . . ." She shook her head at him, like he was making a case out of nothing.

"It's our fault, Gertie. We killed her."

Gertie snorted. She covered her mouth with her hand and wiped up some spilled tea that sloshed over the rim of the cup on the table.

"For Pete's sake, David. Judy was sick with some sort of infection or flu. That's it. What happened was an accident and no one's fault."

She took a sip of tea, then looked him straight in the eye.

Her gaze was clear. The set of her lips tight. Her words pointed.

"Enough of this talk from you. Get that thought right out of your head and focus on those girls of ours. That's what's important. We're family, whole and complete, and we need to start acting like it. Bella and Anna Marie are sisters now, and the faster Bella accepts that, the better."

While Gertie spoke, David thought about something his own father had said to him when he was a young boy.

Little white lies as big as oceans are only that large once we believe them to be.

He'd never really understood what that meant. But seeing the belief in Gertie's eyes at the lie she told . . . he understood now.

"If you have a hard time with that idea"—her words were brisk, cold, hard even—"maybe you need to take even longer routes and not be home as often. I won't have you destroying the bond between our girls." She shoved her chair back and stood, pushing her cup of tea ahead of her on the table.

"Why don't you grab those blankets on the girls' floor and make a bed on the couch? You'll be more comfortable there, I think."

David let her walk away without a word.

Chapter Twenty-Eight
ELLE

Brennley and I sit outside on the staff patio, soaking up the sun and giving our tired legs a breather. All the benches and tables are packed with staff with similar ideas.

She had the stupid idea of going for a run on the beach this morning before our joint shift, saying we needed to burn off energy and clear our minds.

She also had the stupid idea that we should walk to work rather than drive, which is why we are out here, giving our legs a rest before the thirty-minute walk home. It's been a long shift for both of us. A few nurses on my ward are out with the flu, which kept me busy. Brennley lost a patient today, and David isn't doing too well after the attack he had following Charlie's visit. I've been checking in on him but not spending time with him to chat, even though I want to.

While I've been with Mom and traipsing through the countryside finding mysterious crosses, as Brennley likes to put it, she's continued researching whether Judy and Bella were actually real people.

Despite me telling her to let it go, that I am now firmly convinced they were not, she's like a hound dog—once she gets the scent of an idea, she can't let it go.

On our run this morning, she told me all the things she's discovered.

Not surprisingly, there isn't much.

"Are you ready to head home?" Brenn slowly moves her feet off the bench and settles her hands on her knees, like she's trying to find the energy to get up.

"How about we stop at the Shack for ice cream on our way? Maybe that will help motivate us," I suggest.

We don't say much for the next fifteen minutes as we walk down the hill to Queen Street and then toward the downtown area. I think we're both so exhausted and focused on the ice cream that the energy needed for words just isn't there.

"If you haven't come down with that flu, you should go in and see David tomorrow, Elle. I don't think there's much time left." There is a shadow of grief in her eyes. "I wish I had more time with him, you know?" she says. "I mean, I'm sure you do too. To find out about your grandfather right as he's dying . . . he's such a sad and lonely man . . ." Tears gather in her eyes.

"I'm just glad you were there to figure out who he was."

She gives me a look.

"No, really." I might have said something this morning about the craziness of my life since I met him and how sometimes I wish I could turn back time, but that had more to do with Mom and her constant neediness than anything else.

If she isn't calling me three times a day, she's sending me text messages and constantly asking me when I'm coming home, saying then she wouldn't be as bad.

"Is your mom going to be okay?"

I shrug. "She's got the showing coming up, and I think Grace is trying to help her focus on that. Is she okay? She's really fragile right now."

"That might change when David . . ."

She doesn't say it, and I don't think she could say it even if she tried. She's become really attached to the man who is my grandfather. More so than I am.

That should make me feel bad, but it doesn't.

Maybe because it's become more than just meeting a member of my family and trying to create a bond before it's too late. It's about discovering the secrets Mom won't tell me, even now. It's about learning more about my past and trying to work through my own fears of becoming mentally ill like the women before me.

Dissociative identity disorder is caused by a plethora of factors, according to the research I've done. But I've always known those factors include severe trauma during early childhood. I'm still unclear as to what happened to Mom to bring it on. As for Gertie, I would think being raised by a mother with the disorder and then having all those miscarriages would be traumatic enough. I have no idea about my great-grandmother, since I haven't been able to find any information on her. David won't tell me her name; I can't find any records in Mom's files at home with that background information. I already know asking her would be a moot point.

Would finding out my grandparents not only committed a murder but hid it for all these years be traumatic enough for *me*? So far, I don't think so. Maybe that's why Grace is so adamant that I'm fine and should stop worrying.

It's not that this whole experience hasn't affected me, because it has. There's a ball of anger coiled like a snake waiting to strike within my heart. So far it's been aimed at those who've lied to me all my life. I know that's wrong, and I'm trying to understand that something horrific had to have happened to my mother. But that anger, the frustration—it's still there.

I'll also admit that it's hard dealing with the confusion I feel after I leave David's side. I hate how he makes me question everything Mom says to me and then what that, in turn, does to her.

I've listened to his stories, but why hasn't he asked me for any of mine? About my childhood? About Mom?

Why is he so focused on telling a story that can't possibly be true when I could share with him the reality I live?

Why hasn't he asked me about Mom's mental state, especially considering mental health issues run in the family?

I don't know how much time I have left with him, but there are things I need to get off my chest. Things I need to ask.

Like why didn't he protect Mom better?

Like what specifically caused the rift between them?

Like what happened to Gertie? Did she ever get the help she needed?

"Elle, is that Charlie?" We're standing at the crosswalk right in front of the coffee shop where I first met him. I turn to look behind me, to see if I could see him through the window.

"No, up ahead. At the Shack." Brenn nudges me to turn around.

I squint behind my sunglasses. Sure enough, that's Charlie. It's kind of hard to mistake him for anyone else, with his build and booming voice. We're about one hundred feet away from him, but there's no question in my mind it's him.

Charlie must have seen us coming. He meets us halfway down the sidewalk.

"Elizabeth." One word. Four syllables. Often said in so many different ways, but Charlie's voice is monotone.

His hands are burrowed deep in his pants pockets, his massive shoulders stooped so far over his chest, I would have sworn he caved in upon himself.

He doesn't look well, and from the expression on Brennley's face, she's thinking the same thing.

"Charlie, are you okay? Do you need to sit down?" She launches into full nurse mode, checking his pulse, searching his eyes.

"I'm fine, I'm fine." He brushes her off. "How is David? Did I kill him?"

Brenn's mouth gapes open before she reaches over to give him a huge hug. It's awkward, considering she's a tiny thing and he's so large, but the sheen of tears in his eyes before he wipes them away says he appreciates the gesture.

"He's fine, Charlie. You didn't kill him. Is that what you thought? You should have called my desk. I would have told you he's okay. Well, he's *not* okay, but you didn't cause any more damage, is what I mean," she blathers on, stumbling over her words, barely taking a breath until I place my hand on her arm.

"He's fine, Charlie. Thank you for going to see him."

I'm hoping for a sense of relief to run across his face, for the stoop of his shoulders to relax, for the lines of worry on his face to disappear, but they don't.

To all appearances, he's a man in pain. He can't expect to meet up with two nurses and not worry us.

With only a look at each other, we thread our arms through his and make him walk with us back to the Shack.

"In the mood for some ice cream?" I ask.

The Shack itself looks old, but it's all part of the appeal. It could use a fresh coat of paint after a thorough sanding to get rid of the layers of old, but why mess with what works? Two large chalk signs on either side of the Shack show pictures of one-, two-, and three-scoop ice-cream cones and list the available flavors. There are twenty-three of them apparently.

"Best ice cream in town." Charlie catches me eyeing the sign.

Charlie seems to know everyone in the line. Brennley and I just smile. We recognize a few people from around town or from passing them at the hospital.

He points to the board listing all the flavors. "Picked one yet?"

It isn't hard to pick an ice-cream flavor, despite their offering twenty-three different kinds.

"Salted caramel. How about you?"

He wrinkles his nose at my choice.

"Go with the fad. I'm not surprised. That's what kids do nowadays. They don't appreciate the staples." He adds a smile to his mockery.

"Let me guess: you're just getting straight-up vanilla."

He probably drinks his coffee black and eats his eggs runny, his toast lightly buttered, and his steaks medium rare. He's probably the kind of man who knows how he likes things and doesn't deviate.

"Rum raisin, thank you very much."

I'm surprised.

"That's not on the list." I double-check.

"They keep a barrel to the side for me. It's all I ever order. You can't get that stuff anymore. The stores only sell all the new flavors now, like that crap you like or double-churned vanilla and other kinds loaded with so much candy you might as well not call it ice cream anymore."

I eye the barrels in the freezer, then him. "That's a lot of ice cream for one man to eat during a single summer."

"Which is why it's a good thing he buys the barrel ahead of time. He takes home what's leftover at the end of the season."

A man walks out from the side door and slaps Charlie on the back.

"I was wondering when I'd see you two again. It's been a few days," he says to us.

John is the owner of the Shack, and he always seems to be serving ice cream personally whenever we come around.

"John, you know who this is, right?" Charlie asks. "Elizabeth Walker, David Walker's granddaughter."

"Myers," I quickly correct him. "Elle Myers."

John takes a step back and blinks a few times as he looks at me.

I feel like a specimen under a microscope.

"Is that right? Well, isn't this a surprise? How's the old bugger doing?" he asks Charlie.

The slow shake of his head and downcast gaze apparently say it all.

John gives a deep nod and sticks out his hand.

"I'm sorry about your grandfather. How is your mom? Haven't seen her in . . . years. Wow." He shakes his head, as if the memory is too fleeting. "She went off to school, didn't she? Never came back either. Heard she's a famous artist or something. I remember seeing her paintings in the paper."

Both men look at me.

"She's sold a few. She's in the middle of getting ready for a new showing in Toronto later this summer."

"Is that right? Can just anyone come to these showings, or only the rich and famous?" Charlie cocks his head to the side but seems really interested.

"Anyone can come."

They continue to look at me. I try to read what's going on in Charlie's mind, but considering I barely know the man, he could be thinking about the next movie he plans on watching for all I know.

"So"—John clears his throat—"Elle, daughter of our town's most famous painter, how about I treat you girls to an ice cream today?"

"She wants that salted caramel one," Charlie answers for me. "Let me guess . . ." He turns to Brenn. "The one with brownies, right?"

Brennley's face beams with joy. "You remembered. We had this discussion when he came to visit David. He caught me eating an ice-cream bar," she explains.

"The caramel crap and the brownie garbage," Charlie tells John.

"Please." I nudge him.

"What?"

"The caramel crap and the brownie garbage, *please*."

John snickers.

"You're just like your mother, except you're a lot older," Charlie grumbles.

That catches my attention.

"Used to bring her here to get ice cream too, when she was just a little one, though," Charlie says. "She'd get bubble gum, which was pretty new then. Right, John?"

"Bubble gum's been around forever, man. How long are we talking?" He pauses in the act of scooping my ice-cream cone.

"Midfifties, I think." Charlie scratches his head. "God, was it really that long ago?"

"Yeah, bubble gum was probably new then." John bends back behind the lid of the freezer and scoops out even more ice cream. My cone now grows to three scoops.

"Anyway," Charlie continues, "Gertie would get so mad at me for that. Your mom couldn't keep the gum in her mouth, see, and she'd get it all over the place. In her hair, stuck to her clothes, or on the couch. It got to the point where I'd have to get Marie to spit it out before we got home."

I chuckle at that. I wasn't allowed to chew gum as a little girl. Mom scared me by saying that it would get all in my hair if I blew the wrong kind of bubbles. She would tell me stories of girls who lived inside the bubbles made from gum. Those were fun stories, but I remember them being sticky too.

I think the first piece of gum I ever chewed was cinnamon flavor, and I spat it out right away.

I've never really been a gum chewer, come to think of it. Neither has Mom.

"How little was she? Toddler little or kindergarten little?"

Charlie shrugs. "Little. Kneecap little."

"Did you see her much when she was growing up?" I push for more information.

He reaches for the cone John hands him and then gives it to me. "Here and there. More than your grandfather thinks I did, that's for sure."

I pause before taking my first lick.

"What do you mean?"

He snorts. "Don't let that old man in the hospital bed fool you, girl. He was a mean son of a bitch when he needed to be. Best friends for years. Best man at his wedding. Uncle to your mother. Then *boom*, one day he punted me out of his life like you would a football toward the end zone. Your grandpa and me, we'd go fishing most weekends. Sometimes your mother would come along and play with the sunfish that swam close to the rocks. I stopped by the house one Sunday afternoon, and before I even stepped foot out of my truck, he told me to leave."

His face clouds over and his lips do that thing when people get really vexed about something—push hard enough together to resemble a dried-up fig.

"Didn't bother explaining what I'd done or what was wrong. Just told me to leave and not come back." Charlie rubs the back of his neck and looks upward, staring at a dirt spot on the awning above him. "He spouted off nonsense about Gertie not feeling comfortable with me around anymore and that it was best for me to not come around again."

"I'm sorry."

The words come out of me automatically. I don't even think as I respond to the grief in his voice.

"Nah." He hands Brennley her cone, waits for his own before nodding.

"I'm the one who should be apologizing," Charlie says. "This is your grandfather we're talking about. I don't need to be airing dirty laundry when you're just trying to get to know him."

Normally I'd agree with him. But in this case, that dirty laundry he's airing tells me more about my past, about my mother's past, than anything else.

"How about we talk about my mom, then?" I suggest.

"Interested in walking while we talk?"

I think about my sore feet, but the pull of discovering more about Mom's past outweighs the pain.

Charlie isn't a fast walker, and I swear he knows everyone we walk by. If he isn't saying hi and asking how their day is, he's nodding or introducing us, which for the most part is very awkward.

At the corner where we'd normally turn left to head to our apartment, Brenn stops me.

"I'm going to head home, okay? You enjoy your walk, and get some answers if you can." She yawns. "Might even get in a quick nap before you get back. Which is me saying if you need me, you better call."

She gives Charlie a side squeeze, tells him to come back to visit David—but to bring ice cream instead of coffee—and then heads up the street.

We continue on our way, not saying much as we enjoy our ice-cream cones.

"I used to drive by the house every chance I could get," Charlie says out of the blue as we turn down Huron Street. "Sometimes I'd see your mom and Gertie out in the garden. Didn't matter who drove by, your mom would stick her hand up high in the air and wave like it was the most important thing she could do. I'd always honk, even if they weren't out. Just to let them know . . . you know?"

There's a smile on his face as he goes back in time and pictures my mom waving.

I could almost see it myself. Almost.

"Why didn't you stop in?"

Charlie shrugs. "Who says I didn't?"

He points to a restaurant to the right of us. The Erie Belle, famous for its fish and chips. It's a white building with a worn patio but one of the best places to eat locally. "Have you had the fish here? Best in town."

I smile. "It's Brenn's and my favorite place to eat. I was surprised to still see it here, considering Grace used to bring me here at least once a summer when I was younger."

I'd order the junior pollock and fries, with extra tartar sauce.

He nods. "Not surprised. Grace used to work here."

I stumble, bumping him as my foot catches on the uneven pavement.

"You know Grace?"

He gives me a side look. "Why wouldn't I know Grace?"

Good question. The timing is all off, though, unless Grace came into Mom's life earlier than I've been told.

"When did you lose contact with my mom?"

Charlie huffs. "You always have a question on hand, don't you? Your mom was like that too; answer a question with a question. You know what they call that, right? Stalling."

"It's the only way to get answers."

"Guarantee you're not always gonna like what you hear." Charlie's left brow lifts before we cross the street and head toward the lighthouse.

The Kincardine lighthouse has been in the town since 1881 and has become somewhat of an iconic feature. Brenn and I love to walk past the building and sit on the pier while watching the boats in the distance.

"We've got a ghost in there, did you know that?" Charlie asks me as we walk along a pathway bordered by shrubs.

I look at the tall white-and-red beacon, which is now a working museum. I shake my head.

"One of the old keepers?" I assume that would be the only ghost to haunt a lighthouse.

"A phantom piper." Charlie stands with a hand on his hip and looks up to the top. "When the fog is thick, you can hear the bagpipes playing a soulful tune."

"Really?" I follow his gaze. At the very top of the building, there's a small walkway. The piper could walk up there without being seen, no problem.

"Don't tell me you don't believe in ghosts and the afterlife?" Charlie *tsks* as we continue our walk down the gravel path that leads to the pier.

We stop and sit on one of the benches, finishing off our cones before a swarm of seagulls can attack us for any drippings.

I love this spot. The water of Lake Huron gently rolls toward the shoreline while slapping the walls of the pier and rocks along its way. Fishermen stand on the edges of the pier, their rods in the water, their gear at their feet. There are a few older couples; some walk hand in hand while others just sit on the benches situated in the middle of the pier, staring off into the distance, not saying anything but obviously enjoying each other's company.

"Should I?" I ask, coming back to the conversation of believing in ghosts.

Charlie chuckles. "Again with the questions. Yes, you should. Your mother does. Or did. And if she's anything like Gertie, she has a strong belief in ghosts."

"She doesn't." I can see this surprises him.

"Strange. She used to see ghosts all the time when she was little. Scared the bejesus out of me when I caught her talking to them the first time." He shudders.

I turn closer toward him. "What do you mean?"

Is he talking about her imaginary friend maybe? Could this be a tale about Bella? Can Charlie provide the answers I've been looking for?

Charlie scratches his forehead before taking a cloth out of his pocket and wiping the back of his neck.

"Sure is getting warm out here. Let's head back."

He stands, but I don't.

"You coming?"

"What do you mean?" I ask again. "Charlie?"

It looks like he has something to say. For a moment, excitement floods my body. I know, I just know, that the next words out of Charlie's mouth will be the answer I've been searching for. The answers about the imaginary friend, confirmation of Gertie's mental state . . . Charlie could have all the answers I need. All of this, my questioning, doubting my mom, the secrets—it would all be over.

His mouth opens, then closes. He sticks his hands in his pants pockets.

"I can't do this."

And with that, Charlie, the man who professed to know my grandmother, the man who promised to tell me stories about my mom—stories David won't tell me—walks away.

He leaves me to sit there, by myself, and never once looks back.

Chapter Twenty-Nine

By the time I make it close to the apartment, I'm fuming.

Charlie's last words to me before rudely leaving me behind were "I can't do this."

Do what? What *exactly* couldn't he do? Answer my questions? Remember the past? Talk about Gertie? What? What couldn't he do?

I'm so tired of all the secrets. So freaking tired.

My body is too wired for a nap, so I grab a beer from the fridge and sit on our deck, eyes closed, letting the sun soak into my skin. I hope maybe it will scorch the anger simmering on my skin away.

What is so horrible about the past that no one can talk about it?

I feel like I'm chasing a rabbit through a maze. In search of what? I wish I knew.

All my life, I've felt like there's this large hole inside of me, so large that all it would take was a small push and I'd fall into it and be lost forever. When I found out the truth about my father, I thought that hole was filled. I wasn't alone anymore. There was someone else who understood the struggle of living with Marie Walker, someone who had escaped semi-unscathed.

The more I got to know my father, the more I realized how untrue that was. Mitch is just as lost as I am.

Is Mom that strong? Is her touch on someone's life that damaging?

When I went into nursing, I hoped that by finding something else to fill my life with, something other than Mom and her mental health, then maybe—just maybe—I would be okay.

I should have known better. There is no *okay* when it comes to Mom. I'm being sucked back in. Into the cyclone of uncertainty, of instability. Into my own fears of what the outcome could be.

Maybe I've always known there is some deep, dark secret that doesn't need to see the light of day.

My own mental well-being is a noose resting on the curve of my breastbone, just waiting for some traumatic event to force the rope taut. But maybe it doesn't have to be some life-altering event that pulls me under the tide, but rather something minor, insignificant, like a pebble thrown into the ocean of life.

I learned early on never to ask about our past, about our family, because it would always hurt my mother emotionally.

Now that door is open, and after catching a glimpse of the life I could have had, with a grandfather who could have loved me, I want to shove that door open all the way and learn as much as I can before it's too late.

My phone pings with an unexpected text message from Mitch.

Say the word and I'm there.

I know how hard that must have been for him to send. He once admitted that if he never saw Mom again, it would mean he'd lived a good life. He never explained what he meant by that, but I could guess. After all, I did grow up with her.

Thanks, Mitch.

I still don't call him *Father* or *Dad*. I doubt I ever will.

Things are okay for now. David is still telling me stories and I'm still trying to get answers.

Sometimes there aren't any, kiddo.

I can't accept that, though. Not in this case. I lost years with a man who could have been a foundation for me.

It isn't lost on me that I haven't included Gertie in any of my thoughts.

"You should have woken me up when you got in." Brennley joins me out on the deck, stretching with the largest yawn imaginable.

"I would have soon."

She stretches out beside me on a lounger, feet up, eyes closed. "I swear I was a sun goddess in another life. It's like I was destined to lie here, soaking up its rays."

I don't even bother to comment. She's known for saying the weirdest things while waking up.

"We're really bad plant parents. You know that, right?" She reaches her foot out to touch one of the few plants on our deck.

It's true. We are bad plant parents. We bought plants in the spring to spruce up our small deck and promised each other we'd take turns watering them, but . . . I think we both forgot.

"We should never have babies. If we can't keep plants alive, how are we expected to take care of a real human?"

Again, I don't bother to respond.

"I'm serious, Elle. I can't keep patients alive, and you've got murderers in your family. We'll pass those genes along for sure. We're lost causes, babe . . ."

I take a long sip of my lukewarm beer and bite my tongue to keep from replying.

"Oh my God, I'm sorry . . . I didn't mean that." She sits up in the lounger and looks at me. "I should never have had that nap. I'm a groggy mess after. Sorry." She reaches her hand out. "Forgive me?"

"Make me dinner and I'll think about it." Truth be told, I don't want to get up.

"So Charlie . . ." I don't know how to bring up the topic without going off on a rampage.

"Yep. Charlie. Figured something happened between the two of you since you're holding on to that beer bottle pretty tight."

I tell her how he just walked away after assuming I believed in ghosts.

"Brenn, tell me I'm not crazy," I beg.

"You're not crazy."

She says exactly what I ask but not what I need.

"Then why is this happening to me? Why won't anyone give me a straight answer? I just want the truth. How horrible can that be? Are my grandparents psychotic? Did they bury bodies in the ground behind their garage? What happened to my mother that she would pretend her family was dead and let me grow up thinking it was just the two of us?"

"You're not crazy, Elle. Your family is, but you're not. Trust me. Whether the stories David is telling you are real or not, it doesn't matter. What matters is you've known all your life something is wrong with your mom. You finally have the answers as to what happened to her at your fingertips, but you just can't reach them."

The groan that comes out of me is half cry, half laugh.

"I'm so confused," I confess.

"Then clear up the confusion, Elle. Look behind the stories to find the truth."

And how exactly am I supposed to do that?

~

After dinner, I decide to go see David again. Mom sent me a total of three text messages while Brenn made a simple stir-fry for dinner. At least at the hospital, I can put my phone on silent and pretend to ignore her.

The look on Amy's face as I approach the nursing station halts me in my tracks. I'm unable to take another step forward.

Something is wrong.

"Elle, I'm glad you're here." She forces a smile to her face. "I just left Brennley a voice message that you might want to come down. He's okay for tonight, but I know you probably want to spend as much time with him as you can." She pats my arm in sympathy. "He's asleep, but I doubt he'll stay that way for long." A gentleness mixed with pity pours out of her like the sweetest sap from a maple tree.

I hate maple syrup. We used to go to a local farm, less than a half hour away, and have a maple syrup day, where we'd place buckets under spouts and watch the sap drip into the container. We'd pour the boiled syrup onto blocks of snow to cool it and eat as much as we could, to our hearts' content. I ate so much one time I got sick. Grace tried to warn me. Mom said I could eat as much as I wanted, so I did. I think it was her way of teaching me about natural consequences.

When I see David lying there on the bed, the pain he's living with is etched on his face. It takes my breath away. A vein in his cheek pulses to the beat of his heart, and every so often he grimaces.

I pull the chair closer to his bed and watch the rise of his chest, making sure he continues to breathe. I'm not sure I could handle being here as he takes his last breath.

It must be hard, being alone. I don't think he was a very happy man. For that, I feel sorry for him.

"What did you do that was so bad Mom felt she had to protect me from you?" I whisper.

I reach out and want to touch his hand, to have a feeling of connection between us, but I don't dare.

"I wish things were different," I say. "I wish I had known you. Or even"—I lean back in my chair and stare up at the ceiling—"even just known *of* you. I don't know what happened, but I wish she trusted me more. You were characters in a story I never knew the ending to, and it's hard growing up like that, you know?"

Of course he doesn't know.

"You knew of *me*. You built me that dollhouse. But how long did you know of me before that? Were you there for my birth? You knew my father, so why didn't you try to force him to be in my life? Did you keep tabs on me and Mom throughout the years?"

Why am I asking all these questions when I know he won't answer?

"I always watched over you and your mom, from a distance." David's voice is groggy, and he licks his lips as he slowly opens his eyes.

I can see the struggle and feel bad for waking him up. I bring his water cup close to his lips, and after a few sips, he lets go and closes his eyes again.

I think for a moment he's fallen back asleep.

"I've always loved her, you know? Your mother. Always. I knew I had to send her away. It's why Grace came, to be with her. She didn't feel safe at our home anymore, and I couldn't make a choice between the two. I couldn't give up my wife to save my daughter, but I couldn't give my daughter away to save my wife either. I didn't know what to do." Tears run down his face and his voice cracks.

"In the end, it didn't matter." He turns his head to stare out the window.

"So you made your choice, then."

I'm disappointed. I don't know the answer either, and I suspect there was no right decision. Learning he tossed my mother to the side to care for a woman who obviously needed medical attention makes me start to understand where the hatred Mom feels for her father comes from.

"I made the only choice I could. I sent your mom away to someone I trusted more, and I watched over her as much as I could. I lost everything and everyone." He turns to me then, and I can see the grief on his face—in every wrinkle, in the quiver of his lips. He struggles to be stoic. "I don't expect you to understand."

I'm not sure how I can.

"Explain it to me, then. No one else will, and I need to know."

He doesn't say anything for the longest time.

"I'll tell you. If you promise me one thing." His hand shakes as he pulls up the edge of his blanket. "Don't come back. After today, don't come back."

I lean forward. "Why not?" Of course I will come back.

"I don't want you here when I die. After this story, I've nothing left to share." He turns to stare out his window again, and I catch a low grunt.

Even the motion of turning his neck obviously hurts.

I am watching a man die. Not just a man, but my grandfather.

It isn't right. I should have known him when he was younger, when he could have lifted me on his shoulders and taught me how to play baseball. I should have been able to watch his hair turn gray, his wrinkles deepen, his grumpiness grow with age.

There are so many *should haves* when it comes to David and me. I am conflicted—I'm desperate to know the man while confused about him at the same time.

"You need to promise," he repeats, his voice forlorn and full of grief. "It's my time to die, and I'm ready to go. You coming back will only make it harder to do what I know needs to be done."

"What? What needs to be done?"

He keeps his gaze out that window. It makes me want to sit on that side of him, so he will look at me and not out there.

"I need to die."

Chapter Thirty

DAVID

"I'm not ready for you to die," Elle whispers.

I've never been much for rainbows and freaking unicorns, but this girl, she makes my life better, the pain dimmer, and my hope larger.

The other shoe is going to drop any minute now. It always does.

I don't deserve these moments with her, and knowing that eats at my soul. As much as I want more time, more time with her, I can't ask for it.

God isn't my friend. He wouldn't be one to grant me favors like that.

I want to know all about her. Screw my stories about the past—what about hers?

What was she like as a child growing up? Did she laugh? Dance in the field with a crown of daisies on her head? Had Marie taken her to the fair so she could win stuffed bears and ride the Ferris wheel?

She obviously is as smart as her mother. Marie knew how to write before the age of five and could count until she was blue in the face and never miss a number. She soaked in everything we taught her—until she, in turn, became the one to teach us.

I never liked Gertie's drive to homeschool Marie, even though I knew it was the only way. At least for the first few years. It didn't take me long to realize just how much Marie would have hated being in school at a young age. It would have bored her.

Had Elle been like that too?

I'm afraid. I'll admit it. Afraid that if I ask her questions, if I start to learn more about her, I won't want it to stop. Not stopping means not dying, and I've worn out my welcome on this earth.

For every action, there's a reaction. For every decision, a consequence. I thought I paid the ultimate price already, but I guess the way I'm being teased with hope, with more time, is a trick of the devil. He's made me believe in second chances.

I know it isn't a gift from God, that's for damn sure.

"What makes you think you're about to die, anyway? Maybe instead of days, you have weeks or even a month? What if you see the leaves turn colors on the trees outside? Wouldn't you like that?" she asks me.

"Hell no." The sigh that comes with those words is bone deep. The exhaustion in my soul calls to me.

I know I hurt her. She sits back and masks her reaction but not quick enough. She tightens her lips the same way Gertie would, with the edges curling in toward the teeth, and closes her eyes for a fraction too long. Good. Maybe if I hit too close to home too many times she'll promise not to return.

"You're not dying alone." She folds her arms over her chest and gives me that don't-bother-arguing-with-me look of hers. Another Gertie gesture.

It's unnerving how much like Gertie she is. I want to stare at her for hours, memorize every minuscule movement of her eyes, her lips, her hands. To pretend my Gertie has returned to me, whole and healthy.

God, I miss that woman.

I missed out on so much when she was taken away from me. Years of her smile, her touch, her voice. When I got her back, I thought it was our chance to make right so many wrongs, but then that damn cancer wouldn't give an inch. It stole from me in so many ways.

There's so much about her I have missed over the years. The way she'd tell me off, how she'd keep me on my toes with her demands and needs. I even missed the tinkling of that damn bell I bought her after she lost her voice to cancer.

I can still hear it. When I close my eyes, it's there, at the edges of my hearing, always tinkling, always teasing me.

That's what hell will be like. Constant bells ringing, taunting me with the memory of my Gertie.

"You don't need to be here, and that's that. I'll tell Nurse Crankypants that I don't want to see you."

She's laughing. She's actually laughing at me.

"You won't do that. You wanted me here bad enough, so here I am. Don't waste these moments by pretending something you don't feel."

I scowl, or at least try to. My jaw hurts, and it takes too much effort to be grumpy when she's right. I do want her here.

But this has to be our last visit.

I'll make sure of it.

After the story I'm about to confess, she'll go running from this room and refuse to come back, regardless if I want her here or not.

I haven't been sure whether I would tell her the whole story. I'm still not sure I want to, but I need to.

That's the whole point of this, isn't it? To confess my secrets now that Gertie's gone? To tell the truth, for once, after so many wasted years?

I can't make right my wrong. I know that, I've always known that. Charlie not being able to forgive me proves that.

So why am I about to tell her something I've never told a soul? Something Gertie and I promised never to discuss after that horrific day?

Hell if I know.

I do know this, though: she will never forgive me. She'll grow to hate me, just like her mother. I won't blame her.

"You wanted to know if I knew of you when you were a child? I did. We did. Even though we'd never met you, we loved you from afar." A knot of air forces its way up my throat, pushing its way past muscles too tight to loosen, and the pain is excruciating. Feels like a bloody jackhammer freeing itself from my lungs. I hit the button on my left side, out of Elle's sight.

I try to breathe through the pain. *One-killmenow-two-makeitquick-three-ahhhsweetJesus.* The cooling sensation of numbness creeps its way along my veins until the jackhammer hurts only as much as a single heartbeat.

"Are you okay?" Elle stands at my side, her hand inches from my arm.

Am I okay? No. But the drugs help. A lot.

"We saw you once. Gertie and I. Grace, she . . . she told us where you'd be one day. Your mom took you to the beach in Southampton. Gertie and I parked on the main street and walked down to the water. We walked that boardwalk over and over, waiting for you to show up. We were sitting on a bench when we heard laughter and we both knew, instantly, that it was you."

There are damn tears in my eyes, but I don't care. That's a happy memory. A good memory. A memory we would tell over and over. Then I'd remember for us and retell the whole day while Gertie lay in our bed, slowly dying.

Elle slowly sits back down in her chair, her gaze never leaving mine. What? Is she afraid I'll stop talking if she looks away?

"You must have been about three, I think. Grace and Marie were holding your hands, swinging you high in the air. Then you begged to run on the sand. The moment they let go of your hands, you took off, straight to the water." If I close my eyes, I can still see her, wearing a cute little pink bathing suit, her hair in pigtails. Her laugh was like cooling rain on a sweltering day, like an ice cube against swollen lips. It was magic and sunshine rolled into one.

Those were Gertie's words.

"Grace sat on the sand while Marie played in the water with you. We couldn't believe how far out she'd take you—"

"It's because of the sand dunes, they go forever." There's a faraway look in Elle's eyes, as if picturing herself there, in that water with her mom.

"Your mom never noticed us sitting there. We were just two old folks, sitting on the bench on a warm summer day. Gertie couldn't stop crying. We were there for hours, until Grace packed up your things and you all walked down the beach. Away from us."

Grace tried to look at us a few times, lifting her hand in a wave when Marie wasn't paying attention.

She did that for us throughout the years—share details of where Marie would be or where we could see her artwork. It wasn't often, but it was enough. Enough that we could see our girl and Elle.

"How did you know to build me a dollhouse?" Elle wipes at her cheeks before she reaches for a Kleenex, also handing me one.

"Grace stopped by the house one weekend after running errands. I told her I built you a dollhouse and wondered if she'd take it to you. I didn't care if you knew where it came from, just as long as you had it."

"I loved it." The tears run for real down her face. "I still have it. It's in Mom's art studio. We played with that dollhouse for years together. It's one of the best memories I have of growing up."

I just nod, unable to speak past the lump in my throat. Every little girl needs a dollhouse.

Gertie thought I was crazy to make it. It took me months to make it perfect. I fashioned it after the one I made Marie, with a few alterations after looking at different dollhouses in stores. I wanted it to last her for years, to be something she could play with alongside her own daughters, long after I was dead.

I wish there was a way to tell Gertie about her granddaughter. I wish I could describe her, tell her stories about when she came to visit me. I wish . . . for a lot of things that will never come true, but it doesn't change the ache in my heart knowing Gertie missed out on so much.

"Gertie would have liked you."

I don't mean to say it. Not sure why I did.

"I'm not sure I would have liked her, to be honest."

And like that, she pushes a knife into my heart and twists.

How can she say that? She doesn't know. She doesn't understand. I . . . I didn't paint her in the right way. I should have shared the good memories, not all the real ones.

None of what happened to us was Gertie's fault. None of it. She was sick and needed help. I'm the one to blame. Always and forever.

Charlie was right. I knew she needed help, and I should have gotten it for her. Even if it meant putting her in an institution. At least then she would have gotten the care she needed and maybe . . .

"Family is complicated, I get that." Elle leans forward, her soft voice reassuring. "Every story has three sides to it, and I'm not getting the full picture. I get that too. I'm glad I've met you, David."

She places her hand on the bed beside my arm. I can feel heat radiating from her fingertips against my skin. She sighs, and I can tell she's frustrated with herself.

"Spit it out, child." She doesn't need to soften the blow on my account.

She shakes her head. "I'm not saying it right. I . . . I'm glad I met you. But coming to see you . . . it hurts my mom more than I expected it would."

"What's wrong with my Marie?" This is the first I'm hearing that she's not well, and I don't like that.

I didn't want to prod on our other visits. I didn't want to ask how she was because I didn't want to place Elle in a position of breaking her mother's trust. Grace kept me in the loop enough to know she was okay. But now I'm hearing she's not?

"If your mother isn't well, then scoot and be with her. She needs you more than I do. My daughter comes first, don't you understand? She has always come first."

I struggle to push myself up so I'm sitting more than lying. It's hard. My body doesn't want me to move.

Elle reaches for the bed adjuster and raises my head up little by little until I raise my hand for her to stop.

"Mental illness runs in the family, doesn't it?"

Craziness runs in our family is what she means. What she wants to know. It does.

Gertie warned me, but I didn't care.

I should have cared. Or at least listened better, planned better.

"Marie isn't like her mother." Grace would have told me otherwise.

"Oh, come on, David. Open your eyes. If Gertie was unstable, as well as her mother and her grandmother, then why wouldn't you believe my mother could be too?"

I stare up at the goddamn ugly white ceiling and wish to heaven I was anywhere but here.

"Everything I did was to protect Marie from that. Why do you think Marie hates us so much? It sure as hell isn't because we took her to Disney World to see that damn mouse."

Elle leans back in her chair, crosses her arms once again, and taps her foot.

"What?" I spit the word out. I hate when someone taps a foot or finger or nail or anything else at me. Don't patronize me.

"I *don't* know why my mother hates you so much. Why don't you fill me in?"

She gets her sarcasm honestly, at least.

"All I wanted to do was protect your mother. Protect my wife. Protect everyone in my life, including Charlie." The frustration shoots through me like a yo-yo, back and forth from the tip of my bald head to the pads of my feet. It hurts. "That's all I've done, and this is the thanks I get. Fine." Spittle covers the sheet on my lap, I've said it so quickly. "Hate me all you want. Revile me. Rant at me. Walk away from here being glad you never have to see me again. But I loved your mother, and everything I did was for her. Everything."

I jab the air with my finger, anger rising in me even when it isn't justified.

I hate that I'm showing her this side of me. I couldn't care less if anyone else saw it, but not this girl. Not her. I want her to remember me as a nice old man who loved to tell stories, who died with a smile on his face, rather than the cranky old bear too miserable for company.

I half expect her to leave me after my tirade. Wouldn't blame her if she did.

So why isn't she standing up?

"So tell me." She glances at her watch. "I'm not going anywhere, and I want to hear about the father who loved his daughter more than life." She points her finger toward me. "Don't tell me a made-up story about my mother's imaginary friend."

She still doesn't believe Bella is real. Why? Why wouldn't Marie have told her? Explained to her?

"Bella *wasn't* an imaginary friend."

"Of course she was." Elle rolls her eyes.

This pint-size child has the audacity to roll her eyes at me.

"What makes you think that?"

Her cheeks turn a rosy red. "I took a few pieces from the dollhouse in the playroom I found in your garage and brought them home. Mom told me she called the *doll* Isabel."

What game is Marie playing? What lies has she told?

"So my confession was what? A lie?"

"More like a fabrication of a memory."

There's dead certainty in her voice.

Like hell it was.

Chapter Thirty-One

Daddy built us a room that's our very own.

We can have tea parties and play with our dolls here.

There's even a couch full of pillows and blankets that we can read stories on or use for forts.

He let us decorate it however we wanted, even bought new paint for us to use.

I wanted pink.

She wanted yellow.

He's building us something extra special but my sister won't let me see it. She says it's only for her and that I'll have to be nice to her if I want to play with it too.

I'm always nice. She's the one that's mean.

I try to talk to our other sisters. I ask them for help. I think they hear me.

I hope they keep my secrets. So far they haven't told sister. At least, I don't think they have.

Sometimes she looks at me, though, like she knows.

Sometimes . . . sometimes she scares me.

Chapter Thirty-Two

DAVID

December 1956

He'd been away longer than he'd intended. Longer than he should have been, if he was being honest with himself.

He couldn't handle another night in the bed of his new truck. The mattress was as hard as a rock, and all the diner food wasn't doing much for his stomach. He craved a good home-cooked meal, his own bed, and the arms of his wife around him.

Although, the last few times he'd been home, she'd basically refused his touch. He knew tonight would be no different.

Gertie had understood when his two-week haul ended up being three weeks, but she'd all but hinted that if he knew what was good for him, he'd come home after this last load—or else.

She sounded different the last time they spoke, and that more than anything had him increasing his speed.

After dropping off his empty trailer at the yard, David made a beeline home, not stopping at the diner for coffee like he normally did. He knew he'd been gone too long. One second more seemed almost unforgivable.

He knew better than to be away from Gertie, but he couldn't handle being there at the same time.

It had been five long months since Judy's death.

Five months of what they'd done haunting him at every turn. He kept his radio on full blast when on the road so he couldn't hear himself think. He sat with a group of other truckers whenever he stopped and drank way too much whiskey on nights when he couldn't sleep.

The guilt gnawed like a gnat on his soul. Her voice, her face, that *thump* as she fell from his arms. It haunted him until he thought he was going crazy.

But it was worse when he was home.

He swore he could hear her calling to him. She'd be there, standing on the dewy grass in the early morning hours, her hands reaching out for help. He couldn't take it.

That's why he didn't go home as often as he should.

His truck rattled as he drove down the dirt road. The setting sun cast a brilliant aura of purples and blues against the cloudless sky, and he was glad he'd arrive home in time to read the girls a story.

He missed them.

Missed the sound of them calling his name, of the ready smiles on their faces when he'd walk into the room to say good night. He missed the stories they would tell him of what happened while he was gone, the pictures Bella would draw, the clothes Anna Marie would hand sew with Gertie's help.

He missed his girls more than he'd realized.

Gertie didn't meet him at the door anymore when he drove up. He looked around his yard, something he always did when coming home to make sure everything was okay. The first thing he noticed was the Case 320 tractor out of the shed.

Why would Gertie have moved the tractor? She knows I'm working on it, that it shouldn't be used.

She didn't even meet him in the back room, where she used to demand he change from his stinky clothes before setting foot in the house. Now all he found was a pair of pants and a shirt, neatly folded on top of the bench.

She was mad, and he needed to be prepared to eat humble pie.

Opening the door to the kitchen, David expected to find Gertie at the table, a plate of food waiting for him. The kitchen light was off, and the only light that illuminated the way for him was the small table lamp in the hallway between the kitchen and living room.

"Gertie? Love? I'm home," he called out, bewildered.

"In here."

He followed the sound of her voice, which led him to the sitting room. She was curled up on the couch, a blanket over her lap, a book in hand.

"Are you feeling okay?"

Her sitting down, curled on the couch like she was, rattled him.

His Gertie never sat still. Not for long enough to read at least, not unless she was in bed.

"I'm fine. Just reading." She tossed the blanket off and stood.

He expected her to come to him, but she only stood rooted to the carpet beneath her feet.

He held out his arms, needing to feel them wrapped around her. It took a moment, but she forced her feet forward until her body was against him, her arms wrapped loosely around his waist, her head on his chest.

"You're not eating enough, are you?" she complained before leaning back and looking him in the face. "I can feel your ribs."

David followed her into the kitchen, where she took out a casserole from the oven and dished him out a plate of beef and potatoes.

"I'm sorry I haven't been home." David sat at the table and waited while she placed his plate in front of him, filled two glasses with water, and opened an ice-cold beer for him.

She never has beer in the house.

He always had to buy some after going into town. He kept it in the garage, in an old fridge he used just for that purpose.

"You should have been."

"I know."

"We needed you." Gertie's hands nestled together on the table.

"I'm sorry." He didn't have any excuse, didn't even bother to fabricate one.

She was right. He should have been home, and he knew that. He needed to man up, deal with what they'd done, and be what his family needed—a strong pillar of support.

"I thought maybe we could go cut a tree from the field this weekend and trim it? The girls will like that, and it's not too early now. Only a few weeks until Christmas," David suggested, making idle chatter to fill in the gap.

Gertie shrugged.

"Or we can wait till next weekend if you'd prefer?" He was trying to read her, to figure out what she was thinking, but his wife was a closed book.

Damn it. I should have come home last weekend.

"Where's the girls? Where's Anna Marie?"

Gertie glanced up the stairs. "Marie is in bed. She fell asleep a few hours ago."

"Marie?"

She nodded, her gaze fixed on the stairs.

"Since when did we start calling her Marie? That's not her name."

Gertie swallowed hard. "Since last week or so."

"What about Bella?"

Gertie slowly turned her attention to him, and what he saw on her face froze him to the bone.

"Bella is dead."

The bottle of beer in David's hand dropped, smashing against the floor, the liquid covering his legs and feet.

Her words warped in his mind until the dullness of her voice turned into a screech and the tension headache he'd felt all day intensified.

"What did you say?"

It couldn't be true.

Yet, reading Gertie's body language, the way she'd retreated from him, how she'd kept the lights off, the monotone announcement . . . she wasn't lying.

"It was God's will, David. She wasn't strong enough to survive losing her mother."

"What are you talking about?"

How can she be dead? How can Gertie be so calm? Why didn't she say anything to me before now?

"There . . . there was an accident. The girls wanted to go ice-skating down by the creek. I was doing laundry, and they were supposed to be in the playroom. But they sneaked across the road instead. Honestly, David, it's a wonder they both weren't killed."

He shook his head.

What is she saying?

"They know not to go down there." He pushed his chair out and stood, gripping the edge of the table until his knuckles were white. "Why weren't you watching them? How could she be *dead*? Gertie, you're not making sense."

Rather than respond, she stood to clean the splattered beer and swept up the glass at his feet. She was calm, detached, and uncaring. While he was cold with fury, confusion, and grief.

His eyes welled up with tears. He wanted to rush upstairs to see the girls for himself, to disprove Gertie and admit once and for all she'd reached her limit and needed help.

"I was doing laundry, David." Gertie finally said after the floor was cleaned. "The girls disobeyed me, and God intervened. He must have known this was too much, that the girls were too much for me. Bella needed to be with her mother—that's where she was meant to be."

He shook his head as the throbbing in it intensified.

"What did you do, love?"

It was all he could do to keep his voice gentle.

She reached out, as if wanting him to take her hands.

He released his hold on the table and stepped back.

"What did you do?"

"I didn't do anything. Don't you understand? The girls . . . it wasn't right forcing them to be sisters. Bella was never ours. So God helped me, like He's always helped me when He knows something is too much for me."

The soft and serene smile on her face confirmed his fears.

My wife is broken.

David pivoted on the balls of his feet and rushed up the stairs, taking the steps two at a time. He needed to see his daughter, to confirm that everything his wife had said was true while praying it wasn't.

"David, don't. I need to tell you something. Please." Gertie stood at the bottom of the stairs as he reached Anna Marie's room. "Don't wake her please. She needs her rest."

His hand grabbed the handle of the girls' bedroom.

"David, please. Let me explain," Gertie begged.

Explain?

He pushed the door open and almost dropped to his knees.

Bella's bed was empty.

Anna Marie lay like a corpse, her arms stiff at her sides with her blanket tucked tight around her.

David rushed to her side, falling to his knees.

"My God, what happened?" he whispered. "What have I done?"

His daughter's face was completely covered in gauze, her head wrapped like a mummy with only her eyes, nose, and mouth left out—and even those were swollen. Her eyes were as large as golf balls and marbled black and blue. Her lips were cut and misshapen, and her nose was obviously broken.

"Let me explain." Gertie stood at the door, her voice a half whisper.

David reached for his daughter's hands, which were bandaged as well.

"Is she alive?" David asked, his throat swelling with tears and anger.

"She's alive, but she needs to sleep. David, please." Gertie held out her hand, beseeching him to leave the room.

He stumbled to his feet, the room swimming as he struggled to stand upright.

"Tell me, Gertie. You tell me now what happened to our girls. Where is Bella? Why is Anna Marie laying there like that?" He reached for his wife's shoulders and shook her. "God help me, I should have been here. I should have seen the signs. I should have manned up and done what was needed."

"Calm down, David. Come back downstairs and let me explain, please?" She reached up for his hands, dislodging them from her shoulders.

Calm down?

There was not one calm atom inside of him. His thoughts swirled like a vortex, his body a mixture of jelly and fire.

She expects me to calm down?

"Don't tell me to calm down, you crazy woman!" David yelled. "What the hell happened to our daughter? Where is Bella? What is wrong with you?"

He didn't care that she stumbled backward as if he'd hit her. He didn't care that the look of horror on her face was his fault. He didn't care what damage his words inflicted.

All he cared about were his girls.

This is all my fault.

Gertie fled down the stairs as fast as she could to get away from him. He expected her to explode, to match him with fury, with fear. But she didn't.

By the time he followed her, she was seated at the table with a fresh cup of tea.

A fresh bottle of beer waited for him.

"Drink your beer, David, before it gets warm."

Drink my beer? What is wrong with her?

"Gertie Walker, tell me what happened, or so help me . . ." He bit his tongue before finishing his sentence. Red-hot flames of rage washed over him.

"Sit down and I'll tell you. It's fine, David. You should have been home. Maybe then none of this would have happened, but it's all God's will. He's told me things are going to be okay."

She wrapped her hands around her cup and gave him a smile that chilled the blood rushing through his veins.

He'd seen that same smile once, years ago, when they'd visited Gertie's mother in the mental institution and Gertie told her they were having a baby.

The minute Gertie told her, she had smiled the same smile on Gertie's face now. She'd said, "God promised me my heaven babies would soon have a visitor."

Her smile, those words, had sent a jolt right through his heart. After their first miscarriage, he believed her mother had cursed them.

But maybe it was really God.

David sat down and took a swig of his beer, downing nearly half of it before he took a breath. He leaned back in his chair and folded his hands on his lap.

He hoped she thought he was relaxed. Calm. Ready to listen.

He was anything but. Every nerve in his body was tight. Focused. Ready for action.

"I was doing laundry, and the girls asked if they could go out in the yard to play. I didn't have time to watch over them, so I told them they could go play in the playroom for a little bit."

She knew he didn't like them in there alone, not in the winter. It got too cold, and he didn't trust them with the space heater he'd picked up the month before. They weren't always careful with their toys, and those things could overheat or burn anything too close to them. If the girls were to play out in that room, one of the adults needed to be there with them. Gertie knew that.

"They had their jackets and boots on. They would have been fine until I was done with the laundry. They should have listened to me."

She remained so calm, so still.

It scared him.

"They got it in their heads to go down to the creek and skate on the ice. I think they lost their footing. By the time I found them, they were both at the bottom of the hill by the water, cut and bruised. But Bella . . . she landed on the ice and broke it." Gertie swallowed hard, twisting her hands even tighter around the mug. "When I found her, she was facedown in the water, and it was too late. God took her from us to teach Anna Marie a lesson about disobeying me." She shook her head, the first sign of grief he'd seen since coming home. "Anna Marie was hurt, her face was all bloody, hands scraped up pretty good. I think she was trying to stop her fall, but you know what that hill is like, full of rocks—"

"And icy as hell." David pounded his fist on the table, causing Gertie to jerk back. He breathed in through his nose, taking in as much air as he could before rubbing his face with his hand. "They know better than to go down that hill. It's dangerous, even during the summer. It's too steep. God, Gertie, why would they do that?" He could picture it happening. The rocks, mounds of snow and ice, the girls slipping, tumbling down, trying to grab hold of something to stop their fall.

But it all happened too fast, and before they knew it, they were down on the ice.

"Where was Anna Marie? Was she in the water too?"

Gertie shook her head. "No, she was off to the side. She was curled around a large rock halfway down the slope. I think that's what stopped her from landing on the ice."

"Was she awake?" He couldn't get the images out of his head.

Gertie looked down at the table. "No. She was unconscious. Bella was . . . she was already dead, so I picked up Anna Marie and managed to get her back up to the road. It took all I had to get her home and in the house."

"What about Bella? You just left her there?" He couldn't understand what he was hearing. None of this made sense.

"She was already dead."

He heard her, but he didn't believe her.

Sure, the creek was deep enough that a person could drown in it. In the middle of winter, with the ice cracking beneath even the weight of an adult, he could see it happening. But Bella was tiny. Unless there'd been a thaw, the ice would have been too thick.

His girls did the one thing they knew they shouldn't do? Go down the hill to the creek? Hell, even in the summer, they never went down that way. He always made them walk to the bridge, where the slope was gentler.

"So Bella fell down the hill and landed on the ice, which then broke beneath her? But Anna Marie managed to grab hold of a large rock and kept herself from falling all the way? What rock?"

Gertie shook her head, as if that small piece of information didn't matter.

"If you'd been here, David, none of this would have happened."

She has the audacity to blame me?

Is she right? Is this my fault?

David leaned forward, elbows on the table. "How did you know where to find them?"

"Their footprints in the snow."

David covered his face with both hands and pushed them hard enough against his eyes that flares of light danced in front of him.

"The tractor?"

Gertie nodded, seemingly knowing what he was asking.

"I know you said it wasn't fixed, but I didn't know what else to do. I dug a hole and placed Bella in there, beside Judy."

He couldn't believe what he was hearing.

"You . . . dug . . . a . . . grave."

She snorted. "It's not like I don't know how to use the machine, David. I knew I couldn't dig a hole myself with a shovel since the ground is frozen. I probably didn't go as deep as you normally do, but it'll suffice."

"It'll . . . suffice . . ."

He twisted in his seat and looked back upstairs, hoping beyond hope this was all a nightmare and he would see the girls sitting on the top stair, waiting for him to read them a story.

Except they weren't.

Gertie's explanation didn't make sense. None of it made sense.

"Please tell me you took Anna Marie to the hospital."

She scrunched her face up at him. "Her name is Marie now, and why would I do that? I can take care of her here. That way, there's no one asking unnecessary questions. Head wounds heal."

David rocked back in his chair. He was living in a nightmare of his own making. He should have manned up months ago and taken his wife to the doctor, got her seen to—medicated, if needed.

Hell, I should have put my daughter first and placed Gertie in an institution.

What have I done?

"She's fine now, though. God is healing her. I'm keeping her asleep, just like God told me to."

"You've drugged our daughter?"

None of this can be real. It can't be.

"Of course I did. Honestly, David. You're making a big deal over nothing. There's a lot of bruising and still a little bit of swelling, but overall, she looks so much better than she did. Another week and she'll be fine."

David tried to wrap his head around all of this. It was too much, too fast.

Why would the girls have gone down to the creek in the middle of winter to ice-skate? They never skated there. Ever. He'd made a little skating rink for them in their own backyard for this very reason. Why hadn't they used that?

He had so many questions. Questions his wife wasn't answering— or wasn't capable of answering.

How long did it take Gertie to find them? To realize they were missing?

How did she get the two of them back to the house? She isn't that big herself. How long did she leave Bella down there, alone, by herself? Had the girl even really been dead? Could she have been saved? How did Gertie know? And using the tractor when she knew he was trying to fix it? Why would she do that?

It wasn't until later, when Gertie went upstairs to sleep in Bella's bed so she could keep watch over their daughter, that it really hit him.

Bella is dead.

Sweet, caring, beautiful Bella. Gone.

If I'd been here, like Gertie said, could I have saved her?

Absolutely.

The guilt was on him. Her death, his fault. The weight of it all was too much. While his wife and daughter slept upstairs, David stood outside, in the middle of the night, without so much as a jacket, and cried.

He cried for the daughter he'd lost. For the wife he was losing. For the mistakes he'd made and the secrets he had to keep. He cried until there was nothing left inside of him and he was as dry as a desert landscape.

He didn't know where they would go from here. He didn't know what to do.

There were two deaths on his soul now, and there was no coming back from that.

It wasn't just Bella. He'd lost his wife too.

Chapter Thirty-Three

David sat beside his daughter's bed, desperate to hold back the tears as her eyelashes weakly fluttered.

He'd been sitting there for the past hour, reading her story after story, praying that she would wake up. He'd give anything to see her eyes, to hear her voice, to see her move.

She blinked three times and licked her lips.

"Hey, love." David leaned forward. "I'm here now. I'm so sorry."

She turned her head toward him and blinked again. Her lips moved, but no sound came out. He had a hard time taking in the swelling and bruising, the cut lips and black eyes.

I should have been here to protect her and Bella.

He held a cup of water close and angled the straw so she could take a sip.

"Here's some water. Take it slow. Mommy is making you a cup of broth and will be up soon."

Her eyes widened at the words—or widened slightly more than they were already, which was only a bare slit.

Poor girl must be hungry and exhausted. Two weeks in bed like this . . . never again. I should have been home.

"How are you feeling, moppet? Is there anything I can do? Want me to read you another story?" He rambled on, hating this whole situation.

His role as a father was to protect his child, and he'd done a lousy job of that. His own insecurities and shame forced him to break a promise he'd made—to always be there for his girls. Not only did he break that promise, but the consequence was death for Bella and pain for Anna Marie.

How do I even start to beg for forgiveness?

He picked up an illustrated copy of *Grimms' Fairy Tales* and searched for the story of the Goose Girl, one of Anna Marie's favorites, about a princess mistaken for a servant.

Her eyes closed while he read the story and he thought for sure she'd fallen asleep, but when Gertie came to the door, she gasped and tried to form words. Nothing she said made sense.

"I think she hurt her throat in the fall. I've told her not to try to talk," Gertie said as she stepped in with a tray. "I have some warm honey and lemon tea to help with your sore throat."

David moved out of the way while Gertie helped their daughter sip.

She grimaced at the first sip and tried to pull away, but Gertie's hand on the back of her neck wouldn't let her.

"Maybe it needs more sugar, love?" David suggested gently.

"Just a few more sips, Marie. That's it," Gertie coaxed. "You need to drink this to heal. Don't worry, Daddy will stay by your side and continue to read you stories while you sleep."

"Marie?"

Gertie hissed at him over her shoulder, urging him to be quiet. "We talked about this, remember?"

After their daughter drank half the tea in the cup, David pulled her to the side.

"Remind me again why you're calling her Marie?"

"It's what she wants to be called. The girls shared Marie as a middle name. This is probably her way of wanting to remember Bella, that's all. Don't make a big fuss of it, please. And don't, whatever you do, mention Bella. Let's give our daughter time to heal first."

She left the room, blowing a kiss toward their daughter. David returned to his seat.

"So, Marie, huh?" he said. She blinked a few times at him and made what he thought must be a frown. It was hard to tell.

"B . . . ell . . . aaa." Her raspy voice could barely make the sounds to form the word. He winced at the obvious pain she was in.

"*Shhh*, love. It's all right. Just rest now. We'll talk about everything after you're better, okay?"

She slowly moved her right hand up to her chest. Her wrists were wrapped tight, but she managed to point toward her heart.

"Belllllaaa." She whispered this time, her voice sounding like a dying frog.

"I know, love. I know." He reached for the tea, wanting to help soothe her throat, but she leaned away from him.

He took a sip of the tea and almost spat it out.

He hadn't wanted to believe Gertie would drug Anna Marie to sleep, but it was true. He should have known, but ignorance was bliss . . .

Is this what she did with Judy too?

He didn't want to believe it.

Gertie loved Judy, and she wouldn't have given . . .

Nausea rolled in his stomach as the realization dawned.

My wife poisoned Judy, didn't she? Not with alcohol, but something else, something to make her sick.

His mind whirled as he thought back to the summer, how little by little Judy became weaker. How she'd told him his wife wasn't well, how she'd begged him to take her to the doctor.

He hadn't listened.

I should have listened.

"I'm sure your mother has good reason for giving you this tea, but how about I go make you a fresh cup, with extra honey?" The instant relief in her eyes was palatable.

What he saw in her eyes gave him a start. He hesitated a moment before leaning over to give her a kiss on her forehead, careful with his soft touch.

He wanted to ask her about Judy, about the medication she tried to keep from Gertie, about the real story behind what happened with that fall. Gertie's explanation made no sense, but his daughter would tell him the truth. He couldn't ask her right now, though. He would have to wait.

When he made it down the stairs, Gertie was at the kitchen sink, washing their breakfast dishes.

"Have you been giving her alcohol this whole time?"

The look on her face was a mixture of confusion and exasperation. "It's only a shot of brandy. It's not going to hurt her. It's no different than the drugs they would have given her in the hospital."

David snorted. "There's a huge difference and you know it."

He dumped the tea down the drain. He would never let her make another cup of tea for their daughter.

"My mother used to give me brandy in my tea all the time when I wasn't well or couldn't sleep. It didn't do me any harm."

Is she serious? She's honestly using her crazy parent as an example?

"I'm sure she's had enough and is probably tired of sleeping all day. Maybe it's time she got up and moved around a little," he suggested. "Her legs aren't broken, right? Have you taken off the gauze from around her head to see how she's healing?"

"Do you think I'm an imbecile? I know how to take care of our daughter, thank you very much." She spat the words at him while twisting the dishrag in her hand as tight as she could.

She's probably imagining it's my neck between her hands.

He recoiled at that thought and felt immediate shame. That was his anger speaking.

My wife won't harm me and wouldn't purposely harm our daughter, right?

David refilled the teacup with the warm water still in the kettle. He added a squeeze of lemon and an extra spoonful of honey, stirring it while trying very hard to remain calm.

"Gertie? When you found the girls at the bottom of the hill, you were able to recognize them, right? Despite the cuts and everything?"

The spoon Gertie held clattered into the sink.

Without looking at him, she slowly picked it up and scrubbed even harder than she had been before.

"Gertie?"

Maybe she didn't hear me. Maybe she's lost in her own thoughts and my voice startled her.

Or maybe she's ignoring me.

"Of course I recognized our daughter. That's what you're asking, isn't it? You can't possibly think that child upstairs is Bella? I think I know my own daughter. It's understandable that you might doubt, considering you're hardly home and the girls do look so much alike, but . . ."

The accusation in her voice was too much.

"You're right." David nodded, her words fueling the rage that skimmed the surface of his skin. "I haven't been home. Because I'm trying to put food on the table and take care of you and the girls. I should have been here. If I had been"—David fisted his hands at his sides—"maybe this wouldn't have happened. Maybe *none of this* would have happened."

"What do you mean by that?" She turned then, drying the spoon with the towel slung over her shoulder. "Are you saying this was *my* fault?" Her hand shook slightly. "You're the one who brought Judy to the house. You're the one who insisted she stay. You're the one who dropped her and killed her. If anyone is responsible for this mess called our lives, it's you."

She stepped close to him, so close he could feel her breath on his chin as she looked up.

"Maybe God is punishing you for all of this. Have you thought of that? It's your fault our daughter is—" She stopped and stepped back, her body trembling with each step. "It's your fault. All of it."

David wanted to argue with her. He wanted to deny her accusation, place the blame on her for not watching the girls like she should have, but there was a measure of truth to her words.

She's right. I'm to blame and, no doubt, this is God's way of punishing me.

He'd grown to love that little girl as his own, and the hole in his heart from her loss wasn't something he would ever heal from. He'd killed her mother, so God deemed him unfit to raise her and took her from him.

From us.

There was no other way to rationalize it.

"I'm sorry." Gertie wrapped her arms around him. All he could do was stand there. "I didn't mean that. Truly. I can't blame you. God isn't punishing us. All we did was love those girls, and now they're gone. But we still have each other. Maybe you're right. Maybe it's time to get Marie out of bed. Why don't you go cut that tree like you mentioned? She can lie on the couch and watch us decorate it."

She raised herself up on her tiptoes to kiss his cheek before turning back to the cup of tea he'd just made for his daughter, humming while she stirred it a few more times.

"I'll take this up to her and tell her we have a surprise planned for her." She continued to hum a Christmas carol as she walked away, cup in hand.

One minute she was blaming him for the death of both Judy and Bella, and in the next breath she was humming Christmas carols and wanting to decorate for the holiday.

Doesn't she care at all about what happened?

Didn't losing that sweet, precious, and loving girl affect her at all?

Has she grieved already? Is it possible to get over a death in two short weeks?

Not for Gertie.

He knew that firsthand. It took months for her to deal with the loss of any of their children, no matter how far along in the pregnancy she'd been.

For a moment, he'd thought it possible that the girl upstairs was Bella and not his daughter. If that were true, Gertie would be inconsolable right now.

Right?

What does it mean that I can't answer that with certainty? What does it mean that I doubt my own wife's state of mind?

~

For the next two weeks, David stayed home and close to Marie's side.

He caught himself so many times wanting to call her Anna Marie, but the pain in her eyes each time he did so had him biting his tongue.

He always figured she'd want to be called Anna again eventually.

Gertie had him worried. He expected her to fall apart at some point, but she remained chipper, excited about Christmas. Other than their initial talk about Bella, she hadn't mentioned the child or the death again.

In fact, whenever he'd bring it up, she would get a faraway look in her eyes, as if she had no idea who he was talking about.

"Another story?"

Marie's voice still caught him off guard. Where once it was soft and angelic, now it was coarse and rough. Gertie said she'd grow out of it, that her vocal cords just needed to heal. David knew no amount of healing would return the soft cadence of her voice.

She was curled up on the couch, wrapped in a handmade knitted blanket Gertie recently finished. He stoked the fire.

"I need to get some wood, love. How about if Mommy reads you a story this time?"

Gertie sat in the rocker on the other side of the room, knitting a new pair of mittens for Marie to wear once she was allowed back outside.

"Can't she get the wood?" Marie half whispered.

David frowned. He glanced over at Gertie, but she continued knitting away without even looking up.

"Don't you want her to read you a story?"

Marie shook her head.

David knelt down in front of his daughter and reached for her hands. They were still tender. The cuts were healing, and the bruising was now yellow around her knuckles.

This wasn't the first time she'd chosen him over Gertie.

In fact, it was becoming a regular thing. She didn't like being alone with her, to the point where she'd cry if he left the room, freeze up whenever Gertie came in to tuck her into bed. Once, when Marie had woken up from a night terror, he'd even heard her beg Gertie to leave her alone, saying she wanted her real mommy.

"Let me get some wood so we can stay toasty warm. Then I'll be back to read you a story, okay?"

Marie shook her head again, quick little movements, while she played with a stray thread on her blanket.

"Why don't I make us some hot cocoa while Daddy grabs the wood?" Gertie set her knitting down in the basket beside her chair and headed into the kitchen before anyone responded.

Had she heard Marie?

He didn't like the withdrawal happening between Marie and Gertie. He didn't like it from Marie, this not wanting to be with her mother.

I sure as hell don't like it coming from Gertie, who seems to not mind not spending time with her daughter.

What happened to the bond between the two of them? Until the accident, they were inseparable.

In the kitchen, Gertie talked away while she filled the kettle.

"Who are you talking to, love?" David placed his hand on her shoulder.

"Just the babies. They're talking to me again, David. They need to be loved and taken care of, and they're lonely. I like to tell them stories."

A frigid thread of fear snaked along David's spine as he turned Gertie gently around so he could look into her eyes.

They were as clear as the cold, blue sky out the kitchen window, but he didn't see his wife in her gaze.

He didn't even recognize the woman staring back at him.

"Judy and Bella are together, so they've left the babies. Just like they left us. Miserable bitches, the two of them. We need to do something, David, so they're not alone. I can't have them be alone—not again."

She smiled sweetly and innocently, like a cherub without a hint of mischief.

David stole a look at their daughter, who covered her head with the blanket.

A feeling of the rug being pulled out from beneath his feet stole his breath.

This whole situation has spiraled out of my control.

What did I do?

Knowing his wife needed medical help was a kick in the groin.

Who comes first? Who is more important? How can I choose?

He waited until Marie and Gertie were fast asleep before he did the only thing he could think of doing.

David called his baby sister.

She lived in British Columbia and worked at the hospital in Vancouver. It'd been close to five years since he'd last seen her, but he had no one else to turn to.

"David!" She greeted him with a voice full of warmth and light, something he needed just then. "How's my big brother doing?"

Normally he'd tell her all about life, stories about Marie, what they'd done around the house, how his routes were going. But that night, none of it mattered.

"I hate to do this, and I know it's not the best timing. I need you."

There was a brief pause. He heard her inhale.

"I can grab a train and be there in five days."

That's what he loved about his sister. No questions asked, she was there.

"Thank you. I . . ." He choked up. The tight fist holding his heart hostage loosened its grip, but he was unable to really express how much it meant to him.

"Is it Gertie?"

Funny she would pick up on that.

She'd come after Marie was born, to help Gertie for the first few months. They'd sat around the bonfire, David drinking a beer. Before he knew it, he'd confessed the one fear he had—that there would come a day when he'd have to choose between his wife and his children's welfare.

"You choose your family. Always. There's no either or. When that time comes, you call me and I'll be there. Family, David. That's all that matters." She'd leaned over and touched her bottle to his like a handshake agreement.

"I can't choose," he said into the phone. "I need to, but . . ." He swallowed hard and stared through the darkened room toward the stairs. "They're my life, and I can't lose either one."

"I'll buy my ticket tomorrow and get on the earliest train I can."

The instantaneous relief he felt knowing she was coming, that he wouldn't be alone anymore—it was almost too much.

"Thank you." He cleared his throat. "I'll cover the cost of the ticket so you're not out of pocket." He'd do more than just that. He'd pay her a living allowance for coming to take care of things while he worked. It would mean he'd need to take longer hauls, but he'd make it work.

"I know. Don't worry, David. I've got your back." She sounded so sure, as if what he was asking wasn't life changing.

"Are you sure?" He wanted to give her time to really consider what this meant. "You'd be giving up your life in Vancouver, for mine."

"Family, David. Family is all that matters." She repeated the same phrase from the bonfire. "You're my family, which means your problems are mine."

"Grace." He felt like weeping. "Thank you."

Calling his sister was his only hope for keeping his family together, whole.

He prayed it would work.

Chapter Thirty-Four

May 1957

David, you need to come home. Gertie's in the hospital.

He'd called home a few days earlier from Winnipeg, just to check in with Grace to see how everyone was, to remind Gertie he loved her, and to share a funny story about a fellow trucker and his dog he'd met at a stop.

Before he could speak to anyone else, Grace had told him to come home.

She didn't say anything more, just asked him to come as soon as he could. It'd taken two days for him to return, drop off his load, and rush to his family.

Two days of major praying, of begging God to let things be okay, and letting his mind run with worst-case scenarios had exhausted him.

He jumped out of his truck and ran into the house. Grace was wiping a plate she held in her hands.

"What's going on?" He looked around for Marie, but she wasn't in the room.

"Marie is out in the playroom drawing, David. It's okay. She's okay. Now."

"Now?"

Grace slowly set the plate she was wiping dry down on the table, slung the towel over her shoulder—something Gertie used to do—and gave him a hug.

He awkwardly patted her back.

"What was that for?" he asked.

"You look stressed. Everything is okay. Marie is okay . . . now. Gertie is getting the help she needs."

"What do you mean, 'Marie is okay *now*'?" She hadn't said anything about Marie being hurt.

She pulled out a chair and motioned for him to sit.

"Marie and I made a pie. Sit down. While I cut you a piece, I will explain what happened."

He didn't budge.

"What happened to my daughter? Why is Gertie still in the hospital?"

So many questions. He was going to lose it if she didn't tell him everything right that minute.

Grace pulled out an apple pie and cut him a slice. She sat down opposite him and waited until he took a seat.

"Gertie has been hearing the voices of your dead children calling her more and more. You know this."

He nodded. The last time he'd been home for the weekend, he'd noticed she seemed more lost in the past than present in their lives. She would tell him stories of things the babies told her while they lay in bed together. He begged her to stay with him, but he knew the call of the children she'd lost was almost too much.

"I woke up early the other morning and had my shower. I checked in on Marie and noticed her bed was empty, so I knocked on your bedroom door to see if maybe she was in there with Gertie. But your room was empty too."

He frowned. It was unlikely Marie would choose to be alone with Gertie—she still did everything she could not to be.

"I searched the house, then finally went outside to look for them. I found them behind the garden, both of them lying across the graves."

"What do you mean, 'lying across the graves'?"

Grace reached for his hand.

"Gertie said it was time they joined the babies, that they wanted to meet Marie. She'd cut their wrists, David."

His eyes closed in instant grief, then opened again as her words hit him.

"She tried to kill Marie?"

No. I don't believe it. She wouldn't do that.

Everything spun. The room, his sister, his world. It spun out of control, and there was no button he could slam to stop the deadly ride he was on.

"I'm sorry, David. Everyone is okay, though. Marie is okay."

He pushed his chair back. He wanted to rush out to check for himself that his daughter was all right, but Grace grabbed his hand, stopping him.

"I'm not done."

Her monotone voice had him back in his seat.

"She'd barely cut Marie's skin. The girl knew enough to play along, so she lay beside Gertie after she'd cut her own wrists—"

"Gertie cut her own wrists *first*?" David interrupted her.

"She wanted to show Marie it wouldn't hurt. But she couldn't hold the knife afterward, so she barely cut your daughter's skin. By the time I made it out there, Gertie was unconscious. Marie just lay there, shaking like a poor soul."

David wasn't sure he could hear any more. This was worse than anything he'd imagined.

Never would I have believed Gertie would harm our daughter.

"She's under sedation now, under a doctor's supervision. But they want to see you."

"I want to see my daughter."

Months ago, he hadn't felt sure that he could choose between his daughter and his wife, if he could break his word to the woman he loved. But right now, in this moment, nothing was more important to him than his daughter.

Nothing.

He rushed outside and ran across the driveway to the garage. He steadied himself at the door and watched his daughter sit at Bella's drawing table. From the back, she almost looked like Bella with her head down, shoulders hunched while she concentrated on whatever she was drawing. There were still moments when he would have sworn that she was not his daughter, but then she'd smile. Despite the haunted look in her eyes, the love in his heart told him it had to be her.

The pang of missing that little girl pinged his heart.

"Marie?" he called out.

She half turned toward him, pencil in hand. Her wrists were wrapped in large white bandages, and he could see from the expression on her face that she was numb.

Grace suddenly stood beside him. She laid her hand on his back and said quietly, "She's not talking."

"What do you mean?" He didn't take his gaze off Marie.

"She hasn't spoken a word since I found her. What happened was traumatic, and she needs time to heal."

"Maybe she'll talk to me."

David stepped into the room and went to his daughter, placing his arms around her in an attempt to scoop her up in his arms for a hug. Marie started to shake and flail in his arms, and her mouth opened in a soundless scream as she fought against his hold.

David dropped his arms and knelt on the ground.

"Marie, it's okay," he tried to soothe her, to comfort her.

He was scared. He gently touched her arm and she jumped, jerking away from him as far as she could go without falling off the chair.

"I'm so sorry," David mumbled over and over as he watched the fear in his daughter's eyes expand.

"Why is she scared of *me*?" David turned toward Grace, completely helpless. He had no idea what to do or say.

Grace went to Marie and put her arms around her. While Marie huddled against Grace, the tremors subsided. She still wouldn't look at David, and that tore at him.

Why is my daughter so scared of me? Does she blame me for not protecting her? For not being there?

That was the only reason he could think of.

He didn't blame her either.

David stepped back, giving his child room to breathe. He noticed the farther he retreated from her, the calmer she became.

He waited for Grace outside, his heart breaking over and over.

How could this have gone so wrong?

When Grace joined him, she led him inside. He sat woodenly down at the kitchen table.

Numb. That was the only way to describe how he felt.

"You should go see Gertie, David. I'm here for Marie, and your wife needs you."

"My daughter needs me more." The words tore out of the crater where his heart used to be.

"Marie needs time to heal. I'd hoped . . . I don't think your being here is what she needs." Grace handed him a cold beer from the fridge. "Is there anything I need to know? About what happened before I arrived? Is there anything you haven't told me that would explain Gertie's quick deterioration and Marie's response to you both?"

David just shook his head. He'd never told her about Judy or Bella. Never breathed a word about the poisoning or how he'd dropped Judy—killing her by doing so.

Whenever Marie mentioned Bella, Grace assumed it was an imaginary friend. David was more than happy to keep it at that. Gertie never took notice, lost in her own little world since the accident happened.

David still didn't know the full story. He'd been able to piece things together here and there from things said in passing. Like how Marie remembered being *pushed* down the ravine—except David couldn't see Bella pushing her. Or how Gertie would wake up crying, saying she couldn't have saved both no matter how hard she tried, which led David to think that maybe Bella *hadn't* been dead when Gertie found them but she chose to save their daughter first.

No matter how it happened, it was a nightmare. One he'd never wake up from.

He would never tell Grace, though. He would never breathe a single word of what happened from the moment he picked up Judy and Bella. He and Gertie were both culpable in their deaths. From Judy being poisoned, to David dropping her and ultimately killing her, to Gertie choosing which girl to save. Their deaths were on their hands, and he would do everything and anything to protect the ones he loved—even if it meant keeping all of this a secret.

"I don't think Gertie ever got over her last miscarriage," David finally said.

"I agree, but there's nothing else? Something had to have happened for Marie to be afraid of both you and Grace."

David shook his head.

"Could she . . ." He hated to suggest it, but he saw no other option. "Could she have mental issues like Gertie and her mother?" He didn't want to call them crazy, but ultimately, that's what was happening. His wife was going crazy, lost in a world that didn't exist, hearing voices that had never spoken a word.

"If it runs in the family, it is possible. Sometimes there's a catalyst. Almost being killed by her mother when her father was not there to protect her . . . that could have been her breaking point. She needs some time to heal before we can say for sure."

David played with the unopened beer bottle in his hands. "What do I do?" He couldn't lose his little girl. He wouldn't. He would do anything and everything to fix this.

"Give her time. While you're home, be close by, in the same room. Let her hear your voice, get used to you again." She shrugged hopelessly. "Honestly, I don't know, David."

He pushed the beer to the side. "I need to see Gertie. What should I expect? Does she need anything?"

"Maybe take one of her blankets in and some photos of you all? I haven't been to visit her since bringing Marie home. I have been calling to check on her, so they know to expect you today. Gertie has been sedated, but she seems to be . . ."

David slumped in the chair. "I promised her I'd never put her in the hospital, that I'd never let what happened to her mother happen to her."

"You can't keep a promise like that, David. Not now. She won't be coming home, not for a long time. That much I do know. They're aware of her history, and the plan is to send her to London, to the mental institution there."

Every word that came out of Grace's mouth was a stroke of death against the promise he'd made to his wife.

He swore he'd never let this happen, that he'd always take care of her, that he would move heaven and hell to ensure she didn't live the remainder of her days in the hospital.

Chapter Thirty-Five

ELLE

I'm careful to close the door behind me with only a small click. Patches winds her way around my ankles before I pick her up and walk into the kitchen. The stove light is on, and a plate of chocolate-chip cookies with a note to help myself sits on the counter beside a nice tall glass of water.

My hurting heart aches as I think about the love Grace continually shows me.

She's my great-aunt. My family. My real family. How did I not know this? How could I not tell?

I want to hug her and shake her at the same time.

Part of me hopes she'll be up so that I can tell her I know and talk to her about her brother, but there's an even larger part of me that's relieved when I come home to see all the lights out, meaning both she and Mom are in bed already.

My hand is on the stair rail when I hear a sound from the living room. A slight sniffle and the rustle of paper.

I find Grace curled up in the corner of the couch, her legs tucked in tight beneath her, blanket over her lap, folded letter in one hand. She's wiping the tears streaming down her face with the other.

"Grace?"

"Elle, honey. I'm sorry, I didn't mean to bother you." Grace struggles to produce a smile that I know isn't real.

I sit beside her on the couch and can't help but look at the letter she's holding.

"Is that from David?"

I startle her with my question.

"Why would you ask that?"

I thought about this on the drive home. How would I bring it up, the truth about her and David? Did I want her to tell me, or would I just rip the Band-Aid off?

"I've always considered you family, but I guess you really are. Aren't you, *Great-aunt* Grace?"

No sense in beating around the bush. There is so much more I want to know, need to know.

She lets out a very long sigh before leaning over and resting her head on my shoulder. We sit like that for a little bit, the truth wrapped around us like a weighted blanket. It's comforting to just be in the moment.

"I'm sorry I never told you. I wanted to, but I made a promise to your mom a long time ago that I would protect her from her memories and from David. Unfortunately, that meant keeping your family from you." She pats my hand, hoping, I'm sure, that I will accept her explanation.

After hearing Mom's story and learning why Grace became so important to her, what right do I have to argue?

"I understand. I'm not happy about being kept in the dark, but . . . I get it. At least, I think I do."

"What did David tell you?"

"How Gertie tried to kill Mom."

That pretty much sums up my mother's childhood. What else really matters?

"That's it?" she asks. "That's all he told you?"

"He fell asleep in the middle of the story. I think even getting that part out was too much for him." I pull my knees up tight to my chest.

"How was he?"

"Brenn's on shift this morning. She's not sure he'll see the night." I reach for her hand as she inhales sharply, the sound a low whistle of shock. "He made it clear he didn't want anyone there at the end."

It takes her a few moments to compose herself. The tears fall again before she gives a brief smile.

"Stubborn old mule," Grace mutters. "Once he gets an idea in his head, that's it. He's always been like that."

Does that mean he gets his way, though? Wouldn't Grace like to see him, say goodbye?

"Can I ask what happened afterward? How long did it take Mom to talk again? What happened to Gertie?" I have so many questions, so many things I need answered.

"It was sad." Grace takes a deep breath, like she's bracing herself to tell a story more than thirty years in the making. "Gertie had a complete breakdown and was a patient for ten years in a mental ward. Finally she got well enough for David to bring her home. Your mother had what you would call selective mutism, and it lasted for a year. She didn't speak again until we actually moved into this house, when she was seven years old."

The nausea I felt when David told me what Gertie did reappears now as I think of the trauma Mom must have gone through.

"How do you heal from knowing your mother tried to kill you? I can't even . . ." All I can see in my head is the image of my mom lying over the top of a grave, her wrists cut, while her own mother lay beside her.

"You don't. Not completely."

Not completely. I always thought Mom's diagnosis of dissociative identity disorder was hereditary, but now I know it's more complex than I ever imagined.

"What happened between her and David?"

The expression on Grace's face tells me she's as much in the dark as I am.

"I'm assuming he told you about the accident she had? When she fell down the hill and broke through the ice? It was a miracle Gertie found her in time, but from what David told me, she was never the same after that. At first, she couldn't handle being around Gertie. There was a fear that your mother couldn't shake. But afterward, once Gertie was in the hospital, that fear transferred onto her father. I've never been able to figure that out."

When *she* fell down the hill and broke through the ice? No mention of Bella at all.

"So he didn't do anything?"

That doesn't make sense. Why would he be dead to her, why cut him completely out of her life, out of my life, if there was no reason?

Grace leans her head back on the couch. In the dim light, I notice the weariness of age on her face.

"Maybe that's the problem. Every little girl wants her father to protect her, her mother to love her, to know that she's safe. Your mother lost that safety net and she could never quite get it back. He tried, God knows he tried, but your mom worsened each time he came home. That's when I suggested this option. Your grandfather knew the man who wanted to sell this house, so he made a deal with him and the house was placed under my name. It was far enough away from any of David's regular truck routes and from Kincardine for Marie to feel safe, but not too far away for David to be able to keep tabs on her."

I try to wrap my head around that. "He gave up on her, then" is all I can think.

Grace doesn't agree. "No, he realized in order for your mother to heal, he needed to take himself out of the equation. We didn't think it would be forever."

The regret in her voice tells me all I need to know.

"You feel responsible."

She nods. "Of course I do. Did David tell you I worked in the Vancouver hospital before I came here? It was one of the leading hospitals in the country for mental health back in the fifties. Things have changed so much since then. If your mother had been under anyone else's care, she would have been hospitalized, just like Gertie. Looking back, I see there were so many things I could have done to try and save the relationship between your mother and David, but I was too close to it. She became a daughter to me. When she started to speak again, all I wanted was for her to continue healing, even if that meant David had to remain at a distance."

She's tired. I can hear it in her voice, yet I have so many more questions to ask.

"How involved was David in our lives? Even from a distance?" I imagine he would have been. Knowing now about the familial relationship between him and Grace, I can't help but think she would have not only helped him to remain close but would also have encouraged it.

"Close enough. He would come to some of your school plays and sit in the very back, leaving before your mother could see him. Sometimes I'd call and let them know when you'd be at a park or the beach." She smiles then, and I remember the story David told of the day at the beach in Southampton.

"You gave up your life for us." When I look back on my childhood, Grace is always there.

Grace shakes her head.

"It never felt that way to me. Family is the most important thing anyone can have. My brother needed me. Then your mother needed me, and then you came along and . . . there's no other life I wanted than the one I have."

She squeezes my hand while she composes herself.

This is so much to take in. Almost too much.

"Have you kept in touch with your brother throughout the years?"

I'm still having a hard time calling him my grandfather, and I for sure know I can't call Gertie *Grandmother*. Not now. Not after finding out the truth.

"Here and there. We got together for dinner every few months or so. I shared photos of you and Marie. He missed out on so much of your lives, both of you . . ."

Her breath catches on a sob.

She pushes herself up from the couch and sways as she looks down at me.

"I'm exhausted. Would you mind helping me up the stairs? I'm afraid I feel my age tonight."

Without hesitation, I jump up. Slowly, we make our way to her room, shutting off the hall lights as we pass them.

She leans over to give me a kiss and a hug. "Thank you for being there for him and for listening to his stories. He was a good man, with so much love in his heart." She shakes her head sadly while opening her door.

"Grace?" I have to ask. I need to ask. To know for sure. To hear her say it one last time.

She turns and looks at me with the saddest eyes I've ever seen.

"Judy and Bella?"

"Not real. For the year I lived in that house, I never saw evidence they had been there." She gives me the most melancholy smile I've ever seen. "I know you want to believe his stories, to think he was telling the truth, but Bella was your mother's imaginary friend. Don't you think I would have known otherwise?"

I want to believe her. I really do. But David was adamant that they were real . . . it's hard not to be swayed by his earnestness.

"What about the graves?"

I can see the sorrow in her gaze. It's paining her that I can't let this go.

"The graves were for the stillborns." She's ever patient with me, even though I know she's tired of answering the same question over and over.

She sounds so sure.

I want to believe her. I really do.

Chapter Thirty-Six

It's another sleepless night. At two in the morning, Mom knocks on my door and asks if I'll come join her at the fire. Considering I was in the middle of a dream where she bled out over a field of flowers, I have no problem getting up. She makes us cups of hot cocoa, complete with whipped cream, while I stoke the fire.

There's a warm breeze in the night air. It's filled with the symphony of crickets. If ever there was a night I was okay with not sleeping, this would be it.

"Thanks for sitting with me," Mom says softly. "Grace doesn't like me out here alone, and I didn't want to wake her."

I hide my yawn and nod.

"Sorry, love. Why don't you go back to bed? I'll be fine out here," Mom offers.

I can tell from her voice that she really doesn't mean it.

"I wasn't having that great of a sleep anyway."

While Mom stares into the fire, her hands wrapped tight around her mug, I pull out my phone and notice five missed text messages from Brennley.

Her last message was rather insistent.

Wake up girl and call me. ASAP.

Calling her is the last thing I want to do, so I send a reply instead.

Go to bed.
Yowza! Are you seriously awake right now? Call me!

"Let me guess: Brennley? How come she hasn't come out lately?" Mom looks over at me, her body shivering slightly from the breeze. I set my cup down and pick up one of the blankets I brought out, wrapping it around her.

"She's working some weird shifts right now, but she's coming with us to Toronto for your show. I'm going to give her a quick call."

The phone doesn't even get through its first ring when she picks up.

"Oh my God, what took you so long? I was just about to hop in my car and drive up to see you. Seriously, woman, you can't ignore me like that," Brennley says in one breath.

I roll my eyes, thankful she can't see because she'd probably hit me. "What's got you so excited?" I ask.

"Did I ever tell you I had a lead on the story of Judy and Bella?"

In all honesty, if she did, I forgot about it.

"I couldn't drop it. I'm sorry if you're upset about that, but . . ." The level of her voice rises from the excitement she can barely contain.

I hate to burst her bubble, but I'm certainly not going to have this conversation in front of Mom. She waves me off as I stand.

I wait until I'm a good distance away before I speak.

"There is no Judy, Brenn. I found out they really are just imaginary friends my mom made up after a . . . really traumatic experience."

Her groan makes me pull the phone away from my ear—it's that loud.

"Are you kidding me?"

"Sorry."

I wish I were. Honestly, I wish I were. I still can't wrap my head around what Mom went through.

"How sure are you that they aren't real? Like one hundred percent sure or . . ."

I drum my fingers on the back of the phone.

"Pretty sure. Seriously. I'll share about my mom's past one night over wine."

After many, many bottles of wine.

I don't consider sharing what I found out with Brennley an act of betrayal. She's my best friend and knows more about me and my life than anyone else.

"Am I going to need to give your mom one of my famous love hugs at her showing?"

I can't help but smile.

"She loves your hugs, you know that."

"Good. Now, back to Judy. You have no doubts she's not real? 'Cause, dude . . . I think I might have found her. I found a missing persons article in the *Hamilton Gazette* in the early fifties for a Judy Miller, sixteen years old, with a baby. Parents must have had a little bit of money because they offered a reward. Neighbors speculated she ran away with her boyfriend, who drove a truck."

It sounds too good to be true. David never mentioned how old Judy was, only that she was a young mother. So if—and that's a big if—she was real . . . this could have been her.

"David was a trucker, so maybe he came in contact with that Judy or even knew the boyfriend. Maybe he always regretted not helping her, and his mind is now playing tricks on him?" I rub the back of my neck. "I don't know, Brenn. I thought they were real, but everything he told me . . . none of it adds up. Mom had a doll she used to call Isabel—"

"Which is close to Bella." The disappointment in Brennley's voice is contagious. "Well, I'm glad it's not her, then—or that the story isn't real. Could you imagine? Her parents are still alive, those poor people."

"I can't even imagine . . ." My voice trails as I yawn again.

"It was a sad story for Judy anyway. From what I gather, her parents searched for her for years, never giving up, never wanting to believe she could be dead."

That sits between us, the weight of their loss. Even though we don't know them.

"Have you heard how David is?" I can't help but ask.

Brenn inhales deeply. "Still hanging in. I thought I would go in a little early for my shift and sit with him. I'm not sure if he'll wake up or not, but . . ."

But he won't be alone.

"Thank you." I can barely get the words out. They're holed up in my throat, which feels like a small tube stuffed too full with stones and mud.

"I think Grace wants to go in first thing."

She hadn't said so, but I could see it on her face, in her eyes. She needs to say goodbye to her brother.

Family is everything.

He's her family.

"Why would Grace want to see David? Did she persuade your mom to come with her?"

Here is where I drop the bombshell and tell her about Grace and David.

"He's her brother."

There's dead silence on the other end.

"Brother. Sister. Your . . . great-aunt. What the . . ."

"Seriously. I promise I'll explain it all over wine. But for now, know that she's David's sister and gave up everything to take care of Mom when she was young. It's crazy."

Sounds even crazier when I say it like that. I made it sound so simple when it is more complex than a jigsaw puzzle.

"Mind. Blown." She makes an explosion sound. "Literally. Mind blown."

Having a friend like Brennley, who is *like* Brennley—vivacious, larger than life with no filter but the softest heart imaginable—I would be lost without her. I am lost without her.

"Thank you."

The words, the emotions, the tears, they just all flow together. I think about the craziness of my life right now and how the only sane person who keeps me grounded is her.

"You're not crying, are you? Girl . . . I love you. You know that, right? I'm here for you. Every moment, every revelation you find out. I've got your back."

By the time I make it back to Mom, she's curled up in the chair, her legs tucked beneath the blanket and her eyes closed. She doesn't hear me approach, doesn't stir as I sit back in my chair, which means she's finally fallen asleep.

Every time I close my eyes, I keep seeing her as a little girl, wrists cut, lying close to her mother, terrified as hell but trying to remain strong and silent, waiting for someone to save her.

I can't do it. Can't close my eyes, can't imagine her like that. So instead, I watch her. I see her with new eyes, with a new understanding. I stop judging her for how she raised me, letting me believe my grandparents were dead. I can sympathize with her anger toward my father. She feels like he left her, abandoned her.

After everything she's gone through, it makes sense that the only way she can cope is to completely wipe out those who left her. It breaks my heart to think she had to live like that while, at the same time, a deeper, stronger love for her as my mother grows within me.

She had a traumatic childhood full of horrors no child should have to experience. No wonder she wanted to fill my childhood with fantasy and fairy tales.

I never could understand before where the darkness she painted in her pictures came from, but now I know.

Chapter Thirty-Seven

The forty-five-minute drive to Kincardine is a silent one. While I drive, Grace sits beside me, staring out the passenger window, lost in her thoughts. I give her the space I know she needs. No questions, no barraging her with the need to know more about the past.

All of that can wait.

None of that is as important as what she's preparing herself to do: say goodbye to her brother, the man she gave up her life in Vancouver for without hesitation because he needed her.

She grabs hold of my hand, her own trembling as we walk into the hospital. There are moments when we have to stop, when it's evident that the strength to continue is taking more energy than she has.

"Can you do this?" We stop at the doors that would lead us into the geriatrics ward. I've never been in this position before, but I've watched many families walk these hallways, take this journey. I know it has to be one of the hardest things they do.

She shakes her head. I'm ready to lead her away, to take her to the ward where I work—not to get her away from David, but because I know seeing the babies will put a smile on her face.

"If you need more time . . ."

Grace swallows hard. "There is never enough time, Elle. That's something I've learned with all of this."

I push the button to open the door, and I notice an immediate change come over her. Gone is the fear, the hesitation, the unsteadiness from before. She appears to be the strong woman I've always known and counted on.

The sound of our footsteps along the linoleum floor echoes in the quiet corridor. As we round the corner, I notice the way Brennley rushes toward us, her hands outstretched—not in alarm, but almost as a warning.

But before she can say anything, a figure walks out of David's room, which is just past the nurses' station.

"Charlie's here, saying goodbye," she whispers somewhat breathlessly.

I look around her shoulder and nod.

"Looks like he's already said it." I motion behind her.

"Sorry." She winces, knowing how frustrated I feel toward the man. I can't wish him any ill will, though. He's here with David, and I'm thankful for that.

As Charlie walks toward us, Grace slows to a halt.

Neither says anything as he approaches us. He pauses like he wants to talk, but with a rough shake of his head, he mutters something unintelligible and walks on past.

Grace appears unfazed.

"He came, Elle. That says something," Brenn said.

I shrug. If we pass each other in the street in the future, I'll be cordial. But just because he knew my mother—my grandparents—and claimed them as his family doesn't mean he's part of mine.

Grace gives Brennley a long hug.

"It's been too long," Grace whispers. "Thank you for—"

"For taking care of your brother? It's been my pleasure. He's a strong man to live with the pain his body is in and still be able to fight. I don't see that often, not in here."

The three of us walk together toward David's room, all quiet, each lost in our own thoughts.

"You go in alone," I tell Grace. "I'll join you when you're ready, okay?" I know they need some privacy, time to talk, time to grieve with each other.

Brenn and I don't say much as we wait. She continues with her rounds, answering call buttons, filling out her charts. We're both tense. It's there between us, in the air, within our bodies.

How do you say goodbye to someone you barely know?

I'm not sure how to do this. I know it will provide closure, for me and for David, but is that enough?

Grace said there was never enough time, and she's right. Is it wrong of me to want more time with David? More time to build a relationship? More time to let that bond between us grow so that I could finally call him *Grandfather*?

I'm not sure how long she's in there, but it feels like time is standing still. I can only hope that comes as a gift for them both. When she finally comes out of his room, her eyes are sparkling with tears, but the smile on her face is the brightest I've seen in years.

"Elle, love. Come on in."

She wraps me in her arms, whispers how much she loves me into my ear before we walk into David's room together, arm in arm.

I don't think there's any right way to say goodbye to a man ready to die. I wish there was a way to beg him to stay, but I can see from the weariness in his eyes, from the tightness in his smile, that he's ready to go.

With Grace's arm wrapped around my waist, I wish that, just once, I could have felt David's arms around me. What would it have been like to be held in his arms, to cuddle up next to him and have him tell me stories at night?

In that moment, I see what my life could have been like as a little girl with him. The early mornings sitting at the kitchen table with toast and tea, the walks through the fields as he told me stories of what his life had been like as a young farm boy. I could feel his whisker rubs along my sensitive cheek, hear his belly laugh as I giggle during our tickling wars. He could have taught me how to drive, told me about the boys to stay away from, teased me into laughter when all I wanted to do was cry.

I can see the love he feels for me. I know above all things, regardless of everything, that love is real and true.

"Don't you cry, child." The coarseness of David's voice confirms the amount of pain he's in. "I'm not worth those tears."

Grace comes to my defense, even though I know he only said it to help me regain my composure.

"You leave her be, David Walker. Let her cry for you. Consider it a gift you don't deserve."

I wait for Grace to sit in one chair; then I sit in the other. We both move our chairs as close as we can to his bed, but it still doesn't feel like it's close enough.

"If there's one thing my sister is good at, it's not listening to a damn word I say."

Despite his hard words, there's a slight lift to his lips, indicating a smile.

"Why would I start now, you old fool?" Grace shakes her head and wipes at tears sliding down her cheeks. "I don't care what you say—you don't want to die alone, and you know it."

David gives his typical *harrumph* before he closes his eyes in pain.

"Can I hit your button for you, David?" It doesn't need to hurt— not now, not when he's at the end.

"The pain's the only thing letting me know"—his chest rattles as he struggles to take a breath—"I'm still alive."

It takes every ounce of self-control not to hit that button for him.

"I'm ready," he says. He looks at me, his gaze sliding over every inch of my face, as if memorizing my image. "I'm ready to go." He doesn't take his gaze off me.

Is he hoping I'll be the last thing he sees? If so, then I will ensure he sees a smile on my lips, love in my eyes as he takes his last breath.

"I'm not ready to say goodbye," I tell him. "I'm not ready to let you go. I don't care about the past and the mistakes you made. I want more time with you."

I can't look away, no matter how much I want to. So I let the tears fall, never once tearing my gaze from his.

"You're a gift to me." The words breathe out of him, soft as a sword slicing through butter. "Knowing you—it's all I ever wanted. I don't deserve you."

I lean forward and rest my hand beside his. I won't touch him because that will only add to his pain—but I want him to know I wish I could.

"You are my family," I whisper.

His hand grabs hold of mine. His grip isn't strong, but it's there. I can tell it hurts to touch me, to press with the minuscule amount of pressure he's able to give. I can see the shock waves of pain radiate up his arm. I hear the slight gasp, but I don't move my hand from beneath his.

If this is his final act, his final wish—to hold my hand, his granddaughter's hand—then so be it.

"Family," he whispers. The briefest of smiles settles upon his face. "Family," he says again, this time so faint I almost don't hear him.

Nothing else. The monitors that used to beep on a regular basis have been shut off, something Brennley told me had been done earlier, at his request.

There's complete silence among the three of us as he breathes his last breath.

I don't take my gaze from his even as I watch the life—his life—disappear.

Grace sobs then. Large, loud wails tear out of her tiny frame.

I slowly withdraw my hand from beneath his, not wanting to lose that connection but knowing my other family—this woman who's loved me my whole life—needs me now more than he does. I wrap my arms around her, hold her tight as her body shakes against mine. Our tears fall together as we allow ourselves to grieve.

There's never enough time. Never.

Chapter Thirty-Eight

The drive home is as quiet as the drive to the hospital was.

When we arrive, Grace heads upstairs to lie down, needing a little bit of time to collect herself. I go to find Mom, who I know will be in her studio, tucked away in the corner, partially hidden by the large canvas she's been working on. Soft symphony music fills the air. No matter how many times I call out to her, she doesn't hear me.

So I do what I've always done. I pull out a stool, set the coffee I've made down on the bench, and wait.

It only takes her ten minutes to notice me.

"Elle, how long have you been here?" She lays down her brush and heads to the sink to wash paint stains from her hands.

I put the book I've been reading down, careful to use a bookmark to hold my spot and not dog-ear the page.

"Oh, I see you're reading *The Good Liar* by Catherine Mackenzie. Grace picked it up thinking I might enjoy it."

"It's good." I can't remember the last time I sat down and just read a book, but there's something about this one that catches my attention.

"Is Grace okay?" Mom wipes her hands on her apron before taking it off. "I thought she'd be out here with me, not want to be alone."

We agreed not to tell Mom until all three of us were together. Grace said she wouldn't be long; she just needed a little rest.

"She's okay and will join us soon."

She pulls a stool out beside me and rests her head on my shoulder.

"We should be doing something fun together, like working in the garden or going to a movie or farmers' market, instead of being cooped up in this garage while you watch me paint." She straightens and pats my knee. "I'm almost done. Then I promised Grace I'd relax."

"I know you're trying to get it done in time for the showing next week."

She stares at her work area, and her brows knit together while she nibbles on her lip.

"There are a few areas that aren't coming out like I'd hoped."

"Can I see?" I need something, anything, to keep me occupied—and my mind off David's death.

She shakes her head. "Not yet. It needs . . . it needs to be perfect." She chews her lip even more.

"Why don't you come in the house for a bit, for a snack? We could sit out on the back deck for a little while before you get back to work."

It's a long shot, trying to drag my mother away from her work, but I have to try.

The torn gaze she casts toward her easel makes me hop off my stool.

"Tell you what, I'll let you get back to work. I'll bring a tray of fresh fruit out for you."

Her sigh of relief doesn't surprise me. I head back toward the house.

Thankfully, Grace has containers of fresh-cut fruit and veggies in the fridge, so all I need to do is fill glasses with iced tea. I take my time, knowing it doesn't matter when I make it back out there. She won't even notice me. I think about checking in on Grace, just to make sure she really is okay, but I stop myself, knowing she will come down when she's ready.

I add a few more ice cubes to the glasses of tea and make my way outside, careful to sidestep Patches, who lies in the middle of the floor, soaking up the summer sun.

As expected, Mom has no idea when I return. The music is louder, and she's so focused on her painting that I know if I don't interrupt her now, she'll never take time to eat.

I set the tray down on the workbench and make my way past the dollhouse. I stand in front of Mom but off to the side, so if she does glance my way, she'll see me.

It takes her a few minutes.

"Can I see? I promise to keep any opinions to myself until you're completely finished."

She looks at me, then at the painting, before she nods. She carefully puts the brush down in a jar of liquid and steps back, giving me space to walk around the easel and see the painting in all its beautiful glory.

And it is beautiful. Also achingly familiar.

It's a scene I've seen many times. It's similar to what is in the sitting room in the house. I'm not sure how this painting ties all the ones for her show together, though.

"This is . . ."

"It's not for the showing next week. I know that's what you and Grace think I've been working on, but it's not." She picks up a different brush and works on one of the white flowers, adding more shade to the petal. "I need it completed before . . . I just need it done. This is . . ." She struggles to get the words out, to put into a sentence how she's really feeling.

She doesn't need to, though. I know exactly what it is.

Among a field of tiny white flowers, there's a soft yellow blanket. A delicate tea set is arranged on that blanket: two cups and saucers, one teapot, a plate of macarons and berries. It is a beautiful, peaceful painting that makes you wish you were a little girl getting ready for a party. It's everything fairy tales and bedtime stories are made of. Just viewing this painting helps you believe in better days, happier days.

It's a scene Mom has painted many times over, when she's lost in her memories of a happier time. I used to think it was from when she was a young child, but now I believe it's from my childhood, which she prefers to dwell on.

There's one difference, however, on this canvas compared with all her others.

Hidden amid the flowers, so hidden you can barely see them, are four white crosses.

Written on three crosses in a soft shade of gray are the names "Bella," "Judy," and "Gertie." One cross remains plain, unmarked.

Mom's arm sneaks around my waist, and she lays her head against mine.

"This is my way of saying goodbye. Once his name is on that cross, it's done. Over. A memory that can finally fade with time."

There's a sadness in her voice that tethers our hearts together.

"I'm so sorry, Mom." I don't know what else to say. My heart breaks for her, for the memories she wants to forget, needs to forget.

Will she be at peace now, once she finds out David is gone?

"Grace told me you knew. I never wanted you to know. Never." There's a wetness on my shoulder from the tears trailing down my mom's cheeks. She lifts her head. "My memories were never meant to be yours. He should never have done that to you. That's not love, Elizabeth."

I can't take my eyes off the painting. Listening to Mom's words, I know there's more to this than meets the eye. There usually is.

This is her way of saying goodbye. To the childhood she had, to the one she created, to the parents who tried their best, to the memories of the pain she lived with.

Will she be free now? Now that David is dead? Will that be what she needs to calm her soul? To ease that pain?

I hope so.

"I haven't lost you, have I?"

"No, of course not." There's a look of uncertainty on her face that bothers me. "Mom, why would you think that?"

She blinks several times.

"You're the only thing that grounds me in who I am. Nothing else in my life matters. The painting, this house, the memories . . ." She gathers me close for a tight hug. "Being your mother has been the one true thing in my life. I know I didn't make things easy for you, but all I've ever wanted to do was love you completely."

I close my eyes. An overwhelming tidal wave of emotion hits me when she hugs me.

"You'll never lose me. I will always love you." I hug her back just as hard, thankful for this moment with her.

She pulls away, places both hands on my cheeks. "You have always been the best thing that happened to me. Always. You were my fairy tale come true, and you still are. I'm so proud of you and who you've become." She laughs then, wiping away the tears that trickle down her face. "Look at me, a sodding mess. Let's take that tray out to the garden. We'll enjoy the sun for a little while. This painting isn't going anywhere."

She tugs me toward the door, gathers the tray, and waits for me to join her on the walkway.

We round the corner and see Grace sitting on the deck, a glass of wine in hand. She has the emptiest look on her face.

Mom drops the tray she is carrying while my feet became concrete stones. Every step I take toward Grace feels like pushing against a gust of wind determined to keep me away.

"He's finally gone, then," Mom says as I sit on the step beside Grace's chair.

Grace nods and takes a sip of her wine.

The weight of grief is heavy. I don't cry. I can't. Not again. Not right now.

None of us does.

Not the sister who just said goodbye.

Not the daughter who deemed him dead a long time ago.

Not the granddaughter who just met him.

We just sit there, in silence.

Chapter Thirty-Nine

I'm scared.

All the time.

I'm cold too. I sit in front of the fire, and sometimes I wish I could live in the fire, just to get warm again.

I never want to go outside again.

Mommy talks to me, all day, but I pretend to ignore her. She is making me a sweater, a new one that is just for me. But I don't want it to be just for me. I want her to make one for sister too.

Except, sister is gone.

I'm all alone now and I don't want to be all alone.

Mommy says one day we will be with my sisters forever, that it's almost time. She scares me too.

I want my real mommy back. The one who would bake with me and read me stories and braid my hair. The one who didn't scare me so much.

She says I have to change my name. That I have to be two people at the same time and that I can never tell anyone my real name. She says bad things will happen if people find out there were two of us.

Now that Aunt Grace is here, Mommy doesn't talk to me as much. Aunt Grace spends a lot of time with me, she tells me stories, reads me books and makes me the good tea. Not the tea Mommy used to make me.

I like Aunt Grace and wish she was my real mommy.

Chapter Forty

David Basil Walker's funeral is a family affair. He had specific instructions regarding what should happen to his body after his death. No service, no memorial—just cremation and then be laid to rest beside his wife.

We stand at the graveside, the three of us. The sun hides behind heavy gray clouds that look like they could open up anytime, which makes me glad I carried an umbrella, just in case. It would be fitting if it did rain. From the moment we left the house that morning, no one has said a word.

I was shocked when Mom joined us downstairs this morning in a black dress. She made it very clear over toast and coffee that she was only going to support Grace.

But as we stand there, listening to the pastor quote scripture over the ashes of a man who believed he was condemned, I catch the slight tremor that flows through Mom. I hold her hand.

The moment the word *amen* is spoken, Mom pulls her grasp from mine and heads back to the car.

Grace doesn't move a muscle.

"He had a heavy burden," she finally breathes, the words low, like the subtle notes of a wind chime. "But he loved his family more than anything else."

He had a weird concept of love, then. Since his death, I've been trying to work out exactly who David Basil Walker was.

Was he the man in his stories, who buried bodies behind his garage to protect his family?

Was he a man with so much guilt over having to choose between wife and daughter that he finally crumbled beneath the weight?

Was he a man who did the best he could, even to the point of reaching out for help when he realized his best wasn't enough?

I will never know the truth, but I have a feeling he was a mixture of all three.

I wait for Grace, not wanting to leave her alone but, at the same time, torn because Mom is.

"He loved you." Grace puts her arm around my waist. "You visiting him was the best thing to happen to him in years. I can't thank you enough for that."

"I wish . . . I wish I had known him better. Had more time with him." There's an ache in my heart, if I'm being honest. No matter what kind of person he was, he was still my grandfather. Still family—and isn't family supposed to be everything?

"I hope you're wrong, David. I hope you've found your way to Gertie." Grace kneels down and places her palm on the dirt. "Sometimes love is enough, you old grump. I know God had enough love for the both of you, no matter what you thought you did to make Him turn from you." She heaves a long sigh, her body almost collapsing upon itself like a house of cards crumbling from a slight touch.

I wrap my arm around her waist to help her stand.

"I just need a minute," she whispers as she struggles to stand on her own.

"Take as long as you need. There's no rush."

Every time Grace tries to turn away from the grave, she stops. It's as if there's a magnet pulling her back.

"It's hard saying goodbye."

"Then don't," I say. "There's no reason you have to. Not today. It's just for now, until you see him again."

I know there are no words to help ease her pain, her grief, her sorrow. But the slight twist of her mouth, the half smile that isn't quite a smile, tells me it doesn't matter.

"Thank you, love. You're right. This isn't the end, it's just a detour in our journey as a family." She inhales sharply, straightening her shoulders as she does so.

When we turn to head back to join my mom at the car, we see Charlie standing next to her.

"Another casualty in the world of David and Gertie," Grace mumbles softly.

"I wanted to pay my respects but didn't want to intrude," he says.

I'm too focused on Mom to pay him any attention. She's pale, her arms soldier straight at her sides, and her hands are fisted, turning her knuckles white. She's furious.

Why?

Charlie shuffles his feet. I'm not sure who's the most uncomfortable—him or us.

"I don't suppose you remember me, Marie?" Charlie swallows hard, his Adam's apple bobbing, as if in a barrel of water.

"I remember you." She looks back toward the grave, a look of closure on her face. "I wish to God I didn't. Why are you here?"

I look at Mom in shock. The disdain in her voice is unexpected. Like finding out the sweet little puppy you adopted is really a snarling, ankle-biting, rabid wolf.

"Listen, I . . ." Charlie stalls, rubs the back of his neck, and grimaces. "Maybe this was a bad idea," he mutters.

"Why did you come, Charlie?" Grace asks while Mom turns away, her arms crossed tight over her chest.

She won't look at him. In fact, her eyes are clamped shut, as if trying to block something out. But what? The sound of his voice? The memories his being here brings up? Is she remembering something from when she was little?

"I . . . there's something I need to tell you." He coughs and sticks his hands in his pants pockets. "Something that concerns you, Marie."

Mom shakes her head, her lips thinning into a straight white line.

"Please? Let me buy you ladies a coffee or something. I promised . . ." He looks up into the sky and grimaces. "I promised I wouldn't tell until now."

"Tell me what?" Mom still won't look at him.

"This is a story best told sitting down."

I half turn away, just in time to roll my eyes. I can't help myself. Another story. Another lure of untold truths.

"A story? What about?" There's a mixture of fear and anger I can't place in Mom's voice.

I cast Grace a worried look. One moment Mom was ready to leave, disengaged and pale. Now she appears cold and furious.

Mom never gets furious.

"About the last time I saw you." He looks to Grace, then to me, then to Mom. He's unsure of what he should say or maybe how to say it. "When I rescued you after you fell down that hill."

"My mother dragged me back up the hill. You were never there." Mom steps closer to him, challenging his story.

"I was there."

This doesn't make sense.

"Please let me explain over coffee," Charlie begs. He sounds conflicted, like a man who needs to get something off his chest but isn't sure he can or should.

"One coffee, without *any* lies. Understood?" Mom dismisses him, sits in the car, and closes the door.

Grace and I look at each other, completely lost.

Who is this woman?

We agree to meet up at a coffee shop down the road, then join Mom in the car.

"Marie, are you sure? We can leave all this behind now." Grace half turns in the seat to face Mom, who sits in the back. "There's no need to drag all of this up. Not anymore."

I don't start the car. "Mom? Are you okay? We don't have to do this."

She's rock solid, her face edged in granite, her eyes fused with purpose.

"We do, and I'm fine, Elizabeth. Grace, I want to know why he would lie to us, at *his* graveside." She nudges her head toward the window in the direction of David's grave. "He was never there," she whispers, not sounding as sure as she had just minutes ago. "She dragged me up the hill. I'm sure of it. I can still feel the pull on my arms and the pain." She rubs her forearms. "I don't ever remember being in so much pain." She closes her eyes as the memories assault her.

"Marie." Grace reaches out and lightly settles her hand on Mom's knee. "Let's go home, okay?"

Mom shakes her head, her eyes open and as clear as the sky above us. "We can't rely on my memories, we all know that. If he was there . . . maybe he knows what really happened. Maybe"—her voice hitches—"maybe he can tell me why I became Marie after that day."

"You didn't become anyone. You already were," Grace says. She turns to me. "I don't like this. Let's just go home," she says quietly.

I watch Mom in the mirror. She's pensive as she stares out her side window.

What's the right thing to do? What if Charlie really had been there? Maybe it would be good for her to know the truth, to hear what actually happened rather than rely on painful memories that could possibly be distorted.

I'll admit, I'm curious. Is that wrong of me? David only told me what Gertie told him. What if Gertie lied?

"No. I want to hear him out." Mom tears her gaze from the cemetery and looks me straight in the eye via the rearview mirror. "Let's just get this day over with so we can go home and, for once, move forward with our lives without the past hanging over us." She leans forward and pats Grace's hair. "I'll be fine as long as I have you both by my side."

"For the record, this is a mistake," Grace tells her.

Mom shrugs. "Maybe. But there's so much I don't remember, so many things we've always questioned. Wouldn't it be nice to finally get some answers?"

Grace sighs.

"I'm not so sure answers are what we're going to get."

～

Charlie is waiting for us. He's grabbed a corner table where we can be alone. There are four coffee cups on the table and a carafe of coffee in the middle.

No one says anything for the longest time. We all prepare our coffee and sip while waiting for Charlie to find the words to begin his story.

"I made a promise to your mother never to breathe a word of this until both she and David were dead. I'd always hoped I'd be the first to go." Charlie finally finds the courage to speak. "There's no easy way to explain what happened, and I won't be asking for your forgiveness, Marie. But I will tell you I'm sorry, so very sorry, for what happened to you."

It's odd to hear an apology come from his rough-and-gruff voice.

"What exactly do you think happened to me?" Mom keeps her eyes downcast on her mug, her finger running around the rim over and over. She bubbles over with suppressed fury.

I wish I could understand why she's being like this. What is it about Charlie that's setting her off like a wound-up frog that can't stop jumping?

"What do you remember?" Charlie clears his throat.

"Charlie, today's been a long day," Grace interrupts. "Maybe if you could just give us the short version, please?"

She looks tired. Tired and aged. I often forget about how old Grace must be. She's got to be in her late seventies, although she looks at least twenty years younger—and acts like it too. Except for today. Today she's weary and exhausted. This is all too much for her.

I choke on the sip of coffee I've just swallowed when I see the regret on Charlie's face.

"I wish I could," he says. "I never thought I'd be the one to tell you, truth be told."

"And I wish I didn't need to hear it, but we're here. So tell me. Did I really just fall, or did my mother push me down that hill?"

"What?" Charlie leans back, taken by surprise. "Gertie loved you to the moon and back. Why would you think she'd do such a thing? No, no," he sputters, "of course she didn't. She was with me when it all happened."

We all sit there, eyes wide open, mouths gaping at the bombshell he's just dropped.

"You had an affair with my brother's wife?" Grace's brow rises to her hairline, and by the way her lips thin, you can tell she's angry.

"No, no. Nothing like that." Charlie leans back, ruffles his fingers through his hair. "I would never do that to David or Gertie. They were family.

"Listen. Back then, the three of us, we were tight. I loved Gertie, sure, but she loved David more. I never asked her to betray him like that. But I was there for her, you know? I made sure I was there for her. It wasn't until the summer of '56 that things changed. I didn't understand what happened. One day, all was fine and I was sitting at their table eating Gertie's awesome apple pie, and the next, David meets me in the driveway and tells me Gertie doesn't want me around anymore. I knew something was off." He clears his throat, takes a sip of his coffee, and looks off to the side.

"Gertie wasn't a strong woman. Not emotionally, at least. Something broke inside of her after losing so many of her babies."

I watch Mom out of the corner of my eye, judging her reaction to Charlie's memories. There is a slight tremor in her arms she tries to hide, and her breath hitches. It's as if he's knocked the air from her lungs with the mention of the babies.

"I was worried. Worried that something had happened, that maybe she wasn't well and David was trying to protect her, hide her from the gossips in town. But this was me. He should have known I'd do anything to help him protect her. But he pushed me away. I'm a big enough man to admit it hurt. A lot. We both drove trucks for the same company. One month he was on a route that had him home every night like clockwork. The next month, he was on a route taking him away for nights at a time. Eventually he would only come home on weekends. That's when Gertie called me."

"She called you?"

He nods. "At first, it was to help her around the property. A pipe burst, a burner on the stove broke, things she needed a man to fix. Then she'd wave me down as I drove by and tell me she had a pie in the oven. Eventually we devised a system. If the front light was on and David's truck wasn't in the yard, I was to stop by. She was lonely and needed company, you know? It was always at night, after you were in bed."

"And you're telling us nothing happened?" Grace asks. I think we all could see where this was headed. Lonely woman needing the touch of a lonely man. To be honest, the idea disgusts me.

"For Pete's sake, woman. That's what I said, wasn't it?" He pours himself another cup of coffee, muttering beneath his breath something about women assuming they knew men better than the men did.

"There's a reason why I mention I always visited at night. If you'll let me finish, you'll understand." The slump of his shoulders while he rubs his face says this next bit will be tough for him to tell.

"I tried to drop by more often in the winter. I wanted to make sure there was enough wood for the fireplace, that you all were okay. I always expected David to confront me in the truck yard about the wood. I figured he had to notice, but he never did. That wasn't the only reason that I tried to stop in more often, though. I was worried about Gertie. Something wasn't right. She would say things that didn't make sense, talk about her children as if they were alive in one breath and then say something about how her babies had a new mother in the next. I was worried she'd crossed that line, you know, the one where you're mentally stable one day and something snaps the next? I knew about her mother. I even took Gertie once to go see her in the hospital, before things got serious with David. I was worried that had finally happened to her. God, it broke my heart to think so. I was prepared to confront David about it, to tell him she needed help, to force him to get her help. Because I wasn't sure, to be honest, just how safe you were." He stares my mother full in the face, his gaze apologetic, his voice full of regret.

"I wasn't safe."

"I'm sorry."

Mom's brow rises, basically saying *and so?*

"I gave you a doll for your birthday that year. I don't know if you remember."

"I don't."

He shrugs. "You were a little thing; I'm not surprised. Gertie used to tell me stories about you whenever I stopped in, since you were always in bed. She'd show me the pictures you drew, the stories you wrote down in this little paper notebook. I couldn't get over that someone so small could write like you could. She showed me the playroom David built and told me about the tea parties you and Bella would have. I always figured Bella was the name you gave the doll."

I'm in the middle of bringing my half-empty coffee cup to my lips when he mentions Bella. The cup slips from my grasp, hitting the table on an angle and spilling liquid across the surface. My heart pushes against the skin of my chest. All I can hear is the double beat of the blood pumping through the organ. Anything else Charlie says is mumbled.

I can't move. Mom is the first to jump up and grab a handful of napkins to clean up my mess. Grace stares at me with horror—a look I'm sure I mirror.

I try to tamp down the questions going through my brain, but it's like a wind-up jack-in-the-box has been released. There are so many emotions running through me, so many questions I want to blurt out. If it wasn't for Grace's gentle touch on my arm, I'm not sure if I could have restrained myself. I can see her lips move, but I'm not sure what she's saying.

"I'm sorry?" I shake my head, forcing the endless loop of *what-the-hell-did-he-just-say* to stop.

"Elle, do you want more?" she repeats.

"More what?" I'm lost. It takes me a moment to realize she's holding the carafe in her hand and is ready to refill my cup with coffee. "Oh, yes, please. Thanks."

"It was a few weeks before Christmas," Charlie continues once Mom sits back down. "I finished my run early and was headed home. It was close to dinner. I was about half a mile out from the house when

I saw a figure standing in the middle of the road. I slowed down. There was a thin covering of ice on the road. I pulled over when I realized it was Gertie, waving her arms like a crazy woman. She didn't have a coat on, and her teeth were chattering so fast I could barely understand a word out of her mouth. When she dragged me to the edge of the road and pointed down to the creek, I swear my heart stopped."

By now, he has our full attention. No one moves. Mom reaches over to grab hold of my hand and squeezes hard.

"You'd fallen down the hill—you and another little girl. I'm not sure what you were doing there. It was steep, and you would have known better than to play there, let alone try to climb down it in the middle of winter. The ice along the creek was cracked, and there was a body lying on the bank. I rushed down, half sliding, breaking the skin on my hands on the rocks before I reached you both."

His crystal-blue eyes swim with tears as he stares at Mom.

"I didn't know who was who. Gertie was yelling at me from above, but I couldn't make out her words over the wind. I would have sworn you were twins. You were wearing the exact same colored pants and same hand-knit sweater. You were both lying on your backs, blood everywhere, your faces badly battered and bruised. I couldn't tell who was who. I should have been able to—you used to call me Uncle Charlie." His body shakes as he struggles to rein in his emotions. "I checked you both. Only one was breathing. That's who I brought up first." He looks away, his chest heaving as he breathes in deep.

"Gertie carried you into the house while I went back to retrieve the other girl. I tried to clean her face, brush away the snow and dirt, but the skin was all torn from the fall and then the ice. Her eyes were open. I'll never forget that blank look. I could have sworn it was you. I thought it was you from the eyes, and my heart broke. I sobbed. I'm not ashamed to admit it."

"It wasn't me," Mom whispers. "It wasn't me, right?" She directs this question to Grace before leaning forward and placing both palms on the table. "It wasn't me. Say it!" she insists. "Say it!" She slaps the table with her hand, causing everyone to jump.

"I can't." The regret is back in his voice.

"What do you mean you *can't* say it? If you were so close to us that I called you *Uncle*, then why couldn't you tell us apart?" Mom's eyes are wide with fear.

My heart pounds like a native drum during a ritual ceremony.

"You don't understand. I have no idea how long you were down there for, but it was long enough that you weren't recognizable."

Mom begins to shake then, the tremors ricocheting through her body with lightning speed. Both Grace and I reach out at the same time to place our hands on her, let her know she isn't alone. She's so focused on Charlie, I doubt she even knows we're there.

"I brought the other girl into the house and laid her on the couch," Charlie continues. "Gertie was up running a bath, to clean you up and get you warm. You were in so much pain, I could hear you crying through the floor. I didn't know what to do. I didn't know who the little girl was, so I did my best to clean her face and hands with a cloth, but it was hard. I don't know how long she was facedown in the water for, but between the cuts and bruising, her swollen face was unrecognizable."

Mom's hand goes to her cheek while he describes his memory, her fingers lightly follow the contours of her cheekbone, her nose, as if trying to remember that day.

How much does she remember? How much of it did she block out?

"Gertie's explanation never made sense to me. She begged me to dig a hole using David's tractor so that she could bury the little girl next to her babies. She was insistent. I wanted to call David, to contact the police, but she wouldn't hear of it. She told me David had no idea the girl was there, that God had brought her as a gift. She begged me to help her, to dig a hole, said that she would do the rest." He rubs his face repeatedly as he tells this part while we all sit staring at him in shock.

"I don't know why I did it. I don't know why I didn't just take that girl to the hospital, claim I found her somewhere on the road. I should have. But Gertie . . . she was falling apart. I just wanted to help her. So I dug the hole. She begged me to keep this between us, to never tell a soul, that if I breathed a word of it she would hate me forever. I couldn't . . . you have to understand. Back then, things were different. We took care of our own. Gertie, she had a thing about doctors and hospitals and . . ." He turns his coffee cup in his hand, round and round, while he tries to give an explanation that will condone what he's done.

Except there isn't one.

There will never be one.

Everything David told me—it was true.

Judy and Bella . . . they were real. They were real people. Now they're buried behind the garage on David's property.

"So you buried that little girl, then?" The words come out slowly while Grace struggles to put together the pieces of a puzzle she never believed existed. "But who did you bury? Gertie must have known, right? She had to know which one her daughter was. She had to."

Charlie doesn't reply. I'm not sure if it's because he doesn't know or he doesn't want to say.

"As long as she had a daughter, though, that's all that mattered. Right?" The horror of her words settles upon us all.

"Bella was real," Mom whispers as if she can't believe it. "I thought she was someone I made up, someone only in my head. But she was real." The amazement on her face is incredible, hopeful even. Until it isn't. "Or am I Bella? Did you bury the wrong person?

Did you bury Anna Marie?" She covers her mouth with her hands in fear and looks at me, needing help, reassurance she is who she always thought she was.

"I don't know who I buried," Charlie admits. "I couldn't tell the difference between the two of you, but Gertie wouldn't have buried her daughter without telling David. I know she wouldn't have."

"She would if she were crazy." Mom shudders, her monotone voice sending shivers up my own spine. "If we weren't recognizable, she would have just picked the one still breathing to be her daughter."

She turns to Grace, tears filling her wide eyes. "That's why my name was changed. Anna Marie, Bella Marie—it wasn't a hard switch. Oh my God, Grace. I can't . . ."

Grace casts Charlie the deadliest of looks before she pushes her chair away and kneels at Mom's side.

"We will figure this out, Marie." She takes both of Mom's hands in her own. "We'll figure it out, I promise."

"Bella was the artist. She was the one who would draw pictures all the time, not me. I liked to write stories. Remember? I have all those notebooks in my closet. But . . . if I'm Bella . . ." She hides her face in her hands. "Who am I, Grace? Who am I?"

"You are Marie Walker. Daughter of David and Gertie Walker. A famous artist and mother to an amazing woman," Grace reminds her.

"But I'm not always me, am I?"

There's the crux of it. Mom was diagnosed with dissociative identity disorder, just after I was born. During times of stress, and when she felt most out of control, she would resort to another personality. For years, you never knew who was the dominant one.

"You created Marie—you—so that she would never be forgotten," Grace says. "I was there, remember? Afterward? I came to help take care of you, to protect you . . ." Grace catches herself before she says any more.

But she's already said enough.

Mom continues to tremble as tears cascade down her cheeks.

"That's not the Gertie I knew." Charlie tries to be reassuring, but it falls flat.

"The Gertie you knew disappeared when David told you not to come around," Marie says.

We leave Charlie at the table while we help Mom out of the small café and into the car.

No one speaks. For the forty-five minutes it takes to get to the house, we all remain silent, letting Charlie's story, the real story of what happened that horrible day, sink in.

Chapter Forty-One

The storm finally hits.

Grace and I sit at the kitchen table while thunder shakes the house. We lost power about an hour ago.

Every candle we could find is lit, illuminating the kitchen, stairway, and living room with a soft glow. The table is loaded with containers of ice cream that we've pulled out of the freezer.

Mom is up in her room, hopefully sound asleep. Grace stayed with her, talking her through things, until the medication finally took over and she fell asleep, her pillow stained with tears.

The violent storm outside mirrors the storm in our hearts.

I can't wrap my head around it all still. Every time I go to bring it up, I stop myself, unsure of even what to say.

So in the end, I say nothing.

We say nothing. What is there to say? I can't even put into words how I feel.

Mom isn't Mom. Or rather, not the person she thinks she is.

How do you process that? How do you wrap your head around the fact the person you thought you are is actually dead and you've taken her place?

In so many ways, this makes sense.

"This doesn't make sense at all." The disgust in Grace's voice makes me realize I've spoken out loud. "I was there, just after the accident," she says. "There was never any indication from David, Gertie, or Marie that she was Bella."

"Are you sure?"

"Of course I'm sure. A parent knows his child. David would have known right away."

I hate to say it, but . . .

"Unless he didn't want to see it."

The denial on Grace's face says she doesn't believe it. I don't blame her. I wouldn't want to either. For Mom's sake, I hope he never knew.

"Her family . . . ," Grace groans. "Her real family needs to be told." Grace leans forward, her head dropping as she grips her knees. "How . . . I can't . . . after all these years . . ." Her body folds, her shoulders move toward her knees, her head curls into her chest, as if trying to hide from the pain of reality.

"Who do we tell them Mom is?" I'm having a hard time accepting my mother is Bella and not Anna Marie. Of course Judy's family needs to be notified. They deserve closure, but . . .

"And the police." Grace takes a tissue from her sleeve and wipes her eyes. "This is such a nightmare."

I reach for a pad of paper on the table and start to make a list of things that need to be completed.

1.   Contact Judy's family and somehow explain what happened. But what will I say? Hello, I'm Elizabeth, your possible granddaughter? Or the granddaughter of the people who killed your daughter?
2.   Contact the police.
3.   The graves. Who exactly did Charlie bury?
4.   Mom's showing. Do we cancel it or keep it? Explain why we can't be there in person?

Grace is right. This is a nightmare.

So many things don't add up . . . or do, depending on how you look at it.

"Both her wrists were broken. She had to relearn to draw and write." She hems and haws for a moment. "Her reaction was—well, it was reactive, but not surprising. Everyone has a breaking point, and I always thought the accident was Marie's."

My stomach recoils like a rattlesnake about to strike. I feel ready to vomit.

This can't be happening.

"Mom." What must she be thinking? Feeling?

"She's asleep. I hope."

The sound of a door opening says otherwise.

"She's not." I push myself up from the chair and stand at the bottom of the stairs, waiting for Mom as she walks down, a notebook held tight to her chest. "How are you doing? Do you need anything? Some water? Wine? A time machine so we can start this day over?" I attempt to smile and to bring a smile to her face, knowing that trying to ignore everything that has happened would be worthless.

She pats my face and giggles.

"Are you going to be my fairy godmother and wave your wand? Do I get three wishes?" She winks as she passes me.

Why isn't she crying? Or screaming bloody murder? Why isn't she confused and emotional and curled up into a ball, grieving over a girl who used to be her friend?

"Mom?"

"Yes, dear?" She's pouring herself a glass of white wine.

I'm about to ask her if she should be drinking, but after the day we've all had, emptying a few bottles is the least of our worries.

"The worst that will happen is I get drowsy and fall asleep during dessert. I'm an adult, Elle. I want to celebrate my father's death with a glass of wine, so do not say anything to me about mixing alcohol and drugs, okay?" She rolls her eyes as I hold up my hands in surrender.

If she wants to pretend there's nothing wrong, then so be it. After a day like today, a little avoidance is permitted.

"Grace? Could you use a glass as well?"

"I won't turn it down."

We both watch Mom like hawks circling prey. A shared glance between the two of us confirms we're both not only concerned about Mom's reaction but confused as well.

"I'm not Bella," she announces when she sits down at the table.

Her eyes are clear, bright, and focused. The smile on her face is sad but steady, sure. She places a hand on the book she's brought with her and lightly strokes it with her finger.

"I'm not Bella," she repeats. "But Bella was real. She was a year older than me, but we could have been twins, we looked so much alike. She was my best friend, and I loved her like a sister. She was real, not someone I made up to help me get through each day with a crazy mother."

She pats the notebook.

"I know because of my journal. I found it in my closet."

There are tears in Grace's eyes.

"I wrote in this journal. As Anna Marie. Not Bella Marie. I kept my deepest secrets here, my thoughts, especially when I couldn't say them out loud. Grace, you remember that year when I was mute? Selective mutism, I think is what you called it. I might not have been able to speak about what I went through, but it's all here."

"All of it? Even Judy and her death?" I can't help but ask.

Mom nods. "Even that. There's a letter inside the journal Gertie wrote. One of my journal entries says that I found this letter in a drawer and didn't want David to find it, so I hid it from him." She opens the front cover and takes out a folded piece of paper. It has yellowed around the edges, and it crinkles as she opens it and then hands it to Grace.

Mom sips her wine, but I can't tear my attention from Grace as she reads the letter.

The letter shakes as she holds it. I could see the interest in Grace's eyes turn to dismay and then sadness as she reads. Once she's done, she passes it to me to read.

Mom nods that it's okay.

Gertie wrote this letter to Judy—after she died.

> Dear Judy,
> I believe God works in mysterious ways. He brought you and your beautiful little girl into our lives for a reason.
>
> My babies needed a mother to watch over them and keep them company while I'm here, and I needed another little girl to love, a little girl who would be Anna Marie's sister.
>
> Thank you for being God's gift to us. I'm sorry I couldn't wait on Him and His timing, but my babies needed you.
>
> I want you to know, I will love Bella Marie as if she were my own, I promise you that. She will be safe here.
>
> Take care of my babies, and I will take care of yours. Until it's time for me to hold my babies in person,
> Yours,
> Gertie.

"My mother was mentally ill for a long time." Mom takes the letter from me and refolds it, places it back in her journal. "She should have been under a doctor's care, rather than left alone to raise a child."

I expect Grace to speak up, to excuse David for wanting to keep his family together, for trying to keep a promise, but she says nothing.

So neither do I.

"We need to make it right. What happened. It needs to be made right. They need to be buried with their family, not hidden away behind a garage. They deserve a proper resting place, with family." Mom reaches for my hand. "I heard you. Judy's family is still looking for her. We need to make this right. I also want to dedicate my show to them. They're the theme anyway, when you look at all the images as a whole. My mother was right about one thing," Mom says. "God does work in mysterious ways. We may have said goodbye to my father, but because of his death, I finally feel like I know who I am for the first time in a long, long time." Mom raises her glass of wine in a toast. "To memories and stories and family," she says.

The clink of our wineglasses is lost in the boom of thunder directly over the house. I think we all jump at the same time, because we spill our wine all over the table.

We grab as many dish towels and paper towels as we can find to mop up the mess before deciding to forgo drinking any more wine. We finish off the ice cream instead.

"This reminds me of a story." Mom smiles. "One my father used to tell me when I was little and scared during a storm . . ."

Chapter Forty-Two

Dear Anna Marie,

When you were born, I made you a promise. I swore to always protect you, to put you first, to make sure you grew up surrounded by laughter and love.

I'm sorry I didn't always keep that promise.

I know your life growing up wasn't perfect. In fact, it was downright hard. It could have all been prevented if I'd been man enough to do the right thing at the very beginning.

For that, I can never apologize enough.

Since you were a child, all I've tried to do is make right a wrong.

Maybe with my death, that can finally be accomplished.

You were loved, Anna Marie, by both your mother and me. I hope that is something you'll one day be able to see.

Love isn't always pretty or clear cut. It can't be wrapped in a nice little box and presented with a bow. Sometimes it's ugly and hurtful and does more damage than good.

I know you tried to forget about us, and I want you to know I understood. I understand. I don't blame you either.

But we never forgot about you. We never stopped loving you either.

Your mother's last words to me, right before she died, were to tell you she loved you.

Those will be my last words as well.

I love you, my daughter.

Your father,

David Basil Walker

THANK YOU

Of all the stories I have written, this one could not have been completed without the love and support of so many strong women in my life.

A special shout-out and thank-you to all those who are in my amazing reader group, Steena's Secret Society. Your encouragement to keep going, your enthusiasm in helping every time I asked for it, and your love for my stories . . . I would share my chocolate with you all any day of the week! Here's to more stories!

To my writing girls—Dara Lee, Elena, Trish, Tawny, Lauren . . . thank you. You are the best writing partners a woman could have.

To Margie Lawson, who pushed me to tell better stories.

Thank you to Erin Healey, for giving me that push to do better with an idea, and to Pamela Harty, who is the best agent and friend an author could ever ask for!

Danielle Marshall, the first time I met you, you encouraged me to write the story that needed to be told, to believe in myself, and to always trust my heart. I'm thankful to work with you and the rest of the Lake Union team.

To the rest of my Lake Union authors—we are a group who love, support, and nurture one another. I'm thrilled to be on this journey with you all.

But most of all, I want to give a shout-out to my family. Life didn't play fair while I was writing this story, but we made it through and will continue to make it through. As one of my amazing daughters reminded me recently, when life hands you lemons, freeze those suckers and toss them back hard. I love you!

ABOUT THE AUTHOR

Steena Holmes is the *New York Times* and *USA Today* bestselling author of titles including *Saving Abby*, *Stillwater Rising*, and *The Memory Child*. Named to the "20 Best Books by Women in 2015" list by *Good Housekeeping* and *Redbook*, Steena won the National Indie Excellence Award in 2012 for *Finding Emma* as well as the USA Book News Award for *The Word Game* in 2015. Steena lives in Calgary, Alberta, and is a self-proclaimed "travelholic" who can't resist a good cup of coffee. To find out more about her books and her love of traveling, you can visit her website at www.steenaholmes.com or follow her journeys on Instagram @ authorsteenaholmes.